THE LOST BOOK 1

ICE AND MONSTERS

PETER NEALEN

THE LAND of ICE & MONSTERS

THE TEETH
of WINTER
GRICHENCOS'
CITADEL
POHLOJA
SUMNOTH
MENNINKAI
VAHAVA
PAYKHAH
N
W
E
S

WARGATE

An imprint of Galaxy's Edge Press
PO BOX 534
Puyallup, Washington 98371

ISBN: 978-1-949731-65-1

www.forgottenruin.com
www.wargatebooks.com

FOREWORD

WHEN Jason Anspach and I first wrote the *Forgotten Ruin* series, we shared with some fellow authors what we were up to because we felt it was the kind of storytelling people wanted and weren't getting. *Forgotten Ruin* became a big hit, and the desire for WarGate stories is going strong.

We're beyond excited for Peter Nealen to be the first of those authors. He's a great guy, a U.S. Marine veteran, and an excellent storyteller.

But maybe you're wondering, what is WarGate fiction?

We've got an answer ready for you. WarGate is an exciting new genre that blends fantasy, military fiction, and science fiction in a unique way.

A WarGate title is set in fantasy world, you'll find wonderful allusions to Norse Mythology in *Ice and Monsters* while our own *Forgotten Ruin* series is a blend of the traditional *Lord of the Rings* and (old school) *Dungeons and Dragons* fantasy settings.

The next concept we add is a modern military unit. For us it was U.S. Army Rangers, while Peter, a former Marine, went with a U.S. Marine Recon unit—a highly specialized, highly skilled, and highly motivated group of Marines who do a very specific task and do it well.

The third element in a WarGate novel is what we call The Perpetual Taco Machine. To keep a modern military unit acting like a modern military unit in a fantasy world, you've got to keep them equipped. We asked ourselves how we keep the Rangers, Marines, or Special Forces guys fighting through the savage age of Conan from having to turn into just sword-wielding warriors who happen to share the same knowledge of pop culture as you and I.

Ammunition doesn't last forever. Equipment breaks down... and where do you find a can of Rip It in country? It's not like the ye old shop keep keeps skins of coffee and energy drinks next to the wine and health potions, right?

The Perpetual Taco machine keep the ammo from going black and even provides mortars and the occasional Karl Gustav round to keep the trolls, frost giants, and all the other monsters around at bay. That's not as crazy as it sounds. Even now, the United States and other countries are pushing the limits of what can be 3D printed. In WarGate, we just advance the technology out to a point that might make hard sci-fi junkies roll their eyes into the back of their heads and have epileptic fits.

But the end results we're all after is fun. So without further delay, enjoy *Ice and Monsters...* it's a hell of a ride!

Nick Cole & Jason Anspach

P.S. – If you did have a perpetual taco machine, you'd definitely make tacos with it, hence the name. Even the hard sci-fi readers agree with us there.

CHAPTER 1

LOOKING back on it all, given how weird the rest of the world had gotten, taking the Zodiacs into that fog bank was a bad idea. By that time, the government had formally acknowledged that UFOs were real. They hadn't been able to cover up Senator Casimir's exsanguination along with his children. Or his wife having disappeared like a ghost.

Let's not even get into some of the weird stuff I'd seen in the shadows in Syria.

Fog in the summertime, when every atmospheric condition was against it, should have been a warning sign. It definitely hadn't been in the "Situation" part of the brief, either during the Warning Order or in the full, five-paragraph order that Captain Sorenson gave just before we climbed into the CH-53s and took off, the boats partially deflated and "tacoed" so they'd fit with us and our rucks.

Still, looking back, I'm glad we'd been issued a full combat load. The exercise was supposed to end in a live-fire range. We were loaded out. We went without body armor—and boy howdy had *that* been a tough sell—so we carried the standard Recon loadout of twelve mags on the body and one in the gun.

That would come in handy. The body armor would have, too, but in the long run, I'd take bullets over plates.

But I'm getting ahead of myself. Everything seemed normal at first. The helocast went by the numbers—in fact, the pilot was one of the best I'd ever seen. The helos had flared about three klicks off the Norwegian coast, the pilots holding an almost perfect hover ten feet off the water while we shoved the boats out and followed them two at a time, then jumped into the still-frigid water feet-first and swam to the boats.

It was almost too dark to see the Norwegian coast ahead as we bobbed on the ocean, getting the engines mounted and the boats fully inflated, but we could see the *Pyotr Velikiy* battlegroup's navigation lights off to the north clearly enough. The Russians weren't too happy about this round of joint exercises between the US Marine Corps and the Norwegians, and they weren't making it a secret.

"Ready, Conor." Captain Sorenson would probably have frowned if he'd heard Rodeffer call me by my first name. To him, the Marine Corps demanded that my team call me *Staff Sergeant McCall.* But sometimes Recon operates a little differently from the rest of the Marine Corps.

I glanced forward as I took the tiller. The team was in the boat, rucks secured, fins clipped to chest rigs, suppressed M4s—thoroughly drenched in silicone spray to keep the salt water from eating them—pointed outboard. To our right and left, the platoon's other Zodiacs bobbed on the waves, dark and glistening in the dying light.

Bailey, Team 3's team leader, waved at me from the boat off to the left. I returned the signal, then turned my attention toward the CO's boat in the middle. They were a little behind still, and I fancied for a moment that I could see the steam rising from Gunny Taylor's ears where he was riding with Zimmerman out on the far end of the line of boats.

Finally, everyone was ready to go, and the Captain started their engine and sent the lead Zodiac putting toward the Norwegian coast. The rest of us followed, spreading out into a rough wedge.

I looked up at the sky as we went. The stars were out, but there was still some faint, pinkish light in the west. We weren't going to have a lot of darkness to work in, not at that time of year. Which was a good thing as well as a bad thing.

Recon likes darkness. It hides us and lets us sneak around into places we're not supposed to be. But at the same time, we were a lot farther north than most of us were used to, and the North Sea is bitterly cold, even in the summer. The more sunlight there was up to warm things up, the better. I was glad we'd decided to wear drysuits on insert.

We hadn't gotten far before that fog bank rolled up out of nowhere.

I'll admit, I didn't think it was that weird to start with. Fog is fog. And we were all pretty good at nautical navigation that far into the float. I had my compass board on the gunwale, sure that I was holding course. So, we were fine. Sure, the night was supposed to have been clear. But who *really* trusts the weather forecasts in the "Situation" paragraph one hundred percent?

The fog got thicker, and I eased off on the throttle. Within a couple dozen yards, I couldn't even see the boats on either side of us, though I could still hear them. I glanced down at the compass, which was still rock-steady.

We were good. We just had to go carefully because of the reduced visibility.

At least, that was what I thought until we were still chugging through the waves, shrouded by fog, well after the time we should have been at the beach landing site.

I started to question my judgement, but it wasn't like we had a lot of reference points in this soup. The bearing had been spot on since we headed in. I'd chosen to be patient. Maybe we'd slowed down more than I thought.

A sound… almost a moan.

My head came up, and I stared hard into the mists. Other heads came up off the gunwales, too. I hadn't been the only one to notice something.

"You hear that?" Farrar was my RTO, and as usual, his voice was slightly too loud, even in a whisper. He'd never quite perfected the Recon quiet.

Santos shushed him. "We all heard it, moron. Shut up." My assistant team leader wasn't exactly the soul of tact, but Farrar brought out the acid in him fast, quick, and in a hurry. *Especially* when he couldn't be quiet.

But the noise had been weird enough that Santos wasn't going to ignore it just to spite Farrar, either. "What the hell *was* that? A whale?" His voice was still a low whisper that wouldn't carry far.

"Never heard of a whale making a noise like that before, let alone on the surface." I searched the mist around us again. I couldn't see any of the other boats, but nobody had started yelling for help yet. If this had been a real-world combat mission, that might or might not be advisable, depending on the emergency, but since it was a training op, I figured that if anything went wrong with one of the boats, we'd have to go admin to fix it.

The fog was as thick as ever, and the darkness seemed to be even more impenetrable than it had been before. The radios were all in waterproof cascade bags in the rucks; immediate communications without visual contact would be limited to yelling.

And for some reason I couldn't put my finger on, after hearing that strange moan out in the dark, I didn't feel like yelling was going to be a good idea.

"Rodeffer! Stanley! You see anything up there?" I kept my voice to a low hiss projected toward the bow where my point man and slack man were lying on the gunwale, their eyes forward, peering over their rifles.

Rodeffer shook his head, his NVGs sticking out under his bump helmet as he scanned the water around us.

Stanley then said, "Nothing, Staff Sergeant." He was the low man on the totem pole, not only on the team, but also in the platoon. He'd just lat-moved from Supply to Recon and had finished the BRC—Basic Reconnaissance Course—pipeline just in time to join the workup for this float. He might be a Sergeant with six years under his belt, but he was a boot to us, even to Rodeffer, who had just pinned on his third stripe.

Stanley also still had some Big Marine Corps habits. One of the first things Santos had told him when he'd arrived at the Company was *not* to get a haircut for the next two weeks. Recon don't do that screaming high-and-tight shit.

The moan came again, followed by a soft splash somewhere behind us.

Santos swiveled around and craned his neck to look behind us while still lying on the gunwale. "What the hell?"

I let off on the throttle. From the sounds of it, the other boats had as well. Which told me that we'd all heard it.

Letting us drift a little, I turned and looked behind us. Nothing but dark waves disappearing into the fog a few yards away.

Or was there something more out there? Something big and creepy.

I blinked, then stared hard. My NVGs didn't have a lot of light to work with, and they need *some* ambient light to amplify. Even our PVS-15s couldn't see squat in the pitch black. And the fog wasn't exactly letting a lot of starlight down.

Then *something* broached the surface. Not by much, but just enough that I knew it was there. And it didn't look right. It looked almost…human.

I blinked hard and stared at the empty stretch of water I'd just observed.

I couldn't have seen it right. For a moment, I told myself that I'd just experienced the same thing the old sailors who said they'd seen mermaids had. They'd seen a sea cow and thought they'd seen a half-fish, half-hot chick in a shell bikini.

To be honest, I'd never *quite* bought that explanation. Ever seen a sea cow? Nobody who's not high as a kite is going to mistake *that* for a hot chick. Didn't make sense the first time I heard the theory, and I wasn't buying it right then, either.

I was right not to.

Something hit the boat from underneath. Hard. We all froze for a second.

Then they were coming up out of the water all around us.

I caught a good look at the closest one as it grabbed the gunwale right next to me, avoiding the shrouded pumpjet propulsor on the outboard. Its arm was a little too long, its fingers slender and bony, with webbing between them running from knuckle almost clear to the claws at their ends. Its head was blunt and earless, its eyes too big for its head, luminous and practically glowing in my NVGs.

The thing had a mouth wider than the rest of its head, and when it gaped, I saw rows of glassy fangs that looked like they belonged on an anglerfish.

As I stared at the sea monster that was trying to crawl up onto my Zodiac, the first thing that I thought was that I regretted that we'd jumped out of the helicopter into the ocean with our rifles in Condition Four. Which meant that I had an unloaded weapon in front of me when I needed to shoot this thing.

Fortunately, I had a knife.

Actually, I had two with me, but the Bowie that I brought on every op was in my ruck, waterproofed and secured. The titanium dive knife on my vest, however, was easily accessible. I yanked it out of its scabbard, still holding onto the tiller with my other hand as the slimy thing lunged out of the water, its fangs reaching for my throat.

If I'd been thinking straight, I sure wouldn't have tried to hold onto the tiller while getting in a knife fight. But when a sea monster comes up out of the water and tries to grab you, thinking straight kind of goes out the window.

I jabbed at it as it lunged at me, but my blade skittered off its scaly hide, and then it was on top of me, pinning my knife hand against the gunwale, its jaws gnashing for my throat. I let go of the tiller and barely got my arm under its throat, keeping that toothy frog mouth away from my face by inches. I could hear the snap of its teeth and feel a cold breath on my face. That close. I twisted around and threw myself back against the outboard, suddenly scared as hell that this thing was going to drag me off the boat and into the water.

I tried to shove it off me while I fought to get my knife hand free. It kept snapping at my face, but while it was horribly strong, I was a Recon Marine.

For a brief few moments, my entire universe shrank to the stern of the boat as the monster tried to crush me, bite me, or drag me into the water. I was vaguely aware of the noise around me as the rest of the team tried to fight their own attackers, but I couldn't spare the attention.

I hit it with a knee, then an elbow, but none of my blows seemed to faze it. It gurgled and hissed as it pawed and bit at me. It took a swipe at me with its free hand, and I used the momentum to pull my knife out from under its paw and started stabbing.

Have you ever tried to stab a fish? It's harder than it looks; the scales make the skin tough, and the flesh beneath it is rubbery. Without a lot of force, the point just kind of bounces.

My first two stabs didn't go in more than a fraction of an inch. Then I got mad and got one under its armpit, which sank to the hilt.

The thing groaned and reared back. I grabbed hold of the tendrils that hung from the corners of its inhumanly wide mouth. I let it haul me up to where I could straddle the gunwale again, and then I went to town.

Holding it by that tendril, I stabbed it over and over in the neck, trying to do as much damage as possible. Its blows and struggles got desperate, as my hands and my blade got covered in blood, scales, and slime, and I tore open the thing's neck, my knife grinding against its backbone a couple of times. A stench like fish and rotting meat filled my nostrils, and I almost gagged.

It finally went limp. I let it slide into the dark water, where it bobbed on the surface for a moment before it disappeared. I turned toward the bow, my heart hammering and my chest heaving.

Farrar and Smith were still grappling with one of the things in the bottom of the boat. Santos was clubbing another one with his rifle. Rodeffer had his knife out and was trying to get at the one that Farrar and Smith were fighting.

There was no sign of Stanley. His side of the gunwale was empty.

I was about to wade into the fight in the bottom of the boat when Farrar got his dive knife past the thing's desperately flailing limbs and plunged it to the hilt in its eye. The eyeball popped, and viscous and faintly luminous fluid sprayed from the wound. Farrar twisted the knife, grinding it against bone as he cored out the creature's brain, or whatever it had in its place. The monster went limp, its last breath coming out with a disgusting gurgle.

Santos had driven his attacker off and rolled back into the boat, almost landing on Smith. He immediately reached into his vest, pulled out a magazine, and loaded his M4. "Go Condition One, while we've got a minute."

Farrar, Smith, and Rodeffer didn't need to be told twice. Rodeffer quickly slammed a mag into his rifle, racked the bolt, and then was back to the bow, scanning the water.

"Where's Stanley?" Santos beat me to the question by a heartbeat.

"I don't know!" Rodeffer sounded frantic as he scanned the water and the fog around us. "One of those things came up, bit him in the face, and dragged him under!"

"What do you mean, 'bit him in the face?'" Smith was the assistant radio operator, and while he wasn't nearly as boot as Stanley, he only had one float under his belt. The pimple-faced young Sergeant still didn't handle sudden changes well, never mind this kind of weirdness.

"I mean it came out of the water and half-swallowed his *head*, man!" Rodeffer was still looking around the bow, his suppressed muzzle following his NVGs.

"Calm down." I was looking, too, but the fact that I couldn't hear anyone thrashing around in the water, or anyone calling for help, told me that it was probably too late for Stanley. The fight hadn't gone on long, but if he hadn't come up yet…

Another of the creatures breached the surface off to port. Santos shot it, the *crack* of the suppressed round still horrifically loud, echoing across the water.

Then I heard that sound again. The moan.

It was like a deeper, angrier version of a whale song. And something about it tickled the lizard part of my brain and made me wanted to run and hide.

Whatever had made that sound was *big*. And it was *not* friendly. And the odds that we were going to do more than piss it off with 5.56 fire were slim to none.

I looked behind us and saw only fog. But something out there was coming. I could feel it.

Still, I held our position, or at least as close to our position as I could manage. There were zero points of reference in the fog, though I could hear the faint grunts and thuds of hand-to-hand combat and outboard motors in the murk. Were they getting farther away?

I didn't want to leave Stanley if there was a hope in hell of getting him back in the boat.

"Stanley!" Santos's voice was little more than a hiss. I don't think any of the team dared make any more noise than that right then.

Unfortunately, while Stanley didn't make an appearance, an even bigger one of the things suddenly grabbed onto the Zodiac's stern, its mouth gaping as it croaked its hate at me.

I shot it through that open, slavering maw, and then there was no sticking around anymore. Because *something* bigger still had just moved out there in the fog, with another deep, menacing moan, and the Zodiac rocked as its wake rolled past us. Whatever this thing was, it was far too close for comfort.

Gunny Taylor's voice echoed out of the fog, sounding farther away than it should have been. "Get to shore! Get to shore *now!*"

I probably would have tried to stay there anyway, except for two things that happened at the same time.

Something bumped against the bow. Not big. I felt it and slowed, twisting the throttle to back water a little. Rodeffer looked down, then swore as he scrambled back into the boat.

"What?" I demanded. We were still drifting forward, and I didn't have time to guess or wait for Rodeffer to find his voice again.

Turns out I didn't need to.

Stanley's headless corpse bounced against the gunwale and drifted away into the dark and the fog. I knew it was his because I recognized my old load bearing vest. I'd given it to him when he joined the team.

Then that moan sounded a third time, far louder and far closer than before. I glanced over my shoulder and saw a rising shadow in the mist, something huge and dark lifting its head above the waves. Another wake rocked us, and I cranked the throttle, no longer worried about noise.

For a moment, I had no idea which way we were facing. I'd lost all sense of direction in the murk and the dark, and when I looked down, I saw that the compass board had been ripped off during the fight with the sea monster.

But I homed in on the sounds of the other boats—at least, where I hoped I heard the other boats—and revved the throttle as more of the frog-faced, glass-toothed monsters breached the surface, swimming after us.

CHAPTER 2

WE raced through the dark, leaving a rooster-tail wake behind us. Monsters raged and croaked to our rear. The freezing wind and spray stung our faces.

I thought we were going roughly east, but without pulling my own compass out, I had no way to tell for sure. Honestly, that was a minor consideration right then. At that point I was just trying to keep the nightmares rising out of the sea to our stern. I poured on as much throttle as I could.

Finally, I spotted another boat ahead of us, also making waves for the shore. At least, I hoped so. It seemed that the fog was lifting a little, though it was still awfully dark. I steered toward the other boat. There is strength in numbers, especially when everything has just gone horribly wrong.

I still had no idea just *how* wrong things had truly gone. Still, I knew it had to be bad. Sea monsters hadn't even been on the checklist.

"Conor! You might want to open it up a little more!" Santos had just looked behind us. He shifted his weight, turned to aim his M4 back behind us, and popped off about five shots before he gave up. The Zodiac was bouncing off every small wave at the speed we were holding, and it would have been a miracle if he'd hit anything.

We have to have gotten off course, I told myself. *We didn't insert* that *far off the coast.* I wondered if we'd missed a headland and were tearing up a fjord in the fog.

Then the shore appeared, a black mass rising steeply out of the ocean ahead of us. The boat ahead of us turned toward that dark headland, and I had no choice but to follow.

Something in the back of my head, strangely calm in this weird nightmare of an insert, wondered if the shore was really going to be any safer than the ocean. If there were monsters coming out of the North Sea, what was waiting in the dark up there?

But staying out there on the water was not an option. Not with those things trying to eat us.

It took only a few more minutes to get to shore. The fog was lifting, and we could clearly see the other boats, all four of them, now finally closing into formation. We'd gotten so scattered in the chaos and the murk, we were still pretty spread out as we got to shore.

The lifting of the fog also revealed the fact that the things in the water were still coming for us. That deep, roaring moan sounded again, louder than ever. I still couldn't see the thing that made it—it remained shrouded in the mists. Whatever it was, it seemed to be... driving the other monsters on. Now that I could see more clearly, the sight of scores, maybe hundreds, of the ghastly fish-people butterfly stroking through the waves after us, only barely slower than our Zodiacs, made my blood run cold.

Eyes forward again, I noticed that Rodeffer was looking back over his shoulder, watching the same horrifying sight. I needed him on task—I could already hear the surf roaring in the dark up ahead. We were getting close to shore.

"Rodeffer! Eyes front!" If we were going to land this thing, instead of getting tossed on the rocks, he needed to watch where I couldn't see; the bow was out of the water at the speed we were making.

He turned back around, and although the outboard's whine was too loud for me to hear him clearly, I could tell that he cursed rather fervently, throwing up a hand. We were getting shallow already. I reached down and popped the release pin on the motor.

Just in time, because a heartbeat later, Rodeffer slashed his hand down and rolled off the gunwale and into the low waves lapping the shore. I hauled the outboard up to keep the propulsor from getting smashed on the rocks, and then we were skimming onto the short, pebbled beach.

The beach was covered in snow above the waterline. The towering firs just beyond it were laden with white.

With a rasp, the Zodiac skidded to a halt. By sheer force of habit, the rest of the team piled out and started to drag it higher up on the beach.

"Screw that noise! Grab your weapons and rucks and *get off the beach!*" I was already suiting actions to words as I hauled my saltwater-soaked rucksack up out of the bottom of the boat and onto one shoulder. "Rodeffer! Get up there and find us a defensive position!" A glance over my shoulder confirmed that the monsters were still coming. And they were far too close, given how fast we'd made the final run into the beach.

Santos and I stayed with the boat as Farrar, Rodeffer, and Smith shouldered their rucks and hustled up into the hinterland and the snowy woods. I remember thinking, *Why the hell is there snow? It's supposed to be July!* But given the rest of the weirdness that had hit us on this mission, the snow was the least of our worries.

On a knee on that rocky, frigid beach, my hands going numb on my M4, I faced the oncoming horde of slimy, frog-mouthed *things* as they swam toward us, staying mostly submerged in the water until it was less than knee-deep.

The first one surged up out of the sea and I double-tapped it, my suppressor spurting spray and steam, the supersonic reports of the rounds muffled but still achingly loud in the night. It staggered as the 5.56 rounds hammered into its chest, but with a hissing croak of rage, it surged forward, splashing through the shallows toward us.

I shot it four more times, tracking the rounds up from its chest to put the fourth round between those malevolent, lamp-like eyes. It crashed on its face in the surf with a splash.

Another foghorn bellow of a moan came from the fog bank out to sea, and the line of them slowed, still staying on their bellies in the water. I heard Santos shooting on the other side of the boat, but there wasn't a lot to shoot at, not yet. Water's not perfect cover, but it makes for good concealment in the dark, and bullets don't travel far underwater. The heads barely breaking the surface as the horde gathered in the surf zone didn't make for great targets in the dark.

I suddenly realized what was happening. I'd thought that the gunshot had scared them, but with a sudden cold shiver, I understood.

"Vince, fall back to the trees. They're getting ready to rush us." I can't say exactly how I knew that, but something about the way they were just gathering out there put my hackles up. They'd stopped when I shot the first one, but they hadn't retreated. I could see their eyes, gleaming when they popped above the waves, watching us. Waiting.

More suppressed gunfire echoed down the beach. I glanced that way, though I hated to take my eyes off the threat in front of me, and saw that the other four boats were drawn up on the rocks, and the other teams were struggling to either get the boats higher up on the beach, or to hold off the horde. It looked like one team had foundered out in the surf zone, too. The boat was upside down about a dozen yards from shore, and a couple of the team were trying to lift it, while a third Recondo hammered rounds out at the monsters in the surf behind them.

Gunny Taylor was already wading toward them, yelling at them to just get the trapped Marines out and get up on shore.

That team was on the far end of the landing site, so there wasn't much we could do to help. And as I turned back toward the surf, I saw two more of the creatures rear up out of the surf and lunge toward us, too keyed up to wait.

Santos and I shot the nearest one at the same time, six bullets tearing through its scaly hide and knocking it back to fall on its tail in the water. It sat there for a moment, wheezing out its last, then sank backward into the waves, out of sight.

I shifted to the second one, and this time it was close enough that I didn't bother with the drill. I just shot it in the face from about ten yards. It dropped like a sack of rocks and didn't reappear.

"We need to go." Santos wasn't the kind of guy who got stampeded, but he was sounding a little ragged. And I couldn't blame him. This was not a situation any of us were ready for.

This was supposed to be a training op.

"Fall back." I couldn't be sure in the dark, but it looked like the line of monsters out in the surf was creeping closer.

Santos moved first, turning and sprinting as best he could in a drysuit and fin booties and with a ruck on his back, toward the trees and the hinterland. I stayed put for the moment, my rifle leveled, scanning back and forth along the line of frog-faced monstrosities, waiting for the first one to charge and get a bullet in the face.

"Turn and go!" Santos was set. I glanced over my shoulder, made sure I wasn't about to cut off his field of fire, and ran after him.

The rocky shore wasn't fun to run across, particularly not in that cold. The saltwater washing against it hadn't frozen, but the rocks were slick and I was top-heavy. I almost ate it in the first few yards. One foot slipped out from under me, and I stumbled just before reaching the trees.

That may as well have been a signal. With a croaking roar, the monsters surged out of the water and came after us.

I scrambled to the nearest tree and dropped to a knee in the snow beneath it as I turned and leveled my M4 at the surf. Dozens—no, hundreds of the things were splashing out of the surf, croaking and roaring, while that massive *thing* behind them let out another foghorn bellow out in the mist that clung stubbornly to the sea beyond.

Gunfire roared out across the beach as a couple of the M27 gunners let rip. Full-auto 5.56 tore into slimy, scaly flesh and dropped the things into the surf on their faces, but more of them kept coming.

I shot at one, then transitioned to the next one behind it when it disappeared beneath the waves. There were so many that I couldn't be sure that I hit it. And they were coming fast.

More rounds *crack*ed past me to the left. As soon as I'd opened fire, Santos had turned and run, and while we were all running our M4s and the handful of M27 IARs suppressed, there was just too much noise for shouts to be heard clearly. So, we had to communicate by fire.

I struggled up the slope. The weight aside, fin booties are not the best footwear for running in snow, over uneven ground. But there was no time to change over to boots.

I started to slip again as I came alongside Santos. Instead of getting up and pushing on, I stopped behind a fallen tree and got down on a knee, then opened fire on the dim, roaring shapes pushing off the beach.

A big one was shoving its way through the trees, bounding forward on its weird, webbed feet, its toothy maw gaping wide as it bellowed for our blood. I shot it in the mouth, my IR laser dancing with my heartbeat and heaving breath, the hit more thanks to luck than any great skill or timing on my part. I'd been about to just dump rounds at the thing until it went down. But it crashed onto its face in the snow at the first shot.

I forced myself to calm down and just start servicing targets. The sheer panic that I could feel bubbling up in my chest would just get us all eaten.

It's just like any other range. They're just targets. Just keep telling yourself that.

But while I kept repeating that little mantra over and over and over again as I shifted targets and blasted the croaking things plunging through the trees at us, the lizard part of my brain wasn't having it. This was too weird.

The next fish-man, or frog-man, or whatever the hell it was, took a lot longer to go down. I didn't get lucky with a headshot that time and had to hammer five rounds into its chest before I got a bullet into its head, sending it skidding backward as it flopped onto the ground, thrashing like a fish out of water.

By then, a half dozen more were within a handful of yards. Santos was shooting over my shoulder again, knocking one of them spinning into a tree. I got up and moved.

As I turned and struggled into a waddling run, I got a glimpse of our line as we fell back. We'd formed a ragged skirmish line, bounding back through the trees in ones and twos as we poured fire into the oncoming horde. Unfortunately, it wasn't slowing them down. Every time we stopped to lay down fire, they got closer.

Gunny Taylor saw it, too. A moment after I realized we were screwed, I heard his bull-bellow through the trees. "Hold your fire and just *run*!"

Turning back uphill, I quickly spotted Farrar, Smith, and Santos. I couldn't see Rodeffer, but I didn't think he'd fallen behind.

Even as I thought it, I knew I couldn't leave it at that. "Rodeffer!"

"He's up here!" Smith paused just long enough to throw the words back over his shoulder.

With one more glance at the monsters quickly closing in, I turned and ran for my life.

CHAPTER 3

THE forest was old and wild. Which meant that footing wouldn't have been the best under even ideal conditions between the rocks, fallen trees, and decaying remains of even *older* fallen trees. There was no clear path through the woods, and the hill we ran up just got steeper. Add in the snow and ice, and it was murder.

Fortunately, the scaly, frog-faced things behind us weren't having a much better time of it than we were. We like to say in Recon that the water is the Great Equalizer, but these things didn't seem to be that comfortable on land.

Still, while they weren't gaining on us, we weren't outdistancing them, either. The footing was treacherous, and we had to constantly climb over or go around obstacles while weighed down by full Recon and Surveillance rucks, each weighing about seventy to ninety pounds, *dry*. None of ours were dry.

Don't forget the fin booties instead of proper combat boots. That climb was a nightmare.

Farrar slipped and fell on his face, trying to get up over a gigantic, fallen fir tree. I struggled up to him and got my hand under his arm. "Come on, keep moving!" We both almost slipped again as I hauled him to his feet and got him over the tree trunk, where he slipped again and fell once more. But he was over the obstacle.

Turning back, I saw three of the frog-men bursting through the trees, shouldering branches out of their way with showers of snow. I pivoted, still on the wrong side of the tree, put my IR laser on the nearest one, and double-tapped it. The laser was bouncing like mad, and I'm pretty sure the second round missed, but the first one tore into its shoulder and punched it halfway around, making it stagger.

Then I half-climbed, half-rolled over the log and kept going.

Despite the snow, the unnatural cold, and the ice underfoot, I was sweating. I was sure my cammies were soaked under my drysuit. Steam poured from my mouth, nose, and every exposed bit of skin. I knew that we were in for trouble if and when we were safe enough to stop, but we would be in a lot more trouble if we slowed down right now. So, I sweated and kept climbing.

The terrain started to level out as the trees thinned. I caught sight of Rodeffer and Smith as they burst out into a clearing, not far from Esposito and Baldinus from Team 2. Captain Sorenson was even ahead of them. The slope kept climbing, though it was gentler, until it reached the trees on the far side of the clearing.

Even as I came out of the woods and into the snow-covered meadow, I saw that we were in a lot more trouble than I'd thought.

The mountain that loomed against the icy stars above that clearing was as sheer-sided as any I'd ever seen. And the ridgelines coming down to either side weren't much better. Knife-edged rocks half-ringed the clearing. Only a few stubborn pines clung to them, weighed down with snow.

No way we were getting up there in the snow and ice, carrying these rucks. We probably couldn't manage it with proper boots on, never mind still in our amphib gear.

We were trapped.

I looked off to my right, where Gunny Taylor was still bringing up the rear, chivvying the slower guys along. Those were mostly the RTOs, the radio operators. They had the heaviest rucks.

I dropped back to join Gunny. He was huffing, clouds coming off his bald head, even under his boonie. I kept my voice low, or as low as I could while I was panting and trying to speak past the pounding of my own heartbeat. "We're in a box canyon, Gunny."

He looked up, peered through the trees, and cursed. A moment later, we both spun around to face back down the hill, where crashing and croaking announced the closing jaws of the trap.

A massive fish-man clambered over the rock just below us, gripping with the claws at the end of its webbed fingers. Gunny and I both lifted our M4s, IR laser dots dancing on the thing's torso, and fired.

Both suppressors spat, the salt water having been boiled off by the fire we'd already put through them. The thing clung to the rock as the bullets tore into it, its body sagging back and a burbling wail coming from its gaping mouth. I put two more rounds into it, then I had to shift and shoot the next one coming around the side of the rock. That one soaked up three rounds and kept coming. I dumped the rest of the mag into it, and it finally slumped into the snow, staining the white, red.

The snow-laden branches below thrashed and waved as more of them came after us. Gunny Taylor dumped the last of his magazine into the trees on full automatic, then pointed up the hill. "Get moving, Conor!"

I obeyed, then turned and struggled back up the hill, skirting around a tangled blowdown of fallen trees and battering my way through snow-covered branches before I broke out into the open.

Looking up, I could see most of the rest of the platoon getting close to the trees at the base of the sheer rock face at the top of the little hanging valley. For a second, I thought I saw something else, something like a face looming above the trees, but it was too dark to be sure, and I had a few other concerns right at that moment.

I could hear Gunny Taylor behind me, panting and cursing as he moved. Taylor was the oldest man in the platoon and really didn't like running anymore. He wasn't as fast as most of the rest of us. He had no quit in him—he'd catch us all, eventually—but he had one pace, and it wasn't what any of the rest of us would call a sprint.

It didn't feel right to just run across that open meadow. Not only because I was starting to leave Gunny behind, but because that was a long way to go without taking cover. Even though the frog-faced things hadn't showed a weapon beyond their claws and teeth so far, the hard-wired instincts honed by years of training made it just feel *wrong*.

So, I halted about halfway across the meadow and dropped to a knee in the snow. My foot skidded and I almost fell over as my ruck tried to overbalance. If we'd had a chance to wear boots, I expected we'd be a lot farther ahead of those things than we were.

As I caught myself and heaved my ruck upright, catching my foot against a rock or a hole or something under the snow, then leveled my M4, praying that I hadn't just stuffed the suppressor full of compacted snow, I flicked on my IR laser and looked for targets.

Gunny was still struggling up the slope, every other step slipping a little, clouds of steam pouring from his mouth and nose. I looked behind him, playing my laser across the trees, accompanied by not a few more from above and behind me.

At first, I couldn't see any of them. I frowned as I peered through my NVGs. They couldn't have stopped.

But they had. I picked out the first one, even bigger than the brute I'd shot off the rock below, standing just under the trees. It was staring at me, its eyes glowing like lamps in IR. One by one, I picked out more of them. They'd all stopped just before the tree line and were standing there, staring at us.

I held my fire. I was suddenly acutely conscious of just how many of them there were, and how I'd already gone through two mags. I had ten left, and something told me that I had no good way of knowing just how far I was going to have to make those three hundred rounds go.

The big one took a step forward, and I put my laser on its chest. Well, as close as I could get from that distance while on a not-so-stable knee, weighed down with a wet ruck, my chest heaving as I sucked in the chill air. The laser dot danced all over the thing and past it.

It lifted its arms and bellowed, an angry croak that echoed across the hills behind us. It stamped its webbed feet as the horde behind it repeated the noise. Despite the fact that it was just wordless noise, voiced by inhuman monsters, I could still hear the frustration and rage. It was a curse, just not one in words that we could understand.

Still, while they didn't advance, they didn't go away, either. Several of them were pacing back and forth under the trees, somehow reminding me of sharks circling a dive cage. Something was keeping them back, but they hadn't given up. Not yet.

Gunny Taylor kept moving. I heard him panting as he forged past me. "I told you to keep moving, Conor." Even winded and struggling with his footing, he could still growl at me.

I joined him, turning and running toward the trees and the cliffs beyond. I say "running," but given the weight, the distance we'd already scrambled to get away from those things, and the treacherous footing, it was a shuffle at best. We struggled up the shallow slope while a few rounds *crack*ed past us to either side, as the rest of the platoon shot at frog-faced monsters—or at movement and shadows they *thought* were frog-faced monsters.

"Hold your fire!" I wasn't just worried about catching a round from another spooked Recon bubba—though that was *definitely* a factor. We don't train to shoot at shadows, but everybody was rattled, and some of the discipline and training was showing some cracks.

I wasn't immune, but even as Gunny Taylor and I closed the distance, the wheels in my head were already turning, shaking off some of the shock of the weirdness that had just happened.

When we reached the trees a few seconds later, Gunny echoed my own shout. "Cease fire! Only shoot if they advance and you've got a target!" He looked around, scanning the trees. "Consolidate on me!"

I was scanning for my team. Santos flashed his 15s' IR illuminator at me. "Conor. Over here." The whole platoon was in a ragged line along the edge of the meadow, backs to the cliffs that rose almost sheer above us a few yards deeper into the woods. Everyone was down on a knee, weapons pointed down toward the lower edge of the meadow and the croaking, roaring line of monsters down there.

The initial shock was wearing off. I looked up at the cliffs as I joined the rest of the team, scanning for threats behind us. It's always a temptation to get focused on the immediate fight and abandon rear security. And we'd all done it.

As I looked up, I stopped and stared for a second. I hadn't been imagining things before.

A massive, ugly face had been carved into the cliff above us, glowering toward the sea. It had a roughly human arrangement, but it was at one and the same time apish and somehow...*wrong*. It wasn't a skull, not really. But its proportions were off, and everything seemed a little twisted. There was something infinitely malevolent about its stare.

That was the worst part. The longer I looked at it, the less it seemed like a carving. I could almost swear that it was staring at me. There was something just downright horrifying about it. If anything, for that moment, it was worse than the scaly things baying for our blood down below.

I shook the moment of dread off and returned my attention to the situation at hand, getting Farrar and Smith to watch the woods above us as I took a knee and leaned my ruck against a tree. "Everybody up?"

One by one, Smith, Farrar, Rodeffer, and Santos called out their remaining magazines and that they were "up and up," meaning they were unhurt and still had all their equipment. On average, everyone had used about three mags.

"Watch your ammo. Kill shots only." I was still panting, steam pouring off me, and knew that I needed to be careful. We all did. We'd sweated a ton in our drysuits, and if we stayed put, that sweat could quickly freeze against our skin under these conditions.

It was supposed to be July. There wasn't supposed to be snow. Not at this elevation.

I was getting past the denial stage, though, as I was forced to confront the fact that something really, really weird had happened. We had to figure out what would come next. But I wasn't in charge.

"Team leaders!" Gunny Taylor wasn't trying to whisper. There was no point, as much as the atmosphere tended to make me flinch whenever I heard a raised voice. We were in combat, and it wasn't as if the monsters had lost track of us, even if they hadn't followed us across the meadow.

"One at a time, get dried off if you can, and get changed over into boots and out of your drysuits." I would go last, doing what I could to make sure none of my guys hyped out. I struggled to my feet, unwilling to get more than an arm's length from my ruck right at the moment, and headed for the center of our rough formation.

Captain Sorenson had his ruck off and was down on a knee, staring at his GPS. The glow lit his face brightly in my NVGs, and I suddenly thought that if those things down there had eyes adapted for underwater, they could probably see him clearly. But something was keeping them from coming after us.

"Sergeant Fortuna, when are you going to have comms up?" Sorenson's voice was a little high and a little too loud as he looked over his shoulder at where the platoon radioman was bent over the satcom antenna. "We need emergency extract *now*."

"I'm working on it, sir!" Brad Fortuna was one of the older guys in the platoon, a short, skinny man from New York. He was an 0621, a Field Radio Operator, rather than an 0321 Recon Marine, and he'd had some difficulty keeping up at times. And he was clearly stampeded by just how sideways this op had gone. He sounded close to panic. "I can't get a link with a satellite!"

Gunny Taylor was still standing, looming over Captain Sorenson, looking at his own Garmin. He suddenly shut it off and shoved it back in his chest rig. "No GPS satellites detected, either." He looked around, and even past the tube of his NVGs, I could tell he was thinking as he scanned our surroundings.

Something made me look up. I frowned. "Hey, Gunny? Look at the stars."

Staff Sergeants Bailey and Gurke, Team 3 and 4 team leaders, had just joined us. "I saw it, too." Sean Bailey was a lanky, perpetually sleepy-looking man with curly hair, who was a lot faster and a lot sharper than he looked or sounded. "Nothing's where it's supposed to be." He looked up. "Something's gone well and truly sideways. We are not in Norway."

"What the hell are you talking about?" Sorenson apparently hadn't figured things out from the snow, the unfamiliar terrain—this wasn't the first time we'd made a landing on the beach site north of Trondheimsfjord in the last couple of weeks—and the horrible monsters chasing us out of the surf. "What, you think we just *teleported* somewhere?"

I kept my voice low and level. "I don't know how we got here, sir, any more than I know where we are. But we are *definitely* nowhere near where we're supposed to be." I can't say that I'd ever had a very high opinion of Captain Sorenson, but he wasn't exactly adapting well. And this appeared to be a situation where we had to adapt fast or we were going to be food for something with a lot of teeth.

If only that was all we had to worry about. At the time… we had a lot to learn about this place.

The captain didn't have a response to that, at least not at first, so he snapped at Fortuna again. "Get me comms, Fortuna!"

"Sir, I've double and triple checked the azimuth. I can't get the satellite." Fortuna sounded even more frantic.

"Then get HF up!" High Frequency was the old school way of getting comms. You could bounce a radio signal halfway around the world with HF if you knew what you were doing and the atmospheric conditions were right.

Of course, it still depended on having another station out there to pick up the signal. After everything we'd seen and experienced so far that night, I found that I doubted there was any such station out there. I'd already decided that, wherever we were, it wasn't home. There would be nothing familiar here. Fortuna was on a fool's errand.

I don't know why I was adapting to the strangeness so fast. Sure, I was scared. The more I looked around and realized that we were on our own, a very, *very* long way from home with no idea how we'd gotten there or how to get back, the more the terror started to bubble up in my chest. But I was sort of compartmentalizing it all, dealing with one problem at a time.

Maybe part of it was a simple refusal to get stampeded in front of an officer who was clearly losing his shit.

Gunny interposed, his voice quiet. "Don't bother, Sergeant Fortuna. Pack it up. I think we need to be ready to move."

Captain Sorenson snapped his head around to stare at his platoon sergeant. "Gunny..." His voice was rising again.

"Sir, I don't know what happened, but we need to face facts." Taylor's voice was low, even, and hard. "We are on high ground, with a clear view of the sky, and we can't get a single GPS satellite or a lock on a commsat. The terrain's all wrong, we should be able to see lights from a nearby town or village if we're anywhere within fifty miles of Trondheim, and we can't. Hell, we should be able to see the Amphibious Strike Group from here." He pointed out to sea. "There's nothing."

For the first time since we'd gotten ashore, I looked out over the forest. I hadn't realized how high we'd climbed. The land around Trondheimsfjord wasn't that high, and I hadn't completely adjusted yet. But I could see the dark line of the water out past the lingering fogbank.

No lights. No ships. No aircraft. Just that low-lying, stubborn mist and what might have been low, dark islands somewhere beyond.

"It's supposed to be July, but there's snow on the ground. A lot of it. We're on our own, sir. And frankly, I don't trust that whatever is holding those fish-men back is going to last. We need to move."

But Sorenson was reeling. "No, no, no. This is impossible. We just went through some coastal fog. Maybe we're a bit disoriented..." He snapped at Fortuna. "I told you to get comms up, Sergeant!"

Gunny Taylor had had enough. He grabbed Sorenson by the chest rig and hauled him up to where their NVGs almost knocked together.

"We've already lost three Marines tonight, sir, and I'm not going to lose more because you're cracking up. If you can't lead, you're damned well going to get out of my way." He shoved the captain back against his ruck and straightened up. "Fortuna, pack it up. Team leaders, get your boys ready to move."

Gunny Taylor was not a man given to flights of fancy. He had to be as weirded out by the events of the night as any of the rest of us. But he was a Recon Marine, and he would die before he'd quit. This was a situation that would have a harder man gibbering in confusion and fear, but to Gunny Taylor, it was just a new set of problems to solve.

I'd just turned toward my team when something down by the beach let out a deafening screech, and the monsters surged out of the trees with a chorus of croaking roars.

CHAPTER 4

I turned and dropped to a knee, snapping my rifle up and triggering the IR laser again. A ragged volley of suppressed 5.56 fire crackled across the clearing, and half a dozen of the monsters fell on their faces, staining the snow with their watery blood. The rest kept coming. I shot at one, winged it, and steadied myself as it staggered but came on, thrashing through the powder. Letting my breath out, I steadied the dot on it and fired again. With a harsh *crack*, it fell over backward, coughing blood into the air.

Then, before they'd made it ten yards, the face carved in the rocks above and behind us *shouted*.

There were words in that blast of noise, though I couldn't tell you what they were. The language wasn't one I'd ever heard. It sounded old and deep and dark. Right then, as I staggered and almost fell to my knees, feeling like someone was driving an icepick in through my ears, I wished to never hear it again.

Gunfire was silenced as that awful shout drove us to our knees. It wasn't solely the volume, either. There was hate in those words, a bottomless, ancient malice that you could *feel* clear down to your bones without ever understanding a syllable of that mind-shattering language.

The monsters stopped dead in their tracks, staring vacantly up at the face for a moment. Then it shouted again, and this time they turned tail and ran back into the woods, back toward the water, scrambling and thrashing through the snow and the branches, some of them falling over rocks and logs in their haste to get away from that awful face in the cliff.

All but one. Massive, humpbacked, darker than the others, it lingered at the edge of the trees, its long arms hanging nearly to its knees, its fanged mouth agape, glaring its primal hatred at us and the face alike. It raised its arms and croaked its defiance. A dozen IR laser dots danced on its chest, mine included. I started to take up the slack on the trigger, but then it apparently decided that discretion was the better part of valor and turned to vanish into the darkness under the forest.

I looked back at the face. I wished I hadn't. Whereas before it had been a stone face with a vaguely ominous sense of watchfulness about it, now its eyes glowed balefully in my NVGs, and somehow I knew it was watching us as well as the monsters that had fled back toward the ocean.

And it was definitely *not* friendly.

As the echoes died away, I realized I could hear something else in the distance. Horns. Horns and drums. Something about them was savage, discordant. Deep down, I knew that they weren't friendly, either.

I wondered if there was anything good in this cold, deadly place. Or if we'd gone through that fog bank and into a hell like we'd never even imagined.

Looking toward the center, I spotted Gunny Taylor, his head cocked, looking off toward the north. When the captain started to say something a moment later, Gunny Taylor snapped at him, pointing emphatically toward the southern ridgeline. I didn't need to hear what he said to know exactly what had happened.

Captain Sorenson wasn't making the adjustment well. Whatever had happened, he couldn't accept that we weren't in Norway, and that we most likely weren't going to get comms with the USS *Makin Island* anytime soon. If ever. This was so far outside his experience that he simply couldn't wrap his head around it. He wanted the Ospreys to come and get us, to call "End-Ex" and get this over with.

I still didn't know how I was staying so blasé about all this. I think for most of us, adrenaline and training had taken over.

Once we finally found a safe haven—if any such thing existed here—the adrenaline dump was going to be *rough*.

I struggled back to my feet and headed for my team. All but Santos and I had changed over quickly and were now in cammies and boots, their drysuits and fin booties stuffed in their rucks, fins strapped to the tops. Under most insert/extract criteria, we would have buried the amphib gear, but with the boats abandoned and the plan gone completely to hell in a handbasket, we weren't going to leave *anything* behind that might help an enemy track us.

Presuming these enemies tracked using just their eyes. I didn't know, and in that calm within the storm, I found that my imagination was starting to run a little wild. I could think of all sorts of creepy and mystical stuff, leaving aside simple things like the monsters being able to track by scent.

After dropping my pack, I hastily started skinning out of my drysuit as the rest of the team held security. "Vince, get changed over. I think we've got a couple of minutes at most."

Santos did as I told him, even as I peeled my fin booties off, the cold hitting the sweat and saltwater inside like a knife. I had seconds to hastily try to dry them off, get two pairs of socks on, and pull my boots over them. They weren't the insulated winter infantry combat boots, but they were better than glorified Chuck Taylors.

The drums and horns grew louder. Whoever was out there, they were coming fast.

They'd regret tangling with a Recon platoon. Oh, if they had the numbers, they'd take us down eventually, but with on average about three hundred rounds per man, we'd take a *lot* of them down first.

Gunny came forging through the snow toward us. "Two minutes, and we're moving. You're taking trail, Conor, just because your team is out on this end. We'll figure out more once we reconsolidate, but I don't want to hang out under that thing." He jerked a thumb toward the face in the cliff above us.

I couldn't blame him. I could still *feel* that thing staring at us, though it hadn't made any more noise.

I didn't want to look up at it. I'd seen those eyes glowing in infrared, and I didn't want to see it again.

With a thumbs-up, I finished repacking my ruck and shouldered it again. Santos had beaten me by a second, despite the fact that I'd told him to change over after I'd started.

My team was ready. Everyone was rucked up and back up on a knee, weapons pointed outboard. Farrar and Smith were still facing uphill, toward the gruesome face, though neither of them were looking at it, either. Again, I couldn't blame them.

For a moment, I glanced back down toward the shore, just in case. But the monsters that had chased us out of the water still hadn't returned.

Gunny had already gotten Gurke and Team 4 moving. Sergeant Nelson-Hyde, Gurke's pointman, had started to climb the sheer slope of the ridge that ran down the south side of the meadow. From the looks of things, it was not going to be a fun hike. Even in boots, he was struggling with the slope and the slick footing. I saw him fall on his face, catching himself just before sliding back down toward the meadow below. His M4 hit a rock with a *clack* that was audible across the clearing, despite the rising thunder of drums and hooting of hunting horns on the other side of the massif where the face glowered.

We held our position for the next few minutes, while Team 4 clambered up over the ridge. The drums were getting louder. I wanted to grab Rodeffer and head up to the top of the other ridge, see if we could get eyes on the source of the noises, but that would slow our departure.

And I didn't know what the face would do. Maybe it was some kind of automaton, but something about the aura of hatred and malice around it tended to make me think otherwise. It was watching, and if we didn't get away from it as fast as humanly possible, we might find ourselves in a worse situation.

So, we waited. It felt like hours, as each of the teams—the captain and the platoon support team right behind Team 4—struggled up the ridge and over. I didn't hear any gunfire, and nobody came running back, so we might have caught a little bit of a break. I wouldn't have been surprised if we had just run into another hostile force on the other side of the ridgeline. Not with the way the night had already gone.

We didn't stay in place. We kept moving toward the ridge as the rest of the platoon moved over. I could feel the face staring at us the whole way. And once Rodeffer slung his rifle and cinched it down so that he could have both hands free to help him climb, it felt even more like we were bugs being scrutinized.

Scrutinized by a kid with a magnifying glass. And the kid had Jeffrey Dahmer's temperament.

As I followed Rodeffer up the slope, I found that it was every bit as bad as it had looked while watching the other teams climb over. In fact, it was now worse. Those before us had packed the snow down, and it had frozen, making the footing even slicker and more treacherous. Only the fact that we were all wearing shooter gloves kept us from leaving more than a little blood on the rocks, as every one of us slipped and slid and fell on our faces. Rodeffer got halfway up before he slipped, fell, and kissed a rock, then came up with blood oozing from a fat lip.

"You all right?" I had just about caught up with him and helped him back up to his feet.

"Yeah, I'm fine." He wiped the blood away and grabbed a scrubby pine that was clinging to a tiny bit of soil between the rocks to steady himself. He was a Recon Marine. He wouldn't admit that he was hurting and scared and damned near certain he was going to die before he saw the sun again.

It was still dark, though the stars stood out more brightly than I thought I'd ever seen them. Though I supposed I'd never seen *these* stars before. I glanced at my watch but then let it fall to my side in disgust. There was no way of knowing how accurate it was. If we were somewhere else entirely, I couldn't even be sure that I knew when daylight was supposed to come anyway. And the eastern sky was still as black as ever. No early morning nautical twilight to hide in yet.

Not that the dim transition time between night and day was necessarily going to throw whatever freakish things were banging the drums out in those woods off our trail.

I paused, one hand on the boulder ahead of me, down on a knee to keep from sliding down the way I'd come. I was panting. And… I had to stop thinking like that. Sure, a stone face broadcasting tangible malice was weird, but I hadn't seen anything I could definitively call *supernatural* yet.

My mind provided a counterargument: *The hell you say. What do you call driving a Zode through a fog bank and ending up in another world? If everything else seems sort of natural, that's just because it doesn't compare with* that *weirdness. Yet.*

On that happy note, I set my boot, bracing it against a rock, and heaved myself a little higher up the slope. My suppressor knocked against my knee for the umpteenth time, and I ignored it. It wasn't as if every other part of my body didn't hurt by then.

Looking back over my shoulder, I saw that the team was getting strung out. Farrar was lagging, his heavier radioman's ruck slowing him down and making it even harder to get his footing on the icy rocks. Santos and Smith were behind him, though Smith had his head down and was clearly starting to draw in on himself. Fortunately, Santos had his head up, and I saw him catch up with Smith and say something quietly. Smith looked up and saw Farrar slip, and surged forward to keep the radioman from falling. Smith's ruck wasn't light, either. The assistant radioman carries the extra batteries and the backup radio.

I looked up, craning my neck to get my NVGs high enough to see, just as Rodeffer went over the top of the ridgeline. Almost there.

The drums thundered. A new horn call echoed across the snowy landscape. Or was that something else? Was that a horn, or a voice? I couldn't tell.

I had to struggle to get over the last couple of yards to get over the ridgeline. Not only did it get steeper, but the rest of the platoon had churned and packed the snow, which had frozen almost as fast as they'd passed. The last few feet were almost a solid sheet of ice. I had to pull myself up by rocks and the tiny, scrubby trees clinging to the top. I went over the crest on my knees, my ruck threatening to tip over my head.

The slope on the far side was a lot gentler and heavily wooded. Rodeffer was already a dozen yards down, on his feet, his rifle back in his hands. I got my feet under me, made sure I was braced and unlikely to slip and go tumbling down the hillside toward Rodeffer and the trees, and turned to look behind us.

Smith, Farrar, and Santos were getting closer to the top. So far, Farrar was doing okay. I looked off to the north and west.

I stopped, my eyes narrowing behind my NVGs. Were those sparks? At first they looked like fireflies, flickering in and out of my vision against the darker swath of the woods beyond, which faded into blackness in the distance.

No. They were torches. A lot of them. And they were moving through the forest, toward the hill and the face in the cliff.

That must have been what the horns and the drums were all about. The face had shouted, and the summons had been issued.

But who—or what—was answering the call?

Given the hatred that the face had been broadcasting, I sure didn't think they were the good guys.

I had a moment to think as I waited for Farrar, reaching down to give him a hand to get over the crest. We knew nothing about this place. And it wasn't as if the monsters that had come tearing out of the surf after us were exactly brimming with goodwill. Nor was that... *whatever it was* that had been making those foghorn sounds and driving them at us. Maybe the hatred radiating off the face was somewhat justified if it had been put there to fend off those things.

But I didn't think so. I couldn't put my finger on it, but something about that ugly, malice-twisted image had just felt *evil.* And I didn't think that it was just because I was freaked out about being suddenly thrown into another world.

We were Recon Marines. We'd find out where we were and what was happening. We were information gatherers as well as warriors. But that depended on maintaining some standoff.

With Farrar on his feet, Smith right behind him, I turned and followed Rodeffer into the woods. We'd find out more about our adversaries later.

When we could do it on *our* terms.

CHAPTER 5

ROLLING, forested hills descended from the cliffs toward the north and east, fading into the darkness. Another low peak stood against the shore off to the southeast, and I wasn't sure if I could see the profile of another face there, or if it was just my imagination.

The dark and the wilderness can make a man's imagination run away with him pretty quick. There had been a time, doing night land nav, when I could have sworn that I'd heard voices in the wind as it whispered through the grass on northern Camp Pendleton in the middle of the night. The things seen and heard in the dark while sleep deprived during Patrol Phase of the Basic Reconnaissance Course are legendary in the Recon community. And what had already happened that night could certainly lead a man to thinking he was seeing spooks and monsters behind every rock, even when they weren't there.

Something about that peak we'd left behind us bugged me, though. I didn't think that the face had been put there haphazardly. And the monsters that had pursued us clearly didn't want to mess with it. If they were a threat all along the coast, then it stood to reason that the face might not be alone.

Or maybe it was alone and didn't need backup. Maybe it could see more than its eyes could pick out. Maybe nothing in this place really made sense.

But the terrain was the terrain, gravity still worked, ballistics was still the same, and things still died when you shot or stabbed them. Shot or stabbed them enough times, anyway. So, this place wasn't *completely* nuts.

There was some hope in that thought.

I followed Rodeffer as he fell in behind Gonsalves, Bailey's ATL. The platoon was getting strung out into a rough Ranger file, one man behind the other. It was easiest to control while moving fast, and it often became the sort of default Recon formation on movement.

If we took contact again, we'd adjust. For now, we needed to make tracks. Gunny understood that, and if Captain Sorenson had ever been under the misapprehension that he actually ran the platoon, that was being put to rest as reality asserted itself.

Gunny set a fast patrol pace. We were moving quicker than we might have if stealth was our primary concern but still slowly enough that we shouldn't blunder into anything. I could still turn and look back to check on Farrar behind me, even while scanning the darkness under the trees as I did so.

Something sailed by overhead, and I looked up. There was nothing there but the stars and the still, dark branches of the trees. But I'd heard something. When I checked Rodeffer, he was looking up, too, craning his neck to try to spot whatever it was in his NVGs. The tubes tend to pull your head down, whether on a skullcap mount, one of the old halos, or a bump helmet like we were using.

I heard it again and thought that I caught a glimpse of a shape soaring from treetop to treetop just ahead. It might have been a night bird, an owl or something like it, but it gave no cry, only silently gliding from perch to perch.

Something about the sound its wings made didn't sound right, either. I've spent a lot of time in the woods at night. What I heard didn't sound like an owl's wings or any other feathered bird. That thing's wings sounded somehow more...leathery.

Maybe it was my imagination running away with me again. Or maybe there was a perfectly natural explanation that didn't involve spooks and monsters. Maybe they just had big bats here.

Big bats that don't hibernate in the winter.

Hey, it was possible.

There was nothing for it. We just had to keep going. Local wildlife *probably* wasn't working for the monsters. Probably. After all, they're just animals, right?

Still, that thing—or maybe there were several of them—kept pace with us, swooping with faint *flap*s from tree to tree, going back and forth from the point to the rear of the formation. I could *feel* it watching us. And still, it made no sound except for that strange, leathery flapping. Even that was rare.

Try as I might, I couldn't get a good look at it—only an occasional glimpse of movement and shadow. As we moved deeper into the woods, it kept pace. I couldn't help but wonder if it was really there at all. Wonder if maybe it was just a shadow and a whisper of wind. But I couldn't shake the feeling that even if it *was* only an illusion, there was something else behind it, something watchful.

Maybe I was right. Maybe it was this world's equivalent of a drone. Maybe it was a figment of my imagination—but if that was the case, a lot of other guys were suffering from the same fits of paranoia. Or was it truly a critter of some sort that could move faster than we could track it in NVGs?

Without taking a shot at it—and that might not be a great idea if whoever was carrying those torches was hunting us—there wasn't much we could do.

So, we hunched our shoulders and watched the woods and the treetops more keenly as we trudged through the woods.

Fatigue had started to set in. While the sense of imminent threat around us kept anyone from just shutting down, we had all begun to slow. Farrar stumbled a few times, either tripping over roots or having a rock roll under his boot. The weight on his back was setting in, along with the weariness as the adrenaline started to abandon him.

The combat rush only lasts so long. It treats all of us a little differently. That night wasn't my first time, fortunately. I'd seen action in Syria, so I had a bit better idea of what to expect. I get calm in combat—but the otherworldly weirdness of that night had shaken that to a certain extent. Now I was tired, but I was still on my feet. Some of my Marines, though, had just gotten their first taste. And the comedown could only be put off for so long.

It wasn't just my team, either. I was pretty sure Captain Sorenson had just had his baptism of fire, too.

I slowed, dropping back as Farrar caught up. He was a skinny kid, despite the fact that he lifted weights like a madman. I'd told him for months that he needed to ruck more and lift less, but he'd been trying awfully hard to look like Santos, who was a bear of a man—who could still ruck and run Farrar into the ground. Now, Farrar was clearly starting to hit the end of his endurance. His rifle was slack in his hands, his head was lolling slightly, and he stumbled often. He was panting, steam pouring off his head in the cold and dark.

But we weren't in any position to stop. Not yet. We'd been moving less than an hour since the ridge, and we hadn't put nearly enough distance between us and the face. Or the torches and their bearers.

"One foot in front of the other, Farrar. There's no truck to pick you up here. You fall out, and those things back there are gonna eat you." Harsh? Maybe. But what choice did we have? We were already down three Marines. Anyone taking another ruck was going to get crushed, caught, and killed. And all we had to survive with was in those rucks. There was no rear area. Nowhere to resupply. In time, we'd have to figure out how to live off the land, but for the moment, all the batteries, all the extra ammo, all the water we could be sure about, all the food we knew we could eat, and all the meager snivel gear we'd brought was in those rucks.

Falling out wasn't an option. To fall out was to quit.

To quit, to surrender, to give up is to fail.

To be a Recon Marine is to surpass failure. To adapt, overcome, and do whatever it takes to complete the mission.

I didn't have to tell Farrar that. Sure, he was junior, and this was his first real combat mission—even if it had never been intended to be. But he wasn't a boot. He'd done a float with Battalion Recon already. He knew the Creed. And even if you're not reciting it every day, it becomes a part of your very bones. A refusal to stop, to quit, to give up. It becomes ingrained in a real Recon Marine, if it wasn't there in his DNA already.

Farrar snarled silently without looking at me. Consciously or unconsciously, he straightened up, and his footsteps got surer, crunching through the snow and the forest debris underneath it. I nodded and let him pass, waiting for Santos. He'd stick.

He had to. I hadn't been exaggerating. We had three options: march, fight, or die.

Smith was moving slowly but steadily. Smith was younger than Farrar, but he was a tank. Bigger than Santos, he wasn't quite as tall as me, but he probably outweighed me by twenty pounds. Recon Marines don't tend toward mountains of muscle. Oh, we have our Cro-Mags, and Smith was one of them. But as a whole, we tend toward the lean, wiry types. Big guys don't usually handle mountains well under a heavy ruck. They also tend to get crushed by the water.

But ultimately, that "Never Quit" mindset counts for a lot. And Smith had it.

Santos trudged up to where I waited. I won't lie; I was taking a bit of a breather, even though I did want to talk to him.

Santos looked like a cross between a bear and a shaved gorilla. He tended to shamble like a grizzly on its hind legs, but he was built like a silverback, with long arms and heavy features. The fact that he kept his head buzzed, unlike a lot of Recondos who kept their hair right at the limits of Marine Corps regulations, didn't help that impression. It made the thickness of his facial features and heaviness of his brow stand out all the more. He didn't care. In fact, I'd heard him brag about being a Cro-Mag.

Just before he reached me, though, I heard it.

Conor McCall.

I jerked my head around, scanning the woods. I knew every voice in 1st Platoon, and that wasn't one of us. But I couldn't see anyone but us. I could see Smith clearly, Farrar through the trees, and Santos coming down the shallow hillside toward me. But there were no eyes gleaming in the dark, watching me. Just that voice.

I couldn't even be entirely sure that I'd actually *heard* it. Santos hadn't reacted, and he had the keenest hearing of any Recon Marine I'd ever known. Between the gunfire, explosives, and helicopters, most of us had lost at least *some* hearing. Santos's seemed to just get better. So, if Santos hadn't heard anything…

Dangerous, making any assumptions about this place. I had to remind myself of that. *Keep your wits about you.*

Santos had seen me looking around and slowed as he got closer, scanning the woods. "What's up?"

"Thought I heard something." I didn't want to come right out and say that I'd possibly heard a creepy voice calling my name.

Santos stopped and looked around. He might have grimaced—it was hard to tell in the dark, even on NVGs. "You too?"

I frowned. "Who else?"

"I did. Or I thought I did." He looked behind us, peering up toward the hill we'd already come over, but the woods had closed in around us, and we couldn't see more than a few yards anymore. "Could have sworn I heard someone, or some*thing*, call my name, about half a mile back."

Well, that tore it. I wasn't losing my mind. Or if I was, I wasn't alone. We all were, in exactly the same way. "I don't think we're getting away as cleanly as we hoped."

"No, I don't think so, either." He kept watching the woods around us. "You think they already had people in the woods ahead of us, or are they just that fast?"

I didn't have an answer. In no small part because just then I didn't want to say what I was thinking. Because I didn't think anything that could necessarily be classified as "people" was whispering to us.

The fact that whatever was out there knew our names was the other thing that I really didn't want to think about too hard.

"Keep moving, keep your eyes peeled, and if something calls your name that ain't one of us, *don't answer it.*" The warning hardly seemed necessary, but we were all smoked, and sometimes fatigue makes you stupid. Add in the adrenaline dump and just how weird this place was, and it got even worse.

"Don't worry. I grew up with stories about *brujas*. I know better than to follow mysterious voices whispering my name." Santos was still using his Recon voice, but he was scanning the woods as he spoke. He stopped. With a deep breath, he looked squarely at me. "Damn. Hadn't thought about it that way before. But after what we've seen tonight, I guess we should start thinking about that sort of stuff, huh?"

"Maybe." I was still uncomfortable talking about it. I think Santos was, too. Spooks and monsters and magic weren't things we talked about a lot. Sure, there were a lot of closet nerds in Recon—in any special operations community, from what I'd heard—but it still wasn't something we talked about. We usually tried not to get caught reading stuff like that, either. "Let's keep moving."

The weird part was, as uncomfortable as I still was voicing my thoughts about this place, a part of me was reveling in it. Not the kid part that had played *Baldur's Gate* and read fantasy novels when I didn't think my teammates or platoon mates were watching. No, this was something deeper, more primal.

It was as if being cut off from the Marine Corps and everything else, suddenly finding myself in a wild, untamed place full of enemies, something was awakening deep inside. Something ancient. It was the part of me that got goosebumps when I hear bagpipes. The part that reads the *old* stories, the ones my granddad insisted we learn as McCalls, the tales of Cuchullain and Finn Mac Cumhail, and wishes with every fiber to be back in those days. Days of heroes.

I forced myself to focus on the problem at hand. This wasn't a time for hero sagas. This was a time to escape, evade, stay alive, and reevaluate our situation once we could go firm.

Whatever I'd meant to talk to Santos about had fled, driven out by mysterious voices and shadows moving in the dark. I hadn't heard anything flapping overhead for the last few minutes, but that didn't mean that thing wasn't still up there. For all I knew, that was what had called my name. So, I turned back toward the front and resumed my trudge through the snow, rapidly overtaking Smith and then Farrar. That brief breather had given me a bit of a second wind.

But as I moved forward, I saw that I was just about alone in that. The formation was getting ragged, and we were noticeably slowing down. In fact, Rodeffer had halted just a few dozen yards ahead, leaning against a tree and scanning the woods. Ahead of him, Gonsalves had stopped, too.

I passed Rodeffer, bumping him on the shoulder to make sure he knew it was me, and caught up with Gonsalves. "What's up?"

"Don't know." Gonsalves wasn't much of a talker. He wasn't much of an ATL, either, from what I'd seen, but I usually kept that to myself. He was standing in place, staring up toward where Owens had also stopped, instead of checking on his guys and making sure that if they were halted, they could react to contact. Behind me, I could hear the rustle of movement and crunch of boots in the snow as Santos did just that. I headed for the center, looking for Gunny Taylor.

I found him soon, along with Team 4, kneeling at the edge of the woods. As I joined him, I saw that we were at the foot of a massive tor, a blunt tower of rock rising up out of the forest, its shoulders covered in snow and small scrub pines.

Gunny glanced at me as I took a knee next to him. I was shakier than I'd expected, but we'd covered a lot of ground, and the rucks weren't getting any lighter. Not yet. They'd get entirely too light, entirely too quickly.

"Captain thinks we should go firm here and try to get comms up." Gunny didn't sound convinced. But he also didn't sound like he was about to go all, "Sir, shut the hell up," either.

He was probably thinking what was nagging at my mind. While none of us were ready to admit it, we were all just about done in. If we had to, of course, we'd keep moving and fighting until we were dead. But as another old

Gunny had said when I'd been a mere Lance Criminal, "It's easy to be hard. It's hard to be smart."

"You don't think we're actually going to get comms, do you, Guns?" I wasn't going to say the other part. You can't show weakness. We persevere through pain, agony, and suffering. It's drilled into us from the first moment in the training pipeline.

Suffer in silence.

"No, I don't. But I do think that if we keep pushing, we're going to either find ourselves exposed once the sun comes up, or we're going to start losing dudes in the woods." He glanced around, though not at me. "We've been running enough. Has your team seen any sign of pursuit?"

"Not yet. Well, not really." I wasn't sure whether to talk about the voices, or the flapping shadows in the treetops. After all, we'd all hallucinated when we'd been exhausted and sleep deprived. I knew a guy who'd seen a spaceman crossing the road in front of his vehicle in Syria.

"Define 'not really.'" Gunny wasn't having it. And he was right. We were information gatherers. We just reported. We didn't add, didn't subtract, and didn't interpret.

"We've seen some movement, mostly up in the treetops. I thought it was an owl at first, but it doesn't *sound* like an owl. Hasn't hooted once. And..." This was the tough part. "Both Santos and I thought we heard something call our names. When I heard it, Santos should have been able to, but he didn't hear anything."

Gunny nodded. "Thought so. You're not the only one." He took a deep breath. "I hope you didn't answer."

"Of course not." I might have sounded a little indignant.

"Good. Because Dobbin did. I heard him. And now we can't find him."

That sent a chill down my spine that had nothing to do with the cold. "How far back?"

"Maybe half a mile." He shrugged. "We'll look for him. It's too dark to try to track back there right now, even in the snow and on NODs."

I wondered a little at that. Some of the shadows under the trees *had* been strangely darker than others. It didn't seem natural.

"Bring your team up and set up defensive positions here under the trees. We'll consolidate, then put a team together to check out that rock formation. If we can get most of us into the cracks, we might have found our patrol base for a while."

I nodded and got up to move. Before I could leave, though, Gunny reached out and grabbed my sleeve. "Conor? Watch the shadows. Sometimes they move when you're not looking."

CHAPTER 6

IT didn't take all that long to get set in; we were in the rear, after all. I got the team down and behind some cover and joined Gunny, the Captain, and the other team leaders at the edge of the trees.

"Hey, Conor. Do those look like walls to you?" Bailey was pointing up at the tor that loomed against the stars in front of us.

I squinted up at the silhouette. Between the snow on the ground and the stars above, the tor itself was a black mass against the sky. But on further inspection, it did appear that there were walls on top of the mass of rock. Ruined walls, falling down in places, but walls nevertheless.

"That's the most prominent piece of terrain around." Captain Sorenson had apparently gotten over his shock and dismay at what had happened so far and was trying to take charge again. Down on one knee, his ruck on the ground next to him, he was making a little sand table in the snow, as if we couldn't just look at the tor right in front of us. "While it might be a bit conspicuous, it's also probably the most defensible spot. I think I should take a leader's recon and check it, then we can set up our patrol base on top of it if it looks feasible."

"Not much camouflage up there." I didn't think Zimmerman was really that concerned. He was just a contrary, angry man who really didn't like the captain. Granted, I didn't think most of us really *liked* Captain Sorenson, but most of us also made something of an effort not to openly antagonize him.

Of course, Zimmerman would probably turn around and defend the captain in the next minute if one of the other team leaders rubbed him the wrong way. That was the kind of guy Zimmerman was.

The fatigue was wearing on all of us. Also, I think that this place was getting to more than a few of us. That, and the darkness. The sun should have been up by then if we'd been in Norway.

"I think we should send a small team, sir." Gunny was back to playing diplomat. He could do that, though he was usually more comfortable snapping at anyone who got out of line—up to and including the platoon commander. "Leader's recon really isn't where you're supposed to be." He politely left out the fact that without higher to deal with, the captain was a fifth wheel for the platoon. We all had more experience in the Recon field than he did. He'd spent the bulk of the train-up in the ROC—the Recon Operations Center. Sure, that had been a truck in the field most of the time, but it's not the same thing as humping a ruck over a mountain and hiding in a hole in the enemy's backyard for days at a time.

But Sorenson wasn't happy to hear that. He'd never been particularly happy when any of us had kind of shoved him aside and said, "We'll handle this, sir." For a moment, it looked like he was about to argue with Gunny Taylor.

Finally, he took a deep breath. "All right, Gunny. Who would you recommend?"

Taylor looked around at the four of us. "Who's up for some rock climbing?"

There was a pause. I don't think any of us were going to necessarily turn the mission down, but everyone was tired and increasingly cold since we'd stopped moving. It was taking some extra time for the words to move from brain to mouth. We were physically and mentally stiff with the cold.

"We'll go, Gunny." I was slightly surprised that I'd gotten it out first. Maybe I was just warmer, having been the last one to stop moving.

Not that I think any of us were eager to climb that massive lump of rock. Aside from the risks inherent in scrambling over boulders in the dark, covered in ice and snow, it was still night, and after what we'd just seen, there was no way to tell just what we might find lurking in the rocks. Snakes in the desert were one thing—this was something else.

Gunny nodded. "We don't know when the sun's actually going to come up, so don't take too long. But step carefully, watch your backs, and watch your steps."

There wasn't much more to say. I got up and headed back to where my team was set in behind a fallen tree. The massive trunk must have been over a century old before it had fallen.

"Everyone drop rucks." I thought for a second, studying Farrar. He was clearly done in, though to his credit, he hadn't just done the rucksack flop and lay there. He was up on his rifle, leaning against the icy, snow-covered log, but he was obviously about to fall down if not for the tree trunk in front of him. "Rodeffer, Smith, with me. We're going to take a look around that big rock over there, see if we can set up a patrol base on top before the sun comes up."

Nobody said much. I heard Rodeffer grumbling about getting the least time to rest out of the platoon, but he said it under his breath as he set his ruck and got up, slinging his rifle and getting ready to move. If he'd slacked, I'd have gotten on him, but as my first team leader had told me, "If Marines ain't bitching, there's something wrong." Especially in a situation like this, Marines needed to vent a little. So long as he didn't slack off, fall out, or compromise security, then Rodeffer could bitch all he wanted.

It took moments. We all still had our gear on and our rifles in hand. We'd already dropped our rucks. I just had to fill Santos in on the plan, and then I nodded to Rodeffer and pointed toward the tor.

The clearing was larger than I'd thought—the tor was farther away than it had looked at first. The snow was deeper out in the open, too. We all felt considerably lighter without the rucks, but the snow rose nearly to our knees in places, and after a night's fighting and running through the woods with rucks, the footing felt even less certain than usual. We plowed our way toward the tor, though Rodeffer had the most work, breaking trail while keeping his eyes up and out, looking for monsters or whatever new threat was about to come out of the dark.

I looked up. The tor towered over us, and we still had about twenty yards to go. It was a *lot* bigger than I'd initially thought. It was a small mountain in and of itself. The ground was slowly rising toward the base, and it was getting rockier under the snow.

Rodeffer slowed, staring up at the base of the tor. He motioned me forward, so I struggled through the snow to join him.

"Are those stairs?" He pointed toward the base of the stone cliff that rose above us.

"Sure looks like it." I followed the line of the steps as they curved up the side of the cliff and then ended at what looked like a crack in the rock. "Take it slow, watch your angles." I wasn't *entirely* sure of the wisdom of going into an unknown cave with three guys, but we were past the limits of what I knew at that point, so we'd go in until we had to back out.

Rodeffer trudged the rest of the way to the steps, which seemed to have only a dusting of snow on them. In fact, the snow had thinned as we'd gotten higher. It seemed that we were on the leeward side of the tor—the winds off the ocean swept most of the snow into drifts against the other side.

Lifting his M4 to cover the crack in the rock, Rodeffer started up the steps. I closed in to follow.

The steps were taller than I was used to. I almost tripped over the first one and had to slow down as we ascended. Step by step, we climbed up the face of the cliff.

Rodeffer paused at the top of the steps. The ground lay a good ten yards below us. The steps ended in empty space, except for the opening that led back into the dark immediately to our left.

As I stepped up behind Rodeffer, he triggered his IR laser and illuminator, playing them over the rock. Under the bright light, brilliant green in my NVGs, I could see that the opening was more than just a crack. It was a nearly triangular portal deliberately cut into the stone. If there had been a door or a gate on the other side, it was long gone. Some rubble lay on the ground, but that was it.

The passageway went straight into the cliff. Beyond lay only darkness.

I took my hand off my M4's forearm and reached up to squeeze Rodeffer's shoulder. I could feel Smith right behind me. "With you."

He followed his muzzle around the corner, ducking to get under the gateway, though it was tall enough that he really didn't need to. I followed, stepping out slightly wider to bring my own rifle down past his shoulder, putting both muzzles into the gateway. I triggered my own laser and illuminator as soon as we came level.

The two beams shone down the middle of a narrow gatehouse, empty except for faintly drifted snow against one wall. When I played my IR light over the ceiling, I saw holes bored through the rock at regular intervals.

Something told me to stay out from under those, whether the tor was abandoned or not.

We moved carefully through the gatehouse and stacked up just outside the next door. We didn't wait long but pushed through into the next chamber.

We were in a hall, easily three stories from floor to vaulted ceiling. Like the gatehouse, it was empty, though lined with more dark passageways like gaping maws to either side. The hall was echoingly empty, every scuff of a boot sounding achingly loud. Nothing broke the open expanse of leveled rock; great flying buttresses from the walls held the ceiling high above.

It wasn't the quiet or the darkness, or even the awareness of thousands of tons of rock above our heads that creeped me out as we moved around the edge of the open hall, pieing off each doorway as we passed it. The doors led into other, smaller chambers, as near as I could tell. I could even see a window looking out at the woods in one.

No, it wasn't the quiet or a sense of claustrophobia that creeped me out.

It was the eerie familiarity of the place.

I couldn't figure it out. Obviously, I'd never been there before. I'd never been anywhere like it. Maybe I'd seen it in a movie.

I was soon to realize that *that* wasn't it, either.

Rodeffer had paused at the first chamber, but I waved him on. We could clear chamber by chamber later. If we were going to get the rest of the platoon out of the open, we needed to establish that we weren't going to get eaten as soon as we set foot inside. This was just a leader's recon.

A larger gate stood at the far end, with a spiral staircase beyond it. But that wasn't what made me stop, even as Rodeffer moved to the opening.

The gateway was flanked by two statues. They were ancient, worn down by time, ice, and moisture, so there was little detail left. Only the vaguest impression of armor and great axes remained. Or maybe they were maces. It was hard to tell.

But I recognized them. I'd seen them before. And I suddenly remembered where.

I'd had strange, vivid dreams for a couple of days before we'd inserted. They'd been weird enough that I'd kind of put them aside as soon as I'd woken up. It hadn't been the first time—weird dreams often go along with stress, hunger, and sleep deprivation, and Recon excels at doling those out. So, the details had fled, and I hadn't thought about them since.

Until now. When I looked at those statues, it was like a snapshot from one of those dreams came back. I'd stood right there, in that hall, looking at those statues in a dream before we'd ever crossed over into this place.

That gave me the creeps.

The realization lasted just long enough that I kind of stutter-stepped before the urgency of the mission at hand reasserted itself. I really didn't want to go through that door, not after remembering that dream. Even though I couldn't remember anything else except that image. But it was hardly the first time I'd had to reach down, grab hold, and do what needed doing despite the fact that I really didn't want to.

I don't like heights. I jumped out of the airplane anyway.

So, with hardly a pause, I came up to Rodeffer, put my hand on his shoulder while I tilted my M4 muzzle up, and said, "With you."

We went through the gate, guns up and IR lights searching out every nook and cranny where something with lots of teeth and claws might be hiding.

It's surprisingly not that different from regular CQB—Close Quarters Battle—where you have to not only clear your corners and dead space but watch for murder holes in the walls and ceilings, too.

The chamber at the base of the stairs was as empty and barren as everything else we'd seen so far. This place had been abandoned for a long time.

Together, weapons held ready and covering up the stairwell and searching for any openings that might present a threat, we started up.

That was a long staircase. I didn't think to count the steps, but we went up three stories before we came to the first doorway. The pulverized fragments of what might have been a wooden door lay on the floor just inside. Our IR lights revealed a narrow hallway with the black openings of doorways on either side, carved out of the solid rock.

Two figures loomed at the far end of the hallway.

I snapped my light toward one, and Rodeffer, reacting rather than thinking, pinned the same one with his own illuminator. Our laser dots danced on it for a second, fingers hovering near triggers as we watched to see if it was going to move.

But it stayed as motionless as stone. And after a moment, I saw that it *was* stone. Another statue, as worn down and weathered as the two below. I checked the second figure and saw that its condition was the same.

It still felt wrong to turn away from them. We'd seen a stone face shout that night already. Who knew what might decide to get up and move in this place?

Smith took over covering the door as Rodeffer and I continued up. He didn't take many steps after that without turning to check our six, either. None of us knew whether 5.56 might be effective against stone, but we'd damn well make sure any walking statues knew they'd been in a fight.

The stairs continued up. Now that we were above the main hall, the doors opening onto other chambers got more common. Still, the only sound was the faint scrape of our boots on the cold stone steps.

It was frigid in that stairwell. Despite the exertion, I was chilled to the bone. We didn't have enough snivel gear for this place.

Finally, we came to a slanted opening that led into the open air. Snow had drifted down on the top steps, and Rodeffer slowed even more as he approached the portal. The snow was undisturbed. No prints, no nothing.

We came out onto an open courtyard on top of the tor, surrounded by crumbling walls. Snow blanketed the stone, including the four statues who stood on a plinth at the center, staring out to north, south, east, and west.

I got that same sense of weird familiarity. It wasn't as intense as the snapshot I'd seen in my mind of the statues below in the main hall, but I still felt like I'd somehow seen this place before, seen these weathered figures that now looked like little more than rounded obelisks, though their hollow, carved eyes still stared out at the surrounding wilderness.

Despite the lack of tracks in the snow, we spread out and cleared the courtyard. It spanned almost the entire width of the tor, almost fifty yards from one side to the other. And aside from the statues, it was as empty and barren as every chamber we'd seen below.

I moved to the edge and looked out over the ruined wall. The tor stood high above the valley, and as the eastern sky lightened, I could see a lot farther.

The woods on the lower side of the tor thinned quickly, leading down toward a river that wound between the hills. Jagged mountains rose in the distance to the north and east.

Even as I looked back the way we'd come, to see the distant flicker of torches on the ridgeline, something like a big, black bat flapped away from the rocks nearby, heading toward the face in the cliff.

CHAPTER 7

WITH the sun coming up and confirmation that there wasn't a horde of monsters waiting in the dark for us, it was a quick movement to get the platoon inside. Zimmerman's Team 2, down to four men though it was, headed up to the courtyard on top of the tor to establish overwatch, while the rest of the platoon cleared the inside, chamber by chamber.

The place had been a fortress, carved right out of the rock. It was an astounding bit of engineering, especially given how tangibly, incredibly ancient it was.

By the time we'd finished, the sun was fully up, light streaming in through several high channels bored through the rock. It didn't cast a lot of illumination in the main hall, which seemed like it had served as a sort of interior courtyard, but it was enough to see without needing NVGs and IR lights.

While the external chambers and passageways were cleared, the rest of the platoon gathered back in that hall.

"Fortuna, get up to the top and get comms up." Captain Sorenson stood in the middle of the great hall, his hands on his hips. "I don't care how long it takes, I want comms with the *Makin Atoll* or absolute confirmation that we can't get them."

I traded glances with Bailey across the chamber. Everyone had to know by then that we weren't going to get comms. There was no one out there to hear.

Unless there was, somewhere, by some means that we didn't understand. But it seemed to me that if there was anyone nearby in this world who could receive our radio signals, we probably didn't necessarily want them to.

Fortuna heaved his ruck onto his back with a groan, though, and started toward the spiral staircase. I turned back to my team, most of whom were already wrapped in their poncho liners to try to hold off the chill.

"All right." Gunny's voice boomed around the hall. "Which one of you brought a tomahawk?"

Silence fell over the hall as a bunch of Recon Marines tried not to look sheepish. Most of us had some kind of oversized edged weapon, not so much out of practicality as wishful thinking. Everybody wanted to be the guy who got a knife kill. Strangely, the only one I knew of who'd actually done it had ended up accomplishing that coveted feat simply because he was checking out a canal and had handed off his rifle for a moment. When he stepped down into the water, he found himself face to face with an insurgent armed with an AK, with nothing but his bare hands and a folder in his pocket.

Several almost sheepish hands went up. I dug in my ruck and pulled my Bowie out. "It's not a tomahawk."

Gunny eyed it. "No, that's not a tomahawk. That's a short sword. But it'll do." He looked around. "Come on. You nerds who packed extra weight because you wanted to look cool are going to be the foresighted, prepared geniuses who might just save all our hides."

Captain Sorenson was frowning, his hands still on his hips. "What are you talking about, Gunny?"

Gunny Taylor raised an eyebrow and pointed around at the men huddled in their poncho liners and ponchos. "It's cold as hell here, sir. We didn't pack for winter ops. If we don't get a fire going in here, then guys are going to hype out at best, freeze to death at worst."

Sorenson's frown deepened. He didn't like the idea of a fire. If I was being honest, I think all of us had had the same reflexive reaction. Fire means light and smoke. It leaves behind ash and charcoal. It's anathema to men whose entire profession revolves around slipping across the landscape undetected.

But Gunny was right. We weren't equipped for this cold, the stone was going to suck the heat right out of us just by sitting on it, and we were inside.

Not to mention the fact that somebody already knew we were somewhere in the vicinity. There was no hiding that after we'd expended hundreds of rounds killing those scaly fish-men the night before.

Gunny ignored the captain's disapproving frown and pointed. "McCall, I know you and your guys reconned this place first, but since you've got that big pigsticker, I want you to take Rodeffer, Herrera, Applegate, Synar—Applegate? You're an RTO. What are you doing packing that kind of cutlery?"

Sergeant Roy Applegate was a barrel-chested powerlifter who nevertheless could out-ruck most of the rest of the platoon. Which was a good thing for a radioman. He grinned as he hefted the angular, black tomahawk. "Because you never know, Gunny. You never know."

"Whatever. I need you to go out and get some firewood. Enough to last, but don't all get so loaded up that you can't fight."

"I don't think this is a good idea in daylight, Gunny." Sorenson hadn't moved, his frown deepening.

"We won't be going far into the woods, sir." I beat Gunny Taylor to the punch for once. "And Zimmerman and his team will be up on overwatch. Gunny's right—it's below freezing in here, and this is going to be a case of fire or death before too long." I didn't add that trying to maintain stealth at this point was probably moot. I couldn't help but think of that bat-thing I'd seen flying away from the top of the tor.

I mean, I didn't *know* that it was anything but a bird or an actual bat. There was no way to be sure that it was some kind of spy, and in fact, if not for the other weirdness we'd already seen, the very assumption would have sounded crazy.

But once you've seen fish-men come out of the water and tear one of your Marines' heads off, or heard a stone face shout from a mountainside, all after being apparently teleported somewhere you couldn't begin to recognize, you stop taking things for granted.

Gunny Taylor looked around the room. Everyone's breath was a smoking cloud, and a couple of the Marines were starting to shiver violently, even with their Ranger rolls wrapped around their shoulders. "Sir, hypothermia is every bit the threat that the enemy is right now. We haven't had anyone freeze or hype out yet because we've been running and fighting all night. We have to take the risk."

Captain Sorenson looked for a moment like he was still going to say no. I had a sudden feeling that if that happened, things were going to get very… interesting in that hall.

"Fine." He looked at me. "But make it fast, stay under cover as much as possible, and maintain security."

Go lecture somebody else, sir. I was doing this while you were a 2nd Lieutenant in The Basic School. I didn't say it, but I sure thought it real loud. I just nodded, tight-lipped, and bit back my temper. I looked around at the Marines that Gunny had picked out. "Weapons and ammo only. Empty your rucks out so we can carry firewood." That was a risk—if we got hit and had to break out, then they'd be without anything but the survival gear on their bodies. But we didn't have a better way to carry firewood while keeping our weapons in hand.

That took a few minutes, the gear, water, chow, and batteries forming little piles against the stone wall before we slung on the empty rucks and headed for the gatehouse. I could feel Captain Sorenson's eyes on me as we went.

Just before we left, Gunny pulled me aside. "Go ahead and take the time to get a good look at our surroundings. And Conor? If you can, find out what happened to Dobbins."

I nodded. "On it, Guns."

I had to squint as we stepped outside. Though the sun was barely above the mountain peaks to the east, it was already glaring painfully off the snow around the base of the tor. I wanted to get into the tree line fast, if only to get some shade before I went snow-blind.

A glance up at the top of the tor only showed me the ruined walls, starkly silhouetted against the pale blue of the sky. Zimmerman and his boys were up there, but they were staying out of sight. As they should.

We hustled across the meadow, moving fast with the empty rucks. It being broad daylight, we'd shed our bump helmets and NVGs, and my head was cold despite the fleece watch cap I had donned. I'd taken that thing everywhere, winter or summer, and it was getting a little thin, but I was extremely glad I had it.

The snow was still deep enough that we couldn't move as fast as I wanted to, but we got to the trees without incident. I had Rodeffer push a few yards in before calling a halt.

We didn't get right to work. I wasn't ready to throw our tactics, techniques, and procedures out to that extent. We stopped, set security, and waited, watching and listening.

Somewhere, a raven croaked. That sound at least was familiar. The cry echoed across the snowy woods and the valley around us. Maybe my imagination was running away with me, but it sounded almost like there were words in it.

I shook my head. Despite the threatening strangeness of this place, the trees were still trees, the rocks were still rocks, and I had to assume that most of the animals were still animals. Not *everything* here was necessarily out to get us.

Boy, did I have some learning to do.

A clump of snow fell from the boughs of a tree up ahead with a muffled *whump*. All eyes turned that way, muzzles tracking toward it. "Watch your sectors," I hissed.

Nothing showed itself, though. Even the eerily deep shadows had fled with the coming of day. And we had a limited amount of time. Fortunately, a dead tree stood only a few yards away, gray against the dark green and white of the other trees. The trees looked like regular fir and spruce, though somehow they seemed darker, shading toward black rather than blue.

"Come on. Let's go find Dobbins." I got up and pointed to Rodeffer. He nodded and got to his feet, then we started along our back trail.

It wasn't quite a half mile before we found Dobbins' tracks going off to one side, into a thick stand of trees just uphill from our main trail. Spreading out, we moved toward that stand of trees, weapons up and eyes and muzzles moving around constantly. After all, whatever had happened to Dobbins, he hadn't made a sound after answering the voice in the dark.

He hadn't made it far.

We found him face down in the snow, impaled through the throat by a branch sticking out of a gnarled, lighting-blasted tree. He still had all his gear, and his weapon was stuck muzzle-down in the snow.

I didn't touch him at first but scanned the woods around us carefully, my weapon up and my hackles standing on end.

There were no tracks behind him for ten feet. He'd been picked up and *thrown* against that branch.

And whatever had done it hadn't left tracks, either.

"Set security." I wasn't going to leave this to one of the others. I slung my rifle to my side and stepped forward to pull the body off the broken branch. "We'll take him back and then get the firewood."

* * *

"Rodeffer, Synar, and I will hold security." I shrugged out of my ruck. It had taken most of an hour to get

Dobbins' body back and then turn around and head into the woods again, while Zimmerman and his team saw to the body. We probably wouldn't be able to take him with us whenever we left this place, and burying him in frozen ground was out of the question, too. Zimmerman had already found a chamber to lay him in, far from the main hall. "Herrera, Applegate, get to chopping. Once you've filled your rucks, we'll switch out."

After slinging their rifles, the two of them moved to the dead tree. Applegate hefted his tomahawk, but Synar, who had an RTAK, a mutant cross between a Bowie and a machete, held back, looking up at the trees for a moment with a frown. "Hold up, Roy."

"What?" Applegate looked back at him. Synar was one of the skinny guys, red-haired and freckled. He was a quiet dude, too, which often drew Gonsalves's ire. But where Gonsalves was a bully, Applegate was the kind of guy who listened. "You hear something?"

Synar shook his head slowly. "No. It's just… I don't know. What's going to happen if we start cutting into one of these trees?"

"This ain't a Disney movie. The trees ain't gonna come alive and start trying to eat you." Applegate turned toward the tree and lifted his tomahawk.

"No, it ain't a Disney movie." Rodeffer didn't take his eyes off his sector, but he was listening. "Disney movies don't usually have your teammate getting his head ripped off right at the beginning." He spat in the snow. "Let's not take anything for granted."

Applegate sighed. "Look, if the trees were going to come alive and come after us, don't you think they would have done it at night, when we were all strung out and trying to hide in the woods? They're just trees."

Even so, despite his confidence, Applegate seemed a little more hesitant when he swung his tomahawk into the lowest branch.

The 'hawk lopped the branch off with a resounding *thwock* that echoed through the trees. I think we all flinched a little at the noise. There was nothing we could do about it, though. Even if we'd just started cracking branches off, it still wouldn't have been silent.

When no tree monsters opened their eyes and came after us, Synar shook his head and went to work on the other side of the dead tree.

For a while, the only sound was the somewhat rhythmic *whacks* of hatchet and machete as they stripped off and trimmed the lower branches. By the time their rucks were full, they were bristling with good kindling.

"We need some fuel." I eyed the tree as I swapped places with Applegate, hefting my Bowie. Unlike most of the other edged weapons, it wasn't powder-coated or otherwise blackened. It wasn't that shiny though—the blade was darkened by time and wear.

That Bowie had been in my family for a *long* time. The bone handle was as worn as the steel. It looked positively ancient compared to Synar's RTAK. It had been to every war a McCall had gone to fight for almost two centuries. It had been to North Africa and Italy with my grandpa, my dad had taken it to Vietnam, and I'd taken it to the Middle East.

I could still shave with it. It almost felt wrong to use it for this, but what else did I have?

"We need fuel. We're going to have to bring this tree down." I went to work, glad that it was only about six or eight inches thick. I started chopping a notch on one side. After a moment, Rodeffer joined me with his tomahawk, and in a few seconds we had a rhythm going, each man chopping the notch deeper after the other.

It took a while to fell that tree. All the while, those harsh *thwocks* echoed out across the valley. It was making me nervous. I glanced up at the top of the tor, and this time I saw one of Zimmerman's guys, on his rifle, watching over the top of the ruined wall. They hadn't started shooting yet, so nothing was coming to investigate the noise we were making.

Finally, we shoved it over, the last of the trunk cracking as it gave way. After the chopping and the sound of breaking wood, the trunk made a surprisingly muffled *whump* as it hit the snow. It didn't even bounce.

We set to bucking it up, while Synar, Applegate, and Herrera held security. We worked fast, or as fast as we could, given the fact that the tools we had weren't exactly adequate, and I thought that Applegate and I were probably the only ones who'd done this before. Applegate had grown up on a ranch in Colorado, and I'd lived in the mountains for a couple of years after high school and before the Marine Corps.

It felt like the quiet was deceptive, that something was coming. Something had to have heard the noise we were making, and the longer we were out there, alone in the snow, the more easily it was going to swoop down and kill us all.

Or worse.

We didn't try to split the rough log rounds we chopped the trunk into but just shoved them into rucks. Finally, all our rucks loaded with firewood, we started back. If it was possible, I think we were eyeing the shadows under the trees a little more closely as we stepped out into the clearing at the foot of the tor.

I looked up as we came out, squinting against the stark white glare of the sun. In that moment, I saw the figure of the Marine up on top of the tower shift, getting behind his ACOG as he turned and brought his rifle to his shoulder.

I turned and followed the line of his gaze, though I didn't think I'd be able to see anything because of the woods. I was wrong, though. A gap in the trees opened the way toward a saddle on the ridge that climbed off to the northwest.

A lone figure sat atop a massive horse in that saddle, dark against the snow. And unless I missed my guess, it was watching us.

A moment later, my suspicion was confirmed as it lifted a horn to its mouth and a dark, haunting call roared out over the valley.

CHAPTER 8

EVERY nerve screaming in anticipation of an imminent attack, we hustled back toward the stairs. It was rougher going—we'd already packed trails in the snow, and they were getting slick. Add in the rucks full of firewood, and it slowed us down even more.

Santos and Smith were at the top of the stairs, on a knee on the snow-covered stone, weapons out, scanning the woods behind us. "Friendlies coming up!" I probably didn't need to deconflict—there couldn't be many people running around this place in woodland MARPAT camouflage and carrying M4s. But something told me that it would pay to be careful in the days ahead.

Provided we survived.

I scanned the woods and the snowy hills around us as we climbed the steps. I couldn't see that saddle anymore—it was on the far side of the tor. I could see quite a good distance as we got higher, though. I continued to scan for threats, but the hard work of getting firewood so that we didn't freeze to death had brought something else to mind.

Food.

We had about four days' worth of MREs. Maybe six, if we stretched things. After that, unless we found something edible out there, we were going to start to starve to death.

Living off the land in the winter is doable, but it's not fun. And I hadn't seen much in the way of deer tracks so far. Not that I'd been looking all that carefully.

Another horn call drove thoughts and plans for hunting and gathering out of my head as I reached the top of the steps. Santos was listening, his dark eyes moving back and forth across the woods to the south as his gloved fingers flexed around his M4.

"I don't like the sound of that." He kept his voice low, just in case the captain was listening. He'd gotten on us more than once about "complaining."

"I don't either." I paused as Herrera and Synar shuffled inside with their loads, letting them go in first so I could check our six and talk to Santos. "It's a horseman, up on the ridge to the north of where we came over."

He looked a little spooked. "Isn't that where we saw all those torches last night?"

"Close to it." I squinted around at the snowy, sunlit landscape. It was peaceful and beautiful, in a wild, frigid way. And yet, it hid dangers we hadn't even begun to think about. "We covered a lot of ground last night, though. And we don't know enough about this place. We know there are fish-men in the water and a talking stone head on the cliff. That's it. Maybe whoever was carrying those torches were good guys." I didn't believe it. Not after the heebie-jeebies I'd gotten from that face in the cliff. Those torches had come swarming toward the coast not long after that thing had shouted. "We need to step carefully until we know more."

Santos snorted. "That's not exactly our strong point. Especially not with Captain Medal Chaser up there." That last was delivered as a mutter.

I shook my head a little as I turned to carry my load of firewood inside. "No medals to chase here. I think he'll figure that out quick enough. He's not stupid. We're alone and unafraid. We've got the platoon to rely on and nothing else."

"Give him time." Santos didn't sound optimistic.

I'd gotten another step inside the gatehouse when another horn call echoed over the treetops. Santos stiffened as I turned to look.

I couldn't see anything different, but that hadn't been the same horn. The pitch was different. This was an answering call.

"Be ready to fall back inside the gatehouse if things get weird." I turned back inside, suddenly anxious to get the wood unloaded and get back out there with my rifle. "We'll be back out soon."

Gunny already had Rodeffer, Herrera, Applegate, and Synar unloading their rucks. "Since you've got the biggest hatchet, Applegate, start splitting some of that big stuff." Gunny himself was already down on his knees, shaving some of the branches into tinder, a small pile of kindling nearby.

If it had been anyone else in the platoon but Gunny Taylor, I probably would have told them to get lost and let me do it. But the little survival kits we all carried on our bodies at all times, with included fire starters, had been his idea, not mine.

I had just pulled my ruck off and was about to say something about the horn calls when Esposito, Zimmerman's pointman, came tearing into the main hall from the spiral staircase, panting. "Somebody's coming. We've heard horn calls from the northwest and the east."

Gunny looked up from the fire lay. "Do you have eyes on?"

Esposito shook his head. "Just the horn calls, so far. But that first one sounded close."

"It was." I dropped my ruck full of pine logs next to Gunny. "There was a horseman watching us from that saddle to the northeast. He was the one who sounded that first horn."

"He still there?" Gunny looked over at Esposito. But the stocky, red-haired man shook his head.

"He rode back into the trees after he got an answer from the east." Esposito had calmed down a bit as he caught his breath from the descent. "We haven't seen any other movement yet…" He paused and kind of winced. "Unless you count some big black things flying over the trees above that saddle."

"Birds." Captain Sorenson had come out of his corner, where he had a Toughbook laptop hooked up to one of our radio batteries. I didn't know what he hoped to accomplish with it, especially since we didn't have comms, GPS wasn't working, and we had zero imagery for this place, anyway. "Why are we worried about birds, now?"

"They don't look like birds, sir." Esposito seemed a little uncomfortable, and well he should. He'd been the target of the captain's ire before. Esposito had usually turned out to be right in the end, but instead of fueling his own defiance, he'd gotten a bit reluctant to speak up around the platoon commander. "More like really, really big bats."

"This is supposed to be a Marine Recon platoon," Sorenson snapped. "Why is everyone acting like scared kids in the woods?"

Gunny Taylor slowly turned to look at the captain. I couldn't see the expression on his face from where I stood, but I knew that basilisk glare all too well. "We can't take anything for granted here. We still don't know how we got here, or even where 'here' is. Our first contact with anything living in this place was an attack that cost us three Marines, and the attackers weren't anything I'd call natural. Nothing we've seen since has made me inclined to think that we're anywhere that the rules we grew up with apply, aside from the fact that exposure, dehydration, starvation, and violence can still kill you. So, *sir*, I'm inclined to treat anything as a threat until proven otherwise. Even it if is just a big bat. A big bat that doesn't hibernate in the winter and flies around in broad daylight."

Sorenson said nothing at first. It was dark enough in that hall, lit only by a couple of flashlights and the sunlight filtering down through the openings high above, that I wasn't sure if anyone else saw the brief flicker of pure fury that flashed across the captain's face.

My own jaw tensed as I watched him. Something hot and dangerous rose in my chest. I'd clashed with the platoon commander before. Most of us had, team leaders and assistant team leaders alike. Nearly all of us had far more experience in Recon than he did, but he was an officer. Usually, Gunny had managed to maintain a buffer between his team leaders and his platoon commander, alternately getting us to calm down and showing the captain the error of his ways when he could.

Sometimes, Gunny's intervention had been far more diplomatic than ours would have been. Other times—usually in situations that were about to turn into emergencies—he'd simply barked at Sorenson like he was a boot private. And despite the fact that he'd obviously resented such treatment, even Sorenson hadn't wanted to tangle with Gunny Taylor.

Now, I could see that the captain's resentment hadn't gone away. And it was probably stacking on the embarrassment that he'd reacted to our initial contact with what amounted to a freak-out instead of steely-eyed Marine Officer Leadership.

That could get to be a problem. We weren't in a position where we could afford runaway egos.

Captain Sorenson just tried to stare Gunny down for a long moment, then, his lips pressed tightly together, he spun on his heel and went back to his corner.

I caught a glance from Gurke, Team 4's team leader. The look on his face said, "What the hell's his problem?" I shrugged, though I had a pretty good idea.

Bailey just rolled his eyes.

Gunny glared after the captain for a moment before turning back to his fire lay. A quick few strokes of the spine of his knife along the ferrous rod got enough sparks into the tinder that it caught, and a few minutes later, he had the beginning of a good blaze going. "Don't let that go out." He stood up. "Gurke, your team is on gate security. Since it doesn't look like there's another entrance here, we should be able to go to fifty percent until we see enemy forces coming in after us." He looked around at Bailey's and my teams. "The rest of you get some sleep while you can. It's been a long night already. If we're not fighting for our lives again before then, you'll switch out in two hours."

The fact that he hadn't seen fit to say anything about the little confrontation between him and the captain was not lost on any of us.

I pulled Santos and Smith back from the gatehouse, and we settled in around the fire. There wasn't going to be much privacy for the time being, but we were all used to it.

You get new standards for what you can endure in terms of crowded sleeping quarters after you've spent a night with twenty-five dudes in some Syrian's tearoom.

Only as I leaned back against my re-packed ruck, wrapped in my Ranger roll of poncho and tied-in poncho liner, listening to the fire crackle and finally starting to feel warm for the first time since we'd started running for our lives, did I realize just how exhausted I really was. I fell asleep fast.

Unfortunately, the dreams were all about being chased by scaly things that wanted to eat me. And something else was behind them—something darker and infinitely more malevolent.

It wasn't the most restful two hours.

CHAPTER 9

I jerked awake, trying to shake off the horror of the eyes and slavering jaws that had been getting far too close. I half sat up, reaching for my M4 and scanning the darkness around me, my heart pounding.

The fire was getting low, but it hadn't gone out. I quickly realized that I hadn't just awakened because of the nightmare.

Gunny was coming toward us from the gatehouse. "Good, you're up, Conor. Everybody up. Stand to. We've got company outside."

I scrambled to my feet, or I should say I tried to. The cold stone floor and the exertion I'd put myself through over the previous day had conspired to stiffen every muscle in my body. I'd slept with my boots and my chest rig still on, so all I had to do was get up and sling my M4 in front of me.

I suddenly wished for my M110. The longer, heavier 7.62x51 semi-automatic sniper rifle packed quite a bit more punch than my M4. I didn't know what was out there, but whatever it was, I'd prefer to be able to put bigger holes in it. Unfortunately, bringing the 110 had been shot down during planning for this training op that had turned out to be anything but.

Santos was already up. Whether he'd heard Gunny or had just sensed something coming, he'd gotten up just before I'd awoken and was already stirring Smith, Farrar, and Rodeffer from their own fitful sleep.

I started for the gatehouse, but Gunny stopped me. "I want you and your boys up above, Conor. There are a couple of rooms with windows overlooking the gate and the stairs. Get up there and get set up." He grimaced. "Stanley had your M27, didn't he?"

"Yeah, he did." While losing our slack man and teammate had been a blow—one that we'd barely had time to process—the automatic weapon had been another all on its own. The M27 was no SAW—I still didn't understand the Marine Corps' decision to abandon a light machinegun for an automatic rifle—but I had a feeling that we were going to wish we had every bit of firepower we could get our hands on in the days ahead.

However long we survived.

"Well, do what you can. And if it comes to it, make every shot count. I'm going to instruct the other IAR gunners to keep it to semi. We need to save as much ammo as we can." Gunny Taylor was not what I'd call "flippant." Not even when he was giving me a hard time, usually when the platoon commander wasn't around. But right then, he sounded like a man walking through a graveyard at midnight. "Keep your comms on as long as you can."

"Roger." I looked around for a moment—my brief rest had disoriented me a little, and after one clear, I couldn't remember exactly where all the stairs were. While the grand staircase that led up to the battlements on the roof stood at the far end of the hall, there were smaller staircases leading off the side chambers, closer to the gatehouse.

The stone passageways got cold quickly as we moved away from the fire. Fortunately, we'd been next to the fire long enough that our clothes and gear had mostly dried, but we were still somewhat underdressed for the cold. Climbing the steps at least got the blood flowing a bit and loosened up muscles turned stiff and sore during the short nap we'd gotten.

We were plunged into near-darkness as soon as we got out of the hall and away from the circle of firelight. Some pale light filtered in from the windows in the outer chambers, but after Smith slipped and stumbled on the steps, we had to turn weapon lights on, flipping the IR caps open so we could see.

Two chambers flanked the gate, about twenty yards above the ground. A narrow passage linked the two of them, and from the slots and holes bored in the floor, I suspected that it had been intended to not only house a portcullis or something, but was a defensive position in and of itself, in case the gate was breached. Two narrow windows had been bored into the south wall, and the cold light of a winter day flowed in through them.

I pointed to the connecting passage. "Vince, take Smith and get set up in the west chamber." I stepped closer to the nearest window. What I saw gave me pause.

Where there had been nothing but trees and snow when I'd looked out last, there was now a small army.

Hundreds of men, dressed in what looked like buckskins and furs, wrapped in fur cloaks and carrying spears, axes, and short swords, were gathered along the treeline. They weren't formed up, not really, but they weren't advancing yet, either. Several were on horseback, carrying even longer spears.

There was something weird about their mounts. They didn't look like any normal horse I'd ever seen. They were shaggier than any breed I remembered, but that wasn't all. There was something slightly off about their proportions. Their bodies were thicker and longer than any horse's I'd ever seen, and their legs looked almost more like a lion's than a horse's. Their heads were blunt, short, and heavy-boned.

I couldn't see as much of the men. Swathed in heavy fur cloaks and tunics against the cold, most of them wore either mottled masks or helmets under the skin hoods—it was hard to tell which. They looked like they were human, but I didn't see an exposed face anywhere. And after seeing humanoid fish-men coming out of the water the night before, I wasn't taking anything for granted.

Many of them carried round or oval shields, painted in designs that I really didn't care to look at for long. They were all crude, but a moment's study revealed images of monsters, bloodied blades, skulls and other symbols of death, and much more abstract—and somehow more disturbing—symbols.

The lot of them were strangely silent. In fact, many of them seemed somewhat nervous. They were holding their position about a hundred yards from the base of the tor.

"Don't expose yourselves, and if this goes loud, kill shots only." I finally turned away from the window. Santos and Smith were still at the entrance to the connecting passage, watching me. "There's a lot of them down there."

"More of those things from last night?" Smith sounded more than a little nervous.

"No, I don't think so. These guys look like they belong on dry land. But they don't look friendly." Somehow, I doubted that the good guys would be carting around some of those symbols on their shields. Granted, Recon Marines were known to festoon all sorts of things with skulls—the Recon Jack has a skull front and center, often on a rebreather and framed by jump wings. But there was something about this bunch that just raised my hackles.

"Kill shots only." Santos nodded and jerked his head at Smith to follow as he ducked into the narrow hallway and disappeared into the gloom. I turned back to the window.

More figures were filtering out of the trees and joining the army down there. I call it an "army," but it was probably closer to a battalion in size. Maybe three to five hundred men. It was still an awful lot for a Recon platoon that had already taken casualties, especially without supporting arms.

Maybe they weren't there to fight. Not everyone with a weapon in Syria had been there to fight, either. But Recon Marines aren't Special Forces. We don't think about talking first. We think about killing first.

Somewhere off to the east, drums started up. They sounded different, somehow, from the drums we'd heard the night before. No less sinister, but different. There was a more frenetic rhythm to them, and a few of the fur-clad men in the back ranks started to react, twitching and jumping, clashing weapons against shields.

I brought my M4 to my shoulder, braced it against the edge of the window, and started picking my targets. I decided that if—no, *when*—this went south, I was taking down that big bruiser on the gigantic black horse-thing first.

He was staring up at the face of the tor with a stillness that none of the men behind him could emulate. I couldn't see his eyes behind his grimacing mask or visor—which seemed to be the only one in sight made of metal, except for the tusks on either side—but I could *feel* his cold, appraising stare.

That one was dangerous. So, he'd die first.

"Big bastard on the black horse is mine. When this goes loud, hit the horsemen first. I'll bet they're the officers." I didn't take my eyes off my ACOG, but I could sense Rodeffer and Farrar getting into position at the other window. It was just wide enough for two men to barricade on it.

"Would we stop fighting if our officer went down?" Farrar kept his tone light, but it was a question he probably wouldn't have voiced if Captain Sorenson had been within earshot.

"No, but ours aren't out front and staring daggers at the enemy while we hang back and look nervous, either." I kept the chevron right about at chest height on the big man with the tusked helmet. A headshot might be more of a certain kill-shot, but I didn't know what that helmet was made of.

If it was just bronze or even steel, the M855 green tip would punch right through it. We didn't like green tip for a variety of reasons, but when it came to penetration, it was fine. But we'd already seen so much weirdness in this place that I wasn't taking *anything* for granted.

I flicked the selector to "semi" and waited.

The big man on the black horse watched us for a few more minutes as the drums pounded behind him, reaching black metal levels of frenzy. Several of the fur-clad men with axes and spears were twitching uncontrollably behind him, almost like they were going into an epileptic fit.

Or a berserker rage.

The big guy—I'd tagged him as the warlord and was starting to think of him that way—turned in his saddle and gestured at the line behind him. My finger slipped inside the trigger guard, but the charge didn't start then. Instead, the front rank parted, and another figure came through.

My eyes narrowed. This one didn't look like the rest. Instead of furs and buckskins, the figure wore a long black cloak that completely covered it from head to toe, the hem trailing along the ground, the hood keeping its face in deep shadow. Its hands were folded inside the cloak.

The cloaked figure stopped at the warlord's stirrup, and the big warrior looked down at it. We were too far away to hear what he said, if anything, but a moment later, Black Cloak stepped in front of his horse, lifting something out of his cloak with gloved hands.

I couldn't tell what the amulet was made from there, even through the ACOG. Something about it was almost blurry. In fact, the more I tried to look at it, the more my eyes hurt.

After holding it up for a few minutes, emitting a droning sort of sound that got into your head and started to set your teeth on edge, Black Cloak started to walk slowly around the tor.

"All teams, report in." Captain Sorenson's voice was scratchy and weak, his radio trying to penetrate the thick rock walls with what had to be slowly dying batteries, but he still managed to piss me off with just those four words. We were surrounded by what looked an awful lot like an enemy horde, and he was demanding situation reports. All while sitting safe and sound in the great hall down there.

"We have what appears to be a reinforced battalion to regiment-sized element outside." Gurke kept his tone professional, but I could tell that he was a bit impatient with reporting when we had targets begging to be shot about a hundred yards away. "There's a guy in a black cloak doing something weird, circling around toward the northeast. We've still got a shot at him, but we're going to lose him in a minute."

"Hold your fire. We don't know who these people are." After the night before, I would have thought that the *hearts and minds* thing would be secondary to survival, but we *were* completely surrounded and badly outnumbered. "Do you see any weapons?"

I could almost hear Gurke cuss from two stories up and through several feet of rock. "There are a lot. No firearms that we can see, but every one of them has a spear or an axe."

"Then they're completely outgunned. Hold your fire, Marines. Let's see what they want."

I caught a thunderstruck stare from Farrar. "He's seriously trying to play warrior diplomat *now*?"

"If I wasn't up here looking at that, I might be able to see his point." I didn't want to admit it, but even jackasses like Sorenson could be right once in a while. "We don't know anything about this place, and starting a fight with everybody who looks at us cross-eyed could just get us slaughtered. But I don't think this bunch is interested in talking. And there's something about Black Cloak that's just…wrong."

As if to reinforce my point, Black Cloak moved out of my view just then. But the droning noise he was making—or maybe it was that amulet itself—didn't get any quieter. It was still there, boring into our skulls.

And I didn't like what it was doing.

It took a moment to connect the droning with the combined sense of dread and formless disgust that was building in the back of my head. But while a certain degree of dread had been there ever since we'd sailed into that fog bank the night before, it was nothing compared to this gibbering terror that was starting to gnaw at my hindbrain.

"Should have shot the black robe." I hadn't realized that I'd said it aloud until I heard both Rodeffer and Farrar agreeing with a certain heartfelt enthusiasm.

Apparently, I wasn't the only team leader thinking that. The droning intensified for the next few minutes, only to be suddenly cut off as an echoing *crack* reverberated across the valley.

"Who fired?" Sorenson's voice was strident despite the static and skipping. "I told you to hold fire!"

No one answered. Someone had shot Black Cloak, though. That much was obvious.

Sorenson was starting to go on a rant over the radio, but I soon tuned him out as more pressing matters drew all my attention.

The drums had fallen silent at the sound of the shot. The berserkers, or whatever they were, went suddenly still. It was as if the entire horde held its breath.

The warlord didn't even flinch, though. He just sat on his barrel-chested black horse and turned the dark eyeholes in his mask up toward the ruined battlements at the top of the tor, leaning on his saddle pommel. Then he barked a single word over his shoulder.

The front rank seemed to cringe, and then the drums started again. Once more, the fighters in the rear ranks started to shake and twitch.

I thought I understood something of what had just happened, though a part of my brain rebelled at the thought. Black Cloak had been doing something, something weird, as some sort of preparation, and when one of Zimmerman's team had shot him, it must have disrupted that preparation and scared the hell out of the horde down there.

Now, I had no idea what that preparation was, but the fear and disgust that had been clawing at the inside of my skull had stopped. Maybe that droning was some kind of ultrasonic weapon or something.

Just keep telling yourself that.

The drums got louder and faster. A new, weird keening started at the back of the horde, but this was clearly a more natural sound—it didn't carry the strange undertones and effects of the odd droning noise from before.

Through it all, the warlord sat upon that big leonine horse, leaning on his saddle pommel, watching the tor as if he was bored.

The drums and the chanting ebbed and flowed as clouds started to scud in from the north. Several of the front rank were clearly getting into the spirit of the thing, leaping and beating their weapons against their shields, roaring and screaming hoarsely.

Then the warlord raised his hand, and they all went quiet. In an instant.

I leveled my rifle, picking up the reticle right on the warlord's chest.

He dropped his hand. The front ranks surged forward with a roar.

And my trigger broke cleanly, the M4 surging back into my shoulder as I shot the warlord through the heart.

CHAPTER 10

IF I'd truly hoped that dropping the warlord would stop the horde, I was sorely disappointed.

Oh, they hesitated. At least, most of them did. The front-rank berserks… I don't think they even noticed as the man in the tusked helmet jerked, looked down at the hole punched through his mottled breastplate, and then slid bonelessly off his horse to fall face-first in the snow. But the others slowed at least.

Then another voice rose from the woods. It was so loud that it might have been coming from a bullhorn, but I've heard plenty of bullhorns—the BRC instructors friggin' *love* 'em—and that was a full-throated, unassisted roar.

It was a roar that the horde down there was clearly afraid to ignore. Even the ones who had hesitated resumed the charge.

There might have been all kinds of weirdness going on in this place, but the snow still worked against the enemy as much as it had worked against us. There's a reason why ancient armies hadn't fought in the winter much. The attackers had to thrash through the snow, mid-calf deep in places, and their charge quickly slowed.

Which gave us time to engage.

I shifted aim to the nearest target, a big, burly bastard who was foaming at the mouth under his mask as he screamed and waded through the snow toward us, waving an axe over his head. One of my teammates beat me to the shot, punching a bullet through his mask. He fell on his face, the back of his hood slowly turning dark red around a puckered hole where the 5.56 round had torn its way out.

It didn't slow the others down. A smaller fighter trampled the big man's corpse in the snow, a buskin-clad foot pushing his ruined head deeper into the drift. That one didn't make it much farther as I drilled him in the high center chest a split second later.

Unfortunately, while it was still an A-zone shot, that wasn't quite as good as the shot that had felled the warlord. This guy staggered and spat blood but kept coming. He was slowing down, but he wasn't out yet. My follow-up shot blew his brains into the face of the spear-wielder who was catching up with him, but he'd gained about five yards before I made the shot.

Then there were too many of them to pick targets. Despite my own urging to make every shot count, we just had to pour the fire on.

Bullets smashed through armor from above, breaking bones and tearing through flesh, spilling blood on the snow. Dozens dropped at a time, but more of them came on, roaring their hate—and probably trying to psych themselves up as so many of them died in front of their very eyes.

It was insane—a frontal attack in broad daylight across open ground. A frontal attack on a hardened position and with swords, spears, and axes against rifles. And yet, despite the insanity, they were closing the gap fast. There were just too many of them and not enough guns.

The gunfire from below had intensified to a roaring crackle, even suppressed. The carnage was slowing the human wave down as more and more of them had to scramble over the bodies of their dead, collapsed in the snow, which was quickly turning to red and pink slush. Roars and screams were nearly drowned out by the tearing thunder of suppressed 5.56 fire, and further drowned out the groans and wails of the dying.

But it wasn't slowing them down enough. The front ranks were now below us, close enough that I couldn't shoot at them without exposing myself fully in the window. None of them had guns, and I hadn't seen any bows and arrows, or slings, or anything else like that. So, getting tagged up here wasn't really the biggest concern. But old habits die hard.

I dumped the last few rounds in my magazine into the mob still clambering over the dead and dying before I pulled back from the window. "Farrar, get on one of those murder holes in the passageway. Stand by and don't shoot any friendlies. Rodeffer, you're with me." I headed for the stairs, dropping the empty mag and snatching a new one out of my chest rig. It went into the mag well with hardly a thought as I dropped the bolt, chambering the first round. Then I was rushing down the stone steps, heading for the echoing roar of the fight from the gatehouse.

As we came rushing into the main hall, I saw Captain Sorenson at the back, almost barricaded on the doors leading onto the spiral staircase in the back, with Fortuna and Doc Hartsock on a knee close to him. The fire was getting low, but I couldn't see Gunny anywhere.

I ignored the captain and headed for the gatehouse.

The gatehouse's emptiness was working against us. There was no cover between the open gateway itself and the door leading into the great hall. So Gurke and his team—and Gunny Taylor—were crouched or standing at the gateway itself, shooting down the steps and out into the mob surging up the slope toward the tor.

But there's only so much that seven M4s can do against a horde, especially as Herrera, Ridenour, and Chambers all went dry at the same time, right when Rodeffer and I reached the inside doorway.

A new roar went up as the gunfire slackened, and then a hairy form wielding an axe in both hands loomed in the doorway. Gunny Taylor Mozambiqued the raging warrior from about two feet away, thumping all three rounds into him so fast that the shots blended together into one rolling, crackling roar.

Then more of them were charging up the steps, howling like madmen. Gurke shot the first one and went dry, his bolt locking open on an empty mag.

"Turn and go! Keep left!" My own bellow echoed through the stone gatehouse as I snapped my rifle to my shoulder. I didn't have a shot, not yet, but Gurke didn't hesitate, turning and shoving Nelson-Hyde toward the great hall. Chambers did the same a split second later, making sure that Herrera, Ridenour, and Franks were moving.

Gunny was the last one to abandon the position, dumping the last of his magazine down the steps before he sprinted toward the great hall.

Our attackers didn't hesitate. Whatever was driving them must have been something else, because they just kept coming despite the utter slaughter that we'd already inflicted on them. Two of them bulled their way through the gateway right on Gunny Taylor's heels. I slammed three rounds into the first one.

Single-round kills were out. I'd gotten lucky with the warlord. Even if every shot was perfect—which they never are in combat—these guys were too hopped up to go down with only one 5.56 hole in 'em.

Rodeffer and I had set up "high-low." I was standing, leaning out into the gateway with just my rifle and my head behind it. Rodeffer was down on a knee in front of me. We could get two rifles through the opening without exposing either one of us.

Again, it was probably a moot point against axes, spears, and swords. But when things go south, you automatically revert to your training, and this was how we'd trained to fight defensively in close quarters.

The lead howler didn't even slow down, even with three holes in him. He spat blood from beneath his mask and kept coming, his sword held over his head, ready to strike. He bore down on Gunny, moving faster than should have been possible with three bullets in him already.

I dumped the rest of the mag into him, tracking my shots up his armored torso and into his face. Only the last two rounds into his skull finally dropped him, and he crashed in a bloody mess onto the stone floor, his sword clattering out of his suddenly nerveless fingers.

My bolt locked back on an empty magazine, and suddenly there were half a dozen of them right in front of us.

If I'd had a pistol, I'd have simply let go of the rifle and drawn the sidearm. But we'd come equipped for a greenside op, and we didn't usually bring pistols along on recon and surveillance missions. They became extra weight, chafing against your leg as you hiked through the woods with almost half your bodyweight on your back. So now I was facing a growing horde of berserk fighters within bad breath distance, with an empty rifle. I heard Rodeffer go dry with a curse.

We'd trained speed reloads. I could make it happen in a couple of seconds. But my Bowie was right there on my belt, and I didn't think I could reload and bring the rifle to bear before one of them was on top of me, inside the length of the weapon.

So, I slung the rifle and drew the knife.

Now, knife fighting isn't something Marines usually train. Oh, sure, there's a bit of it in the combatives we might practice once a year. But unless you'd had some practice outside the Corps—possibly during some misspent youth—the Marine Corps wasn't going to turn you into any kind of expert knife fighter.

I didn't have the misspent youth, but I was something of a violence nerd, so at least I knew the basics of what I was doing with the Bowie. I wished I had something in my other hand, but there was nothing for it.

It was awkward as hell, having my M4 dangling in front of me as I stepped in front of Rodeffer and met the first man's charge. He was foaming at the mouth and screaming, but he wasn't stupid. He didn't come in swinging the hatchet in his hand like he was chopping wood. He kept in front of him as I brought the Bowie's point around, and with a short, savage hook, he chopped at my hand.

I reacted, only then realizing it was a feint. He drew the axe back as I twisted the knife to try to deflect the blow, then he reversed it and slashed at my head.

I scrambled back, the hot M4 suppressor knocking against my knee, and he surged forward to pursue, pushed along by the growing mob of growling, snarling masked men with axes and swords behind him.

Only that press saved me and killed him. A roaring berserker piled into him from behind while he was off balance, recovering from his missed blow, and he stumbled forward. I saw my opening and ducked under the hatchet, grabbing his wrist with my hand and driving in with the Bowie.

He saw it coming and tried to grab my wrist while jerking the rest of his body backward, away from the Bowie's bitter point. He was as strong as an ox, and I almost lost my grip on his axe hand, but the press behind him was threatening to drive him onto me—and the knife—at the same time it was pushing me backward.

I braced my boots on the stone, and with my teeth gritted and putting every ounce of my bodyweight into the shove, with sheer force of desperation, I tried to drive that knife into his guts.

It was foolhardy—I realize that in hindsight. I'd just pushed ahead of everyone else, and that gatehouse might have been narrow, but it wasn't narrow enough for one man to hold without someone covering his flanks. I was going to be dead in a moment, and I saw that in that split second. If I didn't kill this slavering monster in the next second or two, the three or four behind him were going to get around and cut me to pieces.

Twisting my knife hand, pulling the blade toward me, I got the angle to where I could bend his elbow. Without the arm locked out, he couldn't keep the blade back, and with a snarl of my own, I shoved, hard.

He managed to deflect it a little, away from his stomach and his boiled leather breastplate—which might just have stopped the blade, anyway—but I leaned into his deflection, remembering something about anatomy. The blade plunged into his thigh, and I ripped up as I pulled it back, slicing deeply through the artery.

It takes a few seconds to bleed out from an arterial bleed, but the shock is almost instant. His leg collapsed under him, and he got weak as his berserker rage drained away along with the flood of crimson spurting out of his groin.

I shoved him back into the next man's face, wrenching the hand axe out of his limp fingers, and then I was falling back toward the main hall, bloody Bowie in one hand, axe in the other. I didn't turn and run—that would have been suicide at that point—but stepped steadily back, keeping my weapons in front of me.

I hooked a blade that jabbed for me with the axe, turned it aside, and pulled. The bareheaded man on the other end of the weapon, bald, tattooed, and bearded, with his teeth filed to points, didn't think to let go, and I chopped my Bowie into his neck. It went deep—I'd sharpened it carefully after using it for wood chopping. Hot blood flowed out over my hand, and I dragged it clear, cutting even deeper as I did so. That man sagged and fell on his face, even as the next two behind him tried to leap over his corpse to get at me.

Another step back toward the gate helped pull the knife out of the wound. Then Gunny and Santos were beside me, guns up and barking.

Gunny's failure drill punched the next towering Cro Mag with a mask carved into a crude, leering skull off his feet, spraying blood and brains into the eyes of the man behind him. Santos dumped four or five rounds into the hairy, black-haired one just behind him. That one had so much tangled hair and beard that it had looked like he was wearing a mask, but he wasn't. Santos's bullets cored out his heart, and he fell on his face, the sword falling from his fingers as he dropped.

I took that second to shove my sticky Bowie back in its sheath, jam the axe into my belt, and snatch up my empty rifle. The mag hit the stone as I yanked a fresh one out of my chest rig and slammed it home, long hours of practice making it unnecessary to look where the mag was going. I dropped the bolt and snapped the rifle up to my shoulder as the biggest one yet, wearing what looked like a mutant polar bear's skull for a helmet and wielding an axe in one hand and a sword in the other, stomped over the bodies of the last two that Gunny and Santos had shot.

He roared, swinging both weapons and forcing the others behind him to back up if they didn't want to get cut. That put him front and center, and the three of us obliged him. Almost a dozen rounds tore into him, punching through the mottled breastplate and the bone charms dangling from his bearskin. He staggered but somehow stayed on his feet, spitting blood and swaying for a second before Gunny and I each put a bullet through his forehead.

He fell like a tree.

Then we were falling back through the gateway as Ridenour stuck his M27 through the opening and dumped the entire magazine into the gatehouse, playing the stream of fire back and forth across the narrow space. The roar of the suppressed full auto fire was deafening as the reports bounced off the surrounding rock, drowning out the screams and roars and wails of pain.

Bullets chopped through armor, flesh, and bone, spraying blood and pulverized meat as they tore their way out. The press in the gatehouse was close enough that more than once, rounds went right through their targets and into the men behind them. In a few short seconds, the roars of the attackers turned to screams of agony and the sick gurgles that went along with lung shots.

Reaching the portal, Gunny, Santos, and I turned and added our own fire, getting out of the direct line through the gatehouse but no longer quite as concerned with barricading on the gateway itself.

We poured fire into the cramped gatehouse, no longer all that worried about ammo conservation as the howling mob surged toward us, clambering over the bloody remains of their dead, teeth bared when they weren't concealed by grotesque masks, their weapons clenched in white-knuckled fists. I could barely pick targets, just using my ACOG's chevron as a red dot, putting it roughly center mass on each charging enemy as I shifted back and forth.

I shot one as he tripped over the corpse in front of him, blasting a hole through his eye and punching the bullet into the man behind him. The man behind dropped as well. The one I'd just shot in the head kept coming, his eye a bloody ruin, gnashing his pointed teeth at me until I shot him again through the "T-box." The bullet blew the back of his skull off, and he collapsed, the nasty spiked mace in his hand hitting the rock floor with a clatter that was almost quiet compared to the rest of the cacophony echoing off the stone walls.

They were getting closer to the gate with every step. One of them, another big bruiser with a masked metal helmet, grabbed a body before it could fall all the way to the floor and held it up as a meat shield, driving forward as bullets punched into the corpse with hard *thwack*s. Some of them had to be penetrating all the way through to hit him, but these guys were so wound up that they may as well have been drugged to the gills. It was like the worst horror stories cops would tell about fighting guys on PCP.

Only the drug addicts usually weren't attacking in mobs, wearing armor, and swinging edged weapons.

I didn't want to think too hard about that black cloaked character and the effects his droning had had, either. Fortunately, combat tends to limit how much mental energy you have to spare for woolgathering.

Ordinarily, we'd train to balance out our fire, keep the guns "talking" so that if one man went dry, the others could pick up the fire and avoid a dangerous lull. Unfortunately, that had suddenly been lost in that noisy, blood-spattered little corner of hell that the gatehouse had become. We were so desperate to keep those howling murderers off us that we dumped ammo without a whole lot of coordination.

So, when eight out of the twelve of us had our M4s lock open on empty mags in the same handful of seconds, the pucker factor suddenly went through the roof.

Someone was looking out for us, though. Because at almost that exact same time, a shout went up outside. I call it a shout, but it was a sound that could have come from an LRAD, one of those big sonic weapons used for crowd control. It was so loud that it shook the very rock of the tor. I was in the gateway, and the funneling effect of the gatehouse meant the noise almost drove me to my knees.

The attackers froze for a moment. I couldn't shoot the man directly in front of me—I was empty. I dropped the mag and reached for a reload, knowing that I was going to be too slow and he'd be on me in the next second and realizing that I'd miscalculated and should have gone for the Bowie and the axe.

But I saw the look in his eyes change. In a second, as that horrific noise made the very stones shudder, the fevered rage faltered, suddenly turning to fear, and then to relief as he turned away and ran for the outer gate. The rest had melted away, fleeing out the gateway and down the steps. All that was left in the gatehouse was blood and corpses.

It was over. For the moment.

CHAPTER 11

FOR a long moment, we just stayed in place, hearts still pounding, watching the gateway over our rifles. Gunny finally broke the silence.

"ACE Reports." His voice was a low croak.

The Ammo, Casualty, Equipment report was something that we'd practiced so much that it was second nature. After a fight, you needed to know how many bullets you had left, who needed patching up, and if everyone still had all their stuff, unbroken.

I looked down and checked myself. I was bleeding slightly from a cut I hadn't realized I'd taken during that hand-to-hand with the man I'd stabbed in the groin—or maybe from the one I'd practically decapitated. It wasn't deep, and the blood loss wasn't all that concerning, but I'd need to clean and treat the wound quickly.

I was on my fifth magazine since that first fish-man or whatever it was had come over the gunwale. That wasn't good. Going through four mags in less than a day, when we had zero chance of resupply, didn't bode well. "Eight mags, up and up." Everyone else was in about the same state, give or take a couple mags. We were going to be hurting for ammo fast if they came at us again. And I had no reason to think they wouldn't.

Gunny was thinking along the same lines. He scanned the abattoir that we'd turned the gatehouse into. "We're not going to last long, dumping that kind of ammo." He took a deep breath and stepped inside the gatehouse, glancing out at the bright day and snowy treetops beyond. "Everybody should probably pick up some kind of edged weapon. Find one with some reach."

"Grab a shield, too," I said. When Gunny looked back at me with a raised eyebrow, I shrugged. "Shields are going to be easier than trying to block a weapon with another weapon. And if we're going to hold this in close quarters, we're going to want the shields."

"I don't know how to use a sword, much less a shield," Gurke piped up. "Does anyone else?"

I suppressed a wince. Kind of like reading fantasy books, this wasn't something most Recondos would openly admit. But right then and there, it might just save our lives. "I kinda do. The basics, anyway."

Gunny eyed me with faint amusement. "Why doesn't that really surprise me, Conor?"

"Hey, I'm a violence nerd." I was a little defensive about it. Sure, I had other interests that had fed into learning the basics of swordsmanship, but the truth was, I *was* a "violence nerd." I'd figured it had been a requirement to be a Recon Marine, a true warrior. I'd known at the time that there wasn't a lot of use for swords in the modern day, but I'd been interested, and I had some down time.

Little had I known…

"Well, you heard the man. Everybody grab a shield and a weapon you'd be comfortable hacking someone to bits with." He was already kicking a corpse over, eyeing the single-edged sword that clattered to the floor as he did so.

I stepped out to join him, scanning the blood-splashed heap of bodies. The stench was already horrific, even given the bitter cold in there. I was glad it was winter. If we'd fought this fight in the summer, the great hall would probably have quickly become unlivable, at least until we could clean the corpses out.

I frowned as I looked at the weapons. Most of them were like the sword that Gunny was hefting, or the axe that was still in my belt. They were crude, still showing hammer marks except where the edges had been ground, and the grind work wasn't all that straight, either. The swords were angular, single-edged, glorified brush-cutters, not all that distant from machetes. Their spines were thicker than I would have expected, and they were noticeably blade heavy. That might have made for better chopping, but after a bit of inspection, I suspected they were that thick to make up for lousy metal. Several of the edges were obviously chipped. They weren't *completely* bad—they'd obviously do the job. And they weren't rusting away, either. They'd been coated in some vile-smelling grease to keep moisture off.

But while most of the weapons were that kind of crude scrap, there were others that definitely were not.

I pulled the axe out of my belt and dropped it on the floor as I nudged a dead hand aside and crouched down—careful not to burn myself on my still-smoking suppressor—before pulling the sword that had caught my eye out from under the body. The same blade that the berserker in the polar bear skin had been swinging.

The hilt was wrapped in greasy rags, bound up with rawhide. But the blade was straight, double-edged, and easily a foot longer than the single-edged brush cutters most of the other attackers had used. It tapered nicely toward a bitter point, and it was so well-balanced that it felt almost like I was holding a feather.

"None of these apes made that." Gunny was eyeing the weapon in my hand.

"No, they didn't." I frowned more deeply as I studied it. Why was the hilt wrapped in rags like that? Even the crossguard was covered.

Santos had found a similar treasure—a short sword with a leaf-shaped blade. It was only slightly shorter than the cruder weapons but of considerably higher workmanship. The hilts on that one had been wrapped, too. That was weird.

"Look for more like these," I told the team.

In all, we found about half a dozen such weapons among the dead, even as we held our breath to keep from inhaling the stench of death. Marines who didn't get their hands on one of the higher-quality blades had to settle for the shorter, thicker axes and single-edge swords.

"Team leaders!" I looked up. From the tone of his voice, it hadn't been the first time Captain Sorenson had called for us. "I want to see the team leaders right damned now!"

I glanced at Gunny just in time to see a look that was simultaneously cold and murderous cross his face. I imagined that I'd just looked the same.

We hadn't seen Captain Sorenson in the breach with us.

Gunny gave instructions as he thrust a newly acquired axe into his belt. "Herrera, get upstairs and tell Bailey to get down here and relieve Gurke. Zimmerman's team will relieve McCall's once Gurke's team gets up on the roof." He turned toward the main hall. Gurke and I followed, our faces set and grim.

Sorenson was standing by the fire, his arms crossed and his face pale and angry. If he noticed the cold, angry stares he was getting, he didn't show it.

Zimmerman and Bailey came down the stairs in back, Bailey's team in tow. As they started across the hall to relieve Gurke's Team Four, Sorenson held up a hand. "Hold up. Before anyone else moves a *muscle*, I want to know who fired that first shot."

For a long moment, there was thunderous silence. I think every one of us looked at Gunny, as if to ask what we were supposed to do next. Sorenson noticed, too, and it just made him angrier.

"I'm going to repeat the question just this once. Who fired that first shot?"

Bailey set his jaw and met the captain's eyes. "I did, sir."

Sorenson turned to glare at him. Somehow, it didn't have the effect he probably wanted, not after the fight we'd just been through while he'd stayed back with the radio—a radio with no one on the other end.

"You took the first shot." His voice was low, and he probably intended it to sound dangerous. "One of my team leaders took the first shot." His tone started to rise. "I gave a *direct order* to hold fire. A *direct order!*"

"And if I hadn't and had let that black-robed creep finish what he was doing, we probably wouldn't be here having this conversation right now." Bailey was defiant, folding his arms over his chest rig.

Sorenson scoffed bitterly. "Right. At best, some superstitious local was doing their ritual song and dance—which *you* sure as hell don't know what kind of significance it might have had—and you shot him. None of them had firearms. Or am I wrong?" He looked at Gunny, who stood off to my left, stone-faced. Gunny shook his head, his eyes glinting with a warning that Captain Sorenson took no heed of. "You shot a man who was no immediate threat to us and precipitated *this* bloodbath!" He stabbed a finger toward the gore-choked gatehouse.

Bailey wasn't backing down. "Bullshit, *sir.* You weren't up there." He stabbed a finger at Sorenson. "*You* weren't watching that freak or feeling what his 'ritual song and dance' was doing. You didn't see Owens start to zone out while he bled from his nose, ears, and eyes. You didn't feel everything turning *wrong* around you while that psychopath waved his amulet and made noises that went right into your brain."

Sorenson sneered. "Really? What, you think it was *magic* or something? Or is that just your excuse for disobeying orders and starting a fight that might ultimately get all of us killed? That you shot a *wizard*? Sounds to me like a lousy excuse for poor fire discipline. Just because we're in a difficult situation doesn't mean the rules go out the window, Marine. I'm still your commanding officer, and you will *follow my orders, dammit!*"

Bailey bristled. Zimmerman looked like he was about to step in and say something, but Gunny glared at him and he subsided. Zimmerman... well, Zimmerman didn't have a good record for saying the right thing in a situation like this.

Gunny himself stepped in before Bailey could make the matter worse. "Sir, could I have a word?" He took Sorenson by the arm, and from the looks of it, he wasn't giving the captain an option. I could see Sorenson wince a little as Gunny hit a pressure point and propelled him back toward a corner of the hall. Gunny looked back at us and said, "Get to your positions and get ready for another push!"

Bailey stared after the two of them for a moment, his eyes burning. He looked over at me. "Was Sorenson in the gate during the fight?"

I shook my head.

He cursed. "I knew it. That son of a bitch. He cowers in here while we fight and then has the gall to cuss *me* out for doing what needed to be done. He didn't see a damn thing but wants to act like he's in the TOC on a Pred feed." Bailey looked ready to spit on the floor. "Wants to talk to me about *rules* when he doesn't even know what the hell's going on."

I didn't say anything, though I really did agree with Bailey. Sorenson was still acting like he was part of a chain of command, and that he had higher knowledge and information that we weren't privy to. But there was no Tactical Operations Center here, no Predator live feed from ten thousand feet—not that drone surveillance was any substitute for eyes on the ground. This was down and dirty, tooth and nail survival. And Bailey was right. Sorenson didn't know his head from a hole in the ground in this place, and if he kept acting like he did, he'd get us all killed.

Or worse.

I frowned. I didn't know where that thought had come from. But when I looked down at the fanged skull symbol on my tactically acquired shield, I couldn't *quite* suppress a shudder.

Bailey was right about something else, too, though I couldn't put my finger on how I knew. If Black Cloak had finished what he was doing, we probably wouldn't have lived past the first wave.

Zimmerman shifted his weight, and Bailey turned his glare on him. "Go ahead. Say it."

But Zimmerman just shook his head, an unreadable expression on his face, and turned away. Bailey's bitter glower followed him as he walked away from us. "That little weasel," I heard him mutter under his breath.

"We'd better get into position like Gunny said." I glanced toward the corner, where Gunny was remonstrating with Captain Sorenson. I couldn't hear him, but he was obviously making his point forcefully, in the way that only Gunny Taylor could quite get away with. And Captain Sorenson wasn't happy about it, either.

This was going to be a problem. But only if we survived the next few hours. Or minutes. However much time we had before the next assault.

It took a few minutes for Bailey's team to switch out with Gurke's, and Gurke and his boys to head up to the top of the tor. It took longer to move around the fortress than expected. The place was a castle carved out of the rock, and it was bigger than it looked at first glance.

In the meantime, we moved back to the gatehouse. Bailey took a look at the carnage inside, and his eyebrows climbed toward his hairline. "Damn. You boys killed more people than cancer."

"They made it easy." I stared out toward the woods. "This time."

There wasn't much more to say. We were all exhausted and waiting for the other shoe to drop. I don't think any of us believed that we'd driven the savages off permanently.

Finally, Zimmerman's team showed up, straggled across the great hall, and joined us at the gateway. Zimmerman hadn't climbed the stairs to join them but had waited by the fire. I wasn't sure what to think about that—sure, there hadn't specifically been a *need* for him to climb back up, since he'd come down with his ruck and the rest were coming down anyway. But the fact that he'd been warming his hands instead of getting eyes on the situation at the gatehouse bugged me.

Maybe I was just tired and grumpy.

We got some strange looks from Zimmerman and Nagano, his ATL, at the fact we were all carrying swords, axes, and shields in addition to our M4s. But a look into the gatehouse and a glance down at the decidedly limited number of magazines in his chest rig wiped the look off Bob Nagano's face. Zimmerman still looked like he thought we were getting weird.

Maybe we were. Maybe the only way to survive this place was to get as weird as it was.

I thought about that as I glanced down at my tactically acquired shield while we crossed toward the stairs. I frowned as I looked again at the fanged skull painted crudely on the hide facing. I didn't like that symbol, as much as we used to plaster skulls all over everything in Recon. There was something about this one that was a lot more sinister.

Sure, some of us tended to be pretty sinister ourselves. We were trained killers, and not all of us held the same principles of honor and right and wrong close to our hearts. But that emblem on the shield was something different. Something that gave me the creeps.

On impulse, I bent down as we passed the fire and picked up a charred stick that had rolled out of the blaze and was smoldering on the stone floor. I carried it with me as we headed up the stairs, and I started to scratch out the skull emblem with the charred portion of the stick as we went.

That staircase felt a lot harder this time around. I was breathing hard and starting to sweat a little by the time we reached the top. We didn't take it slow—I wanted to be up there and ready to provide fire support by the time the enemy decided to push again.

Gurke's team was already spread out along one side of the battlements, leaving the other half to us. I let Santos get Rodeffer, Farrar, and Smith positioned while I moved up to the battlements directly above the gate and looked out.

We were still surrounded. The savage warriors had fallen back to the tree line, not that it would do them much good. It was still a pretty easy shot, especially from up on top of the tor. Of course, they wouldn't understand that; they had what I imagined was very limited experience of firearms. As I scanned the meadow around us, it was obvious that as many as we'd killed, it had barely scratched the surface. In fact, the savages appeared to have gotten reinforcements.

Some of them in particular drew my eye. A clump of darker figures gathered around another horseman in a smaller clearing up on the shoulder of the hill to our east.

I lifted my rifle and peered through the ACOG. I felt a chill as I studied the dark figures. There was something not quite right about them, something even more off than the half-crazed berserkers who'd stormed the gatehouse in the teeth of gunfire. They were too far away to see a lot of detail, even at the ACOG's four power magnification, but they seemed strangely misshapen.

The horseman was worse.

He sat atop a massive, shaggy horse, or horse-thing, not unlike the warlord's mount, but bigger and darker. I could have sworn that its eyes glowed red for a moment. It was hard to tell with the snow and the distance, but it looked an awful lot like that thing had claws instead of hooves. The rider was a little too long in the arms and short in the legs—a bit like a gorilla but without the hunched shoulders. He sat tall in his saddle, watching us. I could tell, somehow, that he was staring up at me, even though I couldn't see his eyes beyond the mask of his helmet. Unlike the savages, this mask was unadorned, the faceplate below the eye slits draped with dark cloth.

Someone important had just arrived. And it didn't bode well for any of us.

CHAPTER 12

WE settled in behind the battlements, up on our rifles, watching through scopes, fingers hovering just outside of trigger guards. The next attack could start at any time. They certainly had the numbers and clearly lacked much of the sense of self-preservation that would deter them.

And yet, the attack didn't materialize. The savages in their skins and furs stayed at the tree line, chanting gutturally and thumping their drums, while several of them approached the long-armed figure on the nightmare horse.

I braced my rifle against the crumbling stone that I knelt behind, letting my breath out and keeping my breathing as shallow as possible to keep the scope from jumping too much. That was more easily said than done—it was bitingly cold up there away from the fire, and I was starting to shiver.

I watched a small entourage approach the horseman. He ignored them, even as his lumpy-looking bodyguard loomed over the handful of savages. As they got closer, I could see that most of the newcomers were quite a bit bigger than the savage humans we'd been fighting. Most were at least a head taller, except for one smaller one that looked wiry and somehow insectile.

The savages bowed before the horseman, but he still ignored them. In fact, I could have sworn that he was staring straight at me, his invisible eyes boring right through the ACOG to peer at me. A couple of his bodyguard seemed to laugh, though their faces were covered, just like the horseman's.

Something told me I should be glad of that fact. Thankful to not see what was beneath the veil prior to battle. As it turned out, I'd get to see them closer up a lot sooner than I thought.

Finally, one of the bodyguard, a big, brutish looking character with one arm that looked longer than the other, barked something at the savages and stabbed his spear at them.

I was too far away to see their expressions, but the middle one, the first to have gone prostrate, slowly got up. He drew his sword, about two and a half feet of crude, notched, single-edged brush cutter. Even from five hundred yards away, I could see reluctance in every move he made, but he didn't hesitate.

He lifted the blade and sawed off one of his fingers.

If he screamed, I couldn't hear it over the noise the rest of the enemy army was making. But he held his mutilated hand up and let the blood drip onto the snow for a minute before the big horseman turned his baleful gaze away from our position on the top of the tor and looked at him.

The exchange didn't take all that long. The man with the bleeding, mangled hand drew it back to his chest, presumably trying to staunch the bleeding, and said his piece. The horseman seemed to consider it for a moment, then looked up at us again. I felt a chill as I watched that faceless mask stare at us. There was something even more unnerving about that blank, shrouded visage with its eye slits like pits of pure darkness than any of the snarling masks that the savages had worn.

For a moment, I wished that Captain Sorenson had been up there so that he could *see* what we were facing. Especially since he seemed to have decided that he couldn't trust our word for it.

After what felt like a small eternity as the horseman watched the tor, he nodded and turned his massive, monstrous horse away. He disappeared into the trees and over the hill, his bodyguards in tow. A couple of them looked back, either at us or at the savages who were still beating their drums.

"What the hell just happened?" Santos was next to me, watching the same scene play out. "I don't like this."

"There's nothing *to* like," I answered.

The nastier-looking customers might have cleared out, but we still had a couple hundred axe-wielding howlers down there, waiting for the word to rush us again.

I was in for another surprise, though.

The delegation that had met with the dark horseman and his bodyguards disappeared into the trees behind the line of men still watching us as they thumped their weapons against shields and tree trunks with a strange, off-kilter rhythm. They didn't reemerge for a long time.

When they did, I recognized the man who'd cut off one of his own fingers, if only because of the mask he wore. Like the warlord I'd shot through the heart, his mask appeared to be made of metal and shaped to resemble a dragon or lizard, if slightly stylized. It even had four horns rising from the top, curving back over the hood. Less than practical in a fight but certainly somewhat intimidating.

The man in the dragon helmet was flanked by four more fighters, all hooded and masked, though their masks weren't nearly as ornate as the dragon helmet. They hung back a little as the man in the dragon mask mounted a thick, shaggy, gray horse and rode out into the open toward us.

I put the chevron of my ACOG on his chest. If he wanted some, he'd get it.

But he only advanced about halfway to the tor before reining in. He sat on his horse for a long moment, and while he was too far away to hear and I couldn't see his face, I got the distinct impression that he was muttering to himself. Then he straightened and raised both hands. They were empty, the hand he'd cut a finger off wrapped in a dingy bandage. "Thunder warriors!" he shouted.

Well, that wasn't *exactly* what he said. He didn't speak English. What he said was, "*Tontrom Mailati!*"

I didn't learn that after the fact by studying the local culture. I *understood* him right then and there. And that shocked me almost as much as what he said next.

"We have seen your power!" His voice echoed across the churned and blood-stained snow. His words were strange, and yet I knew what he was saying as clearly as if he had been speaking English. I even *knew* I'd never heard this language before. Somehow.

Or had I? I remembered the eerie feeling of familiarity when I'd seen the strange, worn statues in the main hall. But this was different. There wasn't the same feeling of déjà vu. This was just… odd.

"We cannot best you! The proof lies in our dead, their blood spilled into the snow and onto the stones! You are stronger in battle than we are. Your magic is greater! We must acknowledge it!" He paused, looking up at the ruins atop the tor as if he were waiting for a response. I watched him through my ACOG, my finger hovering near the trigger. I couldn't see his face, or really read his body language, but there was something about him that set my teeth on edge. Something sly. "Shall we talk? This place has not held stores for a very long time. We cannot defeat you, but can you eat stones?"

"The hell do we have to talk about?" Santos kept his voice to a low mutter, his eye to his own ACOG. All it would take would be one wrong move, and Dragon Mask was bug food.

When no reply seemed to be forthcoming—I sure wasn't going to engage this guy, and none of the other Marines up there were going to talk if a team leader was keeping his lip zipped—he apparently decided to change tacks.

"We did not know who you were. When you took shelter in this place, we thought you were the Terrible Ones, come again." He spread his hands to encompass the tor. "This is an evil place. The spirits of the Terrible Ones linger here. We have feared their shades for generations. Could we do anything but what we did?"

I heard the scrape of a boot on stone behind me. With a sinking feeling, I already knew it was the captain.

"How is he doing that?" For once, Sorenson sounded unsure of himself. "I know that's not English, but…"

"This place is weird, sir." Gunny sounded a little distracted, but I felt a momentary wash of relief that he was up there. He could still hopefully mitigate whatever the captain was about to do.

No, I didn't have a lot of confidence in Captain Sorenson. I'd tolerated him during the workup. Team leaders run things in Recon. Officers are there to facilitate and to keep Higher off our backs. But Sorenson didn't get that and would have refused to go along with it anyway. He'd always acted like he expected the enlisted scumbags to get out of line and make him look bad if he didn't keep constant control.

His reactions and behavior since we'd come to this strange, dangerous place hadn't made me trust him any more.

I stayed on my rifle, watching Dragon Mask. He was still gazing up at the top of the tor, sitting easily in his crude saddle. I imagined I could almost see his eyes behind the mask, through the darkened eyeholes, cool, appraising, calculating.

"What do you want to talk about?" Captain Sorenson had stepped up between me and Santos. He was entirely exposed, though I supposed that if they'd had anything that could reach that far, we'd probably already have seen it. The fact that they were hanging back by the tree line after the bloodbath inside the gatehouse suggested that what projectile weapons they did have didn't have a lot of range.

Dragon Mask kind of shrugged. "This is not a good place. The Terrible Ones left their mark here long ago. Their shadow hangs over everything here." He pointed off to the northeast. "Come to our village. There we can talk, away from the shades of the Terrible Ones."

"Not a good idea." Gunny kept his voice down, but his tone was adamant. "They get us out of these walls and into the open, and we're dead."

Almost as if Dragon Mask could hear him—and given how weird it was that he was speaking a language we had never heard before but understood as clearly as if it were

English, that wasn't outside the realm of possibility—he called out again. "Your magic is strong. You have struck down the Great Semos Dheukoh. None of us have ever dared to face him, even those with the greatest magic." He paused again, as if calculating. "We show honor to strength, and yours is great. Come! We would honor you."

Gunny had said his piece. He stood next to the captain, his M4 held easily in his hands, his expression blank. I glanced at the two of them out of the corner of my eye.

Captain Sorenson was watching Dragon Mask, his face thoughtful. Or at least, he was wearing his "thoughtful" expression. I'd seen it too many times to consider it anything but an act, a "leadership tool" that he tried to put on when he'd already made up his mind. I'd seen the man think, and I'd seen him pretend to think. This was definitely the latter.

And when he put on his *I already made up my mind but have to appear to be giving due consideration* face, the decision was rarely a good one.

After a moment, Sorenson nodded. "We will come down to talk." He probably thought his raised voice was commanding, but he was as exhausted and dehydrated as the rest of us, so it was more high-pitched than he'd hoped. If I was being fair, I doubt that I would have sounded much better at that point. "Give us some time to prepare." He turned away from the battlement. "Gunny, I want you and all the team leaders down by the fire in five minutes."

Gunny glared down at Dragon Mask for a moment before following the captain. I returned my gaze to the savages' envoy, too, still keeping my ACOG's reticle right where I could core out his heart and lungs with a couple shots.

I could have sworn the bastard looked smug. This time his body language was impossible to miss. He'd gotten what he wanted.

From what I'd seen so far, nothing this guy was after would have anything to do with our well-being.

"Son of a bitch just wants to be out of the cold," Santos muttered.

"Maybe." I pulled back from the battlement before standing. They might not have guns down there, but I didn't know for sure *what* they had, and I kept thinking about that bat-thing that we'd seen before the rider had sounded its horn. This place didn't operate by the rules we were used to.

I think that was what was making Sorenson freak out so much. He was the arbiter of The Rules, there to keep us iconoclastic, cowboy Recondos on the straight and narrow. The fact that The Rules were all askew, and that as the shock wore off, we were getting that, only made him freak out that much more, tightening his grip lest the whole world spin out of control under him.

He'd be a lot better off embracing that wild Recon heritage. To adapt, overcome, and do whatever it takes to complete the mission.

"Get the team ready to roll." I turned toward the steps as Santos pulled back from the battlement himself and nodded. "And I know I don't have to tell any of you to be ready to kill *everybody* when this goes sideways."

Yeah, I said "when," not "if."

Gurke was already a flight below me on the stairs as I started down. I could hear Gunny's voice echoing up the stairwell, though I couldn't quite make out the words. I didn't really have to—I could imagine.

When I came down, I saw that Gurke was still hanging back by the lumpy, worn-down statues. Bailey and Zimmerman were standing apart, too, on the far side of the fire. Zimmerman's face was blank. Bailey's was a thundercloud, his eyes blazing as he glared at Sorenson.

"This is a chance to fix the damage Staff Sergeant Bailey did." Sorenson stabbed a finger at my fellow team leader. "We're fortunate that these people are superstitious and appear to respect violence as a sign of strength—otherwise we might be in a lot more trouble. We've got an opportunity to smooth over the killing and win these people's hearts and minds. Wherever we are, whatever navigational error led us here, this is their territory, and their culture needs to be taken into account."

Gurke glanced at me. I saw the question in his eyes and couldn't help but agree. Nothing we'd seen of their culture so far appeared to be remotely admirable. Skulls and blood and sorcery that made a man bleed from his ears, nose, and eyes.

Yeah, I said "sorcery." I was coming around to the realization that it was pretty real here. It was the only explanation for some of the things we'd seen already.

"So, we're going to abandon the most defensible position we've seen so far to put ourselves in the middle of a village full of people whose brothers, sons, fathers, husbands, and uncles we just slaughtered like baby seals." Gunny had now discarded any pretense of diplomacy. His Marines were now at risk, and he was going to put his foot down. "You've never been to Afghanistan, have you, sir?"

"Don't take that tone with me, Gunny." Sorenson actually had the guts to knife hand Gunny Taylor. I could see murder in Gunny's eyes, but he held back. "I'm still your commanding officer." He stepped in close. Either he had more balls than I'd ever given him credit for, or he was just that stupid. "Part of the oath is to obey the orders of those placed over you, Gunny. And while we might be lost right now, that won't always be the case."

I expected Gunny to crush his trachea and take over. To my disappointment, he didn't.

I could barely hear him, his voice was pitched so low. "This is a bad call, *sir*. And part of my job as platoon sergeant is to call you out when you make a bad call."

"I don't agree. Your job is to facilitate the commander's intent. And this is the commander's intent, for now." The captain's hand was on his own rifle's firing control. "So, either facilitate, or go ahead and refuse a lawful order. Which under these circumstances, I'm pretty sure might just constitute mutiny."

Did he just make the threat I think he just did? My own rage and contempt surged. This punk of an officer had hung back and screamed at Fortuna about the radio while we'd been fighting for our lives in the gatehouse, but suddenly he was a stone-cold killer when faced with his own platoon sergeant telling him he was wrong?

I almost shot him right then and there.

But I trusted Gunny Taylor. And if Gunny wasn't going to make that move, then neither would I. I just hoped that we survived this little drama. The savages outside might be temporarily cowed by our weapons, but who knew how long that would last?

If you've never seen *The Man Who Would Be King*, just take this as the moral of the story: playing at being a god never works out well in the end. People tend to get a little upset when they realize you're just a mortal, like them.

And that's when they're not setting you up from the get-go.

Gunny looked around at us, his mouth set and his eyes hard. The glance he gave the captain promised that this wasn't over. "Everybody get ready to move. Weapons in the best condition possible, one hundred percent security." He turned his back on Captain Sorenson and moved toward his own ruck.

I saw the momentary look of triumph on the captain's face, and for a brief second, I wanted to wring his neck. But I just turned and headed back up the stairs to get the rest of my team.

All the way up, I was thinking that I'd never expected to be condemned to death or slavery by one of our own.

* * *

Dragon Mask hadn't moved by the time we came out, laden with our rucks, weapons in hand. I still had that sword thrust through my belt, sheathed in a crude scabbard that I'd found to fit it. I could feel the eyes on it as we walked toward Dragon Mask and his odd-looking horse.

The more I looked at that thing, the less certain I was that it was a horse. It looked more like something out of a textbook on prehistoric mammals. I didn't know for sure if it even had hooves, since its feet were buried in the snow. It watched us balefully as Rodeffer and I got closer, but it didn't snort or toss its head like a horse would. It didn't make a sound.

I looked up at Dragon Mask, careful to keep my expression as blank as possible. I'm sure I was tired enough that it came across as a glare of pure enmity. I knew he was our enemy. I knew he was lying. And from his body language and the glint of his eyes on the other side of that mask—which was more ornate close up than I'd been able to see even through my optic—he knew that I saw through him. And he was gloating.

Without a further word—maybe whatever magic made him understandable was wearing off—he flicked the reins and turned his mount to lead the way toward the trees.

The rest of the savages were quiet now, no longer thumping their shields and nearby tree trunks. They parted as we approached, giving us a respectful amount of distance. But the stares that followed us as we trekked into the snowbound forest were not friendly.

CHAPTER 13

THE march took longer than I'd expected, given how quickly the savages had gotten to the tor. There were no roads through those woods—though the savages themselves had left a decently beaten track through the snow. Unfortunately, that compacted snow got slick, especially when we were trying to traverse it with seventy-pound rucks on our backs. After the second time he almost bit it, Rodeffer got off the icy track and started hiking through the mid-calf-deep snow under the trees. It was harder going, but the footing was a little more reliable.

Dragon Mask didn't slow appreciably, but he didn't speed up as his mutant horse-thing forged up the hillside toward the top of the ridge. Apparently, he didn't want to lose the "thunder warriors" he wished to "honor."

It briefly occurred to me that the Aztecs had once considered ripping a man's heart out of his chest while he was still alive "honoring" him. I wasn't all that sure that these people were that much different, given what we'd seen so far.

Some of that might just be my hard-wired paranoia. Deploying to Syria had made me less than trustful of locals, particularly locals who shot at you one minute and then were all sweetness and light, "Mistah, Mistah, why?" the next. I'd been on the receiving end of that kind of treachery before.

Sorenson hadn't. He'd done two floats with the 22nd MEU, or Marine Expeditionary Unit. As far as I knew, the last night and day had been his first combat experience.

I kept my eye on our escort as Dragon Mask led the way over the first ridge and down into the narrow valley on the other side. Most of them were keeping their distance, struggling through the snow out to our flanks. I saw three hulking fighters off to our left, dressed in skins and blue-painted masks, crudely sculpted into roaring grimaces. Two of them carried spears and crude swords, but the biggest one carried a massive Lochaber axe. That thing looked heavy and nasty, but not nearly so much as the man carrying it. I couldn't see his face, obviously, but he kept watching us. I could feel his eyes on me as we trudged up the slope through the snow. I could feel his eagerness at every slip, every misstep. That man was hungry for violence, and the more I watched him out of the corner of my eye, the more I wanted to indulge him.

The men to our right were cut from the same cloth, but on that side, two little, wiry guys who might have been brothers, just going by their build, were staying ahead, rushing to nearly catch up with Dragon Mask before stopping to wait and watch us. One of them had a barbed spear in his hands, and he kept twirling it as he stared at us.

Not once over the ten miles or so we covered that day did I look back at Captain Sorenson. I didn't want him to see the look of pure rage and accusation on my face. We were walking right into the lion's den, and anybody with two brain cells to rub together could see it.

I could only imagine what platitudes he'd spout to justify this insanity. Something about "their land," "cultural understanding being a force multiplier," or some combination of the two.

A nagging part of my mind kept after me that in some ways, Sorenson was right. We'd burned through almost half our ammo already. We had limited food and water, and even the firewood we'd gathered had already been getting low. We wouldn't have survived a siege if the savages had blockaded us.

I just didn't think that trying to make nice with people who clearly wanted us dead—or worse—was the best course of action.

I kept playing the scenario over in my head. The only thing we could have done would have been to break out and try to break contact in the woods. After that? No idea. But I didn't think the captain had much of an idea what we were doing here, either.

Dragon Mask led us over the ridge and down into the river valley below. The trees began to thin as the slope got gentler, and soon we could see the village ahead, wreathed in smoke as the sun began to set.

Several dozen A-frame hide tents were gathered around a wooden structure in the center. That dark, hulking shape was similar to the tents, if far larger, with two peaks instead of one. In the dying light, against the snow, the black structure looked almost horned. The reddish glow of fires beneath the constant haze of smoke rising from between the "horns" only accentuated the impression.

The hide shelters were not permanent. Or so I gathered by the fact that they weren't covered in snow. But that great hall or whatever it was sure looked like it wasn't going anywhere. I wondered a little at that. Was it a temple? A throne room? Or something else?

We trooped into the center of the sprawling village. The tents, while clustered around the central structure, seemed to be placed somewhat haphazardly. The bigger and more ornately decorated ones were all closer to the temple, or whatever it was, while the smaller and poorer ones were farther away, but there was no real pattern, no grid or spoke system in place. It looked like they were set up wherever the strongest, richest, or both decided they wanted to set up, and the others fell in where they could fit.

As I looked around at our escort, I couldn't help but imagine that more than a little blood had probably been spilled over tent sites. These didn't seem like the kind of people who would sort things out like gentlemen.

Dragon Mask led the way through the twisting, turning spaces between the tents, angling toward the towering horns of the soot-blackened wooden structure. Eyes watched us from the shadows inside the tents, dimly backlit by low, crackling fires. As I scanned our surroundings, always looking for the ambush, I noticed that only women and children appeared to be waiting in the village. It looked like all of the men had come out to come after us.

I also noticed that when I could see faces clearly—which wasn't often—none of the expressions were friendly. The women and the kids looked like they were as hungry for bloodshed as that big bruiser with the Lochaber axe who was still lingering near us, still watching.

It was possible that word of the bloodbath we'd wreaked back there had already reached them, but something about the looks we were getting made me think otherwise. This wasn't any kind of *specific* hostility, like that of kin with a vendetta. No, this felt like a more general bloodthirstiness.

Maybe I was just being paranoid. After what we'd seen over the last thirty-six hours, I could hardly be blamed. But I didn't think so.

I was dog-tired, but all the same, I was hyper-alert. It was as if I could see, hear, and smell everything with a vividness that I'd never experienced before. At the time, I suspected that I wasn't nearly as switched on as I felt—I thought it was just the exhaustion and the stress combining into a borderline hallucination. I'd certainly experienced similar things before. During Patrol Phase, I'd only hallucinated for the first couple of days. After that, my body just got used to the sleep deprivation and I pushed through the rest of the week, feeling surprisingly normal. I thought that was all that was happening here, only sharpened by the fact that we had just been in real combat, and the captain had then decided that it was a good idea to accept an invitation for tea and crumpets from the very people we'd been killing in job lots only hours before.

This was like walking into a "formerly" ISIS village in Syria, only ten times worse.

Dragon Mask halted in front of the biggest pavilion in the village, a multi-peaked sprawl of crudely stitched hides facing the main entrance to the wooden building, which I was increasingly convinced was a temple. There were strange designs—all reminiscent of the more abstract and disturbing symbols on the savages' shields—carved into the doorposts. Snarling monsters surmounted every post and beam. I'd say it looked like a Viking longhouse or Norse stave church, but there's a certain beauty to those carvings. These were ugly and threatening in a way I can't quite describe.

The carved human skulls mounted to either side of the entrance to the tent didn't make me feel any more at ease.

Dragon Mask got down off his horse at the entrance and handed the reins to a cringing figure that had come up as we'd stopped. With a wave of invitation, he led the way inside the tent.

Gunny had caught up with me, and he tilted his chin to tell me to wait, even as Captain Sorenson strode past us and into the tent. The rest of the platoon was kind of milling around, turning to face outboard, weapons still held ready, though a few had already done the rucksack flop in the packed down and slightly sooty snow. We were all worn out.

"Team leaders need to come inside," Gunny said. *Before Sorenson does any more damage.* He didn't say that part, but he didn't have to. "Bring your teams in to drop rucks and get warmed up, but I want at least one man per team out here on security until I say otherwise."

"Captain's not gonna like that." Zimmerman might have just been making a point, but right then wasn't the right time. Bailey had just come up behind him, and I saw murder in my friend's eyes as they bored into the back of Zimmerman's skull. "Hearts and minds, that sort of thing."

"I don't give a damn." Gunny was all out of fucks to give. The exertion, the fighting, and the very precarious position we found ourselves in had finally eroded away the last remaining diplomatic bone in his body. "We're maintaining security. We're already in deeper than I ever wanted to be, and I'll be damned if I leave us open to a massacre."

Without another word, Gunny followed the captain inside. Rodeffer was looking back at me as if uncertain what to do, and I pointed him inside. We'd at least get under some shelter. It was cold, getting colder now that we weren't moving.

With Rodeffer leading the way, I ducked inside.

The tent was dimly lit and smoky. Braziers smoldered at the four points of the compass, but most of the light came from a single fire in the center of the room. For the first time, I noticed the smell. It had been too cold outside. It was close and stuffy in here, and the smell of smoke, stale food, sour body odor, and something else, something metallic and even more unpleasant than the rest, almost knocked me over.

Somewhat to my surprise, as my eyes adjusted to the dim, flickering light, I saw no women or children inside. In fact, aside from us and Dragon Mask's honor guard—which included that towering monster with his Lochaber axe—the tent appeared to be empty. There was no furniture except for the braziers. The floor was skins and furs, piled up to insulate against the cold of the snow and the frozen ground.

Dragon Mask had stepped around the fire and removed his mask. When he turned around, the fire threw the lines of his face into stark relief. I looked at the savages' leader for the first time.

He was a tall man with a lean, spare build, and his face was long and sharp-angled. High cheekbones, which appeared to have been ritually scarred, threw his eyes into deep shadow, though the firelight still glinted from their depths. His high forehead ended in a widow's peak, dark, gray-streaked hair falling toward his shoulders. His beard was stringy and patchy. It looked like whenever Rodeffer tried to grow a beard, but greasier.

He lowered himself to sit cross-legged on the skins by the fire, holding his mutilated hand close to his chest as he did so. Captain Sorenson sat next to him, while the rest of us spread out and did the rucksack flop, though I carefully made sure that at least Santos and Smith were positioned where they could watch the shadows around the edge of the tent. Bailey had Gonsalves and Synar watching the entrance, but I wasn't sure that nobody was going to creep up under the edge of the tent. We'd been killing these people only hours before, after all, and they'd been howling for our blood. I didn't trust this sudden friendliness.

I sent Farrar out to take a shift on security outside the door. Bailey had already put Owens out there, and Gurke was sending Herrera. Zimmerman only grudgingly told Baldinus to head out, and then only when Gunny fixed him with that unblinking stare that promised horrible, horrible things if he wasn't obeyed.

As soon as Farrar started for the flap, I turned back in time to see Dragon Mask watching the three Marines head out with their weapons and gear. His eyes glinted in the firelight, and I could have sworn he looked…amused.

Captain Sorenson had shed his ruck—which couldn't have been that heavy; I'd seen him at PT—and he was leaning forward, as if eager to engage with Dragon Mask. Maybe he was.

The truth is, every Recon Marine dreams of being that irregular warfare warlord. Maybe it's because of all the sneaky training we get, coupled with the fact that the Marine Corps is forever trying to put us "back in the box." But there are different ways of thinking about that.

To most of us, it means ambushes, sabotage, running amok behind enemy lines, hunting down their leadership, and generally causing enough havoc that we can break their will by the sheer destruction a highly mobile, highly trained force can wreak. To officers, however, it's a little different.

Sorenson was clearly thinking more along the lines of engaging with the locals and winning their hearts and minds. Unfortunately, I thought that he was suffering from an all-too-common delusion when it came to "hearts and minds."

That delusion was that there weren't people who just wanted you dead, no matter how likeable you tried to make yourself.

I also suspected that he was putting far too much weight on the theory that they were thoroughly cowed by superstitious fear of the power of our firearms. From the look in Dragon Mask's eye, I didn't think he was cowed at all. I thought he was running an angle.

"Welcome to the village of the Dovos nal Uergal." Dragon Mask spread his hands to indicate our surroundings. That bandage was dark with dried blood now. "We have little to offer you. This is a harsh land, and the Younger Gods are often cruel. But perhaps your coming heralds a change in the winds." He couldn't keep the look of cunning off his face, though the captain seemed oblivious.

"I certainly hope so." Sorenson had his officious voice on. It grated every time he used it, which was usually in weekend safety briefs. "We got off to a bad start, but I hope that we can make some amends for the violence we already experienced and move forward as partners."

It was all I could do to keep from rolling my eyes. Gunny's face was blank, but he was watching Dragon Mask like a hawk. Bailey had his rifle across his lap and his fingers were drumming against the pistol grip as he watched Dragon Mask and the silent bodyguard squatting behind him, swilling from drink skins and chewing on some kind of dried meat.

They still had their weapons close by, too.

Dragon Mask waved a dismissive hand. "As I said, the testing of strength on strength has shown your power to be greater. Such is the way of the world. You are honored because you defeated us."

"And what if we hadn't?" Gunny spat out.

Captain Sorenson glanced over his shoulder at Gunny with annoyance clear in his expression, but Gunny Taylor ignored him, his eyes fixed on Dragon Mask.

The leader of the Dovos smiled. It was not a pleasant expression, especially given the scars on his cheeks. "That would have depended on the manner of your defeat. If you fought bravely, you would serve us. If not..." He shrugged.

Captain Sorenson looked a little flustered at that. I could imagine just what that shrug portended, and while he was an arrogant stuffed shirt, Sorenson wasn't so stupid as to miss it, either. If they had decided that we hadn't fought sufficiently hard, we'd have been killed to a man at the very least.

These people made ISIS look like weak sisters.

"If we are going to work together, we need to understand each other." Apparently, the captain was going to try to gloss over that implied threat. He paused, as if thinking. "Where are we, exactly? We seem to have gotten somewhat disoriented while moving through a fog bank and apparently missed our beach landing site."

Boy, that's an understatement. I wondered if he was just trying to sound normal, or if he was still in bald-faced denial about the absolute weirdness we'd already experienced.

"This is the land of the Younger Gods." Dragon Mask pointed outside the tent. "There is one of their great temples, where the fire must never go out." Something about the way he said that, even in his weird language that we were somehow able to understand, told me that he was leaving a crucial detail out there, though I couldn't be sure what it was. "They placed the sentinels along the coast to warn off the sea trolls that serve the Elder God beneath Sunken Chroivah. Those you fought already, I hear?"

Captain Sorenson frowned. "You heard about that?"

Dragon Mask smiled again. "I have ears. The land and the wind carried the news of your fight beneath the Great Watching Thing. I heard its call of warning in the dream world." He leaned forward. "This fog. What was it like?"

Sorenson shrugged. "It was fog. At least, it seemed like normal fog."

I could tell that Dragon Mask didn't believe him, but he declined to push things. I could see the wheels turning behind those eyes. But he leaned back and motioned to his bodyguards. I tensed, my hand on my rifle, but they simply got up and headed for the doorway. The big one with the Lochaber axe, a shaggy brute with scarred cheeks and a bristling spade of a beard, maintained eye contact with me all the way to the flap.

"It grows late, and we have traveled far and fought a great battle." Dragon Mask got to his feet. Captain Sorenson did the same, while the rest of us stayed obstinately on our asses. He glared around at us, but he only got blank, hostile stares in reply. "I will leave you to rest for now. In the morning, we may speak of the future, and what your magic might bring all of us. Until then, my friends."

I frowned. Something about that word... the word for friends. He had said, "*amvik.*" Don't ask me how I knew, but I sensed that *amvik* didn't precisely mean "friend." It was something closer to "servant."

No one else reacted, so maybe I was the only one who picked up on it. I still had no idea how this hoodoo that let us understand him worked.

We still watched him with poker faces and hands close to weapons as he left the tent, not without a single, sly backward glance.

"All right. Set up a security rotation. Fifty percent." Gunny started barking out orders before the captain could open his mouth. "Half the men on security outside, half in here. Don't fucking fall asleep. Everybody else, rack out. I don't want to see anyone who's not on security conscious in the next five minutes."

The rotation took barely two minutes to work out. About thirty seconds later, the tent was practically shaking with snoring.

We all kept our rifles close at hand that night.

CHAPTER 14

IT wasn't a restful night. The stink of the tent aside—most of us with combat deployments had slept in filthier places—what kept us up were the drums and howling that erupted from the temple in the middle of the night. Everyone had been jolted awake except for Zimmerman and Gonsalves. We scrambled for weapons. Only when the guys on outer security reported that the noise was coming from inside the temple did we stand down, sort of.

It was still a long time before anyone got back to sleep.

Everyone was up before our hosts. Most of us were as starving as we were exhausted. We still had a few days' worth of MREs left and made use of them for breakfast. I didn't think anyone was all that eager to sample the Dovos's cuisine, even if they'd brought us any by the time we were ready to eat. Captain Sorenson was probably the exception to that.

About midmorning, some of the women came in with baskets of food and stoppered skins hanging from their shoulders. They laid the food and the drinking skins on the hides by the fire, all of them eyeing us with a strange mixture of awe and hostility.

None of them spoke before they withdrew. Most of us had finished eating by that time, but since Franks is a walking stomach, he went over and picked something out of the nearest basket. It looked like some sort of dried meat, rather like the stuff that Dragon Mask's entourage had been chewing the night before.

He sniffed it. "Venison, I think." He took a bite.

"You're a brave man, Franks." Gurke was leaning against his ruck, apparently dozing. "From what I've seen, I wouldn't be all that confident I was eating deer and not people, if I were you."

"That's enough of that!" Captain Sorenson was awake. "We're guests here."

"And how is that, anyway?" I blurted out. Any reservations that remained about challenging the captain had worn awfully thin. We were way out in the wild, surrounded by enemies, and it would take a *lot* of optimism to think that we were going to get back to the regular Marine Corps' chain of command anytime soon. We were a *long* way from home. "They were screaming for our blood only a few hours ago. I'm pretty sure most of 'em still want to spill it. That big bastard with that nasty-looking axe, especially. He's been mean-mugging us since we left the castle. Which I'm *still* not convinced was a good idea, by the way."

"Are you questioning my orders, Staff Sergeant?" Sorenson was on his feet, his hands on his hips.

I stood and met his gaze levelly, suddenly more confident than I'd expected. If he wanted to make this a fight, I was reasonably sure I could curb-stomp him. "I'm questioning your judgement, *sir*." There wasn't a lot of deference or respect in my use of the word *sir*. "We ain't in Kansas anymore, and you're trying to act like we're only a few miles from the nearest FOB. Syrians and Afghans might play the game carefully because they don't want American air power to come down on their heads, but these people have got no such worries. And I don't know about you, but every symbol I see around here screams 'evil' to me. And you've brought us right into the belly of the beast."

I watched his face turn red as I called him out, but any further argument was cut short by Dragon Mask's arrival.

I call him that, but he was still without his mask, and he wasn't wearing his armor, either. He wore leggings and buskins. His upper body was wrapped in what looked an awful lot like a polar bear hide. At least, the animal that had furnished it had black skin and white fur.

Dragon Mask looked around at us as he closed the tent flap behind him. I watched his eyes as they flicked from one to the other of us, taking in the tableau of confrontation. I could see the wheels turning behind those sly, cunning eyes in his otherwise bland face—though the bland expression was somewhat offset by the ritual scarring—and I didn't like it.

I was suddenly seized with the urge to draw the sword at my side and run it right through his throat.

The time would come when I would think back to that urge with some regret that I hadn't followed through on it.

Captain Sorenson straightened self-consciously, smoothing his own expression as he turned to Dragon Mask. But if he was trying to disguise the fact that we'd just been at each other's throats, it was too late. Dragon Mask had seen it, and he was already planning what to do about it.

The other Dovos might be bloodthirsty savages, but Dragon Mask was something more. He was smart, calculating, and ambitious. He was far more dangerous than any of the rest of them. I had no idea what kind of hierarchy these people had, but he hadn't been in charge until after

I'd smoked the warlord. Now he was acting as if he'd always ruled, despite the mutilated hand that spoke to the fact that he was still beholden to someone—or some*thing*—bigger.

I didn't doubt that he was more than willing to get his hands bloody as well, but there was a brain behind that capacity for violence, and it was capable of cold, detached planning that a screaming berserker probably wasn't. Underestimating this man would get us all killed, or worse.

There was that thought again: *Or worse.*

He didn't get as solicitous as I expected him to. There were no questions about what was happening, or how we had slept or eaten. He just walked past Captain Sorenson and lowered himself to sit by the fire, opening his bearskin as he did so. He was bare-chested, his torso greased over extensive tattoos. Most of them were the sort of abstract glyphs that made my eyes itch to look at them.

"So, let us talk." He waved to the other side of the fire, and after a moment, Captain Sorenson sat down, cross-legged, across from him. "Where did you come from?"

"Like I said last night, we are United States Marines. We launched from the USS *Makin Island* two nights ago and got lost in an unexpected fog bank." Sorenson shifted his weight. "That was when we came under attack by… unknown forces."

Despite Dragon Mask's words the night before, the captain apparently couldn't quite bring himself to say, "sea trolls."

Dragon Mask listened, his eyes hooded, nodding slightly. "Where is this… *Mak-En Island*?"

"I imagine that she's still off the coast of Norway. Unless the Russians made a move after the fog rolled in…" He paused and then shook himself a little. "Oh. The *Makin*

Island is a ship. An amphibious assault ship. We come from the United States of America, but we were off the coast of Norway when this all started."

Dragon Mask's face was still composed, his eyes calculating. "I have never heard of this Nor-way, or Rush-ans. Or the…" He paused, as if struggling with the pronunciation, then gave up. "Or the other place you speak of. You must be from a place far, far away."

Captain Sorenson visibly struggled with that one. We hadn't *physically* covered all that much distance, but it was abundantly obvious that we were a *long* way from home. Furthermore, I saw him glance at Gunny Taylor, who was glaring a warning at him. He was talking too freely, especially given the fact that we'd been engaged in open, bloody hostilities with these same people less than a day before.

"Far away, yes," the captain admitted. There really wasn't any denying it at that point. It wasn't as if we could hike home, or as if reinforcements were standing by to extract us. Fortuna had wasted plenty of time and battery life on trying to make radio contact already, without any response, or even noise to suggest there was anyone else out there.

Dragon Mask glanced down at the rifle sitting next to the captain, then motioned toward it. "Do all of you… Ma-Reens carry such tools of power?" The words he used didn't quite translate that way, but that's the closest I can get. Once again, despite the weird hoodoo that made him understandable, there were subtexts to the words that I could sort of sense without putting my finger on them.

"Yes." Sorenson put his hand on the rifle. "Every one of us."

Dragon Mask reached out a hand. "May I see it?"

I felt more than saw Gunny Taylor tense, but maybe that was just because I did, too. Sorenson couldn't be that stupid.

He wasn't. He shook his head. "We don't hand our weapons over to anyone."

Dragon Mask's eyes flickered with both annoyance and understanding. His gambit had failed, so he was figuring out another tack.

"Of course." He leaned back slightly. Only then did I see that he'd been leaning forward, almost eagerly, inclined toward the captain's rifle. He folded his arms. "We have tales, ancient tales from before the ascension of the Younger Gods, about such weapons of power. Weapons that could take a man's life at a distance, with a roar of thunder, simply by pointing at him." There was undisguised lust in his eyes as he looked at the captain's M4. "No such weapons have been seen in ages. Not in the hands of mere men." His voice dropped, almost to a whisper. "A man with such power might even challenge the Younger Gods and their chosen servants."

So, that was his angle. A relative handful of us had killed dozens, hell, maybe even over a hundred of them without losing one, and he wanted that kind of combat power. We were an asset to be used in his mind, if he could trick us into helping him.

"Who are these Younger Gods?" Sorenson had to have picked up on *that* subtext. Dragon Mask wasn't being nearly as subtle as he probably thought he was. But the captain was playing along anyway.

"Some say that they were men once. But they stole the secrets of deep magic from the Elder Gods and realized their own ascension. In so doing, they tricked the Elder

Gods and imprisoned them in the deep and frozen places. Now the Younger Gods rule, while the Elder Gods slumber. The Elder Gods are truly terrible, more terrible than even the Younger Gods." He stared into the fire for a moment, as if thinking. When he looked up, his eyes were hooded again, trying to hide his thoughts, but I could see that sly look in his face again. "We men are but playthings of the gods. Yet somehow, you have come to us, bearing a power that might even challenge the Younger Gods." Raw, naked ambition lit in his eyes. "Think of it. If the ancient weapons have appeared on the face of the world again, what might a man achieve who holds one of them?"

I thought he was laying it on a bit thick for a few M4s and a couple of M27s, all with rapidly dwindling stocks of ammunition. But if he didn't know how firearms really worked, he might think that they were bottomless, magic death machines.

Rather like some people in Hollywood back home I could mention.

"You talk about these 'younger gods' as if they were real, as if you could actually meet them and touch them." Sorenson was skeptical.

Dragon Mask looked at him as if he were a young child who had just asked if the sun would really rise again the next morning. "Of course they are. Uergal has stood in yonder temple not a fortnight past and taken his fill of the sacrifices we offered. He has led us in battle against his brother, Korgul, and against the sea trolls when they raided far inland some fifteen summers ago. He is a giant who crosses rivers in a single stride and carries the power to crush mountains in his left hand."

Sorenson still looked skeptical, but his certainty was wavering. Dragon Mask had spoken with conviction and awe—but both were tempered with a certain degree of envy and hatred. Again, I wasn't sure if I was the only one picking up on it, or if the others in the tent sensed it, too.

If Sorenson picked up on the subtext, he blithely ignored it. "Well, I certainly think that to overthrow a ruler pretending to be a god is a noble cause." He was starting to put on his "educated officer" lecturing voice, and I had to suppress the pained expression and the groan that threatened to wrench its way out of me. We'd all heard that tone before, and usually when he was spouting crap that even the bootest of our boots understood was crap. "If you truly want to free your people, then we are willing to help, in return for help finding a way home."

Dragon Mask smiled. It was not a pleasant expression. The fact that his teeth were filed to points should have been a warning sign, but Sorenson was probably priding himself on his cultural sensitivity at that point.

"Excellent." While the word in whatever language he was speaking didn't sound exactly like that, the sense was there, along with the almost sibilant hiss that told anyone with an ounce of common sense that this was a deal with the devil that we were going to regret. "If we succeed, you may win the power to bring yourselves home, if you wish."

The fact that Sorenson didn't even question that bothered me more than anything else. When I glanced at Gunny Taylor, I saw him watching Sorenson, not Dragon Mask. His brow was furrowed, more with concern than anger. He caught me looking at him, and in that brief glance I saw that he was as worried about this as I was.

Captain Sorenson leaned forward, unconsciously pulling his M4 across his lap. He flagged Gunny with the muzzle in the process, but fortunately, his hand was nowhere near the trigger. "You seem to have a plan already in mind."

I didn't like the tone in his voice. It was almost painfully eager. As if he'd not only accepted the idea that Dragon Mask could get us back to The World, but that he was already planning what he'd do when we got there. And I had little doubt that it would involve a lot of "disciplinary action" for the Marines who had dared to question him.

Dragon Mask nodded. "Your thunder weapons may well be the tipping point, but they are hardly the only power we will need. Uergal's own magic is great, gathered over many ages, and he has ways to destroy a man that cannot be opposed by ordinary weapons. Or even thunder weapons. We must search out even greater magic so that we might be hidden and protected until we can strike at him. There are protective spells he has wrapped around himself that must be unraveled before even your thunder weapons might touch him." Once again, that cunning look slid across his face. "Only the power of the Elder Gods can do that."

"Well, we don't know much of anything about that, but where we can help with tactics and advice, we will." The captain either wasn't getting it, or he was trying to put on a brave face in front of the rest of us. Either way, he wasn't inspiring a great deal of confidence. Not that that was anything new. "We will, of course, respect any of your traditions or ceremonies. The Marine Corps has always respected the rich cultures of our host nations."

Somebody made a strangled noise behind me. It might have been Bailey.

Dragon Mask was trying to hide his triumphant grin as he stood and drew his bearskin around himself. Something seemed to change in the tent then, as if a door had been shut. I frowned, my eyes narrowing as I studied Dragon Mask. He saw me watching him and met my gaze. His expression was composed, but I suspected he was gloating. I could imagine why. He'd gotten what he wanted.

"Rest, eat, drink." He started toward the tent flap. "There are many preparations that must be made. There will be ceremonies we may do here at the temple, but later we must journey far from here to acquire some of the other things we will need."

He had to walk within arm's length of Gunny Taylor to leave the tent. For a moment, he faltered as he caught Gunny's baleful, unblinking stare. Then he straightened, pulled his bearskin more tightly around himself, and ducked out of the flap.

"What the hell was that, *sir*?" Gunny had waited just long enough for Dragon Mask to have stepped far enough away to be unlikely to overhear, without giving the captain a chance to start talking.

"*That* was winning hearts and minds, Gunny," the captain snapped back. "And you will *not* speak to me like that again, especially not in front of the platoon."

Gunny completely ignored the captain's admonishment. "You kind of have to *know* something about the hearts and minds before you start trying to win them, *sir!* As in, 'are these really people we want to get into bed with?'" He blew out an angry breath, his nostrils flaring. I traded a glance with Bailey. He had stepped back slightly, his eyes a little wide. We'd both seen Gunny Taylor in a rage before—it was hard to avoid it—but this was the most pissed off we'd ever seen him.

Gunny stabbed a knife hand at the tent flap. "Conor said it. I'm pretty sure Bailey's said it. Now I'm saying it. These people were screaming for our blood just yesterday. The looks we've been getting, the demeanor hits, they all tell me that they haven't given up on that. Just because that snake thinks he can get himself some kind of advantage does *not* make these people our friends! Hell, I'd be willing to bet he was rivals with the warlord Conor shot dead, which means we *already* helped him out more than we should have!"

"That is *ENOUGH, Gunnery Sergeant!*" Captain Sorenson was abruptly on his feet, his face livid, his words almost a scream. "You may not like it, but the chain of command is clear, and I am the senior officer here! The decision has been made, and *you will abide by it!*"

His hand was now on his M4's pistol grip, and Gunny saw it. He wasn't the only one, either. The tension in the tent was suddenly palpable. Zimmerman moved then, and while I couldn't see him since I was now facing the captain with my own hand on my weapon, Bailey shifted to face him.

This was awesome. We were in the belly of the beast and at each other's throats. I couldn't imagine a more dangerous situation, and I think that was why Gunny did what he did next.

"Fine. My job is to advise when I think that the platoon commander is making a bad call. I've advised. We'll follow along until this becomes untenable." When Captain Sorenson looked like he was about to explode again, Gunny's voice got harder than ever. "'To obey all *lawful* orders,' Captain Sorenson. It's not a suicide pact."

And that, I think, was why Gunny made the call he did. We were twenty-six men in completely unfamiliar territory, surrounded by enemies. Letting this situation develop to its inevitable—and probably bloody—conclusion would only get us all slaughtered.

Why do I say "bloody," you ask? Because we were Marines, far from any oversight. There was no Big Marine Corps here. And there's something primal that lurks in every Recon Marine, snarling to get out. Something that would eagerly go for the throat over a matter of honor—or of right.

That primal part was waking up in all of us way out here in this strange place. And if we lost control of it, we were all going to die. Gunny, as angry as he was, understood that.

"Everybody sit the hell down." He glared around at all of us. "If we're going to play along with the Dovos' plans, we're going to have to do some contingency planning of our own."

The glower he fixed the captain with warned him not to press his luck. For once, Sorenson heeded the warning.

Bailey came up beside me. "Dude, did that seem as weird to you as it did to me?" He kept his voice low so that only I could hear it. "I mean, he's a dumbass, but he's never been *that* much of a dumbass."

I glanced at Sorenson, remembering that strange feeling when Dragon Mask had closed his bearskin. *Something* had happened then. "No, it was weird. Dragon Mask had something going that was affecting his mind. I don't know what, but when he stood up, it stopped. I don't *think* it affected me—I think it was aimed at the captain alone. But I felt it when it stopped."

"Great. So, we're following a dupe."

"Always have been."

CHAPTER 15

TWO days later, we were trudging into the woods, rucks on over crudely tanned skins that at least kept us warm. It had gotten even colder since we'd arrived at the Dovos' village—and it had already been pretty cold. Ordinarily, we'd keep the warming layers to a minimum during movement. Piling on snivel gear and climbing over mountains under load was a good way to overheat. But it was cold enough, with the wind whipping down from the north to slice right through whatever you put on to try to keep it off, that even the bearskin tunics of the Dovos didn't feel like they were going to be too warm.

Dragon Mask, once again wearing the helmet that caused me to mentally coin the name, was leading our little column. Captain Sorenson was next to him, trailed by a dozen of the Dovos' warriors. We fell in behind them, with another dozen behind us.

It wasn't lost on me that the captain was up front with Dragon Mask, separated from the platoon. It had become the normal state of affairs over the past couple of days—he'd been spending more and more time sitting with Dragon Mask off to one side of the tent where we'd been sequestered. He'd talked more to that greasy, sharp-toothed shaman over the last couple of days than he had to any of us, even Gunny.

That was kind of a blessing and a curse all at the same time, if we're being honest.

What had really put my hackles up was the eagerness with which he'd agreed to participate in the "ceremonies" that Dragon Mask had invited us to. I hadn't seen a thing about these people that suggested I wanted to have *anything* to do with their rituals, and when I saw the blood on the captain's hands and the weird look in his eye after he came back into the tent, I kept my weapons even closer than before.

I'd never especially trusted Captain Sorenson. A lesson I learned well before we got into this mess.

* * *

The dirt under Stanley was rapidly turning to mud from the sweat dripping off him. His arms shook as he held the up position.

"What are we at, Stanley?" I stood over him, my arms folded.

"One hundred eighty, Staff Sergeant." Stanley could barely get the words out. That many eight-count bodybuilders will do that to you. He was nowhere near the Five Hundred Club yet, at least not since he'd joined my team. He should *have joined that club in BRC, but he was shaking by one-eighty.*

"So, what does that mean?" I kept my voice low and easy. This wasn't about me being pissed—though I was—but about him learning.

"Twenty left, Staff Sergeant." His head was hanging between his arms, and his ass was in the air as he tried to keep from collapsing on the ground.

"Twenty and one half. You've still got four counts on this one. Get to it."

He scissored his legs, brought his knees up to his chest, and stood up, his chest heaving. He looked like he was about to puke.

"What's going on here, Staff Sergeant?"

I turned to see Captain Sorenson, our new platoon commander, walking toward us, frowning. I was more than a little surprised to see him there—it was after dark, and he didn't have much of anything left to do there. I'd thought he'd left the range an hour before.

I was not happy to see an officer right then. This was NCO business.

"Sergeant Stanley had an ND on the range today, sir. We're correcting the situation." Stanley had slammed a round into the ground not six inches from Rodeffer's boot. There had been several violations of weapons safety rules there, and I was determined not to see it happen again.

Sorenson looked at me coldly for a moment, before turning his eyes on Stanley. "You're dismissed, Sergeant."

Stanley looked at me with wide eyes for a moment, reading the barely leashed fury in my eyes. I gritted my teeth, but the captain had given an order. I nodded shortly, and he lurched off, too tired to run.

"Come with me, Staff Sergeant." Sorenson turned smartly on his heel and headed back toward his truck.

I didn't exactly have a choice. I followed him and stood there, fuming, as he pulled his laptop out of his vehicle. I frowned. What the hell was he doing?

A moment later, he turned toward me and swiveled the touch screen around. I looked down at a counseling statement. My *counseling statement, not Stanley's. "What the fuck is this?"*

That was not the best choice of words. His face went even stonier, though I could see the rage in his eyes. "That is your counseling statement, Staff Sergeant, for hazing. Speak to me like that again, and it will get a lot worse than a written counseling. Now sign it."

I'm not proud of what I did then. I should have refused. Should have stood up to him. But I wasn't confident that the Marine Corps would have my back—after all, Sorenson's attitude had been Big Marine Corps' attitude for years now. Better to ruin a Marine's career with paperwork than make him sweat and teach the lesson.

So, I signed it. I didn't say another word. I ignored the look of contempt on his face as I turned on my heel and headed toward my own vehicle. My team didn't have range watch that night.

I should have drawn the line. But I was worried about my team with a man like that in charge. So, I played along.

But I knew where we stood.

* * *

Now, that mistrust was only getting worse, at a time when we had to trust each other as a platoon more than ever.

We'd left the village in broad daylight, and by mid-afternoon we were deep in the forest, well out of sight of the temple. The snow was thinner under the trees, all towering firs and spruces that blocked out a lot of the sunlight. They might not actually have been firs or spruces. They looked different enough that an arborist would have classified them as something else, I suppose. They were ever so slightly different from the trees I'd hunted through back home but still close enough for me to call them by the same name. Same with the horse-creatures.

We moved through dappled shadows in near-silence, the snow crunching underfoot as we went. The Dovos made us almost sound clumsy, and they got steadily more and more on edge as we moved downhill toward the river. They hadn't told us about any enemies nearby except for the sea trolls, but a people doesn't live like the Dovos without treating everyone and everything like an enemy.

I was on board with that. Especially if we were including the Dovos in "everyone and everything."

Gunny, Bailey, Gurke, and I had taken full advantage of Captain Sorenson's self-appointed exile, and we were keeping as much separation from the Dovos as we could. We also had flankers out—not a usual Recon thing, but Recon teams usually move by themselves, not in a company-sized element.

The Dovos led the way through the woods, over a low ridge, and down into the river valley. The forest stayed thick until we got within a mile of the river, then the trees started to get smaller and farther apart, often opening into wide clearings, some of them strangely symmetrical. They'd been planted or cleared by something other than nature. The Dovos stayed away from those, and we were more than happy to do the same. There was something *off* about them, even more than every other facet of this place.

While my watch wasn't exactly accurate, as far as I could tell, sunset came early. The Dovos started setting up camp under the trees, and we pulled off a little way to do the same.

I let Santos and the other ATLs handle security, while I grabbed Rodeffer. "Drop your ruck and come with me.

Make sure your gear's still all secured. We can't afford to make noise."

"Where are you going, Conor?" Gunny had appeared at my elbow as if by magic. He was Recon to the core, but it was a mark of how tired I was that I hadn't heard his footsteps crunching in the snow.

"Hunting." I'd divested myself of my ruck and everything else except my M4 and my chest rig. I still had my Bowie, but I'd left my sword leaning against my ruck. For some reason, that gave me a pang, leaving it. I didn't know why.

"Is that a good idea?" Zimmerman had just come over from where his own team was setting in—noticeably not being quite as conscientious about security as the rest of us. "It'll cost ammo."

That did have me a little worried, but Zimmerman's question had me irked. "One shot, one kill, right? Look, we're practically out of chow. We're burning calories like a mother in this cold. And while you might not have noticed, the Dovos aren't all that happy about sharing their food when Dragon Mask over there isn't making them." He'd told the captain that his name was Ekersakar, but I didn't especially care. "That's provided you trust them not to poison it or feed us something we really don't want to eat." Nobody had openly commented about the filed teeth yet, but given the cold and that particular sign, I didn't trust that their diet consisted entirely of pine nuts and venison.

"Step carefully and don't go too far." Gunny was clearly concerned, but there was no getting around our dwindling food supplies. It wasn't as if we had an infinite resupply machine, and he didn't trust the Dovos any more than I did.

His glance toward their camp, where the captain was sitting with Dragon Mask, talking intently, spoke volumes.

Sooner or later, this little divide would have to get addressed.

I met Gunny's eyes, raising my eyebrow in an unspoken question. He shook his head. "My decision. Go. Just try not to bring another horde of trolls or something worse down on us."

I nodded and jerked my head at Rodeffer, then we slipped away into the trees, quickly leaving the glow of the campfires behind.

"Why are they lighting fires if we're in hostile territory?" Rodeffer whispered.

"Maybe they're more worried about what the fires might attract than what they might keep away." I wasn't trying to be spooky. I only realized how creepy that sounded after I said it. But we were in a land of ice and monsters, so there was no telling what might be lurking in the shadows.

The sun hadn't entirely set yet—we still had probably about twenty minutes if things worked the same way here as they did back home. Perfect hunting time. Game usually comes out during the transitional periods, the parts of the day that we called in Recon, "Before Morning Nautical Twilight" and "Early Evening Nautical Twilight." BMNT and EENT.

The two of us stayed closer than we usually did on patrol. Some of that was probably unconscious. Going down to a two-man team in this haunted world wasn't calculated to make any sane man comfortable. As we worked our way through the trees toward where I'd heard a creek gurgling toward the river below, I started to see and hear things that made me check over my shoulder a little more often to make sure that Rodeffer was still there.

It wasn't anything obvious at first. In fact, I was pretty sure—and still am—that most of those first glimpses of movement and furtive sounds were figments of my imagination. I could have sworn that I'd been seeing the occasional shadow moving off to our flanks as we marched during the day. Once again, those could have been explained away, except that they never quite seemed to move in concert with us, or with the faint wind stirring the treetops. When there was any wind, which was rare. Much rarer than the glimpses of movement.

After about half an hour, though, I'd seen enough that I was convinced that there really *was* something out there, something that had been pacing us since shortly after we'd left the village.

If whatever was out there was hoping that I was going to relax my vigilance over time, it probably should have been better at hiding.

Not that I knew for sure what I was going to do if it came at us. If it was flesh and blood, I was going to blow its brains out. Otherwise...

I'd burn that bridge when I got to it.

Rodeffer was getting a little jumpy as we kept going, his head snapping toward every vague sound that might or might not be real, his rifle moving toward every shadow, moving or not. I finally stopped, took a knee behind a towering pseudo-spruce, and pulled him in close.

"Calm down. Whatever it is, it's not coming after us yet. Don't let it get in your head. Watch your sectors, and don't get target fixated on something that might or might not be there."

"You see it, too?" His voice was a hoarse whisper, which just went to show how rattled he was. As young as Rodeffer was, he'd done two floats with Alpha Company, 1st Recon Bn, and he was a good pointman. His fieldcraft hadn't required a lot of honing. He was the kind of guy who could communicate almost without speaking. But this place had him shook, down to his bones.

I couldn't say I blamed him, but we had to be even *more* on our game here.

"I saw what might have been movement." I had to pick my words carefully because I didn't want to panic him, but I couldn't sugarcoat things, either. We had to confront stark reality, as weird as it was, or we'd get blindsided and murdered—or worse—in a heartbeat. "But whatever it is, it's keeping its distance for now. You ever been stalked by a cougar? I mean the four-footed kind."

"No." He was starting to sound a little more collected.

"I have." I scanned the woods around us, but nothing moved. I might have heard a faint whisper, like someone was speaking in the other room where you can't make out the words, but again, it might just have been a faint breeze in the treetops. "There's not much you can do about it except be ready to fight." I took a deep breath. It was cold enough that the air tasted metallic, and it stung the inside of my nose. As much as I distrusted our hosts, I was grateful for the furs I was wearing. "Just don't get so spooked you do something stupid, all right?"

I was watching my sector, so I only saw it in my peripheral vision when he nodded and said, "I guess we're going to have to get used to spooky stuff here, aren't we?"

"Yeah, we are." I wasn't sure that was ever really going to happen, but it really boiled down to keeping our heads attached to our shoulders long enough for the question to resolve itself.

And part of that was finding food so we could keep body and soul together. Violence wasn't the only threat here. I pointed. "That looks like a good spot to set up." A small, tight stand of trees loomed on a slight rise above the creek beyond. The creek itself wasn't quite frozen over—it seemed to be moving too fast for that. I got up and headed for the trees.

As soon as I reached them, though, I wanted to move. There was nothing about the place that stood out—no perfect circle of trees, no strange arrangements of branches, no *Blair Witch* stick figures—but something had just raised my hackles. I scanned the woods over my rifle's muzzle, looking intently for whatever was stalking us.

And then I saw it.

There wasn't much detail. For some reason, the thing seemed *blurry*. All I could see clearly were its eyes, yellow and almost glowing, staring at me from around a tall tree trunk. What might have been a hand was curled around the bark, its fingers too long. Its face was low to the ground, but I got the impression that it was actually pretty tall. It seemed to be hunched down behind the tree as it watched us.

Needless to say, I didn't imagine this thing meant us any good. It glared at us as its hand started to creep around the trunk of the tree.

To make things worse, those vague almost-whispers I'd heard earlier got louder. I still couldn't understand them, but I started to feel a powerful compulsion to put my rifle on the ground and lie down.

Instead, I lifted it and leveled the weapon at the thing, the top-mounted RMR over my ACOG settling its red dot right between those glaring, yellow eyes. I flipped the M4 to "semi" and slipped my gloved finger inside the trigger guard.

I think that surprised it. I don't know if shooting it would have actually done anything, but it was suddenly gone, and the whispers and the compulsion stopped.

Sometimes you've just got to be meaner than the monsters.

I looked to Rodeffer. He acted like he hadn't seen any of it. Maybe he hadn't.

The sun was down. The light was fading. But I could still see enough to spot the game trail—at least, I hoped it was a game trail and not left by something else—heading down to the water. We settled in to wait. I said a little prayer, hoping that God was still listening in this haunted, evil place, both for good hunting and that we'd live through the night.

CHAPTER 16

I didn't say anything about our little encounter at first. Of course, we were occupied with dressing out the small red deer I'd killed on the creek bank, but I also didn't want the captain's input—it would have been useless at best—nor did I trust anything that Dragon Mask would tell us about it.

It took some time to dress out the carcass, mainly because I was one of the two Marines in the platoon who'd ever done his own butchering. We didn't have the time or the supplies to dry any of the meat, but there was about enough to last the platoon for only about a day, anyway. The cold worked to our advantage. The temperature—already bitingly cold—was dipping fiercely with the sun having set. It was a clear night, and what little heat had built up during the day was rapidly fleeing into the sky. While the carcass was still cooling, despite the fact that I'd gutted it while Rodeffer had held security, nervous about the echoing *crack* of the shot that had rolled down the river valley, an hour or two in the snow would probably freeze the meat solid.

Sometimes, adverse conditions can be somewhat beneficial.

I did tell Bailey and Gunny as we split up the meat. "Did Rodeffer see it?" Gunny asked quietly with a glance around to see if anyone else was within earshot.

"I'm not sure. He didn't say anything, but he was trying really hard not to be scared of anything at that point, so he might have just been keeping it to himself." I thought I was doing a pretty good job of being as deadpan as I could be at that point, never mind the fact that the sight of that thing had made every hair on my body stand on end.

"Well, keep it under your hat for now, unless you see it again." Gunny had emptied out a stuff sack and was now filling it with snow before putting his own share in. "The locals have been putting out totems and offerings since just before sunset. I don't want the captain getting a visit from the Good Idea Fairy, and that story might just act as an invitation."

"I take it security's already set?"

He nodded as he closed up the stuff sack. "It is. Which is why I don't want Sorenson getting involved. He might try to keep us on one hundred percent all night, and while we've got to stay alert, guys need to get sleep, too." He looked up at me and Rodeffer. "Speaking of which, you two don't stand a watch tonight." He gestured to the stripped, bloody bones and already half-frozen hide—all that was left of the deer. "This counts. Go get some shut-eye."

I *almost* argued. But nobody in their right mind argues with Gunny Taylor when he glares at you, and he was glaring at me right then. So, I shut up and nodded, then cleaned my knife off in the snow before pulling my sharpener out of my ruck. My dad had taught me that, and the Marine Corps had reinforced it. Always have your weapons and gear cleaned and ready to go before you take care of yourself.

Then, once I made sure that everyone else in the team except Smith, who was on watch, was down, I wrapped myself in my borrowed furs and Ranger roll, my head against my ruck, and tried to sleep.

* * *

I really don't know if it was a dream or not. I stood in the woods. I couldn't tell how close or far from the camp I was—in fact, I couldn't see much at all past the silhouettes of the trees standing black against the stars in the sky overhead. Strangely, I didn't feel cold, despite the fact that the snow was knee-deep.

A faint song echoed through the forest. I couldn't make it out at first, but I tensed. Nothing I'd heard out of the dark so far had been friendly.

But as the song continued, something changed. The woods seemed less dark, somehow, and the sound, in its ethereal beauty, became a comfort in the darkness.

I can't describe it adequately. I don't think any human throat made that music, but somehow, I knew it wasn't a monster, either. And when the glowing figure appeared in front of me, coming through the trees, I wasn't afraid.

The being stood there for a moment. I couldn't see detail, but unlike the thing down by the creek, this figure wasn't blurry. It shone too brightly to see clearly. Now, I knew that didn't necessarily mean much, but there had been a sense of something twisted and *wrong* about the thing by the creek, not to mention the face in the cliff, the sea trolls, the bat-winged thing that had flapped its way out of the tor where we'd taken shelter, and even the Dovos themselves. I didn't get that sense from this figure.

The being raised its hand, and then it was gone.

I woke up as Farrar put few more sticks on the fire. I lay there, watching the stars overhead for a moment, the unspoken but clear message still ringing in my ears.

You are not alone. Stand fast.

Maybe it was just a dream. Maybe it was my subconscious just looking for any comfort in that scary, frozen place. But I didn't think so. Something about it had been too vivid, too real. I've had dreams that felt real before, particularly under stress. Some of the most vivid dreams I'd ever had had been in Syria. This one felt different. As if someone had reached out in the dark to let me know that as desperate as our position was, there was still hope.

It still took a long time to get back to sleep.

* * *

For the next three days, we trekked roughly south, following the river. The Dovos stayed in the trees when possible, and we did the same. Camp was usually pitched about an hour before sundown, and we didn't start moving until well after the sun had risen.

Not that the Dovos slept much after dark. All sorts of weird chanting and worse noises came from their end of our patrol bases well after the sun set. Captain Sorenson only came back to check on us from time to time. He may as well have been joined at the hip with Dragon Mask.

I kept hunting—in fact, I only stood security about every other night, since I was out looking for game the other evenings. I got another red deer the first time and a couple of big, heavily furred rodents that looked like a cross between a capybara and a rabbit the second time. There had been three digging in the snow under a tree, and I got the two biggest with a pair of some of the best shots I'd pulled off in a long time. Those didn't taste that good, but they were better than nothing.

The nights were still unquiet. *Something* was usually prowling around the perimeter after dark. Sometimes we only heard footsteps in the snow. Sometimes we caught glimpses of shadows moving behind the trees, sometimes we saw faint glowing lights. Sometimes there were eyes gleaming in the dim light of our campfires. Nothing ever came close enough to be seen clearly, but whatever was out there wasn't going away, either.

Only ironclad orders from Gunny kept any of us from taking a shot, even though there wasn't much of anything out there to shoot. Marines' first instinct is to kill stuff, so sometimes you've got to be *very* clear when they *shouldn't* shoot.

Granted, Recon Marines take a considerable amount of pride in their marksmanship—our platoon outscored a grunt *company* on one of the ranges at 29 Palms—and we've trained to hard-wire it in that you don't shoot unless you've got a target. But stress does weird things, and there ain't much that's more stressful than watching and listening as monsters that might or might not be physical at all are stalking you. I'd never thought it possible, but I found myself longing for the simple threats, like IEDs on the side of the road and mortar fire.

Of course, it wasn't just the things out in the dark we had to worry about.

On the third night, I woke up and reached for a weapon without knowing why. My hand settled on my sword rather than my M4, and for some reason it lingered there before I moved to my rifle. The hilts were still wrapped, but there was something about that weapon that drew me to it.

Pulling my rifle across my chest, I turned my head to see one of the Dovos, barely visible in the dying glow of the fire's embers, moving toward our perimeter. And from the way he was moving, he was hoping that we couldn't hear or see him. I could barely make out his silhouette, and that's because when there's no artificial light to mess with them, I have crazy night eyes after they adjust. And I'd been asleep for at least an hour.

I was about to throw down when a brilliant red dot started dancing on the Dovo's chest.

"*Hsst!*" Santos was in the trees, all but invisible, though I could just make out the faint glow around his eye from his NVGs. "I see you, motherfucker. You need a reminder what these can do?"

The Dovo froze, looking down at the bright red dot dancing on his chest. I didn't have my NVGs on, but I could feel the hatred in the glare he directed toward the other end of the laser. But he turned and started to slink back toward the Dovos' fires.

"That's right." Santos made his voice deeper and took on a bit of a Southern accent. "Walk on home, boy."

I kept my eye on the retreating Dovo as I crawled out of my furs. I'd warmed up enough under them and my Ranger roll—my poncho liner tied inside my poncho, together forming the greatest piece of gear ever invented—that I didn't notice the bitter cold right away. I moved over to join Santos. "You good?"

"Yeah. I just got out here. I'm not even that cold yet." That was bullshit, but Santos had always held that while it is a truism that, "If Marines ain't bitching, there's something wrong," there's a time and a place, and that time and place are much more narrowly defined for Recon Marines. Being hard was part of the game, and Santos was pretty good at playing it.

"Glad somebody in Recon's still listening to Pantera." I kept my eye on our "ally" as I spoke. There was just enough starlight filtering down through the scattered clouds that had started to move in at the end of the day that I could see my breath smoking in the dark.

Santos snorted. "Master Guns Plummer made it pretty clear—the day Marines stop listening to Pantera is the day the Marine Corps dies."

"Well, it might seem to be a little narrow as far as criteria go, but if Master Guns Plummer said it, it must be true." I wondered a little if we'd ever see our old operations chief again. Probably not. But we'd all carry that mean old bear of a man in our Recon hearts. He'd been an OIF—Operation Iraqi Freedom—I vet, a Fallujah Marine, and he'd probably only die when he got tired of waiting around and walked up and punched Death in the face. At least, that was what I'd heard a few Marines claim. I'd had the chance to talk with the man a time or two and found he was a lot more human and a lot more humble than most people suspected. He was an old school Recon Marine to the core, and he'd probably die that way.

The funny part was, the sarcastic remarks he made were the ones most likely to be turned into proverbs by younger Recon Marines. Like Pantera being the soundtrack to the Marine Corps.

I scanned the dark woods around us, then moved back to my ruck and retrieved my NVGs. Pulling more of my furs over my chest rig, I got the PVS-15s up and running, and joined Santos in the trees.

"You don't need to be up." Santos sounded a little uncomfortable. "Gunny said that when you're hunting, you don't have to stand firewatch."

"We just got probed. I'll stay up." The truth was, there had been a time when I would have welcomed Gunny's exclusion. *I get to hunt and not stand firewatch? Sign me up.* I'm not proud of that. I was a team leader. I had to lead. And that meant putting my own comfort last.

We stayed there in the shadows under the trees, watching the darkness outside and the dim glow of the Dovos' fires inside.

It was a long night.

* * *

The next day, the Dovos turned east, toward the river itself. We didn't have maps or GPS that worked, but some of us still remembered our pace counts, and we estimated that we'd covered about fifty miles over the last three days. The river bottom had been getting wider and flatter, and now as we worked our way out of the forest on the bank and toward the river itself, I saw that it had spread out into a dozen or so shallow, quick-moving streams, partway frozen over in places.

I'd been a little worried about the river crossing. We'd be exposed, out in the open with the nearest cover about ten yards away in either direction. And wading through freezing water while the monsters gathered had not been appealing. But now that we were getting closer to the crossing, I thought I could see Dragon Mask's plan. The river was spread out, the water low, and the ice and snow blocking much of the streams. Just from looking at it, I suspected we'd be able to mostly just step or jump over the water.

Provided the ice didn't collapse under us and pitch us into a deep, freezing pool.

The woods on the far side almost mirrored the forest we'd come from. A towering wall of snow-shrouded trees stood back from the bank, the shadows beneath impenetrable past a few yards.

The Dovos spread out along the riverbank as Dragon Mask and the captain crouched down under a massive, lightning-blasted tree on a little hummock above the water. Gunny quickly and quietly signaled us to set up security ourselves, and in a few moments, we were in a tight perimeter a little farther back from the open, with eyes on the river and the Dovos both.

I had my eye on Dragon Mask. He was crouched under the cracked limb of the tree, a pouch open, chanting quietly and making strange gestures over the pouch.

My eyes narrowed. There was some strange pressure in the air, getting stronger as the chant continued. Captain Sorenson was on a knee next to Dragon Mask, watching whatever he was doing with rapt attention.

I felt my hand creep to my rifle. I could end it right then and there. I stood less than fifteen yards away. One bullet would be all it took.

But we were still surrounded and outnumbered. And if I made a move without the rest of the platoon being ready to act, I'd probably just get most of us killed. Sure, we'd kill plenty of them first, but the butcher's bill would be awfully high.

That butcher's bill was ultimately going to be awfully high, anyway. I was sure of that, as sure as I was that snow is cold. But I had to wait for Gunny to make that call.

Note that I said it would be Gunny's call; I wasn't going to wait for the captain. I didn't trust him before, and the adoring way he was watching Dragon Mask work his hoodoo made me trust him even less.

Something flapped overhead, and I snapped my head back to try to spot it. I'd heard that sound before. It had followed us through the trees that first night. So had several of the other Recon Marines. Weapons tracked up toward the treetops, but nothing appeared. A shadow might have flitted toward the far bank, but I couldn't get a good look at it.

Gunny waved the team leaders down, and we joined him just above the captain and Dragon Mask. We were well placed not only to hear what came next, but also to start killing people fast if it came to it.

Dragon Mask was still sitting there, rocking slightly. I could smell something hot and metallic on the air, even though it was still just as cold as ever.

Then the smell was gone, and the pressure drained away. Dragon Mask slumped a little for a moment. When he got up, his hand was trembling.

"The way is clear." There was something stilted about his voice. Or maybe it was just that it seemed to take an extra moment to understand his words. As if whatever spell he was using to make himself understood wasn't *quite* working right.

"We'll see." Gunny pointed at Gurke. "Team Four, move across and secure the far bank."

Anger flared in Captain Sorenson's eyes. "He *said* we're clear, Gunny."

"And maybe he's right. I'd like to confirm it. Won't take more than a couple more minutes." Gunny Taylor was as unflappable as ever, his own stare all but daring the captain to make an issue out of it.

For a second, I thought that Sorenson was going to lose it. Dragon Mask had drawn up against the tree trunk, watching the interplay. The shaking was gone. Whatever had happened, he'd gathered himself and was once again watching, cataloging everything he saw and heard. I didn't doubt that he'd use any of it to his advantage if and when he got the chance.

Hell, he already was. He'd effectively separated Captain Sorenson from the rest of the platoon, and that was indirectly driving a rift between Zimmerman's team and the rest of the platoon, too. That damned contrary nature seemed to be bringing Zimmerman more and more into the captain's orbit, which I hadn't seen coming.

It wasn't clear whether Captain Sorenson had figured that out, but he struggled to bring his temper back under control. Maybe some element of his training was taking hold again rather than his ego. He nodded shortly. "Okay. It risks damaging the relationship we're building with our local partners, but I guess I can see some wisdom to it. Go ahead. But as soon as Staff Sergeant Gurke has confirmed that there are no hostile forces—which he will—then we're moving out. We have a long way to go before nightfall."

"That brings up something else." Gunny waved at Gurke, who nodded and signaled Nelson-Hyde, who immediately started out of the trees toward the river, his weapon up and scanning. "There seems to be a fair bit of information that's not getting disseminated to the platoon. Such as where we're going and exactly what we're going after."

Sorenson clearly didn't like having to explain himself. Which only went to further illustrate his disconnect when it came to Recon in general, never mind our current situation. But he swallowed his pride, at least for the moment.

"Our objective is a ruined city up in those mountains." He pointed toward the cloud-shrouded peaks to the east, just barely visible above the trees on the other side of the river. "There's an artifact up there that was stolen from the Dovos nal Uergal several years ago. It's of considerable cultural importance to the Dovos, so retrieving it will help Ekersakar's cause." He was acting like those names should mean something to us. He was also still acting as if the weird, sorcerous part of all of this was just native superstition that he was playing along with instead of something very real and very dangerous. At least, he was trying to put that mask on it when he was talking to us. I'd seen him going along with Dragon Mask's little ceremonies a little too eagerly, and the look in his eye from time to time after them was glassy, weird, and disturbing.

It was as if a switch had flipped. He'd been in denial at first, but now he was fully embracing it while trying to deny it when around us.

Gunny didn't comment on that. I wished that he would. But instead, he just nodded. "That's something." He stepped closer to Captain Sorenson, not without a glance at Dragon Mask. "Part of your job is to push as much information to these men as possible, *sir.* They're the ones who execute the commander's intent. They're the ones you need to be talking to, not keeping secrets from. Food for thought."

He turned away before Sorenson could reply and moved back to check on the teams again.

In the meantime, Gurke and his team had gotten across the river without incident or trouble. The water was shallow, and the separate streams were narrow enough to step over and across. They disappeared into the darkness under the trees for a moment, except for Chambers, who stayed on the bank, under a tree, where we could see him.

After a moment, Chambers waved. All clear.

We started across to join him. For some reason, the Dovos hadn't crossed first—maybe they were as wary of Dragon Mask's sorcery as we were, or maybe they were playing Dragon Mask's game and letting Captain Sorenson lull himself into a false sense of security—but now they did, spreading out on our flanks as we stepped it out across the river.

To the Dovos, we were crossing into enemy territory. To most of us, we'd been in enemy territory since we'd gone into that weird fog bank. We'd be calm, cool, and collected while still planning to kill all of them at the drop of a hat.

CHAPTER 17

WHILE the captain had told us that we had a long way to go before nightfall, we moved more slowly than we had for the previous three days, and with greater caution. The Dovos were clearly expecting an attack at any moment. Much more than they had on the west side of the river, as haunted as those woods might have been.

As I watched them, I started to suspect that the river was more than a physical obstacle to get past. We had crossed a border. We were now in enemy territory.

Not that *we*, meaning 1st Platoon, Force Recon Company, I MEF, hadn't been in enemy territory for over a week. But now the Dovos were in enemy territory as well.

I just didn't know who the enemy was. And it pissed me off.

I was fuming so much about being kept in the dark that I caught myself starting to dwell on it to the exclusion of paying proper attention to the woods around us as we hiked through the snowbound forest. I shook myself, feeling the flush of shame over how I'd been woolgathering about conflicts in the future instead of focusing on the immediate threat, here and now.

Nothing about the woods on the east bank of the river seemed all that different from the woods on the west bank. The trees were much the same, the snow might have been *slightly* deeper, and we were starting to move uphill instead of down, but as the whole world closed in to a couple dozen yards of tree trunks and snow, it was hard to see that anything was markedly different.

That included the oppressive sense of being watched and the strange flickers of movement at the edge of your peripheral vision. We hadn't left the spooks behind on the other side of the river. Not that I'd entirely expected to, but that still brought up a troubling thought.

I couldn't help but dwell on it as the question rose in my mind, even while I scanned the shadows under the trees, set in stark contrast by the glare where the sun filtered down through the branches above to strike the snow beneath.

We didn't know who this enemy of the Dovos was. But from what I'd seen of the Dovos, did we *really* want to take their side in a fight? How did we know that their foes were worse than they were? For all we'd seen, whoever's territory we'd just entered might well be the good guys.

What was going to happen when we found out? Would we learn the truth before we killed enough of them to put us irreversibly on the side of what I suspected were bloodthirsty cannibals only playing nice because they were afraid of our guns? They'd already admitted the latter part. I wouldn't bet against the former.

I doubted I was the only one thinking it. For sure Captain Sorenson wasn't. He'd have been a lot less eager to help Dragon Mask if he had. He'd set himself into a "nation building" mindset from the get-go, grasping at the first possibility of local allies that presented itself. I supposed, if I was being somewhat charitable—which I wasn't all that inclined to do—I could understand. We were twenty-six men, all alone, with any support far away in either space, time, or both. He was grasping at the first lifeline that presented itself. I could *almost* sympathize.

But this was no lifeline. I was convinced of that. These people wanted our heads. Dragon Mask was willing to use us to accomplish his aims, and I fully expected him to turn on us as soon as it suited him. With his apparent preternatural abilities, I expected we were going to get blindsided with something weirder and nastier than we were ready for.

Of course, that promise that we'd find a way home if we helped him gain whatever power he was after was a major driving force, too. No use denying that. I just didn't believe it. Unfortunately, the captain had gambled everything on it. Maybe even our souls.

I was still thinking about it all as we halted at what appeared to be a random spot in the woods, and the Dovos started to make camp.

"What the hell?" Bailey came up to join me, peering up at the sky. "It's still at least three hours to sundown."

I watched as the Dovos started to gather blown down trees and drag them toward the camp. "I think they're worried about someone or something coming at us during the night and want a little more time to prepare." I spat into the snow. "Think maybe they know something we don't?"

I was being sarcastic, but Bailey couldn't help himself.

"They know a ton we don't." The glare he shot toward the captain, who was still right at Dragon Mask's side, talking quietly with him while surveying the Dovos' defensive preparations, was downright venomous. "I'm going to rip it out of that son of a bitch soon."

I glanced at my friend and brother from another mother. We were all sporting more than a little stubble by then, and Bailey had gotten as gaunt as the rest of us. The all-wild-game diet had a few things to recommend it, but we were still on restricted calories, given the weight we were carrying and the terrain and the cold. But that wasn't what caught my attention.

No, the burning, primal fury in his eyes was what I really noticed. And it worried me a little.

I knew what I was capable of. It was why I'd striven for a long time to keep my own anger in check. That also meant that I knew Bailey well enough to know full well what *he* was capable of. We really were like brothers. We'd known each other since the Basic Reconnaissance Course, almost eight years before. This was only our second platoon together, but we'd never lost touch even over multiple deployments in different platoons and even different companies.

So, I knew Sean Bailey. I knew him well. And that was why I was worried.

"Easy, brother man." Gunny had uncanny hearing. He joined us, waving Zimmerman and Gurke over as the rest of the platoon set in a tight perimeter, the Marines holding security until we worked up a plan. "Dial it down a bit."

Bailey visibly bit back his hatred. Zimmerman gave him a contemptuous sideways glance as he joined us, and Bailey caught it. I shook my head, even as Bailey snapped, "What the hell are you looking at?"

Gunny's voice was low enough that it wouldn't travel far, but the steel in it was unmistakable. Not that any of us would have crossed Gunny Taylor, even though Zimmerman had bitched about him more than once. "Sean, one more word and you and I are going out in the trees where the boys can't see, and you're going to do eight-counts until you melt the fucking snow, team leader or no team leader, you understand me?"

Bailey took a deep breath. "Roger that, Gunny."

Gunny looked over his shoulder at the Dovos' activity, though not without shooting a warning glare at Zimmerman. He'd seen the look, and he did not approve. "Well, we might not trust these bastards very far, but I think we can trust their own sense of self-preservation, at least at the moment. If they're expecting to get hit, we should expect to get hit." He looked around. "Let's find some brush and build at least some obstacles. Fifty percent security until I say otherwise. Gonna be a rough night, but…"

Gurke groaned a little, prompting another superior look from Zimmerman. I just turned back toward my team. If we were going to cut ourselves a barrier plan before it was fully dark, we were going to have to get to work.

* * *

Getting our defenses set up, unfortunately tied in with the Dovos's, thanks to Captain Sorenson's insistence, at least kept us warm as the sun went down and a deep cold settled under the trees. I was glad that we'd gotten some Arctic warfare training during the workup before we'd gone to sea. The temptation, especially under threat, is to work hard and fast. We'd all done it when building hides after especially long, rough movements, trying to get set in and camouflaged before the Big Orange Ball came up and revealed us. But doing that makes you sweat, and sweating in these conditions could be fatal. Once you stop moving and your core temperature drops, the sweat can freeze to your skin, and then you start the death spiral of hypothermia.

So, setting the barriers of dead trees and branches went more slowly than anyone might have liked. But it kept us from overheating and potentially losing a man to the conditions. The Dovos knew what they were doing, halting early. Unfortunately, even with the head-start, it also meant it was well past dark by the time we finished.

And we already knew we weren't alone.

We'd been making too much noise to hear the footsteps at first. But first Synar, and then Baldinus had spotted movement out in the trees. It had vanished almost as soon as they'd called it out, but a moment later, as I scanned the forest under my NVGs, I could have sworn I'd seen eyes watching us, a brief glint of two lamp-like orbs reflecting the faint ambient light from above before flitting behind a tree.

They'd been awfully high up. I hoped it was just an owl.

It wasn't.

An owl doesn't make slow, crunching footsteps as it circles the camp. And you don't see a wall of white passing behind trees when an owl is passing by. This thing wasn't flying at all. It was walking.

I'd only gotten a glimpse. But from the sound out there, and the little I did see, whatever was out there was *big*.

Then it all went silent, except for the low, whispered incantations coming from the Dovos side of the camp. I'd noticed that unlike before, they'd all camped together instead of flanking us. I doubted it was because of a renewed sense of respect.

I scanned the trees carefully, my rifle already in my shoulder. We hadn't even had time to go down to fifty percent security—every other man up on watch—before this thing had started its approach.

Then a part of the Dovos's branch and tree barrier was suddenly ripped away, and one of their warriors was dragged into the dark with a bloodcurdling scream that was abruptly cut off with a sickening *crunch.*

Every eye and muzzle swiveled toward the noise. That had been halfway around the perimeter from where the footsteps had stopped.

With a sudden sinking feeling in my gut, I realized what had happened. This thing had *deliberately* made noise, then cat-footed it over to where it had hit the camp.

It wasn't finished with the Dovo it had grabbed. The wet *crunch*ing sounds continued for a couple of minutes before everything went quiet again.

Then the Dovo's severed head sailed over the wrecked barrier to land with a *plop* in the snow, smeared with blood, his eyes vacant and staring, his mouth locked open in a gruesome, silent scream.

The Dovos weren't the kinds to wait quietly when attacked. A great roar went up, not unlike the screams and bellows before they'd charged us at the tor. Weapons were clashed against shields or other weapons.

But the thing wasn't there anymore.

This time it came after us.

The Dovos didn't have night vision. We did. So, when I heard a faint rustle at the barrier and pivoted toward it, I got a good look at the massive humanoid figure, covered in white fur, with a pair of curling ram's horns above its glowing, baleful eyes and massive tusks jutting from its gaping lower jaw, as it ripped the felled sapling that we'd wedged between the trees away like it was a patch of weeds.

It had to be twelve feet tall, its arms hanging nearly to its knees. Those long arms darted for Owens, fast as a striking snake.

At least ten of us were already up on sights. Half a dozen IR lasers stabbed out at the monster, though I was one of those who found my RMR red dot with my NVGs. I didn't know how far into what spectrum that thing could see, so I was going to make the first visual indicator of my presence the faint flash from the muzzle of my suppressor, not a glowing white line pointing right back at me.

Twenty rounds tore into the monster's upper chest, throat, and head. It staggered, roaring in pain.

But it didn't go down.

It retreated, then spun around and sprang away into the dark so fast that for a moment, it almost seemed as if it had never been there.

"What the *fuck*..." I couldn't tell who'd whispered it. But I understood the sentiment. Not only was that thing capable of diverting our attention by deliberately stomping through the snow, then moving absolutely soundlessly halfway around the perimeter, but it *should* have been stone dead right there. Sure, 5.56 isn't the greatest killer, but I didn't think even a buffalo could have taken *twenty rounds* and kept moving. Certainly not that fast.

I really wished we had some flares right then. I'd realize later, after the adrenaline had worn off a little, that we could have tossed torches out in the snow, but we hadn't thought of it and hadn't prepared any. And as Recon Marines, we preferred to hide in the dark, anyway.

That might not be the advantage in this world that it had been against jihadis and Russians.

The thing had disappeared into the trees. I scanned our surroundings carefully, straining my ears for any sound that might give it away. Nothing. It was as silent in its suffering as it had been on the hunt.

That was presuming that it was suffering. I wasn't sure about anything that could take that kind of punishment standing up.

The silence dragged on. The Dovos had stoked their fires, and the flickering light still didn't reveal the monster but only intensified the glare off the snow in our NVGs.

"Maybe we scared it off." Applegate had whispered the hopeful statement, but it was quiet enough that his words carried. Even the chanting, murmuring Dovos had gone silent.

Nobody answered. The tension was palpable. I think we were all hoping that Applegate was right, but nobody dared let their guard down.

After a few more minutes, everyone had started to relax, just a little. The first two attacks had come with such rapidity that it didn't seem plausible that the thing would wait this long to hit us again. After all, it had been shot something like twenty times. Maybe it was like a bear, where half the battle is convincing the critter that it's already dead.

I started to hope. I should have known better after almost a week in this place.

It came silently out of the dark on the opposite side of the camp from where it had first hit the Dovos. It dropped out of the trees with a cascade of snow, landed on another of the Dovos, a hulking brute with a heavy brush-cutter of a machete that he used as a sword, ripped the arm holding the blade off by main force, and then, while he screamed, opened its fanged and tusked jaws, before closing them over the top of his skull with a *crunch*.

Then it vaulted over the barrier and disappeared into the dark again, even as half a dozen throwing axes and several gunshots followed it.

The Dovos were muttering, but I had to at least hand it to them. They didn't just collapse into screaming heaps, facing something like that. Even as outclassed as they were—as we all were—they kept fighting. I might not trust them, I might be ready to kill all of them at the drop of a hat, but I could recognize that fighting spirit when I saw it.

"That thing didn't even slow down." Several glares were directed at Captain Sorenson as he said that. We were all scared, but for somebody who was stressing building rapport with our bloodthirsty "allies," he was embarrassing us.

But before anyone could upbraid him for opening his mouth, it was back.

It came right through the gap it had torn in the barrier before. I don't know if it was just pissed, had made a mistake, or figured that since it had attacked from different directions three times now, we wouldn't expect it to come at us from a spot it had already hit. Either way, it was suddenly inside the wire, as it were, a fast-moving mountain of muscle, fur, teeth, and claws.

A half-dozen more rounds slammed into it, apparently without effect. Then Bailey roared his defiance and charged it.

It turned on him in an eyeblink, one paw the size of a dinner plate blurring toward his head. But Bailey had a plan, despite his rage.

He'd seen the blow coming and just barely ducked under it as he jammed his suppressor up under the creature's jaw and fired. The shock snapped the thing's head back, but it just snarled as it staggered for a second, reset itself, and swung for him again.

Bailey couldn't dodge fast enough that time. It grabbed him by the throat and lifted his feet off the ground, snarling as it brought him up toward its slavering, bloodstained jaws.

I was trying to get a shot, knowing it was probably too late, sure that it was about to pop Bailey's head like a grape. But he was in the way, and I couldn't circle around fast enough, even if my bullets would have had any effect.

Then, even as Bailey choked in the strangling grip of the monster's claws as they drew blood from his neck, he jammed his rifle into its eye and pulled the trigger five times as fast as he could.

Blood fountained from the ruined eye socket, spattering the weapon and hissing against the hot suppressor. The thing shuddered, its jaw went slack, and it let go of Bailey, who collapsed into the snow, choking and gasping, as the monster's knees collapsed under it and it crashed to the ground beside him.

The camp had gone silent in the aftermath, every eye momentarily fixed on the monster's corpse. I hurried over to Bailey. "Doc! Get over here!" Those puncture wounds on the sides of his neck were going to need some treatment, and fast.

Bailey looked up at the monster's body. His voice was a harsh, bruised croak. "That's right, punk." He spat blood on the snow, then collapsed.

CHAPTER 18

I hadn't expected the corpse to start to smell so quickly. I'd thought it was too cold. But a stench like a dead coyote began to spread through the campsite after about half an hour, even as we put the barrier plan back in place. Gurke and Gonsalves had hauled the dead monster outside the perimeter, but the stink lingered.

They got some dirty looks from the Dovos while they dragged the ogre, or troll, or abominable snowman, or whatever the hell it was clear. I guessed they wanted to eat it or something. We were probably offending their cultural sensibilities by not devouring its heart. Not that I cared.

The captain did, though. He came over and muttered to Gunny about how the Dovos would have eaten the thing's heart to take its strength, and that we were losing face in their eyes because we didn't. Gunny's blank, pitiless stare actually made the captain blink, and he just kind of slunk away. Apparently, he didn't want to push things, not after that.

The prognosis on Bailey was that he would be all right, provided the monster's claws hadn't been poisoned, which we weren't ruling out. Doc Hartsock had cleaned the wounds as best he could, fully treated them with antiseptic, and bandaged them. The cold made the adhesive on his medical tape a little iffy, but Bailey had wrapped his neck in his shemagh, which he'd been toting around since our first deployment. It was getting threadbare, but it was still a good piece of gear. It had become a tacticool cliché over the years, but it still did a good job of keeping you warm in the cold and cool in the heat. And now it was keeping the bandages in place on Bailey's neck.

We didn't sleep much the rest of the night.

* * *

We were up and moving at daybreak. While daylight movement might have gone against the grain a little, we were getting used to the different rules here. The monsters owned the night more than they owned the day. The savages, who could give these creatures a run for their money in the "evil" department, hunkered down at sunset for a reason.

We kept trudging uphill, tired, gritty eyes turned outboard, weapons ready. There was no respite here. Even with the sun up and the darkest things retreated to their holes (hopefully), death waited in the cold stillness beneath the trees. We were all convinced of that by then.

The terrain only got rougher. The slopes got steeper, and we ran across more and more rocks and sheer drop offs and cliffs. The hillside was more often split by deep draws, and it got rough enough that it took most of that day to cover maybe a couple of miles.

We camped under a towering cliff that made me nervous just looking at it. If the abominable snowman from the night before had wanted to hit us, it would just have to roll a couple of boulders off the top of the cliff.

I pointed to it. "I'm taking my team up there. I don't like leaving that high ground unguarded."

Gunny looked at me and then squinted up at the promontory in the dying light. "I don't like the idea of you boys being that far away from the rest of the platoon."

"We were split up a lot more at the tor."

He snorted. "That was a fortified position, and we owned all of it. This ain't the same thing. What are you going to do if you get cut off?" He wasn't just asking hypotheticals. He was asking for my contingency plan.

I studied the hillside. It looked like there was a way up off to the left. "We won't be directly up on top. We'll set up on the left, where we can keep the way open to that easier slope right there." I pointed where I meant. "I just want to make sure we don't get surprised by someone or something coming up on top of that cliff."

Gunny glanced around. He had to be tired. I'd never seen him hesitate before. "I'm almost as worried about having fewer shooters down here with the Dovos as I am about putting you and your team out in the cold like that."

So, that was it. I looked toward the Dovos' fires, right up against the rock face, and saw a few of them watching us with ever-unfriendly eyes. I could understand. After all, I'd been there when one of them had probed us a couple of nights before.

I studied Gunny with narrowed eyes. I had no idea how much he'd slept—or even eaten—during the trek so far. I was sure that he'd kept one eye open most of the time and had probably witnessed that Dovo trying to sneak up on us, as well as Santos's confrontation. His face was drawn, his usually gaunt cheeks more hollow than usual.

"How long are we going to play this game, Gunny?" I dropped my voice to a whisper. The rest of the platoon didn't need to hear this conversation, not yet. "Just because Dragon Mask's hypnotized the captain, or whatever he's done, doesn't mean the rest of us have to go marching along to hell with him. You said it yourself. Leadership ain't a suicide pact. Why the hell are we still helping these savages? This isn't Syria or Afghanistan. There's no Big Marine Corps here. If he wants to go traipsing on his way to damnation, let him, but I don't want any part of these people anymore."

"Why?" Gunny's voice was low but hard. "Because I've got a responsibility to him as much as I do to you, and in many ways it's the *same* responsibility. Stanley, God rest his soul, was *your* leadership challenge. How many hours did we talk about that?"

I winced a little. I had talked to Gunny Taylor a lot, trying to figure out how to get through to Stanley. The ND on the range that had gotten me in trouble with Captain Sorenson hadn't been his only deficiency. Now he was probably settled, headless, on the bottom of the sea. Unless the sea trolls had eaten him.

"Well, I had twenty-eight leadership challenges. Now I've got twenty-five. And he's one of them. He's been doing this for half as long as I have, and that means I've got a responsibility not to give up on him until I've got no other choice. You don't know him as well as I do, either. He thinks he's doing what's got to be done so that we can survive. He may be wrong. In fact, I'm pretty sure he is. And I don't like how much time he's been spending with Dragon Mask, either." I noticed that Gunny had adopted my nickname for the Dovos's leader instead of using the name he'd given us. "But we haven't reached the point of no return yet. And as long as we haven't crossed that moral event horizon, and there's hope that he might come around, I've got to keep working with him. And so do you."

I bit back an angry rejoinder. I knew how far that would fly. "So, where's the line? How far do we go before we say, 'Enough?'"

"We'll know it when we see it." He gripped my shoulder, hard. "You've trusted me this far, Conor. Trust me now."

I had to nod. I did trust Gunny Taylor. He'd kept the platoon on the level during the rockiest parts of the work-up and then the float to follow. He'd smoothed the waters when the captain and the team leaders had been at each other's throats. He'd put his foot down a few times when we all needed to take a step back. He was the platoon's rock. Without him, we would have been adrift and tearing each other's guts out.

I had to trust Gunny. Despair was the only alternative, and that would get us all dead.

"Fine." I might have sounded angrier and more bitter than I should have. "Permission to take my team up to an overwatch position?"

He might have been a little disappointed in my response, but he nodded. "Make sure you guys get some shelter up there." He glanced up at the clifftop, where a thin veil of snow was whipped off the edge by the wind. "That windchill is going to get bad."

"I'm on it, Gunny." I turned to where Rodeffer, Santos, Farrar, and Smith were gathered in a small perimeter of our own off to one flank. I tapped Rodeffer on the shoulder.

"Let's go. Up that side of the cliff. We're taking overwatch so nothing rolls a boulder on top of the platoon."

None of the team said a word, though I was pretty sure that Farrar, at least, had heard or suspected some of my conversation with Gunny Taylor. He'd been watching. But he kept his mouth shut.

Not that there was much to say. I'd heard Farrar complain bitterly about the captain's arbitrary orders before. There was no love lost there. And he wasn't averting his eyes like he might if he wasn't comfortable with my stance on the mission. There was an understanding in the team.

I worried, as we started to trudge our way up the slope, crawling on our hands and knees in some places, pulling ourselves up by rocks and saplings clinging to the snow-covered hillside, that my own anger and cynicism was wearing off on my teammates. I wasn't worried about Santos—he had a worse attitude than I did. Hell, I'd had to tell him to dial it back more than once. But the others, the younger guys—even though everyone had had at least one deployment already with Recon, except for the late Stanley—they might be picking up on some things that they shouldn't.

Yet, as we reached the stand of trees clinging to the shelf that gave us a good view of the open ground just before the cliff, I wondered again at what I really should be worried about.

Gunny was right. In a way. We had no one to rely on but each other, despite the captain's desperate attempt to ingratiate himself with the locals. So, on that note, to willingly break up the platoon and go our own way was borderline suicide.

But I was right in a way, too. There was no Big Marine Corps here. There was no higher headquarters dictating what we should and should not do from an air-conditioned TOC miles away. The captain didn't have a career to worry about anymore, though he probably hadn't figured that out yet.

That made finding our guidelines a little more complicated.

And I also wondered about that "moral event horizon" Gunny had mentioned. Where was it really? I remembered all too vividly the blood on Captain Sorenson's hands when he'd come out of the temple with Dragon Mask before we left, that almost feverish look in his eyes. I'd told myself that it was probably animal blood. But how could I be sure? And what *was* the cost of dabbling in the Dovos's sorcery?

Had the captain already left that moral event horizon behind? And what did that mean for the rest of us if we kept following him?

I didn't have answers. But I was sure I'd lose sleep looking for them.

We set in under a spreading pseudo-spruce, digging down into the snow under the heavy limbs, keeping close together for ease of concealment as well as warmth. The wind was whipping across the mountainside up there, and while we had some shelter, the icy fingers of the wind still got through some of the limbs. We didn't dare light a fire. That was perhaps a bad decision in that place where the darkness was not our friend, but as they say, you don't rise to the occasion so much as you revert to your highest level of training. And we had trained to lurk in the darkness, camouflaged and concealed.

It was a long, cold, restless night.

CHAPTER 19

WE were half-frozen and sleep-deprived when the Dovos moved past us in the early morning, and the rest of the platoon came up to join us. No monsters had come at us during the night, though I'd seen what had looked very much like an oversized, humpbacked wolf step out of the trees sometime after midnight and stand at the edge of the cliff for a moment before disappearing. I'd had my sights on it, though I was so cold by that point that my red dot was shaking from its shoulder to its tail. It had vanished before I could even take the weapon off safe, so quickly that I started to doubt whether I'd really seen it or not.

Rodeffer had been up at that time, too, and he hadn't said anything. Which only strengthened my doubts.

It was hard to say what was real and what wasn't in those mountains. So many of the vague shadows and flickers of movement that you saw out of the corner of your eye vanished as soon as you turned toward them and left you wondering if you'd caught a glimpse of another monster or were just exhausted, cold, hungry… and starting to hallucinate.

Maybe it was both. I had no way to know.

We kept climbing the mountain.

The trees got shorter, the wind got harsher, and the rocks got sharper and steeper. The snow got deeper, and more and more it overlaid deep, packed ice. On one of the increasingly frequent and necessary halts, I looked over my shoulder and saw the river valley spread out beneath us over the treetops, shrouded in blowing snow and scudding low clouds. A new overcast had moved in, though it was still thin. Despite the dimmed light of the sun, I still had to squint against the harsh, nearly unremitting white of the snow-shrouded landscape.

As my eyes turned north, I saw what looked like a blue-white line along the horizon, far off in the distance, above even the northern peaks. I squinted as I took it in. Unless I missed my guess—and that was possible, given how little sleep I'd gotten since we'd arrived—that was the biggest glacier I'd ever seen.

Looking up, I saw what appeared to be a slot in the mountain ridge above us. And the longer I looked, even as I leaned on my knees, my rifle dangling from its sling, the more I was sure that was where we were going. There didn't appear to be any other viable pathways through that wall of rock and ice rising in sheer, jagged peaks above us.

Our progress got slower still as we fought the terrain, the wind, and the snow and ice. It became harder and harder to maintain security, not only because we were getting strung out into a single file as we worked our way up the mountainside, but also simply because the difficulty of the terrain and the cold was making us start to turn in on ourselves, just putting our heads down and putting one foot—or gloved hand—in front of the other.

The danger became that much more obvious as a rock came sailing down the slope, bouncing off boulders and smashing through a twisted, wind-stunted sapling clinging stubbornly to a crack in the mountain. The booms of its impacts echoed down the mountain, to be quickly snatched away by the howling wind. It bounced off a stony ridge not a yard from my head and sailed out into space, before continuing on down toward the treeline below.

I looked up with a scowl. That rock had been the size of my head. I didn't think that had been an accident.

And from the sound of Dragon Mask's voice, raised and strident despite the fact that I couldn't make out the words over the shrieking of the wind, I was right—it hadn't been an accident. Dragon Mask was pissed that one of his tribesmen had indulged his bloodthirst and put his plan at risk.

His plan was at more risk than I thought he realized.

"Heads on a swivel." My voice was hoarser than I'd expected, but the cold was sucking every bit of moisture out of my body faster than I could drink water. Water, at least, hadn't been nearly the problem food was—we could just melt snow. But my quads burned with every step, my ruck straps were digging into my shoulders, and despite my own shemagh, I could barely feel my ears and nose. My eyes ached from the glare and the cold. "Keep your eyes up and be ready to kill every one of these bastards." At that point, after nearly getting my head taken off by a flying rock, I didn't really care if the captain heard me or not.

Unfortunately, I was so tired, and cold, and focused on the immediate enemy of the Dovos that I almost missed the greater threat.

I didn't realize what I was looking at, at first. It just looked like a rock at first glance. I only saw differently when I noticed the eyes. They were black as chips of obsidian, and if they hadn't moved, I might not have spotted them. It took a second to make out the face, peering over the top of a snow-covered boulder. Its skin was pebbly and pale—it looked almost like frost on stone. A prominent nose jutted over a heavy underbite that exposed teeth like jutting stone arrowheads. Ears like crude stone bowls stuck out from the sides of its head, and a thick layer of frost might have been its hair.

And those black eyes positively burned with hate.

It saw that I'd noticed it, and it let up a grating, ululating cry that echoed across the mountainside as it jumped up on top of the boulder. That was when I saw that it wasn't very big. It might have stood three feet tall, though its arms hung clear to the ground. Its legs were short and bowed, and its sunken chest looked encased in stony scales. Or maybe that was its hide.

It lifted a stone-tipped spear and chucked it at me with terrific force. I ducked, or at least I tried to. My boot slipped out from under me on the snow, and I went flat on my face on the trail. The spear shattered against the boulder immediately over my head.

That was when I realized that I hadn't heard the echoes of the creature's war cry—I'd heard its fellows.

A rain of spears fell on us from either side. I saw Ridenour take one through the throat. He collapsed where he stood, one hand to his neck, blood pouring from beneath his fingers and staining the snow red beneath him. He spasmed for a moment, gasping for air as his throat and lungs filled up with blood. Crimson spouted from his mouth, and then he lost his grip and slid downhill. Only the fact that he fetched up against a cleft in the rocks kept him from wiping out the two teams behind him.

I rolled to my side, my ruck keeping me from going all the way over, and shot at the creature that had thrown its spear at me. The little creature flipped off the rock as I fired, but it wasn't *quite* fast enough. My bullet clipped its ear, and it screamed, a sound like metal being scraped against rocks. To my surprise, it bled, blue-black fluid spraying from the damaged ear.

I hit my ruckstraps' quick releases. It was time to fight, and fighting on *good* terrain with a ruck on is a significant handicap, never mind on that snowy, rocky slope. This wasn't a time to try to break contact, either. The only option we had was the old tried and true counter-ambush.

We didn't have the element of surprise, but we could make up for it with speed and violence of action.

Rolling up to a knee, my boot braced against a rock, I searched for it, but it had ducked out of sight. Another one, alike enough that it could have been the first one's brother, was up on top of a boulder just uphill and to my right, so I shifted my aim and put a bullet through that gaping, snaggletoothed maw. Dark fluids splashed the snow behind it, and it swayed for a second before crashing onto its face and tumbling down the mountainside.

It collided with the first as it went, and the two of them plummeted off the side of a short cliff and out into space, the live one still screeching its hate as it went.

Suppressed gunfire *crack*ed up and down the line. There was no roar as mags got dumped—we'd all come to grips with the need to make every shot count. Fire superiority won't count for much if you run out of ammo before the fight's over, and we had to consider every hour—every minute—in this place as a fight. We only shot when we had targets.

The Dovos were roaring their bloodlust. When I spared a moment to glance up the trail, I could see that a couple of them were down, but most were rushing the little goblins, or whatever they were, with axe and sword. I saw one take a swing, miss, and get another stone-tipped spear thrust under his chin, so hard that the tip punched through the top of his skull.

Those little things were *strong*.

I heard the scrape behind me and pivoted, just as another one seemingly popped up out of the snow on the right side of the trail, its stone throwing axe already cocked and sweeping forward. I shot it center mass from about two yards away, watching the stony scales crack around the bullet hole and more bluish black ichor spatter on the ice and rocks. It tumbled backward, its axe falling from nerveless fingers, its jagged mouth still agape.

Then I was moving up, leaving my ruck behind for the moment. It was a risk, but if we didn't win this fight, the ruck and the gear in it were going to be small comfort. These things weren't likely to give quarter. And they seemed utterly unfazed by the thunder of our weapons.

It was tough going—the slope was steep and most of the snow was already packed down by the Dovos' footprints. I had to find rocks and cracks to brace my boots in. It slowed me down and took the momentum out of my intended charge, but I was still moving, and I still had a weapon that could reach out and touch someone.

I shot another one in the face from about ten feet. Their skulls must have been made of something harder and more brittle than bone because the bullet's impact cracked it open, spilling more dark slime out of the fissure as it collapsed face first into the snow.

I found myself side by side with Nagano, the two of us driving upward, pushing through the ambush. The cold and fatigue were both forgotten in the adrenaline rush of the fight. These things might have caught us by surprise, but we'd trained to react quickly and counterattack ferociously when the situation called for it.

And this situation called for it. High in the mountains, down to the increasingly narrow slot that led up to an even narrower natural pass, we had nowhere to go but through the ambush. And so we were going to kill our way through until they were all dead or we were.

The things refused to get rattled. Another rain of spears came down, though with less effect as more of us had taken cover after the first volley. Several more of the Dovos went down, though. As small as those things were, they were incredibly strong, and they threw those spears *hard.*

Nagano and I ducked behind another rock as more spears shattered against the stones. One embedded itself in a low, scrubby tree, not far from where I'd first seen one of them, the one that had been launched out into the air by the falling body of its kinsman. It stood in the trunk, quivering.

I popped up over the rock, looking for targets, but one of the goblins had closed in and dropped over the top of it, swinging a stone axe as it came.

Nagano knocked the axe aside with his rifle barrel. The axe head left a bright scar in the anodizing. The thing snarled and swung toward him, then leapt on top of him before he could bring his rifle to bear and try to drive the edge of the axe into his throat.

I couldn't shoot it without shooting Nagano. So, I drew my Bowie, slung my rifle around on my back, and waded in.

It had no hair to grab, so I wrapped my arm around its wiry neck and started stabbing it in the side. Its hide was tough, but the darkened blade was good steel, and the point was as bitter as a needle. The hellish little creature felt the prick of the blade starting to go in and tried to twist around, but Nagano had grabbed hold of its axe with both hands, pinning the creature's own hands to the weapon in the process. I'd grappled with Nagano back during the workup. The dude was skinny as a rail but deceptively strong, and if he got his hands on you and decided not to let go, you were in for one hell of a fight. I'd always have to start throwing elbows and knees to get him off.

I shifted my own weight, bearing down and bracing my boot to help push the blade home. The goblin's struggles got more and more desperate as I slid the steel into its chest, struggling to maintain my grip on its neck, hoping that it had a heart I could pierce. It squirmed and squirted black blood all over my hand, rasping and keening in agony as I slowly, inexorably stabbed it to death.

My blade pierced whatever it used for a heart and it stiffened, then went limp. I pried it off Nagano and threw it down the slope. Or, rather, I tried to throw it. Its body was surprisingly heavy for how small it was. It fell short and slid down the mountainside in the snow.

Then I hauled Nagano to his feet, and we resumed our push. By that time, Bailey, Santos, Rodeffer, Synar, and Gunny had joined us.

The Dovos were holding the line up ahead, right where the trail entered the slot that formed the entrance to the pass. They were getting hammered, though. The goblins were pouring down on them from three sides, pelting them with spears, axes, and simple thrown rocks. Despite their own howling and attempts to take the fight to their enemy, the Dovos kept getting beaten back.

For a moment, I was half inclined to let the two forces tear each other to pieces. But the captain was up there, dumping rounds into the goblins when he could, and Gunny wasn't going to leave a Marine in the middle of that.

Gunny was already moving with a purpose, clambering up on the nearest boulder to cover as we scrambled around it. "Up to the left." He gasped the direction in the cold, thin air and then dropped two goblins with two shots. The range wasn't very long, so headshots weren't that hard, which was a good thing given our limited supply of ammo. It took a split second longer to line the target up, but we were dropping these things fast as a result, and while we had to be closer than we might like, the more of them we could kill with fewer rounds, the better.

I struggled up to the next outcrop, shot a goblin through the throat, and held security while Nagano and Synar clambered past me.

Fire and movement usually involves short rushes from cover to cover, while those between rushes suppress the enemy with a high volume of fire. We didn't need the covering fire, not really. The enemy's only ranged weapons were spears, and they'd stopped throwing those. We were still shooting them as targets presented themselves, but the steady roar of gunfire we'd trained for wasn't there.

Half a dozen more goblins tumbled to the snow, bleeding black and blue from shattered skulls and punctured torsos. I still didn't see a single sign of fear or trepidation in any of them. Only stark, inhuman hatred. We were going to have to kill all of them.

Synar, Bailey, and Nagano were set in and dropping goblins like it was a shooting gallery, and Gunny, Rodeffer, and I got up and started moving.

Then a new sound echoed out from the pass.

It was a voice. It was hard to tell at first—it was so deep that it sounded like a volcano or an ice floe breaking off. But like the shout from the face on the cliff, there were words in that rumble of sound, ancient, awful words. Words of command that brooked no disobedience.

The goblins suddenly broke off their attack and scuttled out of sight among the rocks and the ice.

"That doesn't sound good," I mumbled to myself as I kept moving to the next bit of cover, watching the entrance to the pass over my rifle.

For a moment, as the Dovos regrouped, a few shouting their hatred and defiance at the retreated goblins, everything else around us was still as death. The Dovos had taken some losses, evident by the crimson trail leaking down the mountainside in a slow river of bloodstained snow. Bad as that looked, they'd given even better than they'd gotten. Hacked and dismembered goblins littered the rocks around them as they reformed, packed together shoulder to shoulder, hunched behind their shields and weapons as they watched the rocks, waiting for the next blow to fall.

Then the pass wasn't empty anymore.

CHAPTER 20

THE thing that heaved itself out of the shadows under the peaks was massive. It was roughly humanoid, with two legs and two arms, but its knees bent the wrong way, and its limbs were too long for the rest of it. At least, it looked that way at first. In reality its hunched torso was easily proportional to the rest of the body, if it hadn't been bent nearly double. There was still an unsettling, almost spider-like impression to its shape and movement.

A frost-encrusted skull the size of a Volkswagen, with jagged icicles in place of teeth and five eye sockets instead of two, looked emptily at us, and then those sockets began to burn with tiny, cold flames lighting within all five.

It lurched and shambled toward us, looming out of the pass as it roared its curses in a language none of us could have understood, and probably would have made our ears bleed if we could. As it was, the sheer volume of that creaking roar was enough to make my head hurt more than the cold and exertion already had.

With a ponderous swing of its massive arm, it smashed a Dovos' skull to a bloody, pulped ruin, sending the body flying to crash against the cliff face with a sickening *crunch.*

None of us needed any prompting. Almost all at once, the entire platoon opened fire. Those who didn't have a shot scrambled to clear their line of fire.

I had been halfway through another rush up the mountainside when the voice sounded. Now I braced myself against a boulder, putting my red dot on the giant's head and letting my breath out before the trigger broke. Snow and ice crystals blasted away from the end of the suppressor as my bullet joined easily a dozen more, smashing into the frost-crusted skull.

I don't think that I honestly expected it to react any more than the hairy abominable snowman that had attacked our camp a few nights before. And it didn't.

That thing took a hail of bullets to the face, the frost getting blasted away by the impacts, but it showed about as much reaction as a steel target on the range. We were definitely hitting it, but it was completely unfazed. Those same rounds that had cracked goblin skulls in half were barely chipping that thing's head.

For just a moment, I heartily wished that we'd brought explosives, grenades, AT-4s, *something*. Anything heavier than 5.56 carbines and automatic rifles. I had no idea whether they'd be effective against something so obviously preternatural as the hulking monstrosity that crushed another Dovo's chest under a single hand with an impact that shook the ground. Blood sprayed crimson from the dying man's mouth as his ribs were smashed into his heart and lungs.

Recon Marines are used to working with less. Sure, we get more resources than the grunts did. That was why we were better marksmen—Recon got a *much* larger ammo allotment per year than the bigger grunt units. But while we got more and better gear than the regular grunts compared to, say, the Rangers, we got ten-year-old leftovers. Most of us had a lot of our own gear, paid for with our own money, because it was the closest we could get to the top-of-the-line stuff.

Point is, there's a reason why "adapt, improvise, and do whatever it takes to complete the mission" is part of the Recon Creed. The Marine Corps has a long tradition of getting the dregs and making the mission happen, anyway. Those boys on Guadalcanal had been starving, their fatigues rotting off their bodies, and they'd still kept fighting. The Chosin Few had been outnumbered, outgunned, surrounded, and freezing to death, and still killed so many Chinese that they stopped the offensive cold.

We had no explosives or rocket launchers. Our 5.56 wasn't scratching that thing. So, we'd have to improvise.

What did warfighters use before they had explosive shells?

They used big-ass rocks.

I hustled up a few more steps and grabbed Gunny where he was braced in a crack in the mountain. The giant still loomed at the entrance to the pass and didn't seem that inclined to chase after us as long as we kept shooting it in the face. We weren't doing much of any damage, but we were giving it pause. "Try to keep that thing bottled up in the pass. I'm taking Rodeffer up there." I pointed up toward the rocks on the steep slope above the slot in the mountains.

Gunny didn't even look at me. "Make it fast. We're burning through ammo quick." He cranked off another pair of shots at the giant.

There wasn't time for any further words. I slung my rifle around on my back, cinched down the sling, and started up the slope, punching Rodeffer in the shoulder and snarling a quick, "On me," as I went.

If the terrain on the way up to the pass had been rough, we quickly found ourselves on ground that most people would have considered completely impassible. A barren slope of icy, sharp rocks confronted us, in places so steep that it might as well have been a sheer cliff.

In short order, I was on all fours and glad for my gloves, despite how battered they'd gotten over the last week. I had to find handholds and drag myself up by my fingers almost as often as I found footholds. Meanwhile, the fight raged off to my right, the harsh *crack*s of gunshots echoing over the roars of the Dovos and the giant itself. A glance seemed to show the stalemate holding. Our guys were still shooting it in the face whenever it started forward but otherwise—except for the captain—were conserving their ammunition. The Dovos had built a crude, ragged shield wall, with every spear they could bring up pointed up at the giant. But it was only a matter of time before the giant decided that we couldn't hurt it enough to stop it and moved down to stomp us all.

During that split second that my attention had been on the fight at the base of the pass, I put my hand on a rock, only to find that it wasn't the secure handhold I'd thought.

The stone rolled out from under my hand and hit me in the ribs before tumbling down beneath me, narrowly missing Rodeffer's head as he ducked, almost planting his face in the snow to avoid it. For a moment, I was off balance and felt myself start to slip, my right foot starting to give way while most of my weight settled on my left foot and hand. And I was holding onto a narrow shelf of rock with my fingertips with that hand.

For a second, I was sure I was about to go head over heels down the mountainside, and I was probably going to wipe out Rodeffer as I went.

Flinging my hand back toward the ground, I threw myself flat against the mountainside and scrabbled for purchase on the snowy rocks. I felt myself beginning to slide but reached out and grasped another rock with my right hand a moment later, then I dug in and gripped it as hard as my half-frozen fingers could.

I clung there for a second, my heart hammering in my chest. I was secure. I wasn't going to fall any further. Then I lifted my head, looked for the next handhold, and kept going.

Rodeffer had caught up, wisely shifting off to my left to stay out of the way if I grabbed another wrong rock or just slipped. Almost side by side, we dragged ourselves up the slope. I saw another ledge high above, where it appeared that a chunk of the mountainside had broken off sometime in the distant past. It wasn't deep, but it was better than where we were.

All too slowly and painstakingly, we worked our way up toward the ledge. The tide was turning down below, and not for the better. I could hear more than I could see, but the volume of fire had increased, and it wasn't doing much. The giant had advanced out of the pass, and the Dovos and the platoon were both falling back. We were running out of time. And I had no doubt that if the platoon fell back to look for another way around, that giant was going to run us down and crush us all before we got to the tree line.

We reached the shelf, and I pulled myself up first. Looking along it, I thought I saw a route to a precariously perched stand of boulders. At least, I hoped they weren't just part of the mountain, standing above the snow. My plan had been born as soon as I'd laid eyes on that big one. Now to see if it would pay off. I made sure Rodeffer got up beside me, brought my rifle around front, and started to work my way along the shelf, placing each step carefully. There was barely a foot of space in places, and the drop off was sheer once we moved closer to the pass.

But of course, it couldn't be that simple.

I had just moved around a shoulder of stone that jutted out over the shelf when another goblin popped out of nowhere and swung a long stone blade at my knee.

I saw it just in time, and only grabbing the shoulder of rock kept me on my feet as I snatched my leg back. The evasive maneuver put me off balance for a crucial couple of seconds. My rifle was offline, and the goblin had quickly withdrawn the blade and was winding up for another strike.

Still clinging to that little ridge of rock with one hand, I leaned back toward Rodeffer and kicked the goblin off the shelf.

I'd been trying to just knock it back, gain myself some space. I had not expected to send it over the edge given how heavy the little bastards were. But I'd hit it just right so that it went tumbling off the side of the shelf to tumble down the mountain, its scratchy shriek cut off abruptly by a loud *crack* as it hit a rock particularly hard along the way.

After regaining my balance, I swung around the shoulder, only to find myself face to face with another goblin that had popped out of a crack in the mountainside. Fear and shock didn't seem to affect these things at all, so it hadn't really reacted to its fellow getting knocked off the edge and into the abyss. It was already swinging another stone axe, fast as a striking snake.

I was too close to do anything but react. If I'd tried to dodge, I would have been dead. Even if I'd avoided the axe, I would have fetched up against that stone shoulder and gone over the edge. So, with all the speed, surprise, and violence of action I could summon up on that narrow, icy ledge, I attacked.

While I didn't have a bayonet, I still slammed my suppressor into its chest, getting the carbine inside the swing of the axe and striking the goblin *hard*, then parrying the axe before it could bite into my side.

Before I could get the rifle back online to shoot it, the goblin had recovered and swung the axe again, dipping low to try to take my leg off just below the knee. I blocked it again, but this was getting desperate enough that I knew if I didn't end this fast, I was going to get cut. Then it would be the end for me. One slip and this thing would be all over me, chopping me to pieces.

I stepped in again, kneed the goblin in the chin—boy, that hurt—got my off hand wrapped around the carbine's forearm and pried the barrel up under its armpit to rob it of most of its leverage. Then I drew my Bowie.

There was no time or space for finesse. I just brought the blade up and chopped down, splitting the goblin's skull clear between its eyes.

I pried its corpse away from the cliffside and sent it plummeting down the mountainside after the first one.

It took a second to sheathe the Bowie. I didn't have time to worry about wiping the ichor off it. I could do weapons maintenance later—*if* we survived. Getting my carbine back in both hands and ready, I shuffled past the crack in the mountain that the two goblins had appeared from.

There wasn't enough room to cover the dead space as I passed it, but I did the best I could. I really wished I had a grenade, but of course that hadn't been part of the course of fire the captain had laid in for the range in Norway.

That felt like a lifetime ago, when training and courses of fire had been a thing.

I didn't have a grenade, though, and I didn't have space to step back and bring my rifle to bear, so I pulled it back into a retracted position, the buttstock tucked under my elbow, and pointed the suppressor inside as I moved past. Only darkness met my eyes. No movement. It was pitch black a yard inside, and it might have gone back another foot, or it might have gone deep into the heart of the mountain. What mattered, though, was that no more goblins came swarming out of it.

Then I was past the crack and moving along the narrowing path toward the rocks that loomed above the pass. Rodeffer mimicked my own passage, though he wasn't used to the retracted gun—it wasn't something the Marine Corps taught—and hurried to join me.

Things weren't going well below. The giant was shambling out of the pass as the Dovos fell back, sporadic rifle fire no longer holding it at bay. It had crushed at least two more of the Dovos and ripped another in half, blood and offal spraying across the narrow trail leading up toward the pass.

Our Marines were back in the rocks, keeping their distance and still generally out of reach. But that wouldn't last long. Not the way that thing was moving. It was so big that it seemed to be moving in slow motion, but it was covering a lot of ground with each step.

I got to the rocks and paused for a moment, looking for which one might do the most damage—and might be positioned right to drop it on the giant. They were wreathed in snow and ice, and I couldn't tell at first glance if it would even be possible to budge them. They were bigger than I'd thought, too, standing almost as tall as me. And I'm not a small man.

I put my back to the rock, though I wasn't entirely sure of the geometries, either. Dropping a rock on a giant a couple dozen yards below was a bit like long range shooting, but with most of the math being unknown. It was entirely possible that we'd miss entirely, especially as that thing continued down the slope and out of the pass. But the slope below *should* send it careening right into that thing's side, provided we got it moving and timed it right.

Rodeffer joined me, his rifle still in his hands, just in case, and we started to shove.

It didn't budge at first. I dug in with my heels and pushed harder. It might have rocked a little. This boulder was huge, and it was *not* in a particularly precarious position.

"Once more." I grunted the call out through gritted teeth, already mid-shove with a boot braced against one of the other boulders, the other planted on the ground, buried to mid-calf in snow.

The giant lumbered on beneath us—our window was closing.

We pushed, straining against the rock, hoping and praying that this worked. I could hear roaring, crashing, and screaming down below in the pass, but all I could see was the peak above us, the snow glaring white even under the high overcast.

Then the boulder shifted. We both almost fell. My left foot slipped in the snow, and the stone scraped my back as I slid down the rock. Rodeffer kept his feet but shifted his position with a grunt, giving me a chance to reset myself before we both heaved again.

That did it. With a grinding *crunch*, the boulder rocked out of the depression in the mountainside where it had rested for years, if not centuries, and tipped toward the pass below.

It fell in slow motion at first, or it seemed that way. I'd caught myself just before it fell away, grabbing Rodeffer by the arm just to make sure he didn't follow the rock. He was on his feet already, though, pivoting to watch the rock go down, his M4 pointed down toward the giant.

The boulder hit once, the impact shaking the entire mountain. Snow, ice, and fragments of rock sprayed into the air, and the gigantic stone actually *bounced*, then sailed into the air and dropped toward the giant.

It turned and looked up at the impact, a dead, broken Dovo dangling from one clawlike fist. Its five eyes first lit on the boulder, then, even though those eyes were nothing but points of sorcerous flame, I could swear it turned its glare up on us, promising death and worse than death, just before it darted toward the pass.

For a moment, I thought that we'd failed. That thing was suddenly too fast. Not only was it going to dodge the rock, but the boulder was going to crush more of the Dovos, and—much more importantly to my mind—probably a few of our platoon.

The giant wasn't quite quick enough, though. That rock was moving a lot faster than it looked.

The giant had descended too far down from the pass. The boulder hit just above it, bounced even higher, and slammed right into the behemoth's skull.

The thing was smashed against the mountainside like a ragdoll, suddenly swept off its feet by the inexorable force of the hurtling boulder. It absorbed enough of the impact that the rock didn't keep going on to threaten the Dovos or Marines but fetched up against the finger coming down from the pass with a rolling *boom* to pin the dead giant against one side of the pass. It was over.

Then the monster stirred.

It was pinned, but it hadn't been killed. I could almost see the hellish blue glow of its eyes leaking out from under the boulder. One hand was scratching at the rock and snow, twisting around to start to push at the boulder.

We hadn't killed it. Maybe it wasn't truly alive, so we couldn't really *kill* it. For anything to have taken that hit and still be moving…

I was about to sled down the mountain on the seat of my pants to do *something*, anything, when Gunny pushed up through the scattered, confused Dovos, his captured axe in his hand.

He got to the groping arm and went to work. In a few strokes, he'd hewed about halfway through the arm. I could hear the giant's curses, muted by the rock but every bit as poisonous, as he hacked at it. Soon the rest of the platoon was there, adding their own weapons to the cause of hacking this mammoth thing apart like some twisted version of Gulliver's Travels where the little people are savage killers.

It took longer for my team and I to get down to the base of the pass than I'd expected. We had to fight to maintain control, or we were going to go careening down uncontrollably toward the trees and the rocks below, like the goblins I'd knocked off the shelf. But Gunny was still hacking at the monster, accompanied by Bailey, Santos, and a few others. I rushed for my ruck to retrieve my sword.

There was something about the weight of it in my hand that spoke to me. I can't describe it. At the time, I never would have characterized it as *mystical.* There was something to it beyond its balance and the clear quality of its metal, though. Somehow, I knew that it was going to be more effective against that thing than any of the Dovos' weapons. Or even any of the finer blades the others had picked up.

Marines were still hammering away at it by the time I arrived, joined by several of the Dovos. The giant's arm was a grisly mess but still functional. It hadn't shed an ounce of blood, but its groans of pain and furious rages shook the mountain beneath my feet. I moved up beside Gunny. "Step aside."

The first stroke of my blade sheared straight through the iron-hard flesh and bone, severing the grasping hand and eliciting an even louder roar from beneath the boulder. The sword had just gone through a wrist the diameter of a tree trunk with one slice—as though it were nothing.

Gunny's eyebrows climbed toward his hairline. With a sweep of his hand, he stepped aside for me.

I went to work.

CHAPTER 21

WHEN the ACE reports were over, we'd only lost Ridenour. Herrera, Williams, and Owen had taken wounds, Williams a serious puncture to the guts. Doc Hartsock was working on him while Fortuna stood guard, mostly to keep the Dovos back. Many of them were eyeing the wounded man with hands on their weapons.

They'd already slit the throats of their own wounded.

The giant was still roaring and cursing, its voice muffled by the rock that pinned it, forcing it deep into the dirt and snow. I'd hacked off all its limbs, though, so it couldn't get leverage to pry itself loose. The damned thing didn't bleed a drop—it had been like cutting up a tree.

Only easier. I looked down at the sword, with its strangely wrapped hilts. That blade had sheared through the giant's unnatural limbs as easily as a machete going through grass. And without a scratch to the blade itself. Its edge was every bit as keen as it had been before I'd picked it up.

I needed to learn more about that sword. But the middle of the pass in the immediate aftermath of a ferocious fight was not the time nor the place. I sheathed it again, shoving the scabbard back where it would be out of the way.

Each Marine was down to an average of about seven mags per man. We were running through our ammunition awfully fast. Divvying up Ridenour's mags only went so far.

"What are we gonna do with Paul's body?" Franks was crouched next to his assistant radio operator, looking down at the pale, purplish, rapidly freezing meat that had once been his friend. He'd gotten Ridenour's eyes closed. The ragged gash in his neck where the goblin spear had gone in remained open. "Ground's too frozen to bury him, even if it wasn't all rock."

Gunny looked down at the dead Marine. Captain Sorenson was up by the crest of the pass with Dragon Mask, leaving the logistics—and casualty care—to the rest of us. I wasn't the only one who noticed, either.

I could see the conflict written across Gunny Taylor's face. On the one hand, we were deep in hostile territory, with less than friendly allies. We had little time. Building a high enough cairn to protect Ridenour's remains would take too long and put us in the pass at nightfall. I was sure that Gunny was thinking the same thing I was—we might have disabled the giant and put the fear into the goblins, but they'd probably be back as soon as the sun went down.

On the other hand, though, there were principles at stake.

Ridenour was dead. It would ultimately be no never-mind to him what happened to his mortal shell now that he was gone. That said, *I* would sure be bothered by the thought of the goblins desecrating his corpse after we left it there under the pitiless sky, miles from anywhere, in the snow and ice and barren rocks.

Gunny scowled as he cast his eyes around us. "Screw it. It's not like they don't already know we're here." He pointed downhill. "Somebody go back down and chop down a couple of those smaller trees down there." He squinted at the sky. "Probably better make it several. We can't bury him, so we'll have to make him one hell of pyre."

Three of the Marines with tomahawks headed down the slope while the rest of us held security.

Captain Sorenson appeared at the top of the pass, looking down at our position with his hands on his hips. He clearly wasn't happy about the delay, but when he saw that the Dovos were also setting up to burn their dead, he couldn't exactly complain. Hauling the bodies over the pass wasn't an option. It would tie too many hands up when we were probably going to have to fight again at any moment.

The cold was really starting to bite now that the fight was over, even with our furs. We were probably going to have to light a fire even before the pyre got started. Not that any of us were eager to warm ourselves by a brother's funeral pyre, but sometimes necessity is the mother of some pretty gruesome stuff.

Gunny knelt next to me. "That's an impressive weapon." He nodded toward the sword thrust through my rigger's belt. "Mind if I take a look at it?"

For a brief moment, I hesitated. Not because I actually begrudged handing the sword over to him, but I think that I was *expecting* to. There was something strange about that blade, something about the way it just felt *right* in my hand, not to mention the way it had sliced cleanly through the weird, eldritch giant's unnatural bones without a nick or a notch in it.

Something about this place was really getting to me. I can't remember using words like "eldritch" before we sailed through that fog bank.

But that obsessive grasp on the sword that I'd more than half expected didn't materialize. Perhaps I'd watched one too many fantasy movies. I slid it out of its sheath and offered it to him, hilt first.

Gunny took the weapon with what I can only describe as *reverence*. Something about it spoke to him, too. He frowned as he studied the blade, the metal a smoky gray that barely revealed the swirling patterns in its depths. His eyes traveled down to the hilts. "Why is it wrapped up like that? Doesn't look like it was made that way."

I shrugged. "No idea. It was like that when I took it off one of those berserkers in the gatehouse back at the castle."

"Mind if I take it off?"

Again, I shrugged. "May as well. I've got gloves, so if the metal freezing to a hand was the worry, I'm not concerned about it."

After pulling out his folder, he snapped it open and started to carefully cut the rawhide thongs that held the leather against the hilts. Oil, grime, and time had stiffened the crudely tanned hide, so it still took some doing to peel it away from the hilt and pommel.

Santos let out a low whistle. I raised my eyebrows.

The hilts were of the same smoky metal as the blade and inlaid with what looked like gold. The quillons curved gently toward the blade itself, roaring lions, highlighted in gold, facing outward from the core. The grip was wrapped in black leather. The wheel pommel was also inlaid in gold, with a pair of runes that looked curiously like a Greek Chi-Rho, though subtly different.

Gunny's eyes narrowed as he studied the sword, then turned his gaze up toward the Dovos at the top of the pass. There was still a decided distance between us and them.

"Somehow, I don't think that freezing to the grip was the issue."

He didn't say anything more as he handed the sword back. He didn't need to. We were all getting the same feeling about this place and about our "allies."

There's a certain degree to which you have to rely on instinct in a combat zone. Things get weird when danger is everywhere. Unpredictable. Gunny and I had both seen some strange stuff even back in the "real world." I'd known a man in Syria who'd been convinced that he was going to die on the next patrol. He took a bullet through the eye three hours later, when we were ambushed outside Dyarbikar.

Something about this place seemed to enhance that sixth sense. At least, it seemed to be doing that for me. I thought it was doing the same thing for Gunny and Bailey, too. Probably a few more of us, as well. But not everyone had commented on it. We were still in the mindset we'd carried over from The World. We weren't ready to consider such things openly yet.

As more time passed and we continued to move far away from the chain of command we were used to, the question was... where would this sixth sense lead us?

Gurke, Franks, and Chambers were struggling back up the beaten, slick path to the pass, dragging two crooked, scraggly pines. Chambers pulled security while the others dragged the trees. He watched the Dovos just below and behind them more than he was the surroundings. It was clear that he saw them as the biggest threat to our well-being.

I couldn't really say I thought he was wrong.

We stacked the felled trees over Ridenour's body. He'd been stripped of all his serialized gear and as much of anything else as we could use. His sweat-and-blood-soaked cammies had already frozen, and frost had formed on his bloodless, bluish skin.

I could see Franks choking back his grief as he laid the branches over his friend's corpse. Gurke's face was impassive, but his eyes were red and he was blinking a little more rapidly than usual.

We'd lost five brothers in the last week, men we'd trained and lived beside for over a year before we'd ever gone to sea. Only that hard-wired Recon stoicism and the awareness of just how far into hostile territory we were had us keeping it together. We'd all had some practice—some more than others—at tamping the feelings down, compartmentalizing everything until we could safely let it out. All of that practice came to the fore now.

Several of the Dovos were clustering uncomfortably close to where Doc was working on trying to save Williams's life. Williams was in a bad way. He was shaking as the cold set in, and Doc had to keep smacking his hands away from the wound. Awful noises were clawing their way out of his throat, as hard as he was trying to stay quiet.

Gunny moved away from my team and hiked up to join Doc as Gurke, Franks, and Chambers consulted over whether or not they had enough wood to effectively cremate Ridenour, or just cook him. They started back down for more as Gunny reached Doc.

I glanced up in time to see Doc look up at him with something close to panic in his eyes. He turned back to the dressing he was trying to wrap around Williams's torso.

I saw in that split second that Williams was dying, and there wasn't a thing that Doc could do about it.

He didn't dare say it. Probably for a few reasons. For one, it was drummed into everyone in Tactical Combat Casualty Care/Combat Lifesaver that you always encourage the wounded man because you want him to rally—to hold onto that will to live. Nobody talks about what to do when you *know* that no matter how much you work, or how much you encourage the man, he's going to die anyway.

The other thing was not to let the Dovos know. They were already eyeing the wounded man with what I could only describe as "malicious intent."

Gunny rubbed the iron-gray stubble along his jaw. There was nothing he could say, nothing he could do. But he wouldn't tell Doc to stop trying. Even though we might need the medical supplies later on. Some things are more important. Some things might be the wrong choice from a practical standpoint, but the alternative "right" choice will break a man and a unit.

Doc kept trying, tying off the dressing and struggling to warm up an IV bag, right up until the point that Williams shuddered one last time, then went still.

Doc Hartsock was still trying to get the needle prepped, though his hands were shaking more and more violently. Not just because of the cold, either, though that was a factor. He knew what had just happened. He just couldn't admit it. Not yet.

Gunny gently gripped his shoulder. "Doc. He's gone."

Hartsock started to slump. I could see the crash coming. So could Gunny. "Come on. Help me move him over to Ridenour." He had to keep Doc moving, doing something. We couldn't afford to let any man lose it, not there and not then. Least of all our Corpsman.

They lifted Williams's body and carried it with a lot of care over to the pile of branches over Ridenour. Gunny had them lower him before pushing him under the bluish evergreen boughs to strip his ammo and equipment.

Sentiment didn't enter into it. We needed the gear, and we needed the ammo.

Captain Sorenson finally decided to come down and join the rest of the platoon. "We need to get moving, Gunny."

"Once this is done, sir." Gunny's voice brooked no argument, and for once, the captain didn't decide to push the matter.

Gurke and the others came back up, puffing and pouring steam in the cold, thin air. Two more full trees were laid over Ridenour and Williams, and then Gunny went to work with his fire starter.

We all carried them—a ferrous rod on top of a magnesium block—it was part of the on-body survival kit that Gunny had mandated for the whole platoon. He shaved a bit of magnesium into a branch with his knife, then flipped the blade over and raked the spine across the ferrous rod, throwing a fountain of sparks onto the magnesium and the pitch-laden needles and branches.

In moments, the fire was crackling through the boughs, and we finally stepped off.

The top of the pass was only a few dozen yards ahead. On the other side, the path—such as it was—turned sharply to the north, where the mountainside fell away steeply right after the crest.

A high, narrow valley stretched out below, widening as it sloped down toward the south. The tree line was closer to the crest on this side than it had been behind us, the slopes blanketed with dark pines, their boughs laden with snow.

What really caught my eye, glinting in the golden light of the sun as it peered through a tear in the clouds behind us, already much too close to the peaks to the west, was the city.

At least, it had been a city, once upon a time. When I looked at it through my ACOG, I could see that the walls were crumbling, one of the towers completely collapsed, and many of the roofs that were visible inside the walls were falling in. Not only that, but it appeared that at least half of the city had already been consumed by the glacier creeping down from the mountain peaks above. The keep at the center was half-encased in ice.

"Is that where we're going?" Rodeffer had stopped just ahead of me and was looking at the city through his own ACOG.

"Presumably." I glowered toward the front of the column, already a few hundred yards ahead further down the slope, nearly to the tree line. "Captain hasn't seen fit to tell us yet."

"Or else he doesn't know." Rodeffer started moving again, closing in on the Dovos and the captain. We didn't want to let him out of our sight, no matter how much we disliked him. As Gunny had said, he was still one of ours.

I had realized a while back that I didn't want to leave even my worst enemy to the Dovos. Not after some of the things I'd seen.

Behind us, smoke rose against the setting sun, rising above the jagged, icy peaks. Lit from behind and above, there was no disguising our passage through the notch in the mountains.

And if there was some artifact in that city that Dragon Mask wanted, somehow I doubted that it was going to be unguarded.

We descended into the forest as the sun set, lowering our NVGs and hoping that the batteries lasted the night. Because none of us thought we were going to get through it unscathed.

We had no reason to.

CHAPTER 22

THE Dovos at least knew something about warfare and defensive positions. They found a shoulder of the mountain that was mostly level and stood above most of the trees to make camp. They didn't try to set in the brush barricades this time but just set a guard and wrapped themselves in as many furs as they could. They lit no fires. Apparently, the locals on this side of the mountain were dangerous enough that they were willing to risk the dark.

We set in a bit above them in a stand of trees. We had some more standoff—especially if one of them decided to try to take a Marine scalp in the night—but that also put us closer to the goblins. I doubted I was the only Marine who half expected them to come out of the rocks above us that night.

There's no such thing as a free lunch in a combat zone, and this place was far more dangerous than Syria had ever been. We had to accept some tradeoffs.

"Conor, your team's up for first OP." Gunny looked exhausted, his ordinarily gaunt face drawn and dark circles under his eyes. A glance around confirmed that we were all in about the same shape. Grizzled, harried, and just about ready to drop from sheer fatigue, but we'd keep going.

Recon Marines don't quit. It ain't the guy who's naturally the fastest, the strongest, or the smartest who gets through BRC. It's the guy who won't give up, even when his feet are bleeding, he's hallucinating, and every bit of his body aches. He just keeps going, keeps putting one foot in front of the other, until the mission's accomplished.

We weren't all that excited about *this* mission. But survival was a mission all its own, and that was the one we were going to stick with.

"Where do you want us?" I had my eye on a spot, an outcropping about a hundred yards above with good fields of fire and some cover, but Gunny was in charge, and I was tired enough that I was entirely open to the possibility that he'd seen a better position that I'd missed.

He pointed to exactly that outcropping. "Right there. And Conor? I know everybody's tired, but only go down to fifty percent. I have a feeling we're going to get hit tonight, maybe from more than one direction." He glanced back toward the pass, invisible now behind the trees and the curve of the mountains. I took his meaning.

"Don't worry, Gunny. I'm on it." I caught Rodeffer's eye and pointed up toward the outcrop. He couldn't quite suppress the pained look of disgust but put his head down and started trudging back up the mountainside anyway. I fell in behind him, deciding not to call him on the demeanor hit. We were all dead on our feet, and if I started disciplining Marines for a little bitching, it could have the same effect as declaring Williams dead before he'd taken his last breath.

It took a bit too long to get up and into the outcropping. There was a hollow among the rocks, and we set in, putting our rucks in the middle and facing outboard. For a few minutes, we just stayed in place, up on a knee—it was far too dangerous to sit at that point. Someone might fall asleep. We all just watched and listened.

Finally, I was confident enough no monsters or other enemies were coming at us right away. "Okay, I'll take first watch with Rodeffer and Farrar. Smitty, Santos, we'll wake you up in two hours. No fires tonight, so pile on the snivel gear." At that point, we were all too tired and crusty with our own sweat to worry much about the fact that our snivel gear consisted mostly of bad-smelling, poorly tanned skins. It was too cold to smell much, anyway.

Scanning the rocks and the trees through my NVGs, I set in to wait out my watch.

* * *

The night was strangely quiet. The glow of the pyres faded slowly, visible in our NVGs as a faint nimbus behind the peak to our south. The Dovos and the rest of the platoon settled in on the shoulder below us, and soon the only sound was the whisper of the wind through the treetops and the rocks.

It was cold, but I'd worked up enough body heat on the move and gotten into my skins soon enough that I was relatively warm. That worked against me a little, because once I wasn't moving anymore, the fatigue that had been stacking up for the last week really started to set in.

Granted, it set in quick whenever we stopped by that point. I'd done eight-day patrols before. Hell, we'd spent a month in the field in Syria. But that had been different. We'd spent days in one place, taking patrol bases in the countryside, getting resupply by air. We had no resupply, no air, and we'd been on the move or in combat for over a week straight. It was going to get to us eventually.

But once again, survival trumps fatigue. So I pinched myself, rubbed snow on my face, even took off my skins for a few minutes when I found myself getting too warm and comfortable. And I kept scanning the rocks as the stars peeked out through rents in the clouds overhead.

I hadn't seen the moon yet, in part because of the cloud cover. As a pale light started to build in the east over the mountains, I watched it curiously. I wondered if I'd see the familiar moon we were used to, or if I'd see something totally different. It might offer some clues as to where we'd ended up. Were we on Earth still? Just sometime in the distant past or distant future? Or had we somehow been transported to an entirely different planet?

It took some effort to make sure I was still watching my sector as the moon slowly rose. I scanned for movement and strained my ears for the sound of footsteps or other sounds that were out of place.

I thought I'd seen eyes gleaming in the woods below us for a moment, but as I stared at the area and listened carefully, I couldn't see them anymore. Maybe they'd been there. Maybe I'd imagined them. I wasn't sure enough to call it in.

But did I dare ignore it? This entire world was trying to kill us. If there *was* something there, it might kill a lot of us before we could stand to, if I didn't sound the alert.

At the same time, that fatigue had to be kept in mind. I might not have seen anything, and if I got us all stirred up without knowing that I *had*, it would just wear us all down that much more, potentially putting us at even more of a disadvantage.

So, I kept watching the woods, looking for any sign that I hadn't imagined it. The eyes never reappeared.

Just before I had to reach over and wake Santos up, I saw the moon come out through a gap in the clouds. I studied it for a moment. It was just a glaring white crescent in my NVGs, but when I looked at it with my naked eyes, I still couldn't see enough detail to say for sure. The fact that it was still a crescent meant I couldn't see enough of the surface features to tell if it was our moon or not.

Of course, if we were in another time, the moon might not look the same, anyway.

It was weird, thinking about time travel and everything, but there had to be *some* explanation for what had already happened to us, and conventional, non-nerdy ways of thinking obviously weren't adequate for our situation.

I reached over and shook Santos, who started a little and reached for his rifle before he realized where we were and what was going on. I whispered my turnover, he sat up, got himself awake and his weapon ready, and finally nodded. "I got you."

I leaned back against my ruck and was asleep in seconds.

* * *

I sat straight up, panic clawing at my chest. I'd fallen asleep. I reached for my weapon, wondering why I didn't have my NVGs on, looking for the goblins I was sure were about to cut us all to pieces.

The night was silent and still. Santos was a dark silhouette right next to me, watching the darkness through his NVGs, his M4 across his lap. He turned toward me. "Dude, what the hell? You just scared the hell out of me."

I let out a shuddering sigh, trying to will my pounding heart to slow down. "Fuck. Sorry, dude. Thought I'd fallen asleep on security."

"You've got another hour and a half. Go back to sleep. Don't worry. I'll give you a good whack if things get weird."

Suppressing the shakes, I leaned back against my ruck and tried to go back to sleep. It took a surprisingly short time, given how amped up I'd just been.

CHAPTER 23

WE heard the movement before we ever saw anything. Whoever or whatever was out there, they weren't trying to stay quiet.

Branches snapped, snow crunched, and tools or weapons clattered against trees and each other. We might have been able to hear voices, too, though what we could hear sounded more like grunts and hoots than words.

Dragon Mask called a halt about an hour after sunrise. Naturally, he didn't talk to the rest of us but drew Captain Sorenson aside and spoke to him in hushed tones at the edge of the Dovos' formation. We had to hold security and listen to the noises in the forest while he spoke to the captain. The Dovos watched us as much as they watched the woods around us.

We returned the favor.

To my great irritation—but complete lack of surprise—we moved out again without the captain passing along any information he might have gotten from Dragon Mask.

The platoon wasn't following the Dovos anymore, not the way we had before. The terrain had leveled out, though we were still moving downhill through the forest toward the rushing river at the bottom of the valley. Instead, we'd moved up and onto their left flank. It was better for our own security and made it less likely that they'd lead us into an ambush.

That also meant we didn't need to wait for the captain to explain the situation.

With the platoon set in a modified wedge, my team was out front, on point, with Gurke's team on the left, and Zimmerman's team on the right, closest to the Dovos and the captain. Bailey and his team were taking up the rear, with Gunny in the middle with Doc.

Fortuna was with the captain, next to Dragon Mask, in the middle of the Dovos.

The woods had looked thick from up on the mountainside, but now that we were among the trees, there was plenty of space between the trunks, which rose straight from the forest floor for almost fifty feet before they started to sprout branches. If there was any undergrowth, it had been crushed flat by the deep blanket of snow, crisscrossed with strange tracks.

Movement caught my eye at the same time as Rodeffer snapped his M4 up, only to lower it as another red deer came bounding out of the trees, halted as it saw us, and then turned and sprang away, before vanishing into the woods, heading up the valley toward the mountain.

The whole team had frozen at that, and we looked and listened for whatever had spooked the deer. But as its footsteps faded into the distance and the other sounds didn't seem to be getting any closer, we started moving again. After all, the Dovos hadn't stopped. As little as we trusted them, it wouldn't be good to let them out of our sight in the middle of hostile territory.

We continued to thread our way through the woods, scanning the shadows under the trees. It was hard to tell just how far we could see as the pattern of overlapping tree trunks seemed to blend together over time.

That meant we were far too close for comfort when the first of the locals stepped out of the trees.

At first glance, I could have taken him for one of the Dovos. The young man was unshaven, unkempt, and dressed in poorly tanned skins. He had a javelin in his hand and another couple thrust through the crude sash that held his equally crude hide tunic to his chest.

That was where the resemblance ended, though. He wore no armor, carried no other weapons. And when he looked up and saw us, his eyes got wide, he froze for a second, then he let out an almost animalistic yelp and turned and dashed into the woods, yelling at the top of his lungs.

Rodeffer had him dead to rights, but hadn't been expecting that reaction. The man was gone, vanished into the forest, before he could pull the trigger.

I wasn't sure how bad that really was. On the one hand, the alert had just been raised that we were in the vicinity. That was never good. Recon Marines don't like the locals to know they're there. It's called "compromise," and it's usually our cue to pop smoke and head for extract.

Except there was no extract here. We had nowhere to run to. Which only made the compromise worse. If Rodeffer had been faster, he might have shot the man before he could yell.

But that wasn't really an option, either. While there might not be any established rules of engagement for whatever far distant place in time or space or both where we'd ended up, only a few of us would really be comfortable with shooting a man who was running away without having attacked us first, and those were generally restrained by the threatened wrath of Gunny Taylor.

Yes, Gunny's wrath, not the captain's. Gunny was the heart and soul of that platoon. Always had been. And to some extent, that made him our conscience, too. The same way that a good father is his sons' moral guide.

Besides, a gunshot—suppressed or not—would have been every bit the compromise that the fleeing man's yells were.

Gunny moved up to join us as we moved to cover behind nearby tree trunks. The Dovos had also stopped, their own weapons held ready, watching the woods around us as more voices took up the cry. A moment later, a horn sounded in the distance, and the hooting cries of alarm faded away. Almost as if they had been answered, and no longer needed to call out.

That was ominous. And something about that horn didn't sound right, either.

Captain Sorenson came hustling over from the Dovos' position. "What the hell did you do?"

Gunny turned his glare on the captain before I could answer, which was probably a good thing because my hackles were already up, and that question was calculated to make me see red. Who did this punk of a college-educated *boot* think he was? How was it that he trusted his savage new friends more than his own Marines?

It was a mindset I *had* seen before, in Syria. Never understood it there, either.

"They didn't do a damned thing. Nothing but pure, dumb luck that one of the locals' scouts stumbled on us instead of them." Gunny's voice was a growl, and the absence of the word "sir" was deafening in its silence. "I think it's time we got the intel dump your buddy gave you, that you didn't bother to pass along."

Sorenson blinked, shocked for a second. But, predictably, that shifted to affronted anger a moment later. "That was need-to-know information…"

Gunny cut him off with a vicious stab of a knife hand to his sternum. "If you think for a second that *any* information about this place is too 'need-to-know' for the rest of the platoon to hear, I will fucking *end you.*" That last was delivered in a low, deadly whisper that I probably wasn't supposed to hear. "We are so far out in the wind that if you're not going to be an asset to this platoon, you are officially a liability, and I will *not* put these men's lives at risk for the sake of your pride. Do you hear me clearly, Sorenson?"

I was watching the two of them closely, letting the rest of my team watch our exterior security while I kept an eye on the more immediate threat—the captain and the Dovos. I saw the captain blink as he suddenly realized that he wasn't really in charge of Gunny Taylor.

Gunny wasn't threatening him. He was warning him of what was inevitably going to happen if he stepped too far over the line. Gunny had been in Iraq and Afghanistan. He'd killed more people than cancer. He'd totally cut the captain's throat in a heartbeat if he thought he had to.

Captain Sorenson looked around at the rest of us. I wasn't the only one watching him. I could see the realization dawn in his eyes that he really was alone. Zimmerman was the only team leader who wasn't glaring daggers at him, and he was studiously attending to his team's dispositions rather than looking at the captain or anyone else.

For a brief moment, rage flared in Sorenson's eyes. The fact that "his" Marines weren't following him unquestioningly infuriated him, and even as he tamped down his anger and clenched his jaw, I saw the promise in his eyes. A promise that he might be forced to do the right thing now, but eventually we'd all bend to his will. Whether it was at the hands of Big Marine Corps when we got back to the world or through whatever sorcery he was learning from Dragon Mask.

Cold day in hell, bud. I'd seen scarier dudes in Syria. We'd *killed* scarier dudes in Syria.

For that matter, I was pretty sure we'd killed some scarier dudes back at the tor when we'd been killing the Dovos, before he decided to fall for their "truce."

Finally, he took a deep, angry breath. "Ekersakar says that this side of the river is ruled by a Younger God named Taramas. And that she has a thing for control. She tends to dominate her subjects' minds. He warned me that most of them will be somewhat animalistic. They have their tasks, and they are not encouraged to think beyond that. In fact, from what he told me, most of them can't." He folded his arms over his chest rig. "So, the best way to get close would have been to stay quiet and maintain a small footprint, because most of her subjects wouldn't be looking for us. But since some of you decided to be on your own program instead of following the Dovos like we originally planned, now we're compromised." That horn sounded again in the distance, answered by yet another. "And now it sounds like they're coming, which means our chance to sneak in and take the athame is probably blown."

"What athame?" The captain's face went completely still as Gunny asked the question.

"That's the artifact that we've come to help the Dovos retrieve." He looked around as the horn sounded again. "We couldn't go into detail before because we were still in Uergal's territory, and Ekersakar was concerned that he had spies within their camp." Somehow, I got the impression that he wasn't going into all of Dragon Mask's concerns, but the captain had been dismissive of the sorcerous element of this strange world since we'd arrived, despite his own dabbling, which was becoming ever more obvious. It was as if he thought we couldn't see. I suspected that Dragon Mask had been worried about things like that bat-winged creature that had carried word of our presence at the tor to his masters. "Uergal knows the significance of the athame and that Ekersakar can use it to..." He stammered, just for a moment. "To claim a greater authority."

"So, now that we're right in the enemy's backyard, *now* is the time to brief this?" Gunny was at the end of his patience.

"If we hadn't gotten compromised, then the briefing would have been given in the last covered and concealed position, Gunny!" The captain started to stab a finger in Gunny's face, but then he thought better of it. "There was a plan in place!"

"That plan was about as useful as tits on a boar hog as long as it was only in your head and not disseminated to the rest of the platoon." I half expected Gunny to out-and-out snap, but he kept his words short and his voice low. "Now there's nothing to do about it but adapt to the situation and fight through until we can get somewhere secure." He stabbed a knife hand at the captain's sternum again. "This is on *you*." He turned to me. "Conor, take your team, move up, and see if you can get eyes on. See what we're up against and where they're coming from." He pointed to each team leader in turn. "The rest of you, shift right and get low. I don't want anyone left in this position when the bad guys show up."

I didn't wait around to see how he was going to coordinate that with the Dovos. I was, frankly, glad that we'd gotten tapped as the scout team. I'd rather be on the hunt.

We stepped off, keeping our rucks on, just in case. They would make maneuvering difficult, but I didn't want our supplies far out of our reach if things went pear-shaped and we had to escape and evade, or E&E. When we had no rear area, no safe haven to run to, the contents of those rucks could mean the difference between life and death.

I got Rodeffer moving off to the northeast, angling slightly up the valley and getting off our original line of march, much like the rest of the platoon was doing as they repositioned behind us. He was moving even more slowly than before, but he was being careful, slipping from tree to tree and doing his best to make as little noise as possible.

We would need to pause and make snowshoes at some point, I realized. We were leaving a lot of signature as we struggled through knee-deep snow.

We still reached the bottom of the valley in a fairly short time. A narrow creek ran down through the broken ground, with the trees growing right up to the banks. Several had been dropped across the creek, and from the looks of the scraps of snow and ice clinging to the sides and the snapped-off branches, they were being used as footbridges, probably by the skin-clad locals.

I thought about it for a second. Using the local footbridge went against every instinct I'd formed as a Recon Marine. In BRC Land Nav, if you got caught using the roads, you got thrashed, then you still had to find all your points by drop-dead-time. And in some parts of Syria, using the roads was a good way to get blown up. Here, using the locals' passage across the creek put us in a high-traffic choke point and made detection by the enemy that much more likely.

On the other hand, wading across that fast, rocky stream didn't seem like a good idea, either, especially not in the depths of winter.

In the end, though, since we could still hear plenty of movement out in the woods around us, security and caution won out. We moved upstream, getting into thicker woods and looking for a better crossing point.

We found it about a hundred yards up where the trees had gotten close enough together that the shadows beneath were like an early twilight. Trees bent over the creek, their gnarled roots curling around and over the boulders that lined the creek bed, forming an arched ceiling of intertwined boughs over the rushing water.

There were enough rocks above the surface that we could get across without wading, provided we moved carefully and didn't slip.

Rodeffer ventured out first, finding that he could grab hold of low-hanging branches all the way out into the middle of the stream to keep his balance. His boot slipped on the icy rocks once, but he caught himself and was across in seconds, then he took a knee and scanned the trees around him with his M4 up as I followed.

One by one, we got across the stream as the horns got closer.

* * *

The diversion to get across the creek had slowed us down, so we stepped it out as soon as the rest of the team was across. I wanted to get eyes on the enemy as quickly as possible. I'd have preferred to be in position to see them coming out of the city, but we were already too late for that, judging by the nearness of the horn calls we heard.

They were moving fast. We hadn't gotten more than five hundred yards from the stream when we saw their vanguard.

We'd come to the edge of a clearing uphill from the stream, masked from the rest of the platoon by thick woods. Rodeffer froze and slowly sank to a knee behind a tree as the lead elements came out of the trees and into the open, just over fifty yards away.

It was a strange group that came out of the trees, driven forward by horns and drums and the will of the dark horsemen in their midst. A mob of men dressed much like the scout we'd spooked half-walked, half-jogged through the snow, armed with javelins, spears, and crude axes.

There was something odd about the way they moved, and it took me a moment to realize what it was. The mob ebbed and flowed like nervous animals. They were afraid of what was ahead of them, under the shadows of the trees, but even more afraid of the figures who rode in the center of each milling cluster.

The armored figures riding on the same thickset, mutant horse-creatures that the Dovos' leaders had ridden back at the tor were massive. I wouldn't call them giants, but each one was probably close to six-foot-six. None were of the same build, nor did any of them wear exactly the same armor. One wore blackened mail, another darkened lamellar of overlapping plates, another a coat of scales the color of old blood. Their helms were similarly different, ranging from a tall, peaked helmet with a black cloth covering the face beneath the nasal to a full-face helm with a T-shaped slit, the metal painted black, to another full helm sculpted to look like a fanged skull.

Only one wore no helmet. His neck seemed slightly too long, his pale, bald skull creased by scars, a thick, black mustache and chops framing a slavering mouth full of pointed teeth that were too long for him to close his lips over. His deep-set eyes actually glowed red.

All of the armored, manlike monsters carried much more finely crafted weapons than the mobs that swirled around them. Axes, lances, and long swords all gleamed dully in the hard winter sunlight. Axeheads and shields were carved with strangely shaped glyphs that made my eyes hurt if I looked at them too long.

There were at least a dozen of the armored commanders, or warlords, or knights, or whatever they were. Each one led what I estimated to be at least a hundred of their foot soldiers. While those wild-eyed, shaggy, flighty spear-wielders probably didn't make the most competent fighters, there were a *lot* of them.

I was watching them through my ACOG when one of the mounted warriors, his head encased in a blackened iron helm with an equally dark mail veil covering his face, turned toward me. I saw glimmers of lambent fire behind the eyeholes in the masked nasal as he looked straight at me.

I felt my guts go cold. I believe that is what we call a "hard compromise."

And there's only one way to react. Especially when you've got only five dudes.

To this day, I'm still amazed that I made that shot. Granted, it was only a hundred yards, and I had a 4x scope on my rifle, but putting a bullet right through an eyehole at a hundred yards is still quite a feat, and I can't pretend otherwise.

At the time, I would have put it down to luck. After some of what I've seen here… I'm not so sure anymore.

The bullet tore through that sullen, glowing red eye and pulped the brains behind it. At that range, the green tip penetrator should have retained enough energy to punch out the back of the helmet, but as the massive warrior's head snapped back and he slowly slid off his horse's back and into the snow, his head turned and I saw that it hadn't exited after all.

The corpse hit the snow with a crash. The sound echoed through the clearing, and the horns and drums stumbled for a moment.

We were already moving. I hadn't had to say a word. The team knew exactly what that first shot meant. And they'd all seen what I had. None of us wanted to stay put when that many enemy fighters were about to descend on us.

A deep, inhuman howl went up behind us. We were already thrashing through the snow, plowing our way back toward the stream. I knew there was no way we were going to outrun those horses, but giving up wasn't in any of our natures.

I caught up with Rodeffer and pointed him toward the thicker trees higher upstream. "Get us in the thickest woods you can find!" I let him push on, turned, dropped to a knee, and looked for a target.

Plenty of them were coming through the trees, dozens of hooting, grunting men on foot with spears and javelins. One of the horsemen was behind them, driving them on.

Ammo was precious, but I still remembered the plaque in the Battalion area, somewhere far, far away. *Lord, if it be my time to die, let me die with my barrel hot, my mags empty, lying in a pile of empty brass.*

I turned, leveled my M4, and went to work.

CHAPTER 24

MY first shots slammed into the leader, a big bruiser with his eyes open so wide I could see the whites all the way around his irises. He was wrapped in furs that were cinched around his chest, waist, arms, and legs with leather thongs, and he held a spear over his head, ready to throw it or thrust it at me.

Two shots took him in the chest, ripping straight through as green tip is generally wont to do. He staggered but didn't stop. I wasn't surprised. I'd seen a lot more rounds to the chest than that fail to stop ISIS fighters when they were all hopped up on adrenaline and whatever other substances they took before combat.

And this guy was no different. He kept coming, thrashing through the snow, still too far away to hope to hit me with that spear.

I shot him three more times before I hit something vital enough that he sagged, coughing blood, then crashed onto his face in the snow.

The rest of the mob behind him hesitated at that. For a handful of seconds, their charge faltered, and I turned and ran. The rest of the team had gotten another twenty yards toward the stream, Santos and Smith had stopped and taken a knee, and I surged past them, fighting the snow with every step.

Rounds *snap*ped past me, thudding into flesh and bone behind me. Those spear throwers didn't have a hope in hell of hitting us unless they pulled out bows, and I hadn't seen any so far. But we had to keep them at a distance or we'd be overwhelmed. Shooting them dead was a good way to do that.

I got halfway to the stream, found a tree growing at a weird curve around the boulder at its base, and dropped to a knee. Steam billowed from my mouth and nose as I leveled my rifle and braced it against the tree trunk to keep it steady despite my heart pounding and my lungs heaving.

Several more of the mob had dropped, and the rest were clearly hesitant to continue to advance. They seemed like spooked animals more than men. But then the armored rider, the bald one without a helmet, spoke in words harsh, inhuman, and unintelligible. Considering those fangs, it was a wonder he could speak at all.

Whatever he said, it got the mob moving again. They were scared of our rifles but even more scared of him.

So, I shot him.

My shooting wasn't nearly as good as the last time. The first shot broke on his breastplate, and to my surprise, it didn't penetrate. It was like shooting a steel gong target. The bullet disintegrated in a puff and spray of spall, licking blood from the monstrosity's neck and face. He didn't even seem to notice.

So I did what I'd trained to do against body armor. None of the Syrian jihadis I'd shot had been wearing plates, but we'd known that they had them. So, when we couldn't hit their vitals, we went for the stomach/groin area and the head. I couldn't hit his groin without shooting through that horse-thing's big, bony head, so I shifted to his skull.

That's still an awfully small target at a hundred fifty yards. My first shot missed. I cursed under my breath, shifted my aim, let my breath out, and tried to time his movements.

He'd looked up, straight at me, as soon as the bullet had *snap*ped past his head. How he knew exactly where the shot had come from, especially since we were still all running suppressors, I didn't know. But he'd miscalculated and stopped moving, completely still as he stared at me where I crouched behind the tree.

He was doing… *something.* I could feel it. My skin crawled, and a headache that had nothing to do with the cold started to squeeze my temples.

My trigger broke just before it got immeasurably worse. With the M4 braced against the tree and as I was leaning hard into the buttstock, the recoil hardly moved it at all. So, I got to see the impact as my bullet punched into his T-box, just to one side of his nose and below one of those glowing red eyes.

His head snapped back, and for a brief moment, I was afraid that even shooting him in the head hadn't worked. Maybe there was a reason he wasn't wearing a helmet. Maybe the bullet hadn't gone all the way in. Maybe he didn't even keep his brain in his skull.

But he slumped, slowly, in the saddle. He didn't fall off the horse-thing, which still stood there placidly. Every other horse I'd ever seen would have bolted as soon as its rider was shot. The dark armored warrior sagged backward, his head lolling on his too-long neck, until his lifeless eyes were staring at the sky.

The mob stopped dead. Some of them bolted. The rest just sort of hunkered where they were, looking around with wide, frightened eyes. Santos and Farrar smoked a few more of them, anyway. Not because they just wanted to murder them, but because it hadn't registered that they weren't trying to rush us anymore.

There's no magic switch that tells you not to shoot the guy who was just coming for your blood, but suddenly hesitates. Maybe he just tripped. Maybe he saw that not everyone was online with him anymore, and he paused to check. You don't know. And in combat, sometimes things don't register immediately as the adrenaline both focuses your attention and narrows it.

"Turn and go!" We couldn't kill all of them fast enough. We just had to kill enough of them to buy us some time.

Santos and Farrar turned and burned, though right then the depth of the snow and the weight of our rucks made their sprint back toward the stream look like more of a lumbering stumble.

I stayed in position to cover them, which was the only reason I saw what was happening.

The mob *was* hesitating. Without the armored rider driving them forward, they were either too scared of our guns, or they simply couldn't function without direction. Their wide eyes, clearly visible through my ACOG, weren't really all there. For a just a moment, I remembered what Captain Sorenson had said that Dragon Mask had told him, that their supernatural ruler dominated their minds. I was seeing the truth of that right in front of my eyes.

I waited for the other riders to close in, but as I shifted my aim to spot one of them through the trees, I saw that he was just sitting on his horse, watching.

A moment later, as Santos roared, "Turn and go!" a new sound rose over the valley, echoing out from the walls of the city above. It wasn't a horn or a drumbeat, but a high-pitched, keening scream. The sound of it was like having icepicks rammed into my ears, and I stumbled for a moment.

Once again, even through the pain, I could tell that there had been words in that cry, words of hate and fear and anger, but I couldn't understand them. It didn't really occur to me at the time, but the contrast between that and the way we'd mysteriously been able to understand Dragon Mask was pretty telling. Apparently, the strange phenomenon that made him intelligible didn't work with everyone in this place.

I got to a tree right at the bank of the creek, then turned and braced my rifle against the trunk again. The rest of the team had held their fire, even as they kept bounding back to join me. The mob wasn't following. In fact, they were streaming back uphill into the woods, with a few wide-eyed, frightened looks over their shoulders, leaving the corpses to freeze in the snow.

The armored figure I'd shot in the head was still bent backward unnaturally in the saddle, staring at the sky without seeing. The horse had started to wander back toward the city, seemingly ignoring the weight of the corpse on its back.

I didn't know why they'd given up the pursuit. But I'd take it. If I wanted to be especially optimistic, I might think that we'd hurt them badly enough in the opening moments of the fight that we'd scared them off.

I'm not that optimistic. "Let's go. Get across the stream and back to the rest of the platoon."

* * *

It took longer than I'd hoped, given the terrain and the snow. The valley had fallen silent after that scream. And the longer that silence stretched out, the less I liked it. Something was brewing, and I already knew it wasn't good.

At least we knew for sure that the humans here were every bit as bad as the Dovos. Maybe even worse.

We finally linked up with the platoon, set in within a stand of taller trees and ready to ambush anyone who might be coming after us. Santos got the team set in on one flank while I reported back to Gunny.

Once again, there was no sign of the captain. I didn't comment on it.

Gunny listened to my SALUTE report in silence, his eyes still scanning the woods below us. I told him everything I could remember from the brief clash, including a rough estimate of the enemy's numbers and the weird way the mobs had acted, as if they were mindless drones swarming under the central control of the riders.

Under different circumstances—like our old lives in the Marine Corps—I might not have said anything about that weird, crawling sensation and the accompanying headache that had gone away as soon as I blew the rider's brains out. But after all we'd seen here, reporting on the weird stuff was every bit as important as Size, Activity, Location, Unit, Time, and Equipment. Call it SWALUTE and always add the weird, I guess.

I also told him that I really didn't think that they'd been scared off by the power of our weapons.

He nodded. "Yeah, I doubt that anything that could make that scream is worried about some M4s. Even if it doesn't know what they are." He looked up toward the city, what little we could see of it through the trees. "You're sure you broke contact cleanly?"

"Sure? No. Not here." I didn't need to elaborate much. We were still learning the rules here, and the blatantly supernatural elements to this world made the rules a bit more malleable than we were used to. "But if they do come after us, I doubt that it'll be that bunch. They'll find a different angle."

Almost as if something had heard me, a shadow passed overhead, and a strange whisper hissed through the treetops. I looked up but couldn't see anything.

"All right, let's move. The captain's still determined to get up to that city and find a way in. If we're not in imminent danger of taking contact, then we might be able to reset and reattack this without getting into a pitched gunfight." Gunny stood up. He was still wearing his ruck. "Ruck up and get ready. I'll go find the captain."

CHAPTER 25

WE could still hear movement in the woods around us but didn't come under attack again, even though it took far longer to get the Dovos moving than any of us would have liked. We pushed upstream, toward the top of the valley, getting into steeper and rockier terrain as the woods closed in around us again.

That's the Recon way. We go into the nastiest terrain we can find, where no one else wants to go, because if nobody goes in there, they can't stumble on you and compromise your team.

I didn't know how well it was going to work in this place, but it was worth a try.

We slowed as the woods got thicker. Unfortunately, while the main force had pulled back, the Younger God Taramas, or whoever was calling the shots in that city, had sent something else. And as we slowed, they got to catch up.

The first indicator that trouble was coming our way was when a hooting cry went up on our right flank, answered by a similar cry behind us.

Everybody stopped for a second at that. Eyes scanned the trees around us. But the forest was really thick there, and we couldn't see more than a few yards. Another hoot went up, echoing through the trees. That one sounded closer.

"Keep moving." Gunny's voice was a low hiss from just behind my team. I signaled Rodeffer to keep going and Farrar to follow him, while I took a knee next to a tree. I wanted to talk to Gunny for a moment. Apparently, I wasn't the only one, either; Bailey was forging through the snow to catch up.

"Okay, what is it?" He saw me crouched there, and Bailey moving in quick, and simply came up to take a knee next to me, his eyes still out and watching the rest of the platoon as well as the forest around us.

"If those things are hunting us and they're anything like the riders we killed on the other side of the creek, then they *are* going to catch up with us," Bailey said as he glanced at Zimmerman's team while they trudged past. "These things ain't human, at least not anymore. We have to expect that they're going to move faster than we can."

"What's your plan?" He knew me well enough to know that I hadn't just stopped to bitch.

Another hoot went up. *Much* closer this time. Bailey jerked a thumb at it. "Let me take my team and set in an ambush. If we can kill at least one of these things, it might give the others pause." I wasn't entirely sure of that, but whatever was out there, it was closing in fast, and we were going to have to deal with it sooner or later, anyway.

Gunny looked from one to the other of us. I hadn't spoken yet, but Bailey's plan was pretty close to what I'd had in mind. Of course, his team was the trail team, so they'd probably get the duty. "And if they don't?"

Bailey shrugged. "Then we run. It's still a better idea to whittle them down instead of waiting for them to close the noose."

He thought about it for a moment. Then he nodded shortly. "Do it." There was no time for indecision, and Gunny had long been the type to say that a poor decision is always better than no decision.

The captain might object, but he wasn't there, and whatever was stalking us was getting closer by the second. Bailey gave Gunny a thumbs-up, turned, and hustled back downhill as fast as he could to link back up with the rest of his team.

We kept moving, though I kept my team moving slowly, just in case Bailey needed backup. I didn't like the idea of leaving Sean down there to face whatever new and nasty surprise this place had in store by himself.

It might have been another three hundred yards up the hill before we heard everything go to hell behind us. Howls and hoots echoed through the woods, punctuated by the harsh *crack*s of suppressed gunfire. Bailey and his boys were getting stuck in, all right. But it didn't sound like it was going well.

I made my decision.

"We're breaking off." I paused, just for a second. While I didn't like the idea, we'd fight a lot better without the rucks. We'd pulled it off before, but from the sounds of things, Bailey's team might not have a lot of time, so we needed to move fast. "Drop rucks. Weapons and ammo only."

There wasn't time to brief anything in detail. I didn't really need to. I pointed to the higher ground off to the right, which should give us a flanking position on Bailey's target. We hadn't gotten far when the plan suddenly went sideways. Bailey and his boys were still invisible through the trees, though we could hear the noise pretty clearly as it echoed through the woods. That was why we *almost* missed the second creature just ahead of us.

Rodeffer stopped dead, his rifle raised, and I followed suit, stepping behind a tree and looking for whatever he'd seen.

I couldn't see it at first. I couldn't hear its movement over the racket downhill. If not for the fact that it was talking to itself, I might not have heard it at all.

Once again, I couldn't understand it, though in the quiet as I settled in behind a tree, looking for it over my sights, I could make out words, even though they were gibberish to me. They sounded vaguely Slavic, but that wasn't the part that really struck me.

It was the tone of its voice. That thing out there wasn't a mindless animal, like a dog making noises to itself or a cat chirping while it stalked a mouse or a bird. No, this thing was obviously intelligent, and what's more, it was *enjoying* itself.

In fact, the longer I listened to it mutter and chuckle to itself, the more I was convinced that it wasn't actually talking to itself. It was talking to *us*.

And it was telling us just what it was going to do to us, and how much it was going to enjoy doing it.

I spotted movement and shifted my rifle toward it, but it wasn't there. Maybe I'd seen it, maybe I'd seen the wind stirring a branch, or an animal running for cover as that hunting *thing* came closer.

Then it was right in front of me, barely twenty yards away.

It was humanoid in that it had two arms, two legs, a head, and only two eyes. That was about where it ended, though. It was gray-skinned and appeared to be hairless aside from a forest of porcupine-quill-like spines running from the back of its head down its back. I could see that mane of spines from where I was because it was down on all fours. Its fingers were too long and tipped with black claws, and its knees bent the wrong way. Its head might have been human at one point, but its jaws were thrust out into a muzzle, sharp teeth pressing against the inside of its lips. Its ears were long and pointed, thrusting out and swiveling from side to side. Its nose had receded into its face and looked more like the nostrils of a skull.

Its eyes, though. They weren't the glowing red coals that the riders had peered at the world through. They were all too human. Cold gray eyes swept the woods as its triangular nostrils quivered with a loud snuffling sound.

Those eyes locked on mine as I looked at them through the ACOG. My finger was already tightening on the trigger.

I wasn't alone. Farrar and Rodeffer opened fire at the same moment. Six rounds smashed into the thing with a ripping crash, punching through gray flesh and white bone.

The wounds didn't even slow it down.

It leapt forward, its twisted muzzle stretching into a vicious grin, snatching a long, wicked-looking, broad-bladed knife off its belt. It was wearing clothes, cut to fit around its spines and its freakishly long limbs. It was even wearing boots. I didn't know why since bullets tearing through its torso didn't even seem to faze it. The cold must not bother it at all.

"*Ah, the meat fights back! So much the better!*" No, it hadn't switched to speaking English. But as its attention turned to us specifically, I could suddenly understand it. I didn't find that comforting. "*Come, let us dance!*"

I hammered two more rounds into its chest before I gave up. The 5.56 rounds weren't doing squat. I slung the weapon to my back and drew my sword.

Don't ask me why I decided to do that. It just seemed like the right thing to do. When one weapon goes down, you transition to the secondary.

I was no great swordsman at the time. But I knew that I wanted to keep that big pigsticker between me and it, and that I didn't want to overextend to the point it could get slapped out of my hand. Of course, if that thing was as fast and as strong as it looked, it probably could take the blade away from me anyway, but I was bound and determined to draw some more blood before it did.

The sight of that blade gave it pause, though. It stopped an arm's length short of the point, its own knife held loosely at its side. "*Well, now. Where did you get* that*?*" Its eyes searched me. "*Unfortunate for you that the blade does not pass on the skill of the one who first wielded it.*"

I wished I'd brought my shield, as crude as it was, but it was still lashed to my ruck. So, I kept the sword directly in front of me, one hand on the grip, the other on the pommel. It was slightly too short to get both hands on the hilts, but I'd do what I could with what I had.

The thing wasn't circling or otherwise moving. It stayed where it was, stock still except for its eyes, waiting. The rest of the team had ceased fire—either they'd also realized that the bullets weren't doing anything and we needed the ammo for things that did die when you shot them, or they were worried about hitting me—and the woods had suddenly fallen silent. Even the calls of the other hunters had stopped.

When it struck, it was blindingly fast. I didn't block the knife with my sword, I blocked its arm. The creature's blade was already inside my reach. Only the fact that I tried to parry it kept the point from going into my neck. As it was, the point pricked my shoulder, the puncture immediately starting to burn horribly, and my hands on the hilt were jarred as if I'd just hit a tree with a baseball bat.

I'd always read that you were supposed to parry with the flat of the blade instead of the edge. The only thing the latter gets you is a good notch in your edge. After enough hits, your sharp sword becomes a hacksaw blade. But I'd instinctively turned the edge into the oncoming arm, and it bit deep.

The creature snatched its knife hand back, dark red blood flowing from the wound. Unlike the bullet wounds, this one didn't close. "*Fortunate. But it will not happen a second time.*"

It was maneuvering on me now. It flipped the knife to its other hand, sidestepping around to my left. I tracked it with the point, determined that I was going to sink that blade to the hilt in it if it charged me. It was about all I had. My forearms ached from that blow, and I worried that I'd lose the sword if it hit me again.

If I could even get the blade between me and its stroke.

Santos and Rodeffer had spread out to either side, their own melee weapons in hand, having apparently figured out that shooting this thing wasn't going to stop it. Of course, I wasn't sure those blades would, either. There was something about the sword I'd taken off a dead Dovo in the tor that made it more effective. I didn't know what, but I wasn't going to look a gift horse in the mouth, either.

The creature suddenly pounced at Rodeffer, swinging that knife at his throat. He jumped backward, or he tried to. He tripped and fell, and while that meant he evaded the slash, it put him on his back, and the thing was on him in a flash.

I seemed to be much too far away as I thrashed through the snow toward them. Rodeffer had grabbed the thing's wrist as it tried to stab him, and while Rodeffer was a strong dude, I could see that he had seconds before it drove that knife into his guts. His teeth were gritted as he was driven down into the snow, and his arms were shaking as the thing leered down at him, leaning on one hand next to his head while the other slowly, inexorably forced the knife point toward his flesh.

That thing must have either been really confident, or it had underestimated how strong Rodeffer was. The point had nearly touched his chest rig when I stabbed it in the side.

My blade didn't go in very deep. The thing sprang away again and skidded on all fours in the snow about fifteen feet down the slope. It had only barely avoided slamming into a tree trunk by shoving off with three limbs. It glared up at me, and then it was coming for me, murder in its eyes.

I hacked at it as it came in. My combat calm had overcome its momentary lapse at the realization that this thing was tougher by far than anything we'd faced except that damned giant that was probably still howling its curses from under the boulder we'd dropped on it. So, while I wasn't what you might call "relaxed," I was in control, my awareness clear. I could see every spine on its back, see the glare in its eyes, and more importantly, I could see the arc of the knife as it came at me.

And I saw where my sword had to go. I just wasn't quite fast enough to get it there.

My arm plus the length of the sword blade just about equaled that thing's reach with the knife. I ducked to the side, hopefully getting my head underneath that arc, and stabbed for the armpit.

But it was too fast. I pricked it, but it twisted in midair and slapped me hard enough that I saw stars as I realized I was flying through the air, just before I landed on my face in the snow. I'd lost my grip on the sword. I could barely breathe, desperately fighting to suck some wind back into my lungs as I clawed my way out of the snowbank. I rolled onto my back, realizing then that I didn't have the sword, my M4—as relatively useless as it was against this thing—was still on my back, and I was now lying on it. I snatched at my Bowie, knowing that I was already too slow and I was going to die. It was already almost on me.

Then Gunny came in with his axe.

I hadn't even known that he'd followed us. Now he went to work on that thing like a lumberjack on meth.

His first blow hammered into its spine. That thing was so tough that it hardly did anything, but he wasn't expecting a single hit to take it down. He wrenched the blade out, reversed it without arresting its momentum a bit, and slammed it down into the thing's hamstring.

It roared, but he'd blindsided it, and he'd done enough damage with those two strokes that it couldn't heal fast enough to jump away. And he kept up the flurry of blows, moving back and forth as he hacked away at it, battering it hard enough to keep it off balance just long enough that I could get back up and try to find my sword.

There it was. It had left a perfect, sword-shaped hole in the snow, and it took a second to snatch it out. I pivoted, my chest and head aching, and waded in despite the pain. Gunny's sheer savagery was doing more than my calm had. Blood was starting to flow, though the wounds weren't nearly deep enough to kill it. But it was as if it was in shock, having turned to face him, knocked off balance, trying to block his flurry of blows with an arm that was getting bloodier and bloodier. The axe wasn't doing much more than our bullets had, but he'd managed to block every thrust of the knife and do enough damage that he'd taken up all of its attention.

Which gave me my opening.

Every fiber of my body hurt, though I was getting some air back into my battered lungs. I wrapped my fingers around the sword's hilt and waded in.

I didn't hack at it. While I was pretty sure that the sword would bite a lot deeper than Gunny's axe, we needed to end this. I could hear more hooting calls from out in the woods. This had already gone on too long. So, while I had no way of knowing for sure if it would work with an unnatural monstrosity that could shrug off multiple 5.56 rounds, I went back to the simple target zones. A T-box shot to the head will usually punch through the brainstem. That's a "circuitry kill." That wasn't that doable with a blade at the angle I had. But the other "A-zone" is the heart and lungs. And that thing had its arms up, one of them trying to hold off Gunny's frenzied, berserker axe blows, while the other looked for an opening to slam that wicked knife into him.

Its armpit was wide open. And I stabbed it right under its arm, one hand on the hilt, the other on the pommel, driving it toward its heart and lungs as hard as I could.

The point skittered off a rib, then sank deep as the thing threw back its head and howled in pain. It swept its arm back, knocking me flat again as I lost my grip on the sword hilt. But it hadn't hit me nearly as hard as it had the first time. I was back on my feet in a second, my Bowie in my hand, ready to make it hurt as much as possible before it snapped my neck or cut my throat.

But it was dying. It sagged around the blade in its torso, a terrible gurgling noise coming from its throat. Gunny stepped in one more time as its arms lost their strength. He brought his axe down with terrific force on the center of its forehead.

Whatever had kept the thing from succumbing to our bullets no longer seemed to be working. The axe went deep, splitting its skull clear to its nostrils. It quivered once, then went still.

Gunny wrenched the axe loose and wiped the gore off on the snow. He eyed the edge, his expression as dispassionate as ever. It was badly notched, bent, and dull. It would probably need a *lot* of work before it was a useful weapon again, except maybe a particularly hard club.

I dragged my sword out of the thing's corpse. The monster was already starting to rot before our eyes, despite the cold. I pulled the blade out of a viscous, liquid mess that smelled like an open sewer. Strangely, the blade itself wasn't stained. A couple drops of brownish gore slid off and dripped onto the snow without leaving a trace on the metal.

"Let's go," Gunny rasped as more hoots sounded in the woods. They sounded different this time, as if they were calling the thing that we'd just killed, and they didn't know what to make of its silence. Then a new scream came from the city. The hoots stopped. But I could have sworn I saw a flicker of movement down the hill somewhere. They hadn't given up the hunt. That scream had sounded...*imperious*, somehow. They were under orders. And like the humans we had faced earlier, I thought that they were more afraid of whatever made that scream than they were of us.

We started back up toward where we'd left the rucks, leaving the steaming puddle of ichor that had been that unnatural predator melting the snow behind us. As we climbed uphill, we met Bailey and his team. I breathed a little easier, seeing that they were all still alive, even though we'd been diverted from helping them out. Bailey was still wiping rotting gore off his own leaf-bladed sword. So, they'd killed their target.

I glanced back just before we lost sight of the disintegrating remains and noticed something, a little detail that stuck in my mind. I wasn't sure what it meant, not yet. I'd learn more later. But just for a moment, in that split second before it died, I'd seen terror like nothing I'd ever imagined in its eyes.

CHAPTER 26

IT took seconds to ruck up and get moving again. I felt like I'd been hit by a truck, and it was a struggle to pick up the pace as we continued up toward where the Dovos had found a high crossing over the stream. Every part of me ached, and my head was pounding. My throat was raw from the exertion in the searing cold. And I might have twisted an ankle at some point because it was *throbbing*. I was pretty sure it wasn't broken, but it hurt like hell.

It could have been worse, given what we'd just endured, but there were more of those things out there, and we couldn't afford to slow down because I was hurting.

I could hear Sergeant O'Neill in my head, back long ago and far away, as we'd been doing flutter kicks in a mud puddle, in the rain. "*This is what it's all about, gents. When you're cold, wet, tired, and hurting, but you reach down, grab hold, and keep going. That's what makes a Recon Marine. When everyone else gives up, you keep going.*"

So, I gritted my teeth, ignored the pain, and kept climbing. I couldn't put my head down. This wasn't a road march. I had to keep my eyes up, watching our surroundings and my team. Somehow, that hurt worse, but I kept at it.

I looked back down the hill, my eyes narrowed. I realized that I hadn't heard one of those hunting calls in a while. But as I peered through the trees, I could have sworn that I saw a long-limbed shape flit from shadow to shadow.

I saw it again when we got to the crossing. It hadn't gotten any closer. I frowned, and Gunny saw me looking. He raised an eyebrow questioningly, then moved up to join me under a gnarled, lightning-blasted tree that had to be at least a century old. "You see something?"

With a nod down the hill, I murmured, "They're still back there. At least one. I've seen it twice now, moving in the trees behind us. Here's the weird thing, though. It hasn't gotten any closer in the last twenty minutes."

He followed my gaze down the hillside. "I thought so. Pretty sure I've seen something a couple times, too." He rubbed his chin for a moment. "I wonder if they're too scared of whatever screamed at them to give up the hunt or if after we killed the other one, they don't *really* want a piece, either." He scowled. "I don't like having them back there, especially since we don't know what kind of comms they might have with the rest of their *compadres*, but unless we're ready to get into another knock down drag out, I'm not sure we can do much about it."

"*Especially* if they don't want to engage." I spat, or at least I tried to. I needed to drink water. Between the fight and the cold, I was getting severely dehydrated. "Those things are fast. At least the one we killed was." I realized that I really hadn't needed to say that. Gunny had been there. "But we can't just leave 'em back there."

"I'm open to suggestions."

I glanced up toward the front. "I'm sure the captain has some ideas. Or I should say, Dragon Mask has some ideas that the captain would be more than happy to pass on." I was tired enough that some of my bitterness and cynicism leaked out.

"Careful, Conor. He's still the captain. Remember what I said before." Gunny didn't raise his voice. He wasn't even looking at me but still watching the shadows under the trees below us.

I gritted my teeth. Gunny might still have some hope for Captain Sorenson, but at that point, I didn't. Every slight, every bad idea we'd had to go along with, every arrogant assumption of superiority over men with far more experience, going back to the beginning of the workup, weighed on my tired, strung-out mind. He'd been an adversary more than a leader for the entire time he'd been our platoon commander, and now that he had embraced these savages over his own Marines, I couldn't help but mentally exclude him from our "tribe."

I also didn't know if Gunny was putting any credence in the promise to get us home if we followed Dragon Mask on his quest for power. I had always figured he was lying, but now it was starting to claw at the back of my mind that maybe he wasn't. I'd certainly seen enough spooky stuff so far not to discount the possibility.

But what would the cost be? Would it be better to stay stranded here than trade our souls for the chance to go back home?

Through my weariness and my anger, I could still see Gunny's point, though. He remained detached, still looking at the entire situation dispassionately and with an eye to keeping us all alive. He hadn't yet succumbed to the atavistic, primal urge to strike out on our own that was tugging at the rest of us, Bailey and me in particular.

I wondered just how long that would last. What would be the breaking point? How far were we going to go with this charade of an alliance before Gunny said, "Enough," and let us loose?

And how far out of position and behind the power curve were we going to be when we hit that line? How much ammo were we going to have left when we found ourselves surrounded by enemies, both within and without?

How far would we have gone down that road to hell? How much would we have helped an evil man get the power he was willing to sacrifice us all for?

We were in a crack, and the longer this went on, the deeper and darker that crack got.

As time went on and I learned more about the world we'd been thrown into, I would come to understand the Dovos and what had molded and twisted them into the savages they were. My loathing would only increase, but alongside it I would come to pity them, in a way. But right then, my reaction was more instinctive. I knew never to trust anyone who was trying to kill me one second, then acting like a bosom buddy the next.

Some of my reaction to our current situation was conscious. Some of it was simple, animal survival instinct. We know, deep down, when we're among enemies no matter what else we're "supposed" to know.

But at the same time, I trusted Gunny. He and Bailey had been the only two other members of the platoon who I really had trusted for most of the last six months. Gurke was an okay dude, but we weren't close. My team was solid. But the two I could really confide in were Bailey and Gunny.

I didn't agree with him here. But he had a point. The fewer we were, the more easily we'd get picked off. That was why he wasn't willing to write the captain off. That, plus his own fatherly sense of responsibility.

That wasn't something I felt. The captain might be a leadership challenge to Gunny, but he was a thorn in the side to me. I wondered if even Gunny was letting his emotions override his judgement.

This wasn't the time to have that argument, nor the place. Gunny was still Gunny. Unless I was willing to strike out on my own and reject the man who had held us steady through all the captain's and Big Marine Corps' crap. I couldn't do that. So, I'd trust him. For now.

But when it blew up, if we survived, you'd better believe I was going to say, "I told you so."

I just kept moving, letting that long monologue to remain inside my head, unspoken. I didn't have a suggestion as to how to deal with the hunters on our trail, and neither did anyone else, it seemed. So, I leaned into my ruck straps and kept going toward the crossing.

The Dovos had found another log bridge across the stream. We were a lot higher up than we had been when my team had crossed to scout out the enemy, so the streambed was narrower and rockier. The bridge was built of felled trees that had clearly been there for a long time—the bark was worn off along the top, scarred by many pairs of feet. I was pretty sure I'd seen tracks moving off through the snow where we hadn't gone.

Security was set in at both ends of the bridge. Everyone knew all too well how bad a linear danger area could be. When crossing a linear danger area in a high-trafficked area—like, say, a local footbridge—it got worse. A firebreak or stream could *potentially* expose you as you cross, as someone *might* be up or downstream and happen to look across. But a footbridge meant there might be regular traffic that could stumble on you. And with those hunters still lurking behind us, it was anyone's guess what kind of ambush might have been set in ahead of us.

We got across without incident. My team was well away from the stream by the time Bailey's team crossed and continued on behind us.

I couldn't see the hunters anymore. But I knew they were there.

* * *

We kept going up, higher and higher, as the trees got shorter and thinner again. I could get glimpses of the whole spread of the valley below when I looked back through the trees. A few high clouds drifted in an otherwise cold, hard, blue emptiness. Sunlight glared off the snow on treetops and the icy ridge we'd crossed over.

I was squinting hard. We'd been set up for a summertime greenside op, so I hadn't brought my Oakleys. They were in my berth on the ship, wherever and whenever that was. So, I had to squint, risking snow blindness every step of the way.

I stopped a moment after Rodeffer. He was already peering back toward the pass we'd crossed. "You see that, Conor?"

I squinted harder. There was movement there. I brought up my rifle and looked through the ACOG.

There was more than just movement. A column of men in furs and carrying weapons was wending its way down the mountain from the pass, with more riders in between formations. They rode the same odd horses, though some of them were obviously human, arrayed like Dragon Mask and the warlord that I had shot from the tor. Several were draped in black, hooded cloaks.

Others were noticeably different. Misshapen, outsized monstrosities, they reminded me of the rider I'd seen up on the ridge above the Dovos just before they'd assaulted the tor.

They also reminded me of the riders we'd fought just down the hill from where we now stood. No two of them were the same. Though I couldn't make out a lot of detail at that distance, I could tell that some were shorter and broader, some taller and thinner. A couple of them were gargantuan mountains of muscle and hide, too big to ride.

I scanned up toward the pass. There were a *lot* of them. And as I got to the entrance to the pass itself, I lingered, watching the massive, shaggy mount and its equally massive rider as it paced down the snowy slope.

The beast was built like some cross between a lion and a gorilla. Its hind legs were slightly shorter than its forelegs, and its back was humped. Its head was massive and silver-furred, with a mane that narrowed to a point beneath its chin, vicious tusks meeting equally nasty fangs in its mouth, protruding from its lips. A double set of ram's horns curled from behind its eyes.

Judging by how much detail I could make out from across the valley, and the size of the Dovos, or the Dovos' kin, who were walking nearby, that thing had to be the size of a rhino. And its rider was scaled to match it.

Thickset, barrel-chested, with hardly any neck and an oversized head that looked too large even for its massive body, the figure was clad in armor that looked black until the light hit it just so, when it gave off a greenish sheen, like a beetle's carapace. The point of the spear jutting over his shoulder gleamed the same color. That spear looked like it was fifteen feet long and as big around as a baseball bat, and that rider had it over his shoulder like granddaddy's shotgun, like it barely weighed anything at all.

I didn't know who that was, but I was fairly sure he was bad news. The army he had with him was even worse news.

Another shriek went up from the city, louder than before. We must be getting close. But it wasn't aimed at us. At least, I was pretty sure it wasn't. Especially when that massive, armored monstrosity on the silver-furred beast lifted that huge spear in a gesture that was unmistakably threatening and defiant.

Either we had just walked into the middle of a war, or Dragon Mask's god had figured out his game and come after him. Which might still amount to the same thing if Uergal and Taramas disliked each other enough.

Looking forward, I'd seen that the Dovos had halted, and several of them were arguing fiercely, though still in hushed tones. I scanned the slope beneath us again, looking for the hunters on our trail. No sign of them. Were they closing in, anxious to finish the job before the new threat got too close, or was the arrival of the army of monsters and savages on the other side of the valley altered the calculus enough that they'd been pulled back?

I realized that I was still thinking in terms of near-instantaneous radio comms. I had no idea how these things communicated battlefield orders. Maybe they had telepathy. Everything else here was certainly weird enough. Or maybe that scream had included orders to the rest of the ruined city's forces in the valley. I didn't think so, though. That had sounded like a cry of rage and challenge, not orders and coordination. Language barrier or not, emotion is emotion, and that shriek had been full of it.

The captain hustled down toward our position, following Dragon Mask. The Dovos' leader was obviously agitated, muttering behind his mask. "Can you see?" His trick to make himself understood seemed to be strained. He was still speaking his own language, but it took some extra effort to understand him. As if he was mumbling on the other side of a door.

Rodeffer pointed as I grimaced and got the rest of the team set in, mostly watching down the hill toward the last known position where we'd seen the hunters. Dragon Mask clambered up to the side of a tree growing out of a crack between two massive, snow-draped boulders, and the captain joined him, ignoring the rest of us as we set in security, looking for the hunters who'd been hounding us.

On the one hand, we were in a better spot to counter the hunters if they attacked us rather than getting jumped on the move. On the other hand, we were halted in enemy territory with at least one group of enemies already right on us.

"It is Uergal." Dragon Mask's dread was palpable. He uttered a curse, which I couldn't understand, but the sense of it was downright vile. "He must not have taken the bait." He spat the same curse. I briefly wondered just what the "bait" had been.

At the same moment, a series of hooting calls went up from the woods around us. My eyes narrowed as I scanned the forest. That hadn't sounded like a recall. That had sounded more like, *get in there and finish them quickly.*

I got behind a tree, bracing my M4 and scanning the woods. I was using the ACOG as a spotting scope more than I was looking to shoot anything. There's a first time for everything, but the last one hadn't gone down fast enough to 5.56. It was possible that a direct hit to the brainstem might drop one, sorcerous monster or not, but they moved so fast that a reliable headshot was iffy, at best.

No, I'd go for the sword again if it came to it. I'd still rather be moving than sitting there waiting for them. But the captain and Dragon Mask were up there muttering about what the plan was, and when Gunny approached and started to try to suggest that we get moving again, the captain shushed him. We were going to be stuck in place, waiting to get hit as the hunter monsters moved in. One had been more than a handful. Four or five at once were going to tear us apart.

Another chorus of howls went up. They were closer. And there were a lot of them.

I dropped my ruck, slung my rifle behind me, cinched the sling down, and drew the sword. There was a sudden, choked-off exclamation from up behind me.

"Staff Sergeant McCall, put that away!" I looked over my shoulder to see the captain pointing at me, his eyes wide with what might have been fear or anger. He hustled down toward us, lowering his voice as he reached me and Gunny. "I don't know why you saw fit to remove the coverings, but that sword could disrupt what Ekersakar is trying to do!"

I looked up at where Dragon Mask was making strange gestures in the air, holding up an amulet as he swayed from side to side and chanted. Unlike before, I couldn't understand what he was chanting, but this time I was pretty sure

I didn't want to know. Something about the sounds he was making made my eardrums ache. And his voice wasn't that loud.

Looking down at the sword in my hand, I took in the runes on the pommel, the hilt, and the smaller ones in the fuller running down the center of the blade. "What the hell is this sword going to do that'll 'disrupt' whatever he's doing?"

"He says that it was a prize claimed from that old fortress, and that it was touched by the same evil that lived there." I glanced at Gunny, who was watching the captain with narrowed eyes. Since when did the captain buy into even the notion of "good" and "evil?" He'd condemned us more than once for talking in such terms. How deep did Dragon Mask have his claws in him? It was uncharacteristic, and seeing it, I wondered if there wasn't more reason behind Gunny's refusal to give up on him than I'd thought. If he was being actively manipulated…

"They tried to ritually cleanse it, but they could never quite manage it. That's why the hilts were wrapped. You shouldn't have unwrapped them." He sounded like he really believed it, too. And he suddenly realized that. I could see him try to reel it back in. Had to maintain that image, even if we all knew it was a fraud. "We are in a fragile situation here. We don't have a great handle on our allies' culture. We *cannot* risk damaging this relationship by crossing their cultural taboos."

Now, I'll admit that I was pretty much running on gut instinct at that moment. And my gut instinct was telling me that this sword, this deadly work of art in my hand that had been the only thing that had pierced that hunter's heart, wasn't evil. Wasn't "touched by evil." And I was pretty sure the only reason that the Dovos said the tor was an evil place was because whoever had lived there in the distant past had been their enemies. And while I would be the first to say that the enemy of evil is not necessarily good, I was getting that feeling. The feeling that whoever had been there, whoever had forged my captured sword, they weren't just a different flavor of evil, like Taramas and his, or her, or its lackeys that were currently hunting us.

And if the sword disrupted whatever Dragon Mask was doing that was making my head hurt, I was not inclined to think that it was a bad thing.

But the captain didn't, and as long as Gunny said so, he was still the CO. "Put it *away*, Staff Sergeant!" His voice was a low hiss as he glanced over his shoulder, as if afraid that Dragon Mask would see that I still had the sword in my hand and get offended.

Gunny nodded fractionally. With a glare, I sheathed the sword and turned toward the trees, just as three more of the hunters came out into the open.

No two were exactly alike. They all had similar oversized, carnivorous teeth and were long-limbed and lean, but that was about where it ended. One was horned, with goat-like legs and horrifically long arms. Another had tusks amid its smaller fangs and looked like a starving gorilla, its legs considerably shorter than its arms. The last one was, if anything, far more human-looking, but that just made it weirder. It walked slowly and calmly on long, thin legs, clad in a long tunic of what looked like leather, though I got the sudden horrifying impression that it was made of human skin. Its equally long, thin arms were clasped behind its back as it walked up the slope with an air of total unconcern. Its head was bald and gray, its teeth pressing at its lips, but its face looked otherwise human. Wizened and cadaverously thin, but still human.

I got behind my rifle and got ready to sell myself as dearly as possible.

But as soon as I got the ACOG's chevron on the tall, straight, disturbingly human one, something happened.

The last word of Dragon Mask's incantation hit us like a freight train. I think I actually blacked out for a second. When I cracked my eyes back open, my vision felt blurry, and something was running down out of my nose into my week-old mustache and shemagh. It was blood.

Something was happening behind the hunters, who had stopped dead where they were. At first, I thought that I was seeing things, but the snow was rising up in a massive hump, as if the ground itself was swelling into a hill right behind them. And as it got higher, it got...dirtier. It started to turn brown, then darkened more and more until it was black, almost as if a bubble of crude oil had swelled up out of the ground.

The air around it was blurred, as if an oily mist was coming off of it. I suddenly realized that I could hear a horrific buzzing, and the trees seemed to creak and sway, as if under the buffeting of a stiff wind—except there wasn't any wind. And they were all swaying away from that oily black...thing.

The hunters had forgotten us. They had all turned quickly to face that thing. One of them—or maybe all of them, it was hard to tell with that strange buzzing in the air—started keening, a high-pitched cry of despair and terror.

Someone opened fire on the blob, but the gunfire was silenced as suddenly as it had begun. It had sounded strangely muted, as if I had double earpro in—which I didn't. My watch cap and shemagh were all I had on my head at the moment.

What happened next is hard to describe. I'm not entirely sure just *what* I saw. At one and the same time, it was as if the black thing spat a part of itself at each of the hunters, engulfing them in something like thick, black tar, and also as if they were yanked toward the thing and partway consumed.

It makes my head hurt just thinking about it and trying to put it down on paper. It was unnatural. It defied every law of physics I'd ever thought I'd known. Just like the black, oily thing itself, it was *wrong.*

I might have blinked. I might have blacked out again. I lost track of time for a moment, and when I could see clearly again, the black thing was gone, the hunters were nothing but puddles of steaming gore and tar, and there was a sulfurous smell on the air that made me want to puke.

That urge only got stronger when I looked up the hill and saw that one of ours had similarly been turned into red and black mush. Only process of elimination showed me that it was Nelson-Hyde, Gurke's pointman.

The hillside was suddenly silent. Even the cries and horns and drums from both Uergal's army and Taramas's defenses had stopped. The entire valley seemed hushed, stunned, and horrified.

I turned on the captain. "*That* was a better option than *this*?" I drew the sword and pointed it at his face. He was in such shock at what we'd just witnessed that I'm not sure he even noticed the blade barely an arm's length from his face. "Never again." I gulped back bile as I stepped forward, still careful not to *actually* stab him. "You hear me, *sir*? *Nev-*

er. Again." I glared at Dragon Mask, who was watching the blade in my hand rather than me, then sheathed it. I looked at Gunny. His face was blank for a moment, but then he took a deep breath and nodded. We were on the same page. We'd found that line, the one that could not be crossed.

But the captain was recovering, and he hadn't gotten the message. "It was necessary." His voice was thick, as if his mouth was full of spit, almost as if he was on the edge of vomiting. "We didn't have another choice."

I stepped closer. Right then I didn't give a damn about his rank or his position. "Yes, we did. And we do. We might have gotten blindsided this time, but if he tries to do something like that again, I'm going to kill him myself." I looked up at Dragon Mask and saw that he'd understood me. And he knew I was dead serious. And when I turned my eyes back to Captain Sorenson, I saw that he'd picked up on the unspoken part of that threat. *And if you get in my way, I'll kill you, too.*

"*Get the hell out of my way, Zimmerman*!" All eyes turned up the hill to where Chambers and Gurke were vying for a shot at Dragon Mask. Zimmerman's team—with varying degrees of willingness—had interjected themselves, though even Zimmerman wasn't so retarded as to try to stand directly in front of the other Recon Marines' muzzles. They were trying to hold the two back, while Franks and Herrera were both still staring at what was left of Nelson-Hyde in shock. "I'm going to kill that son of a bitch!"

"Stand down, Staff Sergeant!" Captain Sorenson was probably trying to sound authoritative as he turned aside from me and started back up the slope. But his voice cracked, and he sounded more desperate than in charge. "That is our *ally*, and you *will* treat him as such!"

Gurke stabbed a knife hand at Dragon Mask, not bothering to look at the captain. Even from where I stood, I could see the hate written in every line of his face. "That 'ally' just killed Clarence!"

"It was an *accident*, Staff Sergeant!" The captain had reached the struggling knot of Marines, grabbing Gurke by the arm. I saw that most of the Dovos weren't watching us. They were every bit as horrified as we were. That was saying something. "He wasn't the target!"

Gurke turned with a jerk and stared at the captain, his eyes burning with so much rage that Sorenson took a step back. "What the fuck does that matter? I never heard of a green-on-blue just getting dismissed just because the bad guy was an 'ally.' And *this* was a hell of a lot worse than some Afghan turning his rifle on his trainer."

He stabbed a finger in the captain's chest. Sorenson was so rocked that he didn't react right away. "You're so married to your 'alliance' that you're trying to ignore the fact that whatever that was, it was the equivalent of setting off a fucking claymore inside the perimeter without warning anyone. That fucker's dangerous, he's not our fucking friend—no matter how much you try to lie to yourself and us about it—and if you don't kill him, I will."

"That is *not* your call, Staff Sergeant!" The captain had gotten over his shock. "What happened to Sergeant Nelson-Hyde is tragic, but remember that this is a combat situation, and bad things happen. I thought I had Marines in my platoon, men who understand that this is a dangerous profession. If you're too scared to do the job, tell me now so I can fire you and find a team leader who will."

I really don't think he understood just how close he came to getting murdered right then and there.

Gunny interjected. "That's enough. Gurke, set in security up top." When Gurke didn't move or even blink, his voice got hard. "*Now*, Ross. I'll take care of this."

With one final glare that promised hell to pay in the future, Gurke turned aside, pulling Chambers with him. Chambers looked even less willing to let it go, his hand still on his rifle, his face red, staring sheer murder at Sorenson. But Gunny stared them both down until they did what he'd told them before turning to the captain.

"This can't go unaddressed." He had his hands on his rifle but still managed to convey the impression of a disappointed father. "I've turned a blind eye to all sorts of other red flags, but this one can't happen again. We might be allies for now. That's only because these people offered a truce, and we're way out in the cold. *And* it's apparent that their opponents are every bit as monstrous as they are, if not more so. But this? This is across the line. Whatever he did, he killed one of ours." He didn't address the sheer unnatural horror of whatever phenomenon Dragon Mask had summoned. That bothered me a little.

"And if Sergeant Nelson-Hyde hadn't shot at it, he might still be alive." The captain wasn't backing down, and I could almost see Gurke turning around to go after him again. Hell, *I* almost went up the mountain to rip his throat out for that. And I'd never particularly liked Nelson-Hyde.

"Doesn't matter. He was one of ours. That can't happen again." Gunny stabbed a finger down toward the darkened, dead spot where that…thing had materialized. Or whatever it had done. "I don't know what that was, but Gurke's not wrong. That was calling fire on our own position without warning the rest of us."

My eyes narrowed. Once again, he hadn't mentioned just how *wrong* that had felt. Like somehow we'd all been contaminated just by being close to it, never mind benefiting from it.

Maybe that would take time. Maybe we were still too unaccustomed to just what this place was, how things worked here. The supernatural still wasn't a part of our internal calculus.

We had to make that adjustment. But most of us were so focused on survival that we hadn't gotten that far yet.

Finally, the captain nodded. He looked up at the Dovos. Those whose faces we could see were as pale and wide-eyed with terror as many of us. "I think that I can convince him to avoid using that…technique…again." He turned away and headed back up the hill toward Dragon Mask.

We should have walked, right then and there. That we didn't, but simply tried to compromise and drive on with the paper-thin promise that we weren't going to use whatever black sorcery had killed those hunters and Sergeant Clarence Nelson-Hyde, was a mistake that those of us who survived would have to live with for the rest of our lives.

However long they last in this nightmare place.

CHAPTER 27

A shocked hush had fallen over the valley following that hellish summoning. When I got a look through the trees toward the far side of the valley, I saw that Uergal and his army had halted, holding their position on the mountainside as Uergal and a clump of his mutated minions conferred. At least, it looked like they were conferring. Uergal himself, from what I could see through my ACOG, appeared to be sitting on his mount, stock still, staring toward the city. I was pretty sure that one of the dark riders next to him, uninvolved in the conference but staring at the city alongside his "god," was the same one who had demanded Dragon Mask mutilate himself.

Whatever that was that Dragon Mask had done, it had been so horrific that it had even frightened the monsters into taking pause to consider what to do next.

The Dovos hurried on, while we trailed behind. I was too absorbed in holding security—and getting up the damn mountain—to look around at the rest of the platoon much, but I could still tell that there were decidedly mixed reactions to what had just gone down.

More than a few had the same reservations that I did. None of us really understood what had just happened, or just *how* bad it really was. Again, it was mostly a matter of gut instinct. We recognized that whatever it was, it was simply *wrong*, unnatural. Whatever that black stuff had been, it simply did not belong in this world.

Before you say that *we* didn't exactly belong…we belonged there a hell of a lot more than that thing.

Bailey, I could see, was torn. On the one hand, he'd felt the same twisted, awful evil of what had happened. He knew as well as I did that—even though neither of us might have been able to articulate it at the time—there was something soul-killing about summoning that kind of power. Something unforgivable.

At the same time, though, there's not a Marine alive who can't appreciate some serious destruction. And that had been the single most awe-inspiring act of destruction we'd ever witnessed—and Bailey and I had both seen entire city blocks leveled in Syria. Still, I could see in Bailey's face that he was wondering if the power represented by what Dragon Mask had just done wasn't our only hope to get through this alive.

Bailey wasn't the only one to think that way. I saw a couple of glances from Marines who'd seen me threaten Dragon Mask—and by extension the captain—with looks that suggested I was an idiot for turning down that kind of destructive power.

Marines kill people and break their stuff. We don't always think deeper than that. Not all of us, anyway. There were always going to be those who would grab at any way to better kill people and break their stuff. And that spell, or summoning, or whatever it had been had turned three monsters that we'd have had a hard time killing at the best of times into puddles of smoking goo. Why would we turn down a weapon like that?

Zimmerman especially seemed to be dwelling on that question. He'd been farther away, so he hadn't borne the brunt of the mind-shredding insanity that had been that dark intrusion into reality. Nor had he seen up-close what it had done to our brother.

Plus, his contrariety had, weirdly, drawn him closer to the captain since we'd come here, and he was probably pissed at me for pointing a sword at our platoon commander. Tough.

I found myself worrying about the whole situation from every angle as we climbed higher and higher up the forested slope. After about another half hour, the half-wrecked, partially glacier-encased wall of the ruined city of Taramas came into view through the trees.

I didn't have time to worry about it anymore.

We stopped on a wide shelf about fifty feet below the bottom of the glacier. The trees were once again getting shorter and scrubbier, and the wind was kicking down off the mountaintops, lashing us with icy blasts that threatened to freeze our extremities even through our warming layers. I hadn't realized how much the forest had been sheltering us until then.

Dragon Mask had moved up to the front of the formation, beside that big bruiser with the Lochaber axe. We were still below the base of the city walls and about five hundred yards to the north. I hadn't expected to stop here—we were a good four hundred fifty yards away—well out of arrowshot—but we were still in plain view and would easily be spotted by things that could probably find ways to hurt us even without throwing pointed sticks or rocks at us.

Dragon Mask and his compatriots were crouched around what looked like a rockslide that appeared to be pretty recent. It formed a dark gray scar across the snowy slope, without any fresh snow on the slide itself.

There was a dark gap just on our side of the slide, where the slumped hillside had torn off part of the shelf. It looked as if there was a cave there, and Dragon Mask and his big bruiser of a lieutenant were looking inside it and conferring.

Once again, the Marines had to set security while the captain hustled up to join them. I glared my contempt after him, then turned to the perimeter.

I had a pretty good view of the valley below us. Which meant I also had a good view of what Uergal was doing.

Apparently, the council of war was over. The army was threading its way down the hillside again, disappearing into the trees on the slope, while Uergal sat atop his beast and stared toward the city. He was much too far away, as huge as he obviously was, to see much detail, but I had the distinct impression that he wasn't just staring at Taramas's city. He was scanning the whole ridgeline, looking for us. Or at least, he was looking for whatever strange, mysterious force had just thrown the whole balance of power out of whack.

As awful and costly as that had been, it had bought us time. But I suspected that it had come with a higher price than just the life we'd lost.

Leaving aside the metaphysical price that I could just kind of sense more than articulate, I had a sudden suspicion that even if Uergal and Taramas absolutely *hated* each other, they might just put any such feud aside to come after us now. After all, if you're not *completely* insane, joining forces with an enemy to quash an even greater threat that could wipe you both off the face of the map just makes sense.

I'd seen absolute fanatics who I'd call completely insane do just that. Team up to kill Marines so they could hurry back to killing one another. What remained to be seen was what these monsters would do.

The captain signaled, and Gunny came around our rough perimeter. "Team leaders up."

With a snarl that might or might not have been suited to the situation, I turned the team over to Santos and followed Gunny up the hill. Zimmerman was already nearly at the captain's side. Gurke followed close behind Gunny, but Bailey dropped back to join me.

He didn't say anything. He didn't have to. The look he gave me spoke volumes. We were brothers from another mother, and while the Recon Creed says that "A Recon Marine can speak without saying a word," it isn't always true. But the two of us really could.

He knew that I knew how torn he was over what had happened. He also knew that I knew that he wasn't sure about my reaction, but he wasn't going to dismiss it or me. Bailey trusted me as much as I trusted him. And given the fact that neither of us trusted the Dovos, he gave me a nod that said he was willing to err on the side of figuring that I'd made the right call.

I nodded back, thankful that Bailey, at least, had my back.

We trudged up through the snow, fighting the slick footing on the increasingly steep mountainside. We kept to the trees and the rocky outcrops and put them between us and the looming wall of Taramas's city. Obviously, there was no longer any hiding the fact of our presence, but that didn't mean we had to make things easy for the enemy.

We reached the edge of the slide and the cave in the mountainside where the captain was crouched with Dragon Mask and his crony—who I had started mentally calling Bruiser—plus Zimmerman, Gurke, and Gunny. We took a knee next to them, and I saw that the cave was really more like a crack that led into what appeared to be a deeper cavern, stretching away to the right and left, vanishing into the dark under the mountain ridge.

I glanced to the left, following that passage when something that stood like a jagged tooth on the ridgeline above us caught my eye. It might have been a ruined tower. It had a commanding view of the whole valley. That didn't make me any more comfortable about our position, which already felt exposed as hell.

The captain turned to us, his "leadership" face back on. "So, Ekersakar tells me that there was once a network of watchtowers all along this ridge, connected to the city by tunnels. His original plan was to work our way up to one of those watchtowers and then descend into the tunnels to infiltrate the city that way. But this slide appears to have opened one of the tunnels, so we won't have to go as far."

I eyed the dark opening while Bailey asked the question that had to be on most of our minds. "How does he know all this, sir? What's the source on the intel?"

Captain Sorenson glanced at Dragon Mask, who was wholly absorbed in studying the opening in the mountainside. "The Dovos nal Uergal have been trying to retrieve this artifact for a long time. Ekersakar has made it a subject of study for most of his life. There are temples throughout these northlands that hold volumes of knowledge, and they've even raided some of Taramas's temples, as well." Sorenson had adopted that professorial, lecturing tone that he seemed to think lent him gravitas but just made him sound like an overbearing schoolteacher to me. "There's a lot of lore these people have collected and passed down about this artifact and where it might be hidden. And from what I've been able to gather, they have preserved a lot of history about this particular city." The captain looked a little uncertain. "It's even possible, given what he's told me, that the artifact was lost when the city was taken. That's a little unclear."

Bailey was watching Dragon Mask. The Dovos's leader was still raptly peering into the darkness under the mountain. I glanced at him but then turned back to the captain.

"When did he tell you this?" I had my suspicions. I also suspected that whatever 'history' Dragon Mask was drawing on, it was, shall we say, *slanted*, at best. My first thought was the stories about both the tor and the sword at my side being "evil" should be weighed against the fact that they came from someone who had apparently drawn power from the depths of hell itself, power that had disintegrated Nelson-Hyde as *collateral damage.*

It reminded me of some of the "history" cited by any number of terrorists back home. Rewriting the past to justify all sorts of atrocities in the present.

Then, almost as one—except for Zimmerman—we looked over at Gunny, waiting for him to make the call. Hoping—again, almost as one—that he'd finally make the decision that would end this.

But he didn't. I could see that he was worried, that he didn't think that this was a good idea. I know I sure didn't want to go down into that blackness under the mountain. Looking around, I could see the stony faces of the other Marines, none of whom wanted to go down there, either.

And yet none of us were willing to show fear or be the first one to say, "Screw that noise."

Being a tunnel rat wasn't something that any of us had signed up for. We'd volunteered to do all sorts of dangerous stuff, to include jumping out of airplanes into hostile territory, with only five other dudes and whoever we could get on the radio for support. But tunnel rat takes a whole different level of crazy.

Sure, there were probably a couple would-be tunnel rats in the platoon. Or, rather, there had been. I'd known that Ridenour had been just that crazy.

But the captain had one of his "Good Ideas," and he wasn't going to let go of it. And while Gunny pulled him aside and remonstrated with him quietly, I could see that Sorenson was dead set on following through with the plan.

Gunny's voice was low, and I'm still slightly surprised that I could hear him as well as I could. "This is a point of no return, sir. If we go down there, we're trapped. And after that last little display, I'm not sure we should even be here in the first place."

The captain grabbed Gunny by the sleeve. "This is hardly the right time or place, Gunny." Never mind that we'd been after him about this since back at the tor. "We have nowhere else to go, no other allies. We have to work with what we've got. I would think that you, at least, would understand that. This kind of unconventional warfare environment requires some compromises." He furrowed his brows at Gunny, not without a glance at me. "Do you have another option? Anything besides fighting to our deaths back in that cave?"

"Sometimes fighting to the death is preferable to the alternative." Gunny's teeth were clenched, and I thought I knew why. On the surface, the captain had a point. We'd been surrounded, and we had no knowledge of the area, the local tribes, or even if there was any place where we could have found sanctuary. If Dragon Mask hadn't offered a truce, we might have been slowly strangled in that place.

But what was the alternative? To become the tools of a local warlord, one who, it was increasingly evident, was every bit as evil as any of the other monsters prowling the darkness around us?

I'd have preferred to have gone down fighting in that tor than get dragged into Dragon Mask's game. I'd been there before. My first platoon sergeant, Gunny Aguilar, had been through something similar in Afghanistan, and he'd hated and distrusted every militia leader in Syria as a consequence. I'd never gotten the whole story, but I'd gathered that there were a lot of dead people who hadn't been valid targets, thanks to a local Pashtun chieftain's games.

Now here we were, trapped in the same situation—only worse—thanks to the captain. And unfortunately, given the nature of the place we'd found ourselves, we didn't have a solid alternative plan. We simply didn't have enough information.

Under the circumstances, I would have thought that striking out cross-country, hunting for our food and avoiding contact until we found a better place to take shelter, would be far superior to the situation we found ourselves in.

Captain Sorenson nodded at Gunny's words and said, "Well, I don't agree. And I'm still in command." He turned toward the tunnels. "Staff Sergeant Zimmerman, take point. We'll have to use NODs and the IR illuminators on our PEQ-16s to see down there. The Dovos will follow, but we'll be in front since we have greater capability."

I waited for Gunny to refuse. Waited for that final break. After all, what was keeping the captain in command, here in this far, strange place? There was no Big Marine Corps here. There was nothing and no one to enforce the chain of command.

No one except for Gunny.

Looking back on it, I know why he didn't make the break then and there. I know why he hung on, trying to keep the platoon together at all costs. If the chain broke down, what was to keep all of us from splintering in a savage land where we'd be devoured piecemeal within a desperately short time if we struck out on our own without a plan or a destination? If he turned on the captain, what was to prevent any of us from turning on him?

I don't know if he imagined what the cost would be, even then. We were making it up as we went along. Gunny didn't make the break. He didn't draw the line in the sand then and there, before another line was crossed. A line that would change all of us forever.

We went into the dark.

CHAPTER 28

THE tunnel was rough-hewn and cold, though once we got deep enough in, it actually felt slightly warmer than outside. The deeper you get underground, the less the surface temperature penetrates. Soon we were moving down the darkened tunnel, moisture dripping from the walls, steam pouring from our mouths and noses. It was still cold down there, even if it was above freezing, and the moisture made the cold bite that much more bitterly than the deep freeze outside.

Marines were in front on the captain's insistence. The more I looked at it, the more I saw what an untenable position we'd been put in. Taramas's monsters lay ahead, inside the city, and the Dovos were behind, blocking the exit. Despite the losses they'd taken, they still outnumbered us by about two to one. So while I couldn't say there was no turning back, it would have been a hard fight if we tried it.

The pale light of day had long since vanished behind us. The Dovos lit torches to keep themselves from stumbling into each other and our trail element, which Bailey had taken up. These torches weren't exactly roaring bonfires on a stick like you see in the movies. Their flickering light only penetrated a few feet in the damp blackness, though the feeble glow went a lot farther in our NVGs.

Between the torchlight behind us and the PEQ-16 IR illuminators on Zimmerman's team's rifles, we could see fairly well, albeit limited to the narrow green circle where we had our heads pointed.

There just wasn't much of anything to see. Only damp stone walls and stone floor, chipped away by some long-ago laborers through solid rock, receding into the dark in front and behind. The tunnel descended steadily as it paralleled the ridgeline toward the city below. Its age was apparent; centuries of earthquakes, ground shifts, and simple landslides had opened cracks in some places, sometimes faintly and sometimes resulting in openings that looked to lead deeper into the mountainside. Other stretches had nearly collapsed, making passage more difficult. We had to crawl through a few times, one by one, squirming through spaces so narrow that some of the bigger guys had to shuck their chest rigs, never mind their rucks. Thankfully we never found our passage fully blocked by a cave-in

Time crawled as we crept closer and closer. I know I wasn't the only one that was tensing up, waiting for the inevitable ambush. Every crevice, every partial cave-in, every hole in the wall looked like it might hold a monster waiting to pop out and munch on a Marine's skull.

We moved ever deeper into the darkness without walking into an ambush. And we'd come across multiple spots that were ideal for one. Even when we had to toss rucks and jump across a gaping crack in the floor, nothing came out to eat us.

Finally, after what felt like days, we came to the gates.

Well, they weren't *gates*, really. More like ancient, cracked, iron-shod doors set into the rock. Again, the shifts in the mountainside had taken their toll, and the metal frame was crooked, the doors partially hanging from their hinges. One was clearly wedged in place and probably wouldn't budge short of blowing it to pieces. The other hung loose, offering a way deeper into the city.

Zimmerman moved up, joining Esposito at the door and shining his IR illuminator through the gap. Finally, the team leader nodded and heaved the door open as Esposito ducked through.

No gunfire sounded on the other side. Zimmerman and Baldinus went through, with Nagano following, not without some reluctance.

The rest of the platoon followed, slowly, one or two men at a time. Even with that door wedged partially open, we had a narrow space to move through, which made for a bit of a bottleneck. Given where we were, that wasn't helping my nervousness.

We finally all filtered through and found ourselves in a larger but still cramped room, with another reinforced door, standing ajar, opening onto a courtyard beyond. Both were empty and silent except for the rustle of gear and the faint scrape of weapons against gear.

I moved up to join Zimmerman at the door, peering through the opening at the courtyard. Scattered piles of rubble lay at the base of the glacier where it had slowly encroached on the open space, surrounding the massive, blocky edifice of black stone that loomed overhead.

"Holy crap. We got right to the citadel." Zimmerman craned his neck to look up at the tower above us. "Why isn't this guarded?"

"You're assuming that it's not guarded, versus we just can't see the guards," I answered. Looking up at the dark face of the citadel, I could see plenty of loopholes where someone—or something—might be watching. "There's no way they aren't ready for *something*, not after we showed up with Uergal and his army on our heels."

Zimmerman grunted in agreement. We didn't like each other very much, but the tactical situation wasn't subject to our likes and dislikes. We were still Recon Marines. The fight came first.

He peered at the tower, which was half-encased in bluish ice and snow. "I don't see a way in."

I scanned the courtyard, only then noticing the noise rising from outside. It sounded like most of Uergal's army had already closed in on the city, and I was pretty sure that they were not unopposed. That had to be the sound of an ancient battle—reduced down here to a distant roar of voices and clanging steel. I wondered if that was why Taramas didn't have visible guards on this particular hole in her defenses. I couldn't imagine that she didn't know about it, no matter how ruined the city appeared.

"There." I pointed. Stone steps led up to a landing about twenty feet above the courtyard. "That's probably the way in."

Zimmerman squinted at it.

Gurke was at my elbow. "I don't like that. That's a fatal funnel and a half."

"It might be our only way in, though." I chewed my lip. That was a mistake—despite the dampness in the tunnels and caves, I'd been so dehydrated by the cold that my lip cracked immediately. "Damn, I wish we had some frags."

"Flashbangs, you mean?" That must have been Baldinus's idea of being helpful.

"No, I mean frags. I don't care if anyone inside survives. From what we've seen, I seriously doubt there's anyone in there whose death I'd cry over."

The monsters that had come after us had convinced me that Taramas was hardly a good guy. Or girl, god... whatever.

Granted, we weren't on what I'd call the side of the angels right then, either. I was starting to wonder if there was any such thing here. All I'd seen so far were monsters, savages, and more monsters.

Ultimately, though, we didn't have frags. And there was no way that anyone inside that tower wasn't going to notice when we sprinted across that empty, windswept courtyard and ran up the steps. Which meant that forcing that tower door—provided it was open and we didn't have to breach a barred door every bit as thick as the heavy, iron-bound doors we were currently peering around—was going to be a meat grinder.

There had to be another way in. And, as if to prove that he'd been planning this for a *very* long time, Dragon Mask obliged.

"There is another way. Come." He turned toward a darkened, shadowed portion of the guardhouse, or whatever that room was. He cast around for a while, then started pulling at the rubble piled in the corner. "Yes! Here it is. The Scrolls of Skoloth described the citadel in some detail. This place was fought over for many years before Taramas overthrew the old evil that built the city. There are passages throughout the mountainside. Remnants from long ago when the defenders had to reach the outposts without exposing themselves aboveground." More of the rubble cascaded away with a rattle of stone, and he reached out for a torch. In the feeble light, amplified by our PVS-15s, he revealed an ancient trap door.

It opened with a horrific shriek of rusty metal and a dry breath of musty air, revealing crude stone steps leading down into utter blackness.

"This will take us to the cellars beneath the citadel." Dragon Mask stood back from the opening, waving us forward. I didn't like that. But it had already been established that we were there to do Dragon Mask's dirty work since we had the guns.

"Team Three has point." Of course Captain Sorenson had to step in, micromanage, and put the one team leader who wasn't daydreaming about slitting his throat on point. Zimmerman.

Esposito led the way down, and one by one, we all followed.

* * *

The catacombs beneath the citadel itself were far less battered and damaged than the passage that had led us under the ridgeline into the city. Lined with cut stone, it appeared that a lot more effort had gone into their construction, too.

That didn't make them any less creepy.

As we moved through, peering at the stone hallways through the narrow green circles our NVGs provided, I could have sworn that I heard whispers, rustles of movement, and distant cries and screams. When I stopped and tried to focus on them, the sounds faded, and I could only hear our own movement and the rasp of my own breathing in my ears.

Esposito stopped abruptly, and the whole column backed up. A moment later, the word filtered back. They'd reached a four-way intersection, and neither Esposito nor Zimmerman knew which way to go.

Unfortunately, judging by the whispered conference between the captain and Dragon Mask right behind us, they didn't seem to know which way to go, either. Dragon Mask, despite his insistence that he had detailed information about this place, didn't seem to have expected a labyrinth. He'd probably figured that the tunnels went straight to a primary guardroom or cellar under the citadel.

That was, of course, assuming that there was *one* cellar. I could envision a bunch of chambers hollowed out for storage, prisons, guardhouses, and refuges. I was no tunnel rat, nor was I an expert in catacombs, but what I remembered about historical tunnel systems—especially in places like Iwo Jima or Cu Chi, places that the Marine Corps had made a point of studying—they were rarely linear or symmetrical.

Before the route could be decided, though, all hell broke loose.

I couldn't see what was happening, but gunfire erupted down at the intersection. Even suppressed, the reports were brutally loud in the enclosed rock walls. Rodeffer and I pushed forward, dropping our rucks as we went. We'd have to retrieve them later, but trying to fight in close quarters with a ruck on is a recipe for disaster.

We reached the intersection, where Zimmerman, Baldinus, Nagano, and Esposito were pouring rifle fire down the cross passage. They weren't paying any mind to the other two passages, and as we came around the corner, it was easy enough to see why.

The cross passage was swarming with gigantic, pale, spiny worms, writhing toward us with gaping mouths like leeches. I couldn't see any eyes, even in the PEQ-16s' bright IR illumination. Not that it should have been a surprise with subterranean worms, but it was just that much more unsettling as those things squirmed toward us, moving far too quickly for their size.

They also weren't reacting much to the 5.56 rounds zipping through their pale flesh, either.

I quickly checked the two passages that had no guns on them. They were empty, still, and dark. I didn't know how long that would last, now that the thunderous announcement of our presence echoed down through the rock, but for the moment we were clear. Which didn't solve the problem of those worms, which were getting closer by the second.

Zimmerman and his team started to back up and retreated into the passage we'd already come down, before one of those things could get close enough to bite. The bullets *were* slowing them down but didn't appear to be doing much more than that.

"Reloading!" The fire slackened as Nagano dropped his empty mag and slapped in another. Thirty fewer rounds left to fight with.

We were all going to be down to blades, 'hawks, and sticks before too long.

And then where would we be with Dragon Mask and his savages?

More immediately, of course, was the problem of how to fight giant cave worms that didn't die when you shot them.

Gurke thought faster than the rest of us, fortunately. He shouldered past Santos and Smith, holding two burning torches he'd taken from the Dovos. He handed one to me, and we waded forward as the worms reached the intersection and Zimmerman and Esposito fell back around the corner.

Without eyes, they didn't react to the light. But they sure reacted to the heat.

The closest one reared up, its mouthparts glistening in the flickering glow of the fire, and I hammered my torch into it.

The thing *sizzled* as the flames licked at it and the smoldering, pitch-soaked knot was thrust against its pale, damp flesh. I'd gotten a little overly enthusiastic—the torch guttered and almost went out as it came up against the worm's slime. But the torch stayed lit, and the worm's flesh shriveled and turned black as it reared back with a hiss.

Gurke had been a little more cautious, but while he swung the torch at the next worm, bringing the flames within a few inches of it, the thing was apparently so insensate that it didn't react. Even as I pressed my attack, jabbing at the one I'd burned and the next one behind it, he was forced back as his target stretched toward him, its mouthparts working. Only when he jammed the torch right into its gullet did it hiss and fall back, blistered and burned.

Several long minutes went on like that, jabbing and swinging at the pale giant leeches with our torches, holding the line as they tried to reach us and suck us dry. My arm was getting tired, but the worms hated the fire. Once burned a couple of times, they retreated, making awful gurgling noises. The trouble was, as soon as one fell back, two more came slithering out of the dark.

Santos and Gunny had joined us with two more torches. Gunny looked back over his shoulder. "Somebody watch those other tunnels!"

I didn't hear any more gunfire behind us, so that was a good sign. I focused on the monstrous worms coming out of the blackness. I'd flipped my NVGs up so that they wouldn't get whited out whenever I swung my torch in front of my face, so all I could see was when a glistening, white lump of slimy flesh humped up out of the dark and into the torch's guttering circle of light.

The four of us kept fighting, using the torches relentlessly against a seemingly endless foe in the subterranean blackness.

It took me a second to realize that darkness and quiet had replaced the writhing worms. We stood there with our torches held out, panting and sweating despite the damp underground chill. The worms had retreated, burned and shriveled and in mindless pain.

"Ruck up," Gunny croaked. "We have to keep moving before somebody comes down to investigate all the noise."

He'd barely finished speaking when Rodeffer opened fire down the passage in front of us.

CHAPTER 29

THE echoes of suppressed gunfire died away as I turned to join Rodeffer. "Whatchya got?"

"Don't know for sure." He lowered his rifle. His suppressor was still glowing slightly in IR. "I just saw eyes, teeth, and one of those single-edged blades like the Dovos carry. Not sure if I hit it."

I scanned the dark passage that sloped slightly upward and away from the intersection where we were holding, looking for any more monsters coming out of the shadows to try and eat our faces off. Our IR illuminators only reached to the bend about fifty yards beyond. Whatever had been there, whatever Rodeffer had shot at, it was gone.

"It'll be back, whatever it was." I didn't doubt that Rodeffer had seen *something*. And if it had been armed, I had zero issue with him shooting it. Hell, if it had big enough teeth that he'd noticed on NVGs, that counted as "armed" in my book, after everything we'd seen so far.

I turned back toward Gunny and the rest where Dragon Mask and the captain were huddled just short of the intersection. "We need to move while we still can. If we get pinned down in this damned tunnel, we're fucked."

Dragon Mask was consulting something in his hand, then pointed straight ahead.

"Go straight," Captain Sorenson said, apparently thinking none of us were looking at Dragon Mask's hand signal.

I tapped Rodeffer. Zimmerman's team had fallen back from the worms, and I wasn't inclined to stay put long enough to reshuffle to the captain's preferred movement order. He got up, but that was when I remembered that we'd left our rucks about twenty yards back. I was *also* not inclined to leave them behind. Who knew when we were going to have to run for our lives? This was hardly a secure area.

So, we let Zimmerman and Esposito move up while we worked our way back to grab our rucks. That put us in the trail element, right in front of the Dovos, as we moved through the intersection.

I could have sworn that I heard noises from both directions as we passed back through the intersection. I scanned with NVGs and PEQ-16 but only saw blank, dark, stone walls. But I had no doubt that Taramas's monstrosities were going to respond to the noise we'd already made fighting those worms.

As we hustled down the passage, the glow in my NVGs grew more intense. That wasn't just IR illuminators. After a few more paces, I started to see the dim, greenish glow in my peripheral vision, around the outside of my NVGs, too.

We slowed as Zimmerman and his team neared the portal into the next room. That was where the greenish glow was coming from. They paused, though I didn't know what they were waiting for. There wasn't a door to stack up on. Finally, they flowed into the room, weapons up and sweeping across a vaulted stone chamber.

By the time my team got there, the chamber had been cleared. It was roughly octagonal, if you counted the passage we'd just come down and the matching one leading deeper in. The room was empty except for four sconces set on pillars in the floor, lit with flickering green flames.

That was disturbing. If this place had no function, and there was no one here, who turned on the lights?

I clearly wasn't the only one thinking that. M4s were still up, and the tension was written on every man's face. Zimmerman's team covered the eastern passage, Gurke's the southern, and we turned back to watch the north. The Dovos had come in after us, and of course that meant we had to watch them, too.

Even with the visible threats and danger areas covered, it didn't *feel* like we had security in place. I joined Gunny, Gurke, Zimmerman, and Bailey in the center of the room. Dragon Mask and the captain conferred beneath one of the green torches, not far from us. Every Marine kept both hands on their rifles, scanning the walls, the floor, and the ceiling, as if we were all just waiting for *something* to pop out to ambush us.

There was something very unnatural about that place. Maybe it was the green light. Or just the fact that the green lights were *lit*, in a place where there was no reason to have them lit.

Dragon Mask looked up as Gurke fixed his gaze on one of the green flames—looking curiously at them. I hadn't looked directly at them, part of a habit formed by a relatively long career in which looking directly at light sources was a bad idea, given that it destroys your night adaptation

Dragon Mask stiffened. "Do not look at the lights!"

The warning was almost too little, too late. Gurke was staring, his eyes locked open, his body fixed and immobile. I lunged at him, knocking him away from the pillar and the flickering green flames. My tackle almost didn't dislodge him. It was as if his feet had nearly become rooted to the floor. I'm not a small man, and with my ruck on my back, I weighed almost two hundred fifty pounds even after a lot of calories burned on not a lot of food for over a week. With the full force of my legs pushing me, I knocked Gurke sprawling, and his rifle hit the stone with a clatter as he fell.

I interposed myself between him and the light. As my shadow fell across him, Gurke blinked and looked around, as if confused as to why he was on the floor. He looked up at me, and I could see his bewilderment even past his PVS-15s.

"What the hell just happened?"

I reached down to help him up. "You got an eyeful of one of those lights. Dragon Mask says that's a bad idea. From the looks of things, he's right. You locked right up."

He started to glance up at one of the green flames but checked himself and ran a hand over his face. "Damn. Thanks, brother." He looked around. "Nobody look at the fucking green lights!"

The captain looked at him as if he'd just taken a dump in the punchbowl at the Marine Corps Ball, never mind that it was a warning that everyone really did need to hear. But Captain Sorenson was ready to brief our next move, so he was put out that Gurke had upstaged him, or something.

"Ekersakar says that he's certain that our goal is on this level, right over there." He pointed to the east. "He doesn't know what we'll have to face to get it, but this is the final push before we get out of here."

He made that sound so simple. As if escaping from the catacombs beneath one enemy monster's fortress with some kind of artifact so valued that it was buried in said catacombs, while another monster who wanted our ally's head on a platter was outside, was just going to be one more regular tactical problem to solve.

Meanwhile, we were strung out, low on ammo, and increasingly starting to dread whatever else was coming. We were allied with savages led by an evil sorcerer, and being hunted by monsters. There was no light at the end of the tunnel. I don't think any of us except maybe the captain and Zimmerman actually believed that Dragon Mask was going to send us home if he got the kind of power he was after, or if it would be worth it in the long run if he did.

But we were already deep in the enemy's fortress, outnumbered and surrounded by the Dovos, never mind Taramas's monsters. The only way out—unless Gunny was willing to give the word to turn on Dragon Mask, and by extension, the captain—was through.

So, we moved. Heading out of the green-lit room and into the darkness of the passage to the east, weapons up and looking for threats, even as shouts and the shuffle of feet began to filter down the tunnels behind us.

The monsters were coming.

* * *

The passage split again into a T-intersection with the joining tunnel to our right. Another lurid glow spilled from that passageway. It looked rather less than inviting, so naturally, that was the direction Dragon Mask pointed us.

Zimmerman didn't hesitate, though he still popped the corner in a high-low with Esposito, one man taking a knee and the other standing above and behind him before they leaned out at the same time, presenting two rifle barrels at any threats while still shielded by the stone walls. Nagano covered down the long passageway ahead of us that disappeared into the blackness a lot quicker than it should have, given that Nagano had his PEQ-16 shining its IR spotlight down the tunnel. The spot disappeared within about fifty yards, if not less.

Neither man opened fire, but soon Zimmerman stepped out into the hallway as Esposito got to his feet and joined him. Nagano moved up to continue covering the long passage, while the rest of us followed Zimmerman and Esposito.

That tunnel ended in a low-ceilinged antechamber, with a single brazier burning with what looked like normal fire at first glance, until you noticed the lines of purplish lightning racing through the flames. I didn't look too closely, and this time none of the others did, either.

The walls were lined with little alcoves, in which stood suits of armor. They were unlike anything I'd seen in this frozen, barbaric place. Each one was slightly different, but they were all suits of full plate, like something you'd see in some preserved castle in Europe. Each held a massive weapon, blade down, in gauntleted hands.

And they were watching us.

I don't mean they seemed somehow watchful. Every helmet was turned toward us, their empty eye slits trained on the Marines and Dovos flowing into the room.

At first, it might have been explained as just a trick, every suit arranged so that its helmet was trained on the entrance. The psychological effect after what we'd been through on the way in there would be undeniable.

But then they started moving.

The first one came off its dais and swung for Esposito. He wasn't ready for it, and the massive, rune-carved axe came crashing down on his shoulder, cleaving through his collarbone and sinking deep into his chest with a sickening *crunch*. His knees buckled under him as his blood painted the rocky ceiling, and the suit of armor ripped the axe clear.

Zimmerman shot it at almost point-blank range, but while the bullet punched through the helmet, it had no effect at all.

That was all I needed to see. We were way too short on ammunition to waste it shooting at things that didn't die when you filled them with bullets. I slung my rifle, hauled my shield down off my ruck—I'd worked up a cool little sling system with 550 cord—and drew my sword.

The captain might not like my using it with the hilt uncovered, but I didn't care. I deflected a rushing mace with the shield—even without being stupid and trying to fully block it, the impact still hurt like hell—and jabbed my sword at the base of the thing's helmet.

The first blow didn't go home but skittered off the faceplate, leaving a bright scar on the pitch-black metal. But to my surprise, the thing retreated. Not far, but it retreated.

"Get back to the doorway!" Gunny bellowed. Somebody fired past my shoulder, hammering a Mozambique—two to the chest, one to the head—into another of the armored figures, but he may as well have spat on it.

I took a step back, even as the line of armored figures advanced on us, coming around the brazier and forming up, shoulder to shoulder. They made no sound except for the clank of their plates and the creak of ancient, dried-out leather. There was dust on every one of them.

We were out of time, though. Even as the closest armored figures took another step, their weapons poised to strike, an inhuman scream echoed from the rear, followed by Dovos war cries, the clash of weapons, and the rending sounds of flesh being torn asunder. More high-pitched screams of agony reverberated through the rocky halls, mostly human.

We could fight the monsters coming at us from behind, or we could drive through and possibly capture what they were trying to protect. That was *if* we could figure out how to kill these silent, ominous, armored figures that continued to slowly advance. The animated suits of armor on the flanks closed in behind the vanguard as they neared the door.

To my right and left, Zimmerman and Baldinus dumped more rounds at the oncoming figures, bullets punching right through ancient plate where they should have pulped hearts and lungs, or smashed through brainstems. Nothing so much as fazed them.

"Melee up!" I never imagined I'd ever hear that as a Recon Marine, and I doubt that Gunny had ever thought he'd say it. But he shouldered past Baldinus and joined me, that battered, blunted axe in his hands. It was probably better than nothing.

Baldinus slipped around behind me, drawing out a spiked club he'd picked up somewhere along the way. Zimmerman gave him a withering look, but the yoked, blond young man didn't seem to notice.

"I'll take lead. Keep them off me." I had a hunch at that point. I was too strung out for anything more. But there was something about that sword in my hand. One of them had backed up when I'd hit it, even though I'd only scratched its armor.

I waded in.

Blows rained down on my shield, and the wood splintered behind the glued rawhide facing. If I hadn't already defaced the symbols on it, that few minutes in that tiny, cold stone room would have done it.

An axe ripped half the facing off. Gunny got his own axe between me and a sword blow. Baldinus brought his club crashing down on a helmet in the split second the axe I'd deflected with my shield was out of action. He dented the helm, but the blow didn't seem to have any more effect than the bullets had.

That was when I stepped in and stabbed my blade into the tiny gap in the armpit that had opened in that momentary exchange of blows.

It didn't kill it. My angle was wrong to hit whatever the stygian knight used as a heart. I might have hit a brachial artery if it had been truly alive. But it wasn't.

It wasn't even close.

Living things don't have an armored sleeve just suddenly fall off and leave…nothing. The armor was hollow.

I brought the blade back, unconsciously doing what I'd been trained to with a knife in the Marine Corps Martial Arts Program, which we'd all sort of laughed about back in the day. Back in The World. Before we found ourselves in a position to fight face-to-face with knives, swords, and axes.

I was jostled from behind as the screams and other sounds of desperate fighting grew louder. We were caught between the hammer and the anvil, and if we didn't unleash some serious violence of action in the next few seconds, we were going to get crushed.

Gunny saw that instinctively and faster than I did. He'd also seen what had just happened when I'd stabbed that animated suit of armor in the armpit. While I was still trying to wrap my head around the fact that I was fighting *animated, empty suits of armor*, he took advantage of the situation.

Ducking beneath another swipe of a mace, he brought that battered, blunted axe up with a hard uppercut that knocked the now one-armed suit of armor's helmet back, opening a gap between the faceplate and the gorget. "Hit it!"

The point of my sword was already in a position aimed right at that gap. I made the thrust.

The sword went inside—all the way back to punch through rotting, crumbling leather padding before hitting the metal with a *clang* that was almost inaudible over the rest of the cacophony of battle around us. The crash that followed as the suit suddenly collapsed into its component parts on the stone floor, however, was pretty loud.

Even as that first one fell apart, another brought its sword down on my shield, cleaving through the wood and hide nearly to my hand. I let go just before it was wrenched out of my grip, but I still had that sling around me. I was yanked off my feet, which probably saved my life, as another axe whistled through the air where my head had been a moment before.

As I stumbled and fell, Gunny was going to town, swinging his own axe like a madman, crashing its already notched and blunted edge into joints, helmets, or whatever he could reach. He wasn't trying to kill any of them—not that they could be *killed*, since they weren't alive—he was just trying to keep them off balance and off me.

He wasn't just flailing, either, I saw as I rolled on top of my ruck and hammered the point of the sword up into an armored skirt, cutting the spectral "ligaments" that kept an armored leg—I forget the technical term—upright. That suit crashed to the floor, and I heaved myself up, untangling myself from my ruined shield. I tackled it before it could bring that sword to bear. Pointing my own sword down, I put all my weight on it and forced it down under the helmet. It met no resistance, again, and the suit fell apart under me.

A ringing clash and a grunt sounded above me, and I rolled off the pieces of armor in time to see Baldinus clinched with another stygian knight, his club held with both hands, trying to fend off the spike of that thing's warhammer as it bore down on him. It was trying to force the spike into his throat by main force.

I hacked at the back of its knee and it went down to one knee, dragging Baldinus's club down with it. The unearthly knight didn't think to let go of one end, and he was pulled down, until I got a knee under myself and stabbed down into the breastplate, roughly where the neck would meet the shoulder. The animated armor froze for a split second, then fell apart.

Gunny was desperately keeping the other three off my back, blocking and deflecting a rain of blows, his axe moving faster than I would have imagined possible. He never once overextended, keeping the blade and the haft between himself and the stygian knights, striking as quick as a rattlesnake and then drawing back before they could find an opening.

We'd always looked up to Gunny Taylor as a hell of a Recon Marine. He was a great shot, a sound tactician, and he knew all the little tidbits of the job that made Recon Marines "jacks of all trades." I don't think any of us ever thought that Gunny knew how to fight in close quarters with medieval weapons, though.

Maybe he didn't. Maybe it was something about this place that had awakened a talent that even he hadn't suspected. I don't know.

But for those few seconds, that blinding speed and sheer ferocity kept me from getting chopped to pieces, even as the rest of the platoon and the Dovos were forced into the antechamber by the savagery of the fight out in the passageway.

I surged to my feet, grabbing the sword hilts with both hands, just like I had when fighting that hunter in the snow. My first thrust missed, the point ricocheting off the armor's pauldron. I almost lost my head as the thing riposted. Only that quick retraction I'd learned saved me, allowing me to get the blade just barely between the axe and my skull. My bump helmet wasn't going to protect against that.

On instinct, I grabbed the axe blade with one gloved hand—by some miracle it didn't slice me open—and shouldered into the thing, getting under the knight's arm and jamming the blade up where it would have had a chin if it were a living, breathing man. The helmet went flying as the rest fell apart, getting underfoot as the next one swung for my knee.

Fortunately, I was getting a rhythm as Gunny battered the last one back and gave me some space to deal with this opponent. I kept my balance as the armor collapsed under my weight and quickly backstepped to avoid the coming blow, countering with a stab for the faceplate. I wasn't trying to get a kill—I just wanted to make that thing back off a little. Under most circumstances, that's all I would have accomplished. But somehow, I hit just right, and the blade went in through the eye slit.

The armor collapsed under the helmet, but now the helmet was wedged on the end of my blade. Gunny was getting forced back as he tired and the automaton rained a pitiless series of blows against his axe. Most of the platoon was now in the antechamber with us. I could see the movement and the glow of torches as the Dovos fought and died in the passageway behind us.

I kicked the helmet off the end of the sword and closed in on the last hollow knight, even as Dragon Mask dashed for the darkened chamber that had been our objective, with the captain, Zimmerman, and a handful of the Dovos at his heels. I wanted to curse at them, but I had more immediate concerns.

The armored automaton hadn't budged, even while Gunny whaled away at it, leaving big dents in the armor. I didn't have much of an opening to get at it, especially with how crowded the antechamber was getting. Taramas's guards were pressing the fight, hard.

I jabbed at the armored figure, my blows skipping off its plates until I timed one badly and it swatted my sword aside before a riposte that almost tore my throat out. I jerked back just in time, but its axe clipped my chin, putting a notch in my helmet's chinstrap and drawing blood.

Gunny hit it one more time, then shoulder-charged it, hammering it back into the wall and trying to get under its weapon arm. It battered at him with the other gauntlet, but the blows landed on his ruck and bump helmet. Gunny gritted his teeth and bore the attack, driving the thing into the rock behind it.

I checked the passageway we'd come from. Towering, gray-skinned warriors with glowing red eyes were cutting the Dovos to dog treats in the tunnel. In that momentary look, I saw one of our savage allies nearly hacked in half by an upward stroke from the base of the ribcage that ended at the collarbone. The Dovos's mottled armor barely slowed the angular, single-edged sword down. Another nearby had just had his skull split to the chin by the same weapon.

The Dovos were wavering. I could see it. More of them were falling back as the monsters kept coming.

I turned back to Gunny and his opponent. It appeared that my sword was the only thing that could kill these things. But I didn't have an opening. Gunny was in the way. And he couldn't move without opening himself up to that axe, which was already moving remorselessly toward his neck.

But I remembered that I didn't need a lot of force if I could get the point into a gap in the armor. I grabbed the axe, lending my strength to help keep it off Gunny, and jabbed the point of my sword under the gauntlet. The axe was released into my hand. I dropped it, reached inside before the thing could swing at me with the empty vambrace, and stabbed it in the "neck."

It fell apart under Gunny, and he collapsed on top of it for a moment, until I got my hand under his arm and helped him up.

The two of us turned as the last of the Dovos broke, howling in terror, and sprinted away from the looming, gray-skinned warriors in the doorway.

CHAPTER 30

I didn't have time to sheath the sword, but that was why I'd tied a lanyard of 550 cord behind the pommel. I had to drop it and snatch my M4 back up, letting the blade dangle from my wrist. I dumped five rounds into a leering, red-eyed face from ten feet away as one of those gray-skinned, black-armored monstrosities came charging at me, jagged blade held ready to strike. My first round went into the rim of the black shield held just below his eyes. The next four walked up his nose and forehead, spattering blood and brain matter across the armored mask of the one behind him.

More were coming, and they were moving fast. Gunny blasted a masked one and fell back behind the brazier. I followed as four more, one of them so big that he almost filled the portal alone, spilled inside. That one, a gigantic cyclops—not even joking, he had a single, massive red eye in the center of his forehead—swung a hammer at the nearest Dovo, a burly, screaming berserker who wouldn't have stood a chance even if he'd tried to block. The hammer smashed his skull to bloody fragments with a sickening *crunch.*

Gunny, Rodeffer, and I dumped rounds into that roaring cyclops, but it was not going down. It was hurt, it was bleeding, but its skull must have been grizzly bear thick. Even as I shot it twice in the face, it *still* didn't drop but came thundering after us. One swing of that hammer smashed the brazier in half. Sparks and little purple lightning bolts flew as the coals spilled out or went flying.

Baldinus yelled in pain as one of them landed on him, and his weapon's fire ceased as he tried to frantically shake the burning coal off.

More of the black-armored monsters poured into the room. Space was running out as we were steadily forced back toward the far door. Bailey killed one with a contact shot, his suppressor punched into its cheek, just before it could swing its sword into his neck.

Then all hell really broke loose.

Something happened in that chamber Dragon Mask had disappeared into. I can't really describe the sensation that went through us. It was almost like an earthquake, except that the ground didn't move. It was as if reality *blinked*, just for a fraction of a second. A shudder that had nothing to do with the physical went through everyone and everything in that room. Even Taramas's gray-skinned warriors froze.

Then the nightmare came howling out of the portal and right into the middle of the fight.

It was hard to look at. My eyes and brain rebelled at its very existence. As I think back I have to fight my memory, which doesn't want to remember that thing. It was almost skeletally lean, with too many limbs, wings, and an overabundance of eyes. It looked like it was made of tar… except when it looked almost like smoke. Smoke with eyes and a wide, leering mouthful of razor teeth.

It tore through the Dovos closest to the portal first. The first one it hit turned to pink mist and spattered across the wall as if he'd exploded. The second it grabbed, wrapping talons as long as my forearm around his throat, and lifted off the floor as the savage screamed in abject, animal terror, before being ripped in half. Lengthwise. The shower of blood and guts hardly added to the carnage already sprayed across half the room.

We were all shooting at it, but we may as well have been throwing spitballs. Whatever it was, it came from the same place as that horror that had turned Nelson-Hyde to red mush. It shot toward Fortuna, moving so fast that it *blurred*. Our Comms NCO's head simply *disappeared* when it hit him, a fine red spray adding to the gore coating the antechamber, sizzling in the spilled coals that were still spitting purplish lightning bolts.

We had all stepped into hell.

Then, a second horror, bulkier and sprouting several dozen tentacles around easily as many eyes and mouths, appeared in the doorway as the first threw Fortuna's corpse into the cyclops' face.

No one needed to be told. Marines and Dovos alike fell back to the passage across from our entry. The gray-skinned, red-eyed mutants fell back, too, fortunately in the opposite direction.

Running away might stick in our craw, especially with at least two of our own cut off on the other side of those horrors. Facing Taramas's twisted minions was preferable to that unwinnable fight.

At least we could kill *them*.

The next few seconds were a mad scramble. Gurke and his team set up on the door, and Gurke screamed, "*Set!*" because he couldn't just start shooting with so many of us in the way. The rush through the door was less of a flow than a desperate flood, as gibbering panic threatened to overtake more than a few of us.

As soon as he had an open field of fire, Gurke started dumping rounds into the antechamber, most of them going into the monstrous warriors of Taramas as they were torn apart by the black, oily horrors. It wasn't going to do much, but it might slow down any pursuit.

I got past Gurke and paused just long enough to sheathe my sword, before grabbing Smith and Rodeffer as we rushed through the door and into the darkness of the tunnels again. "We're taking point!"

Not that I was so eager to run away I had to shout about it, but right then it didn't look like anyone else was paying enough attention to the direction we were *going*. Everyone was pretty focused on getting away from those Things That Should Not Be. Those Dovos who'd gotten out even more so than we—they were already almost out of sight in the darkness.

That single-minded retreat almost cost us everything. As we got to the next intersection, more of Taramas's warriors came howling up the passage toward us.

Rock, meet Hard Place. Deformed, mutant warriors to our right, blank rock ahead, a gibbering horror from the depths of hell itself behind us, blackness to the left.

Smith opened up, tearing into the lead warrior, a horse-faced giant with four arms. His bolt locked back on an empty mag even as his last round tore the monster's brain stem apart, and the massive corpse crashed onto its face on the stone floor. I brought my own M4 up as he pivoted away and shot the next one in the mouth. The corpulent thing with a yard-long tongue and a cleaver in one meaty fist slowed, stopped, and then slumped to the floor. It had taken a second for the news to penetrate that it was dead.

Gunny ran past me and slapped my shoulder. "Last man!" I turned and followed, immediately hugging the left-hand wall as Santos poured fire down the right.

Only then did I realize that we were running *down,* deeper into the mountain. Deeper into the dark. Taramas's monsters were between us and escape. We'd bought ourselves a few minutes, but we might not get much more than that.

I should have been thinking about my last moments. Should have been making my peace. Death was inevitable at that point. But I was too focused on staying alive and killing as many of these monsters as possible before they got close enough to tear us apart.

We got a bit of a reprieve as the tentacled horror behind us burst into the intersection, ripping a barrel-chested, skull-faced, three-eyed monstrosity to bloody pieces. Taramas's ghastly warriors slowed, faced by something even weirder and more evil than they, as it shrieked and threw bits and pieces of their fellow against the walls and ceiling of the passage. One of them started to chant, and the air *crackled.*

Gunny grabbed Santos, and we hustled away into the blackness.

Whatever was about to happen back there, it wasn't good. But it might buy us a little more time.

The passage led downward, and even as the noise of battle receded behind us, the creeping dread got worse. We kept getting farther and farther away from the light, farther and farther from hope. I couldn't see how many of us had made it out of that antechamber, but there were only a handful of Dovos, and I was pretty sure we'd left some Marines behind, too.

I hated it with every fiber of my being, but the alternative was suicide. Going back into that hell of monsters and sorcery would be a good way to die horribly and do our brothers zero good.

Of course, it looked like we might die horribly anyway, either starving in the dark or being hunted down by eyeless *things* that we'd never see as our batteries died and left us blind under the roots of the mountains.

I turned back, checking our six. I'd ended up in the rear, with Gunny just ahead of me. As a team leader, I probably should have been farther up, but right then, there were no billets, no rank. There were only desperate men, tired, strung out, and being chased by monsters out of our darkest nightmares.

Shining my IR illuminator up the passage, back the way we'd come, I caught a glimpse of movement and then saw the footpad they'd sent after us. So, the monsters hadn't just let us go while they focused on the horrors in their basement.

That thing *probably* wasn't going to try to attack us. It was small, pale, and scrawny. It crawled on all fours, creeping along the floor at the base of one of the walls. Despite our making a bit of noise, our rucks creaking and boots thumping faintly on the stone floor, I could still tell that this thing wasn't making a sound.

They had sent it to pace us and spy on us. They wanted to keep tabs on us for later, after they'd dealt with the horrors Dragon Mask had summoned.

I had no doubt that Dragon Mask had summoned those things.

I lifted my rifle and peered through the RMR mounted to the top of the ACOG. I could have used the PEQ-16's IR laser, but something made me hesitate. The slinking little creature shouldn't have been able to see us. One of the Dovos had kept a torch, but they were far ahead, the faint, flickering glow lost in the shadows. The only light most of the platoon was moving on was from IR illuminators on NVGs and PEQ-16s.

If the spy could see in IR, pointing a laser at it might just give us all away.

So, I lined up the red dot on it as it crawled forward. I waited as it got closer, its eyes wide, staring lamps in my 15s.

It suddenly jerked its head up and stared at me. It had noticed that I'd stopped. Too late.

The harsh *crack* of the shot reverberated up and down the tunnel, and I couldn't help but wince. The creature let out a keening scream as the bullet tore through its torso, and it flopped and thrashed on the floor, howling in agony, until it finally went still, its arms and legs tucked in like a dead cockroach.

"That could have been quieter." Gunny was at my elbow. "Let's hustle."

CHAPTER 31

WE went deeper into the dark. I can't tell you how far we went or for how long. I didn't dare look at my watch. I wasn't even sure that it was keeping accurate time anymore, anyway. It had seemed off for a while, and we'd never been able to figure out what time it was here to begin with.

After what felt like a small eternity, the lead element slowed and halted. Gunny moved forward to check it out, while I held rear security with my team. All of us had made it. Santos rounded Farrar up and joined the three of us in the trail element. We spread out across the passage, taking a knee on the cold, damp stone, feeling every ache, bruise, and ounce of weight in our rucks and chest rigs. "Ounces equal pounds, and pounds equal pain," went the old Recon saying. It had never been more true.

The adrenaline had started wearing off as we'd moved away from the fight, and that was dangerous. Exhaustion was setting in. None of us had eaten in a while, either. But we were hardly in a secure position where we could go down for even a couple of hours.

I blinked repeatedly and bit my tongue until it was about to bleed to force myself to stay awake and keep scanning the tunnel behind us. Damp, rough-hewn stone walls receded into total blackness past the dim green circle of my IR floodlight.

I heard the rustle of movement and boots on stone behind me. A moment later, a whisper came back. "Move up."

We got up far too slowly, fighting our rucks all the way, and moved further down the passage. After a few paces we came to where Chambers and Herrera were holding security on the tunnel, just outside another opening to the right. Gunny appeared in the opening. "In here. Watch your step and keep to the walls. There's a big pit in the middle of the floor."

I stepped inside and then ushered the rest of the team in. "Last man," Santos called quietly as he came in, tapping Chambers on the ruck. Chambers and Herrera fell in behind, moving to take security on the doorway but out of the tunnel.

Looking around, I took stock. There were about sixteen of us left. Most were rucksack-flopped around the walls of the chamber, weapons across knees, heads either back against rucks or bowed toward chests. Gunny and Doc were the only headquarters element guys left. Nagano and Baldinus were all that remained of Team 2. Bailey still had Synar and Applegate. Gurke was down to Chambers, Herrera, and Franks. My team had gotten lucky—we hadn't lost a man since Stanley had been pulled overboard by that sea troll, what felt like a lifetime ago.

About half a dozen of the Dovos were still with us, huddled in the far corner around a guttering torch, holding their axes and crude, single-edged swords loosely. I watched them narrowly for a moment and realized that they weren't going to be a threat for a while. They looked shell-shocked, staring into the darkness with expressions that looked haunted even in the blurred shades of green that my PVS-15s showed me.

I looked over at Gunny as Gurke and Bailey joined us. Nagano was still sitting against his ruck, staring at nothing. Gunny didn't call him over but let him recover a little. We all probably needed it, but we were far from out of danger.

"Is this it?" Gurke sounded a little strung out. "Is everybody else dead?"

We'd inserted with twenty-nine men. We'd lost almost half.

"Maybe." Gunny's voice was grim, but there was no give in him. We were still alive and still in the fight, so he was going to keep his head up and keep driving forward. "Nobody's dead until we've seen a body. Until then, they're MIA." He looked around. "We're moderately secure here, but that won't last. Take a breather and get ready to move. We might have to fight our way out—though that might mean we stay down here for a bit until things settle down. Conor smoked the tail they sent after us, but that probably only bought us time. How's everyone doing for ammo?"

That took a minute. When it all shook out, we were down to about three mags per man. Frankly, I was surprised we still had that much left after the chaos of that fight back up in that antechamber.

We'd just finished the ACE reports when I thought I heard something outside. I lifted a finger for silence as I stepped over to Chambers by the door and strained my battered hearing for what I thought I'd just heard.

Gunny was watching me carefully, but he shushed the rest as I cocked my head and listened.

I couldn't quite believe what I was hearing at first. In fact, the more I listened, the more I thought it was a trap, some new terror playing particularly sick mind games.

Somewhere, down in the dark, in the direction we'd been moving, a clear, lilting voice was singing softly. I couldn't make out the words, but while there was a mournful note to the song, there was something pure to it—something comforting.

I didn't trust it.

No, that's not quite right. I should say, I was afraid to trust it. I didn't *want* to trust it. For all I knew, it was the musical equivalent of an anglerfish's lure. But there was something about the voice and the song that called to me, and something—rather like the dream I'd had in the woods all those days ago—that told me that whoever or whatever was singing, it meant us no harm.

"Rodeffer. On me." I lifted my M4 and stepped to the doorway.

"Rod, you stay put." Gunny joined me. "With you."

We flowed out into the tunnel. I went right, Gunny went left. We cleared our sectors and then Gunny collapsed on me, stepping up beside me where I could see him out of my peripheral and blinking his IR flood.

The two of us moved forward carefully, following the sound of the song. The more I listened, the more it sounded like a hymn. An ancient hymn, one that evoked the glories of heaven with just the human voice. It sounded like nothing that belonged down there, beneath the mountain. Out of place in that domain of darkness and horror.

As we moved forward, another tunnel loomed dark on the right. I tracked in on it, clearing as much as I could on

IR as Gunny covered down the long axis of the tunnel. The singing was definitely coming from in there.

The opening led into another chamber identical to the one we'd taken as a refuge. This one had another pit in the center, as well. The rest of the chamber was empty. The singing was coming from the pit.

With Gunny posted on the door to watch the tunnel, I moved toward the pit, keeping my M4 up and carefully easing my eyes and muzzle over the lip.

My IR flood shone on five faces looking up at me from the bottom of the pit, about twelve feet down. Four men and a woman stared up at my light, and from their body language, they could see me as clearly as I could see them.

Their clothing was dirty and torn but clearly better made than anything the Dovos had worn. The men wore padded jerkins, loose trousers, and soft, hide boots. The woman wore a dress, but while it was richly embroidered, its cut was simple and utilitarian, fitting for travel. She wore a cloak over the gown, the hood drawn up over her hair. But none of those details were what immediately caught my eye. They came later.

The woman was… I can only say *staggeringly* beautiful. Dark hair cascaded in waves from under her hood. Her eyes glistened even in IR, set in a heart-shaped face with a small, slightly upturned nose above full lips. Even through NVGs, those eyes were captivating. It was as if she could see past the IR flood and through my NVGs, into my soul.

I tore my gaze away from hers and scanned the four men. Each was similarly perfect, almost inhumanly so.

Note I didn't say "beautiful" when speaking of the men because I don't want to give the wrong idea. That word is usually associated with slender, feminine features, like you see a lot of depictions of elves in fantasy. That wasn't these guys. Every one of them was a lantern-jawed Hercules. Even after however long they'd been in that pit, they looked like they could break me in half. And I'm neither small nor a pushover in a fight.

The men had stepped in front of the woman as I came to the lip of the pit. The tallest one, his hair swept back and sporting a massive handlebar mustache, looked up at me with his head slightly tilted. Even in what had to be pitch blackness to the unaided eye, he was inspecting me.

"If you are a servant of Taramas, you are different from the usual savages she sends. Who are you?" His voice was deep and resonant, with a lilting music to it. He wasn't speaking English, but I understood him. And for some reason, despite the fact that he was apparently pulling the same trick Dragon Mask had, it didn't disturb me nearly as much.

"We're United States Marines. We're no friends of Taramas." I didn't know if that trick of understanding worked both ways with these people, and at first I wasn't sure if they'd comprehended what I said because the four men didn't move but watched me with stony, suspicious expressions.

The woman continued to study me with that penetrating, unblinking look. She reached up and put a delicate hand on the man's shoulder. "They are not our enemies, Mathghaman." She took her gaze away from me for a moment and seemed to stare into space, concentrating. "They have fought Taramas and her Fohorimans, I think. And they have not had the best of it." She pinned me with her eyes again. "What is your name, sir?"

"My name is Conor." I hadn't lowered my M4, despite the fact that I didn't *feel* like these people were a threat. I was that strung out. "Who are you? And what are you doing down here?"

Her hand still on Mathghaman's shoulder, the woman stepped forward. "Conor. I am Nuala. We came from the Isle of Riamog in search of one of our own who fled here after a terrible crime. Unfortunately, before we could find him, Taramas's servants surrounded us and took us prisoner. We have been imprisoned and tortured here ever since." She held a hand up toward me. "Please. Will you help us?"

Gunny had joined me. He didn't say anything at first as he looked over his shoulder, down into the pit, then turned his attention back to the doorway.

"What do you think, Gunny?" I really didn't know what to think, myself. I *wanted* to believe that they were real, that we had found allies—*real* allies—down here in the dark. But a part of me was still afraid that it was all a clever deception, an illusion that Taramas had put down there to mess with our heads. That these were actually her creatures, masked by sorcery and illusion, and that as soon as we brought them up, they'd turn into more of the fanged, red-eyed monsters that we'd been fighting.

He took a deep breath, his eyes still on the doorway. "You've got a better feel for this place than I do. What's your gut telling you?"

Thanks, Guns. I looked back down at the five of them, trying to think.

The woman—Nuala—closed her eyes for a moment. "I know. Taramas is a powerful witch, and her sorceries twist men's minds as much as their bodies. But we are not of her." She spread her hands. "We have no token to show you to prove we are not her creatures. Our fates are in your hands."

Gunny thought of it before I did. "Conor. The sword."

He was right. These things had shown a remarkable fear and revulsion of that runed blade that I'd picked up, that it seemed some Dovo had taken as a trophy, then wrapped the hilts so as to avoid looking at the runes. And if it had disrupted Dragon Mask's sorcery…

I kept my M4 up with my off hand, just to keep the IR flood pointed down into the pit, and drew the sword. "If you're not Taramas's creatures, then you should be able to touch this without harm." I knelt down at the edge and lowered the sword. I wasn't being particularly courteous at that point. I held out the point, not the hilts.

Nuala's eyes widened. "Where did you get that?"

"Took it off a dead man who'd wrapped the hilts in deer hide." I held the sword steady. "The locals don't seem to like it very much."

"I would not imagine." She was too short to reach the blade, but the man she'd called Mathghaman stepped forward, something like awe on his face. He reached up and touched the blade, almost reverently.

He didn't disappear, turn into a slavering monster, or burst into flames. His fingers lingered on the blade and he looked up at me. "You do not know the treasure you bear, Conor."

"I've got some idea." I stood up and sheathed the sword. If these people could handle it without even so much as revulsion, I figured they were okay. "This has been the only thing that has been able to kill some of these things."

"It would be. A blessed weapon has a certain efficacy against the cursed." Mathghaman looked up at me. "Will you help us, then?"

"We'll get you out, but you might be climbing out of the frying pan and into the fire. We're not in the best position ourselves." I stepped back and stuck my head out the door while Gunny covered me. "Rodeffer!" I didn't yell, but the hissed words carried. "Bring two sling ropes and get over here."

Most of us still carried sling ropes in our rucks. They were useful for a lot of things, not least of all hauling rucks and weapons up really steep slopes. Or retrieving a downed teammate. Our Roper days, when we'd had to run everywhere with the ropes tied around our shoulders, were over, but we never put the ropes away. Rodeffer hurried over with two of the eight-foot sections of coiled climbing rope in one hand, his other on his M4's pistol grip.

It took moments to splice the two ropes together using a sheet bend, and then I lowered one end to Mathghaman while I looped the other around behind my hips. He clambered up, hand over hand, faster than I would have expected. He was heavy, but he moved with such agility and grace that it felt like I'd barely taken his weight before he grasped the stone lip of the pit and pulled himself the rest of the way up. "I will take the rope." I handed it off and he pulled it around his own waist as another of the men climbed up.

As soon as he was up on the floor, another of the men lifted Nuala by the waist, holding her up toward the lip of the pit, where the second man reached down to take her by the hands. Both men lifted her as if she weighed nothing.

The last three came up quickly. Mathghaman coiled the ropes and handed them back. "Thank you. We have no weapons. They were taken from us."

"Don't thank us yet," Gunny told him grimly. I was taller than Gunny, and Mathghaman stood almost half a head taller than me. "We're cut off down here. There was a hell of a fight up that way, and we couldn't even scratch some of the things that got unleashed."

Mathghaman frowned. "Not even with the sword?"

"Didn't have a chance to use it." I felt suddenly defensive. "Not sure I could have even hit one of them, though. They seemed to turn to smoke when you looked at 'em wrong."

That prompted several worried looks among them. "What did they look like? Exactly?" Nuala asked.

"Like they were made of tar or oil. Sometimes smoke. Too many limbs, too many eyes. And they were fast. *Really* fast."

"Did she dare?" The man who spoke was slightly shorter than Mathghaman, whip lean and with only pale stubble on his jaw. "Would Taramas grow so foolish that she would call on Vaelor in his sleep?"

"It wasn't her." Gunny visibly steeled himself. "It was a man named Ekersakar, a man who came here with us. He was trying to steal something from Taramas."

Nuala nodded gravely. "The Athame of Urkartikar. A man who sought to supplant one of the Warlock Kings *would* seek it."

But Mathghaman turned troubled eyes on us. "What brought you here with such a man?"

Gunny sighed. "We don't know how we came here—this world, I mean. We're…not from around here. We come from someplace far, far away and this Ekersakar promised our captain that if he got the power he wanted, he could send us back." He shrugged helplessly. "The captain believed him. Now he's missing, and half of us are dead or missing, too. We're caught between a rock and a hard place down here. I'm sorry you're here with us, too."

Almost on cue, a hooting, gibbering howl echoed down the tunnel from above. The enemy was coming.

I turned to Mathghaman. "I'll give you the sword." I really didn't want to part with it at that point—it had saved my life more than my rifle—but it seemed like the right thing to do. But he shook his head.

"You have borne it this far. I will not take it from you unless you truly wish it." It was almost as if he could read my mind, and I wasn't sure if I liked that. Even so, I drew my Bowie, flipped it around, and presented him with the handle.

"You'll need some kind of a weapon. For however long we last."

He took it, with a slight bow of his head. I still didn't know how he could see, but these people were spooky enough with their ability to make me understand their language and apparently see into my mind that being able to see clearly in the pitch dark wasn't all *that* surprising.

Another cry reverberated down the tunnel. The sound was full of anger and hate. They must have found their spy. They were closing fast.

"Let's link up with the others and get ready to kill some monsters." Gunny started moving, but the barrel-chested, curly haired man reached out and took him by the shoulder first.

"Wait." He held up a hand. "Do you feel that?"

"Feel what?" All I could feel was the dampness and the oppressive dread of being trapped under millions of tons of solid rock while the monsters came to tear our heads off.

"I feel it too." Mathghaman sniffed the air. "A faint breeze." He turned down the passage, deeper into the mountain, and pointed. "There is an opening, somewhere that connects to that tunnel. There might be a way out." He turned to Gunny. "Gather your men. We might not die today, after all."

Gunny looked at me, and I suddenly realized he was asking my opinion. He was the platoon sergeant, and he'd been our de facto platoon commander for almost two years, anyway. But even with the captain's regular visits from the Good Idea Fairy, Gunny had always had some kind of commander's intent to work with. Now there was only him. And somehow, he trusted me to check him if he jumped the wrong way.

I nodded. I couldn't articulate it then, but there was something *good* about these people. The test with the sword aside, I got none of the heebie-jeebies I'd felt dealing with Dragon Mask and the Dovos nal Uergal. Maybe that just meant they were better at the mind games, but for some reason I didn't think so, especially after Mathghaman's reaction to the sword at my side.

"All right, then." Gunny turned toward the door where Chambers was watching us. "Bring it in! We're moving out. Let's hustle."

CHAPTER 32

WE didn't move quite fast enough to avoid contact. The monsters—"Fohorimans," Nuala had called them—were on us in moments.

Chambers and Herrera punched out to cover the tunnel while the rest of the platoon headed deeper into the mountain. They opened fire as the first attackers appeared in the tunnel, the harsh *cracks* of their suppressed rifles still deafeningly loud. The people of… Riamog, I thought it was, looked around at the noise but didn't seem as awestruck as the Dovos had been. Curious, maybe. But not afraid.

"Turn and go!" I hadn't followed too closely as Gunny got the rest of the platoon moving down the tunnel. Something had prompted me to hang back, to be ready to cover the rest as we broke contact. Maybe it was the sword at my side. Maybe it was just me being ornery and wanting another crack at the Fohorimans.

But it wasn't Fohorimans in the lead. It was more Dovos, or Taramas's equivalent, whatever they called themselves. At any rate, they were men, clad in skins and untreated lamellar or boiled leather armor, stirred up to a frenzy as they ran down the tunnel with axes and crude swords in hand.

They died quickly, frenzy or no. Double-taps work fine when you put the bullets in hearts, lungs, or heads.

Chambers held his position for a few more seconds as Herrera turned, checked behind him, and ran up the middle of the passage. I moved to the wall he'd just vacated, clearing a path for him and clearing my own field of fire so that I could engage. Only then did I realize that Mathghaman had stayed with me, my Bowie in his hand. I hoped we wouldn't need it.

We killed half a dozen in almost as many seconds. The mob kept coming, driven forward by the Fohorimans behind them. I could see the glowing red eyes in the darkness behind Taramas's human fighters. A rolling, thundering challenge that was shouted from even farther back sent ice water up my spine.

Mathghaman put his hand on my shoulder. "We need to go. Taramas herself is coming. And we are not prepared to face her."

I dumped the rest of the mag into the oncoming savages. They had slowed, but not enough, and not because they were afraid of our guns. They were more afraid of the Fohorimans behind them than they were of the boom sticks spitting noisy but invisible death at them in front. But the bodies we'd already dropped were presenting an obstacle that even the frenzied berserkers were starting to stumble over.

As I stitched rounds across the front rank, more of them crashed to the floor or stumbled as their blood spilled out of little 5.56 holes and their strength slipped away. They blundered into each other, and at least one got stuck on his neighbor's weapon. The advance slowed further as the dead and wounded piled up.

The Fohoriman behind them was getting pissed, I could see that even as I turned to fall back. Mathghaman wasn't finished, though. He stood his ground, and I slowed as I noticed that he wasn't with me.

I didn't know what he could do without a weapon more formidable than my Bowie. It was a good blade, but, c'mon. I tensed a little, wondering if I'd miscalculated, and he was about to do something like Dragon Mask, summoning monsters or something.

Mathghaman simply went down on one knee for a moment, looking up at the ceiling. His lips moved, but I couldn't hear what he was saying over the howling of the berserkers coming after us.

I stepped back as I swapped mags and shot a massive, bearskin-clad howler with wild eyes and a filthy beard down to his chest as he leaped over the body in front of him, nearly scraping his head on the ceiling. He was so close that I shot him through the teeth, spraying gore across the stone overhead, and when he landed, his knees buckled and he fell on his face.

Then Mathghaman rose to his feet. And once again, I find I have a hard time describing just what happened as he did.

There was a flash, only for a brief fraction of a second. I could hardly tell that it even happened. But it broke the savages' frenzy in a heartbeat, turning it to confusion and near panic.

Mathghaman stepped forward and took the sword from the slack fingers of the sav I'd just shot. It wasn't one of their crude brush cutters, but it wasn't of the fine craftsmanship of mine, either. Ancient, discolored, and notched, it was still a formidable weapon, nevertheless. He turned and grabbed my arm as he hurried down the tunnel. "Come. We must go now."

Then we were running down the tunnel after the rest as Taramas screamed her hatred after us.

* * *

The tunnel itself didn't go much farther before it ended in a crack that opened on a much bigger chamber. Bailey and Baldinus led the way down the pile of rubble below the crack, their IR floods sweeping around the inside of the cavern, while Fennean, the light-haired man who had felt the faint breath of wind that had led us down here, trailed right behind them.

The screaming, yelling, and curses behind us had faded somewhat, though none of us thought that the pursuit had stopped. Regardless of what we had done in that antechamber, regardless of what had happened after we fell back, I imagined that the prisoners we'd freed must have some value to Taramas. She wouldn't want to let them go.

Gunny halted at the crack, making sure everyone made it through. The Dovos who had escaped the antechamber with us had stopped dead when they saw us return with our new companions and retreated, visibly terrified. After that, it was just Marines and the former prisoners who were scrambling down that slippery slope of scree and rubble into the cavern.

The IR illuminators shone off towering stalagmites and stalactites, some of them grown together into rippled columns nearly ten feet thick. The chamber's ceiling rose high above us as the floor dipped and then began to rise again, angling away to the south. Presuming that my sense of direction hadn't gotten all turned around.

Now I could feel that faint breath of air. There was a way out of this cavern somewhere. I just hoped that it wasn't as bad as where we'd come from.

Mathghaman had paused, looking back into the darkness behind us. He was one of the last, along with Gunny and me. "They are coming. We must make haste."

I looked back, wishing I had a claymore. Or even just a satchel of C4. Bringing down the tunnel would be every bit as effective as turning the whole mob behind us into pink mist.

"Go, Conor." Gunny's voice brooked no argument. "We'll be right behind you."

With one more glance back into the dark, I started down the slope.

I skidded and slid more than I climbed, but I was at the base of the fan of rocky debris in a matter of seconds. When I looked back up, I saw that Gunny and Mathghaman were indeed right behind me. I stepped off after the rest of the platoon and the other former prisoners. Fennean was still in the lead, with the other two keeping close to Nuala in the center of the formation. Fennean and Bailey's team were almost out of sight amid the stone columns and stalagmites.

Rocks bounded down the slope behind us. I pivoted, bringing my M4 to bear. Half a dozen or so of Taramas's human attack dogs stood in the crack, unwilling to descend into the cavern. Some of that was probably because their torches only illuminated a short stretch of the slide leading down into the cavern. But they were clearly afraid, despite the curses in whatever guttural language that the Fohorimans used booming from behind them.

Gunny pushed my M4 down. "Save your ammo. They can't see us from up there." He pulled me toward the nearest stalagmite. "Let 'em lose us in the dark."

We faded into the cavern. But from the rattle of rocks and faint curses behind us, I knew that they were still following us, however reluctantly. Hopefully, that reluctance would slow them enough that we could open the gap.

In short order, we'd put enough of the rock formations between us and our pursuers that I could barely see the glow of their torches even on NVGs. Utter darkness surrounded us, broken only by our IR illuminators.

We'd used them an awful lot. Batteries were going to die soon. Most of us had already had to change batteries at least once since we'd inserted. I still had a couple of spares in my ruck, but who knew how long they were going to last?

The point element had stopped. Gunny, Mathghaman, and I moved up as Santos fell back to cover our rear. It was quickly evident what they'd found that had prompted the halt.

A shallow depression, surrounded by a half-circle of stalagmites, was scattered with bones, skulls, and the torn, bloodstained, and shredded remnants of the savage hide clothing and armor, perhaps the Dovos or perhaps belonging to some other wild tribe. Several of their weapons were rusting and crumbling amid the debris, including a single-edged sword that had been snapped cleanly in half.

"Well, I think we know why they were hesitant to follow us down here." Gunny looked around, scanning the surrounding stone columns. "The only question comes down to specifics. What's been eating any savs that stray down into these caverns?"

"*Nuathair Tellain.*" The barrel-chested, black-haired man named Bearrac spoke the words under his breath. *Tunnel Serpent.*

That didn't sound good.

The sound of the name had barely faded from our hearing when a new noise met my battered hearing. A slick, slithering sound rasped around the shadows behind the wall of stalagmites, accompanied by a wet, rumbling growl. A moment later, a pair of baleful, lamp-like eyes opened just above one of the lower, more rounded formations. Claws as long as my hand curled over the top of the stalagmite.

A dozen IR floods stabbed at the thing, and I saw what I can only describe as some weird cross between a lizard and a sabertooth tiger. It was hairless, black, and covered in scales, but the features of that massive head were clearly feline. The wickedly curving fangs were vaguely translucent, dripping with saliva.

The thing hauled itself over the top of the stalagmite, revealing a long, winding tail in place of a body. Its only two limbs were the taloned arms pulling it over the rock. It opened its toothy maw wide and hissed at us.

Then it moved, fast as a rattler, and struck at Doc. It was far too close, and Doc had never been the swiftest of us. He was doomed.

But Fennean was faster.

He caught the sword that Mathghaman tossed to him, and then he was suddenly between Doc and the cave serpent so fast that it seemed as if he'd moved when I'd blinked.

His first blow stopped the serpent's lunge cold, and it recoiled as fast as it had struck. What might have been blood, dark against the pale fangs, dripped from its nose. But Fennean didn't hold his ground. He pursued the monster, a single leap taking him halfway up the stalagmite before he clambered up as if the slick, damp, rippled stone had steps carved in it.

A swift stroke of the sword drew more blood, and the serpent reared back still more, its tail flicking. Only then did I notice that it had a stinger on the end of that tail, like a gigantic scorpion's. It wasn't just thirty feet long with claws and fangs, but this thing was also apparently venomous at both ends.

That stinger came in like a bullwhip, but Fennean saw it coming. Balanced atop the stalagmite, he swayed aside and hacked at the tail. If he'd been wielding my sword, I think he might have severed it altogether. As it was, the blade cleaved through some of the scales and sank deep into the muscle, just short of the stinger itself. It was enough to block the strike, if not to wound the serpent too deeply.

I was moving by then, slinging my M4 again and drawing my sword. We had to finish this quickly or our pursuers were going to catch up. We couldn't afford this delay.

Unfortunately, there was a lot of rock between me and the serpent. I had a bit of time since Fennean was holding its attention, but I had to clamber over some rubble and squeeze between a stalagmite and a floor-to-ceiling column of stone. It was a tight fit, and I had to lead with the sword and suck in my already shrunken stomach to get through the opening. As it was, my chest rig caught until I lifted it high enough to fit through.

In the meantime, though, Fennean had struck.

The enraged serpent had yanked its stinger back, oozing blood or ichor from the wound he'd given it. Hissing with rage, it swung a taloned paw at him, only to take the point of the sword in the palm. It tried to yank the paw back, but he'd already moved, leaping forward again and getting inside the striking limb. He stabbed it in the armpit and swung by that fulcrum around onto its back, then dragged the blade out and cut deeply into the softer scales under its foreleg as he did so, then rammed it, point first, deep into the serpent's head, right behind the strange, hairless ear.

The cat-faced serpent stiffened and shuddered, transfixed, then it collapsed. Fennean rode the carcass to the floor, dragging the sword clear as it crashed to the stone.

He wiped the blade clean on his cloak before handing it back to Mathghaman. "Pray that there are no more of them here. This one was old and slow. If there are mature whelps…"

"We shall deal with them as we come to them." Mathghaman turned to Gunny. "We should make haste."

Gunny nodded, acknowledging Mathghaman's courtesy. "Move out."

With Bailey and Baldinus taking point again, we plunged deeper into the cavern, hoping and praying that we found the source of the breeze—and that it wasn't just a narrow crack in the mountain that only a field mouse could get through.

But some hope is better than none. If we came to such a tiny crack, we'd dig our way out.

To quit, to surrender, to give up is to fail. To be a Recon Marine is to surpass failure; to adapt, overcome, and do whatever it takes to complete the mission.

CHAPTER 33

THE cavern narrowed as we got higher, and the breeze coming down into our faces got stiffer. If that was a rabbit hole we were heading for, then the wind on the other side was *kicking.*

Regardless, I hoped that it didn't open onto a sheer cliff a hundred feet tall. If it did, we may as well have come to a dead end.

The tunnel ahead of us began to brighten, at first only within the green circle of my PVS-15s. The temperature was dropping again, too, as the wind intensified. We were getting close to an opening. Bailey, Baldinus, and Fennean stepped it out, Fennean keeping behind Baldinus, though he clearly wanted to go first. Having handed the captured sword back to Mathghaman, though, he saw the wisdom in letting the man with a weapon go first.

The passage bent before the opening, and I looked up to see the point element disappear around the curve. I kept climbing, forcing one foot in front of the other. My ruck straps rubbed at my shoulders, and its weight felt like a ton. We'd come a long way and with little rest or food.

No gunfire sounded, and no alarm was passed back. We pushed up and around the bend.

The opening was a crack in the mountainside atop another fan-shaped slide of gray, broken scree. The slide was old, lying under a blanket of undisturbed snow. We stood at the top, blinking in the sudden brightness, flipping our NVGs up out of the way after making sure to switch them off to save batteries. Taramas's glacier-encased city loomed off to the north, still far too close for comfort.

It must have been near evening, though it was a little hard to tell since a leaden overcast covered the sky. The wind was biting, and I could smell snow on the air. A part of me dreaded it, but another part, that deep, hard-wired Recon part, welcomed it. The risk was higher, but at least Taramas's warriors would have a hard time coming after us.

Recon loves bad weather. Just because most people don't want to be out in it.

I didn't know about the Fohorimans, though. Scary as they were, they still feared death, that much was clear. But how affected were they by the weather? I gathered that they weren't exactly human. And what kind of sorcery could Taramas—or Uergal—send after us?

Bailey already had Baldinus working his way down the edge of the slide, making for a narrow ledge encircled by stunted, wind-twisted trees. Bailey being Bailey, he wasn't going to stick around and gape at the scenery. We needed a more secure spot to recock and figure out the plan, and the barren side of the mountain, within sight of the enemy's fortress, wasn't it.

Spread out into a Ranger file, we picked our way down the slope as Baldinus and Bailey set up amid the trees. The footing was treacherous, made worse by the grinding fatigue that was really starting to come down on us, but nobody bit it. It took longer than it should have before we were gathered in a rough perimeter in the trees, somewhat sheltered from the stinging wind, our new allies in the center.

Bailey, Gurke, and I joined Gunny and Mathghaman in the middle, under the gray shell of a lightning-blasted spruce. For a moment, we just looked at each other, almost too tired to speak. Mathghaman appeared fresher than the rest of us. He waited for us to gather ourselves.

In the open and in the light of day, he looked like even more of a paragon. Reddish hair and beard framed a chiseled face with keen, gray eyes. He stood almost half a head taller than me, and I was one of the tallest of the platoon. Despite the fact that his dark blue gambeson, green cloak, and green trousers seemed hardly adequate to the weather, he didn't even seem to notice the cold, while the rest of us were already starting to shiver.

"We have little time, but perhaps we should speak." Mathghaman looked around at us, his eyes measuring. "Better to know each other's intentions and minds. How did you come here, and what would you do now?"

Gunny gave him the wavetops of what had happened since we'd inserted off the *Makin Island.* He didn't so much as flinch as he described every step that had brought us to a city full of monsters, allied with someone who it was increasingly clear was an evil megalomaniac. That was Gunny Taylor. Face the bad along with the good, without blinking. Take the lessons learned and do better. Don't try to hide your faults. That only makes things worse.

Mathghaman listened in silence, his eyes occasionally flicking to one or the other of us as Gunny told the story. He seemed to be taking in a lot of the unspoken subtext, not that there was much. Gunny wasn't leaving anything important out.

Finally, as Gunny finished and the first flakes of snow began to fall, Mathghaman nodded, though not before a glance at Nuala, who inclined her head as if she approved whatever he would say next. "You would not be the first to be led astray by such promises. And in an unfamiliar land full of unknown dangers, a man who makes a bad choice among worse choices might not be wholly blamed." He stood, looming over us. "You rescued us from the dungeons of Taramas, and therefore we owe you a debt. Time will tell whether that debt might lead to true friendship. Yet we have little time."

He glanced up as the snow fell more thickly, and that was when I thought I could hear a faint flapping sound. A sound that I'd heard before. The last time, the Dovos had come out of the woods and attacked us shortly after.

"We must go." He held out a hand. "The *Tuacha da Riamog* pay our debts. If we can escape from Taramas and her creatures, we shall do it together."

Gunny gripped his hand, and we had an accord. I got the feeling that how long this agreement lasted would depend more on what *we* did, than them.

Mathghaman pointed to the south along the line of the ridge where we were perched precariously. "The coast lies there. While I do not know how long we were imprisoned below, if it has not been too long, our ship should still be loitering in the misty islands off the shore." He glanced up again. "Fennean knows the way."

Almost at the same time, a braying horn went up from the valley just below the city. My guess was that whatever had overflown us had reported back to either Uergal or Taramas. Or both.

Gunny got us moving. "Conor, take point. Take Fennean with you."

I nodded, looked around, and pointed to Rodeffer. He struggled to his feet, got his bearings, and stepped off, as Fennean joined him. I fell in behind them and we started along the mountainside, heading down into the trees.

Behind us, another hate-filled cry of summoning went up into the cold air, the echoes deadened by the thickening snow. The hunt was on.

* * *

The next four days and nights blurred together as we trudged, scrambled, and ran when we could over some of the nastiest mountain terrain I'd seen in a long time, through dense evergreen woods and snow that had drifted hip-deep in places, where the rock wasn't so sheer that the snow couldn't accumulate. Seriously, there were places we clambered over that I think a mountain goat would have looked at and decided to find another way around. We weren't hiking in some of those areas, we were rock climbing.

We didn't dare slow down any more than the terrain forced us to for that whole four days. Once, when we paused for a breather on the far side of a particularly tortuous hanging valley, having had to descend farther than we'd intended just to get around the dirty blue glacier that had encroached deeply toward the lowlands below, we heard that horn again. I'd looked back the way we'd come just in time to see movement on the ridgeline above. Bringing my M4 up, I peered through the ACOG and saw fur-clad savages and Fohorimans streaming over the ridge through a gap in the trees.

A moment's pause, and I'd noticed a figure atop a massive beast sitting at the upper tree line. I couldn't make out features, especially since the snow had started to fall again, but the figure looked enormous and vaguely green.

Uergal was coming after us.

He wasn't alone, either. Another hulking beast, dark-furred and horned, padded up to join his mount, carrying a smaller figure all in black.

Mathghaman had seen me watching the far ridgeline and joined me. He had no magnified optics, but somehow I wasn't surprised when he said, "Taramas. So, she has been forced to admit our presence to Uergal." He glanced back to where Nuala had sat against a tree, wrapped in her cloak. "She must truly be desperate to reclaim her prize. It takes a great deal for the Warlock Lords of the Fohorimans to put aside their hatreds." He turned toward Gunny. "We should move."

We moved out and struggled down the other side of the ridge.

* * *

There's a reason why Patrol Phase is so brutal. From insert until extract, eight days later, you *might* get two hours of sleep out of every twenty-four. When you're not moving or executing the mission, you're holding security and planning for the next mission. It's a frag-O a day. Ropers quickly get so strung out that they hallucinate, dreaming even while on their feet and moving.

Patrol Phase was nothing compared to that movement down the mountain. It drove us to our limits and beyond them. And we kept going, because the alternative was to let Uergal and Taramas, with their combined army of Dovos, Fohorimans, and other creatures, catch us.

The Tuacha had told us nothing of what they had endured at Taramas's hands. I could guess, though. Even though they were strangely serene most of the time—and their endurance put every one of us to shame—there were moments. I awoke during one of the all-too-brief rests we had on the third day to see Bearrac sitting against a stump, awake, staring into empty space. I'd seen that stare before. Seen it in a Marine's eyes after that fight outside Al Busayrah. Seen it in a Yezidi girl's eyes after we went through an IS camp in the desert below Mount Abdulaziz.

While I suspected that the Tuacha weren't entirely human and were probably longer-lived and more insightful than we were, I knew the thousand-mile stare of someone who had seen hell, up close and personal, when I saw it. Bearrac had witnessed and endured things no one ever should have to.

From what I'd observed so far, I expected that Taramas's imagination for such things vastly surpassed even the Daesh animals who we'd killed in eastern Syria.

That stare alone was sufficient reason to stay ahead of the monsters on our trail. And so, when the time came, we got up and kept moving, ignoring the exhaustion, ignoring the pain, ignoring the gnawing hunger that had begun to bite as we'd run through the last of the meat we'd hunted before reaching Taramas's valley. Just put one foot in front of the other and drive through until the mission's done or you're dead.

* * *

As the light waned on the fourth day, we came down out of the mountains and saw the sea.

We also saw the sprawling ruins of a port city draped in snow and half-engulfed by the coastal forest. Mathghaman pointed from the promontory where we'd come out of the woods. "Teac Mor Farragah. Long has it been since my father last set sail from her quays while the Fohorimans burned the city behind him." If he was tempted to reflect on history, he dismissed the temptation quickly. "We must light the beacon atop the Tower of Rabhadh. If our ship still waits for us, they will see it."

I glanced up the mountainside behind us, catching another glimpse of movement. The pursuit hadn't slackened for the entire four days. They were still coming for us. "How far out are they? If they're still there?"

He looked over his shoulder, sensing my meaning. "We will have to hold our ground for some time. Perhaps as long as a day."

"We don't have that kind of ammo." Gurke had joined us. "We'll go black within the first hour with the numbers they've got coming for us."

"Well, that's why we've been picking up close combat weapons for the last couple of weeks." Bailey had just clambered up onto the rock, and he hefted the warhammer that he'd grabbed somewhere along the line. It looked like one of the ones those animated suits of armor had been wielding. I had no idea when he'd had a chance to grab it.

"That's great, but we're twenty guys. Numbers count for a lot more when it comes to hand-to-hand." Gurke just sounded beat down. His ordinarily lean features and deep-set eyes now looked like a skull, despite the two weeks of beard and increasingly shaggy hair curling out from under his bump helmet. "And we're all dead tired and half starved."

"We can use the ruins to our advantage." Mathghaman clapped Gurke on the shoulder, his huge hand making the smaller man stumble a little. "Come. We must make haste. Nuala will hurry to the tower and light the beacon, while we prepare our defenses."

* * *

Night fell as we reached the crumbling walls, overshadowed by towering trees. We dropped our NVGs and carefully moved through a breach, guns up and looking for targets. Half-destroyed stone buildings lined a narrow street on the far side of a twenty-yard stretch of what had been open ground on the inside of the wall, though it was now as overgrown by forest as the outside of the walls. There were a lot of shadows, broken doorways and half-collapsed windows staring at us like the eyes of skulls. Lots of places for creepy crawlies to hide and wait for tired Marines to wander past.

We spread out into a rough, two-team skirmisher's line as we came through the gap, keeping our rucks on just in case as we advanced through the trees while Gurke's team hung back by the gate to watch our backs. Uergal and Taramas seemed to have halted their army on the lowlands about a mile outside the city walls. Before we'd plunged into the trees on the inside, I'd seen the campfires start to flicker out on the plain by the half-frozen river that ran down to Teac Mor Farragah from the mountains above Taramas's citadel.

Maybe even the monsters were afraid of the dark in this place. Or maybe there were yet other monsters that came out at night that could challenge even the Warlock Lords.

That was comforting.

We had barely reached the street when Nuala suddenly moved, flitting ahead faster than I would have imagined possible. She didn't run like a normal person, either, but seemed to simply glide over the ground like smoke as she quickly vanished into the streets.

Santos made a strangled sound, and I think about half of us surged forward, but Mathghaman put up a hand to forestall the frustrated rush to cover her. "She will move faster on her own. We should see to the defenses."

And indeed, by the time we'd moved a block into the city streets, light flared from the Tower of Warning. Nuala had moved fast, indeed.

We kept going, muzzles pivoting to cover each corner, door, window, and shadow as we worked our way deeper in, heading for the quays by the shore.

* * *

The city was far too big to cover every approach the enemy might take. But we had to try. If we just set in an Alamo at the docks, we'd be overwhelmed in minutes. It was time for the Recon Way of War.

Mathghaman led the way to a large, roofless stone building with a half-collapsed pillared portico. It stood right at the edge of the quays, which lay in a rough spoke pattern around an almost perfectly circular harbor, sheltered from the sea by the crumbling remains of a fortified sea wall. What looked almost like a still-intact mast rose from the dark water next to one of the quays. We cleared the inside, then dropped rucks and gathered around Gunny and the Tuacha near the entrance.

Under the glow of a red-lens headlamp, Mathghaman swept aside the snow and sketched out the rough layout of the city with a finger in the dirt. "The streets are set in rings around the harbor, with connecting spokes. I cannot say how many may have been blocked by debris after the siege. It was long ago. As you can see, the city has been left in ruins. There were gates here, here, and here, with main thoroughfares that ran to the harbor, though passing through the inner walls here and here."

"Seems awfully heavily fortified to the landward side for a port city." Chambers was peering over Gurke's shoulder, his hands folded on his M4's buttstock.

"These shores have been a battlefield for many lives of men," was Mathghaman's response. "The Fohorimans to the north, and worse things beyond them, were as great a threat as the sea trolls in the mists."

"All right." Gunny frowned down at the rough map, scratching his beard. "We're going to have to split into two-man teams and set ambushes in along the likely avenues of approach." He grimaced. "Conor, I want your first team here…"

CHAPTER 34

WHILE I think we all would have braved the dark to get into position, Nuala forbade it. She had appeared back in our midst as if by magic, slipping past security without a sound. That had us spooked, and if we hadn't been so dead on our feet—and in such dire straits—I think that Nagano would have had everyone except for team leaders and assistant team leaders—and maybe Doc—doing eight counts until they puked.

"The ruins are not safe." Her lilting voice sounded at once enchanting and motherly. "The Fohorimans and their servants might shun and fear this place because of our ancestors' imprint upon the very stones, but there are other things prowling the darkness this night, things that will not fear even your weapons. To venture out in such small numbers would be folly." She looked around at us. "Even such warriors as yourselves would lose half your number by dawn."

Gunny grunted. "If we're not in position by the time the enemy starts to move in, we're dead anyway."

I might have expected even Gunny to use a different turn of phrase, but something about Nuala was making all of us watch our language. Cussing in front of her felt like dropping an f-bomb at Thanksgiving in front of your saintly grandmother.

"They will wait for dawn." Bearrac spoke with certainty, his massive arms crossed in front of his chest. "They, too, fear what creeps in the night here. And with good reason. Things were unleashed during the fall of the city that never should have walked in the waking world."

My hackles were all the way up as I turned to watch the shadows beyond the walls and our all-too-small security perimeter. Extract is always the most dangerous part of any mission, but this was taking things a step farther.

Diarmodh, the smallest of the Tuacha, a quick, slender man with slightly pointed features and a swept-out blond mustache, suddenly appeared as silently and unexpectedly as Nuala had. These people were quick and quiet. He had a bundle in his arms and laid it down next to the map, then unrolled it to reveal five swords with short quillions and leaf-shaped blades. "The armory was where you said it would be, Mathghaman, but it had been despoiled. These were all I could find."

"They will do." Mathghaman drew my Bowie from his belt and handed it back to me, hilt first, before he selected one of the swords and presented it to Gunny, hilt first over his arm. "This will serve you better than that axe, I think."

Gunny took the sword slowly, inclining his head to indicate his thanks.

Mathghaman selected one of the remaining leaf-shaped swords and hefted it experimentally. I noticed that only after he had taken one did the rest of the Tuacha men reach for their own. "We will set a guard for tonight. Let each man get what rest he can. Come the morning, they will be upon us.

"Pray to Tigharn that our beacon was seen and that the winds bear our brothers to us quickly."

* * *

It wasn't a restful night. With only twenty of us to hold security, we had to switch off a lot, which meant only getting snatches of about two hours of sleep at a time. And those were restless.

I woke up about half an hour into my rest shift, where I was half-lying, half-sitting against my ruck just inside the partially collapsed doorway in the wall, while Rodeffer watched our sector. I didn't know what had awakened me, not at first. I wasn't disoriented—didn't think that I'd fallen asleep on security—but I came to alert and feeling the heebie-jeebies like I hadn't in a long time.

After grabbing my M4, I rolled off my ruck and came to a knee, barricaded on the doorway across from Rodeffer. I strained my eyes into the dark for a moment, my gut absolutely convinced that something was about to hit us. I didn't even have time to grab my helmet and NVGs.

But while Rodeffer was every bit as alert and at the ready as I was, nothing came. The feeling that we were being watched by something dangerous and predatory didn't recede, though.

Finally, I reached over for my helmet, keeping my gun hand on my weapon's firing control, and hauled it over to me, then lifted it onto my head with one hand. It wobbled a little as I pried my NVGs down and turned them on. Getting the chinstrap fastened was more complicated than it should have been, but I finally got the helmet settled and my 15s in front of my eyes.

At first, all I could see was the stark lines of the ruins outside of our refuge. Nothing moved. The snow still reflected the faint glow from the beacon in the Tower of Warning above our heads.

Then I saw the eyes.

Deep in the shadows, in an ancient house that still had a mostly intact roof, two points of baleful light gleamed. They were invisible when I turned my head to look into the shadows out of the corner of my eye, so they only glinted in IR—or they were reflecting just enough of the ambient glow from the beacon that my NVGs could pick them up.

I stared at the eyes, trying to make out what kind of monster they belonged to. But I couldn't see anything except the eyes in utter blackness.

Finally, I decided to risk it. I triggered my PEQ-16's IR flood, shining the infrared light in through the gap at the eyes. They flared with reflected infrared light, and something about the way they narrowed told me that that thing wasn't happy about having light shone in its eyes.

Despite that, nothing else about the creature was revealed. It remained hidden in utter darkness, as if my flood hadn't illuminated anything about it at all.

The eyes blinked. They glared at me and then vanished. The darkness persisted for a few moments and then faded to the point that my IR flood splashed a circle of green on the far wall of the ruined, empty house.

Only then did I hear the scrape of a footstep behind me. I glanced around to see Bearrac standing at my shoulder, his sword in his hand, staring out into the dark. He saw me looking at him and nodded. He said nothing but laid his hand on my shoulder for a moment before moving off to another part of the perimeter.

I stayed up for a few more minutes. Rodeffer stayed in place—it was still his watch, and he wasn't going to stand down, though he also wasn't going to tell me to go back to sleep. Finally, knowing that we were in for a hell of a fight come morning, I lay back down to get a few more minutes of rest, at least, before I had to get up and take security again.

I could still see those eyes staring when I closed my own.

I didn't sleep.

* * *

While the sun wasn't up yet, the long night was nearing its end as Rodeffer and I worked our way through the empty, rubble-choked streets toward the northern gate. It was still dark but turning to that pre-dawn pale that washed out NVGs and reduced contrast to the point that they were next to useless.

We were moving as fast as we could while still scanning every darkened corner, hole, door, and window we passed. While neither of us had said a word about it, we both had the memory of those eyes in that impenetrable shadow all too fresh in our minds.

Yet as we progressed toward our ambush position, we saw no movement, no gleaming eyes full of malice in the shadows. Everything was still except for us and the frigid wind blowing in off the ocean. It moaned softly through the ruins, slightly muffling the faint crunch of our boots in the snow. I could smell the salt in the air, but there was no refreshment there. It smelled like rot and dead sea troll.

As the light brightened—though still filtering through the clouds that lowered over the hills above the ruins—I saw that there were other footprints in the snow. Monstrous prints from humanoid feet with claws and too many—or too few—toes. Whatever had made them seemed to have vanished with the coming of dawn.

I prayed that they stayed that way. Horns and drums began to sound to the north as Uergal's and Taramas's armies started to move.

Since we didn't have a chance to recon our positions the night before, we had to pick a good spot quickly. A crumbling manor on a slight hill that overlooked the north gate in the inner wall made for a decent overlook, and we quickly cleared it as the dawn intensified and the sounds of the advancing forces grew louder. There wasn't much to clear. The inside was gutted, leaving little but crumbling walls of stone and a few piles of rubble, not to mention what might have been the frozen, near-petrified remains of burned-out timbers, cracked and fallen in during the fires Mathghaman had told us about.

I would have kind of liked a second-story lookout position, but we had to settle for the collapsed north wing. Rodeffer and I crept into the rubble, getting down and crawling to a position in the shadow of a towering section of stone wall that hadn't fallen, standing like some weird, ragged obelisk in the snow. I heard movement behind me and turned to see that Mathghaman had joined us. He moved up to another spot on the other side of the rockpile and crouched behind it, peering toward the gate, that leaf-bladed sword in his hand.

"If you end up needing to use that pigsticker, we've been here too long," I said and then wondered a little that I'd had the stones to speak to him like that. Mathghaman had what I could only describe as a *regal* bearing, the kind that officers like Captain Sorenson only dreamed of. The man was a leader, born and bred, and he radiated it with his every move, word, and even look. His very existence seemed to demand respect. It was weird, but it resonated.

He gave me a faint, devil-may-care smile. "I gather from what you and your chieftain have said that your own weapons will not last forever."

"They won't." I had two and a half mags left. My M4 was going to be useful for considerably less than "forever." "But we don't intend to hold the line here, either. We're going to kill a few of them and fall back past Smith and Farrar."

"I know." He turned back toward the gates. "And when you move, I will join them. And then rejoin you when they retreat. I will stand at the front of the fight until we come to grips with our enemies or the ship arrives." He shrugged. "It is my place."

Like I said. Something about the man demanded respect.

Rodeffer chimed in, "Well, if we'd managed to grab another rifle, you'd be welcome to it." My pointman suddenly looked abashed, as if he'd just put his foot in his mouth. But Mathghaman took the words for what they were.

"I would thank you for it. They seem to be superior weapons than the greatest of our bows. But best not to pine for what cannot be." Mathghaman could give Gunny a run for his money.

Then the first of the Dovos appeared in the gateway, and there was no more time for talk.

They advanced carefully, cautiously, their shields up, daubed with foul symbols and images, their weapons held ready and their eyes peering over shield rims. They hadn't quite formed a shield wall. In fact, their formation was more of a mob than a formation. Not that it made much difference to us. We didn't plan to engage them hand-to-hand until there was no other choice, and the plan was to do that in a very narrow choke point where their numbers wouldn't count for as much.

Rodeffer was down flat on the rubble, his M4 braced against a block of stone, clamped in place with one gloved hand, his eye to his ACOG. He was ready. He was just waiting for me to open the ball.

My target was easy to pick. The hairy, blond giant with black streaks in his hair and beard, and black paint or dye daubed around his eyes as if to make them look like a skull's eye sockets. The brute had pushed nearly two paces ahead of any of the rest. He was twitching, and we were close enough that I could see that he was foaming at the mouth, spittle dribbling into his filthy beard and freezing as it ran down away from his bared teeth.

I put my ACOG's chevron on his head, let my breath out with a faint cloud of steam, and squeezed the trigger. The *crack* of the suppressed round echoed across the ruins, and the berserker's head snapped back, a faint cloud of red spray spattering from the back of his skull. He crashed onto his back, his axe tumbling from nerveless fingers.

Unfortunately, if we'd been hoping that that first killing would give the rest pause, we were doomed to disappointment. An inhuman roar went up from behind, and if the rest of the Dovos stutter-stepped for a moment, they quickly got over it and charged with a chorus of ululating screams, weapons raised and murderous frenzy in their eyes.

I quickly switched targets and gave the skinny, masked Dovo with a spear a double tap that ripped through his boiled leather cuirass and his throat. He kept moving forward, but fell on his face, his fallen spear tripping another behind him, but that one only got shoved out of the way and trampled by two more behind him.

Rodeffer was shooting steadily, his M4 rocking with a rhythmic *crack, crack, crack.* I was engaging as fast as I could switch targets, drilling heart and lung shots with every pair. The leader had been barely seventy-five yards away when I'd shot him, and the rest were closing the distance fast.

We'd probably each dropped a dozen when I made the decision, as they came howling for our blood, scrambling up the little rise where the ruined manor stood. "Fall back." I scrambled up to a knee, then surged to my feet and headed for the back of the manor, Mathghaman right beside me, Rodeffer following. A flung javelin—or a really big arrow—clattered off the stones over our heads, and then we were behind the bulk of the manor's ruined walls and running for the gap that would let us move to our next position.

We wove quickly through the smaller foundations and half-standing walls. We'd left our rucks back by the harbor, so we were a lot lighter than we'd felt for days. Exhaustion and hunger still took their toll. We weren't nearly as fast as we should have been. But we were fast enough to maintain our distance from the enemy as Farrar and Smith opened fire from their own hiding place, bullets spitting down the lane and knocking more Dovos off their feet, staining the snow-covered stones red.

Mathghaman, true to his word, broke off and sprinted to join Smith and Farrar. He had to be chafing to get into the fight, but he was as composed and calm as ever in the last glimpse I got of him as Rodeffer and I pushed to our next hidey hole, another roofless ruin surrounded by broken columns at the edge of what might once have been a square.

Gunfire rattled across the city as more of the platoon engaged. We were vastly outnumbered, and neither Uergal nor Taramas appeared to have wanted to chance a single approach. If we *hadn't* spread out, we probably would have already been flanked and surrounded.

The cold air burning my throat and lungs, I jumped over a low, fallen wall and dropped to a knee behind it, then laid my M4 across the stones and waited for Rodeffer to get all the way out of my line of fire. Smith and Farrar had already ceased fire and were sprinting down the street ahead of us. The Dovos were closing fast.

I opened fire before Smith, Farrar, and Mathghaman had passed us. We were running out of space and time real fast.

My first shot was hasty, my breathing and heart rate still too high for pinpoint accuracy. I hit the Dovo with a notched, brush cutter sword and a fanged helmet in the shoulder, spinning him halfway around with the impact. My follow-up shot punched through his armpit, and he sagged as pink froth started to flow from under his faceplate's fangs as his pulped lung started to fill with blood. Three more shouldered past him, knocking him into the snow as they raced at us.

Rodeffer shot one through the throat. I got the next one in the guts. Without waiting for him to stumble and fall, I shifted to the hulking, bare-chested berserk behind him and hammered three rounds into his chest.

Then, even as Mathghaman vaulted the wall behind us and crouched by my side, I saw that they were too close, and Smith and Farrar hadn't opened up yet. So, despite myself, I switched my M4 to burst, briefly wished that I had one of the older A1s that had full auto, and started dumping the mag into the onrushing mob.

Bullets punched through their crude armor like it was cardboard, ripping through ribs, guts, limbs, hearts, lungs, and throats. They were close enough—less than thirty yards—that I didn't waste too many rounds. Most of my shots hit. So did Rodeffer's. But we both went dry, bolts locking back on empty mags, at almost the same time.

Smith and Farrar took up the fire. They hadn't gone far, taking shelter behind another nondescript pile of stones only about fifty yards back from our position. In fact, they hadn't gone nearly far enough according to plan, but the Dovos were coming at us faster than we'd hoped.

As we lunged away from our position, Mathghaman noticeably took up a position *behind* us, keeping himself between us and the Dovos. I glanced back and saw why.

Twenty Fohorimans rode those mutant, Neolithic-looking horses about fifty yards behind the mob of Dovos. Twisted and monstrous, no two looked exactly the same, but none of them looked quite human. One had an elongated face that looked like a nightmare cross between a horse and a man. Another had an apish face that bore tusks and looked like a fantasy orc from some video game back in The World, except he was gray instead of green. Another's face was completely obscured by lank, black hair, except for two glowing, red eyes. Several others wore full-face or veiled helms, draped with mail or black cloth, but I was sure they were just as twisted beneath them.

And behind them rode Taramas.

Her beast was bigger than I'd thought, standing head and shoulders above the biggest of the horse-things that the Fohorimans rode. Horned and fanged, her mount snarled and slavered as she urged it forward.

It was the first real look I'd gotten at her, and while it was little more than a glance, that image burned itself into my mind.

She was skeletally thin, clad in black robes over black lacquered scale armor. Her face was elongated, her chin sharply pointed, her cheeks sunken like a skull, her nose narrow between burning red eyes. Horns had grown from her forehead, and she had wrapped them in wire from which dangled a pair of gilded fangs from some beast I probably didn't want to meet in the dark. Her cloak billowed out behind her, moving against the wind like some living thing.

She was infinitely more monstrous than the Fohorimans who rode in front of her. She radiated hatred and cruelty in a way that her mere physical description can't communicate.

If only we had more ammo. And claymores. And mortars. And air support.

For a brief moment, I thought I knew just what it must have felt like to be one of those SOG teams in Laos back in the day, compromised and hunted before they could get comms up to call for help.

We raced past Smith and Farrar, panting and sucking at the freezing air, feeling our lungs try to cramp as we frantically reloaded. Less than one full mag left.

There was no time to look for our planned fallback positions, the ones we'd marked on the way out to the initial ambush site. We had to sprint to the next bit of cover behind our teammates, set in, and open fire again. Drop about ten to a dozen Dovos while Smith and Farrar bounded back behind us, then repeat. Block by block, twenty yards at a time. While the enemy closed in on us every moment.

By the fourth or fifth bound, they were on us. We were still almost five hundred yards from the harbor.

I dumped the last of my half mag into a mob that hadn't seemed to thin nearly enough for all the bodies we'd left littering the snowy, abandoned streets in our wake. Half a dozen more fell, blood spilling from holes punched through chests and skulls, and then my bolt locked back for the last time. I slung the M4 to my back, cinched down the sling with a single tug, and drew my sword. They were ten paces away.

"Not here." Mathghaman grabbed me by the arm and turned me back toward the harbor. "Run. Like you have never run before."

He'd already grabbed Rodeffer and launched him down the street. I followed, noticing once again that Mathghaman waited for me. He didn't stay behind me but loped along by my side as we sprinted for the harbor.

Smith and Farrar opened fire as we ran past, killing a few more and dropping their bodies to slow the men behind them, but then they went black too and turned to run after us. Mathghaman fell back to pace them.

As hard as I was running, that was easily the longest and hardest five hundred yards I've ever covered, before or since. The snow was slick beneath my boots, and I ran in terror that the next step might be the one that slipped out from under me and left me to die beneath Dovo blades.

Provided Taramas was feeling merciful enough to let them kill me right there. But I kept my balance and kept moving, even as my legs burned, my lungs ached, and every fiber of my being screamed at me to just stop and rest.

I reached our Alamo just behind Gunny and Santos. About half the survivors of the platoon had already gotten there, along with Fennean and Diarmodh. From the looks of things, nobody had any ammo left. Gunny and Diarmodh had them forming up with blades, axes, and clubs, ready to fight hand-to-hand.

The beacon still burned above our heads. I didn't know what Nuala had done when she'd lit that beacon, but it had burned unattended for hours on end without fading. We could only hope that it wasn't burning futilely, only there to mark our deaths.

I found a position in the forefront, holding up the blessed sword as my justification, even as I forced Nagano to step back. He grimaced and handed me one of the handful of shields we'd brought. It wasn't the one I'd picked up back at the tor, but it would have to do.

We formed a shield wall at the opening in the wall as the rest of the platoon raced in, followed by Bearrac. And then they were on us.

The Dovos had slowed and parted, and the Fohorimans spurred their mounts forward. They must have driven their servants ahead of them to soak up our bullets, and now that they were pretty sure we were black on ammo, they wanted to close in and make the kill themselves.

The first, a towering figure entirely encased in armor, his face hidden by a horned great helm, eyes invisible behind black pits of eyeholes, came in fast, swinging a massive poleaxe that split Applegate's shield in two and bit into his arm. Applegate sagged with a groan but still managed to strike out with his own sword, hacking at the Fohoriman's arm. His first blow bounced off the armored gauntlet, but he recovered, despite his other arm hanging uselessly at his side, quickly drawing the notched blade back and swinging for a knee as the Fohoriman drew the bill back for another stroke.

That next blow glanced off the Fohoriman's armored leg. Applegate might have died then and there if Bearrac hadn't whipped his own sword in front of his face, stopping the bill cold with a terrific *crack*.

Then the duel began.

The gap in the wall was too narrow for more than one of the Fohorimans to attack, particularly given the size of this armored monstrosity. So, as Bearrac stepped into the breach and Doc pulled Applegate back from the line, the fight became a contest of strength, skill, and ferocity between the black-bearded Bearrac and the armored Fohoriman.

Blade and bill darted and clashed, moving almost too fast to see. Sparks flew from the blades as they came together and parted, deflecting or deflected as they sought each other's lives. A vicious swing at Bearrac's knee was suddenly reversed and redirected at his head, countered a handspan from the man's skull by a lightning parry. A thrust was batted to one side by the bill, only to have Bearrac seemingly ride the blade over his opponent's weapon and send the point darting in once again.

That one went home. The Fohoriman shuddered for a moment, and when Bearrac drew his blade back, there was black blood on the point.

The Fohoriman had been hurt but quickly responded, his bill slithering in as fast as a striking snake. That stroke also drew blood, slicing through Bearrac's gambeson and cutting into his shoulder. In moments, his sleeve was turning red, stiffening as the blood cooled and began to freeze.

But instead of recoiling from the blow, Bearrac stepped inside it, whipping his wounded arm up and wrapping up the bill's shaft under his arm. He wrenched it to one side, nearly ripping it from his opponent's hands, and then he twisted, driving his sword home as he did so.

I couldn't see exactly what had happened—whether he had found a gap in the armor or if he had simply rammed the point straight through the scales by main force—but black blood suddenly gushed from under the helm, and the Fohoriman sagged, his knees giving way. One hand clawed at Bearrac's gambeson, and then he fell.

Without hesitation, another came in from the flank, swinging a wicked black sword at Bearrac's head. I took a half step forward, got my shield under the sword, and deflected it upward. The force of that glancing blow felt like I'd just gotten hit by a truck. If I'd taken it straight on, the impact would probably have shattered my arm, shield or no shield.

That block committed me. I had put myself between Bearrac and the Fohoriman, and so I had to fight. What I'd seen so far told me that I was completely outclassed, but it wouldn't be the first time. I'd have to make up for it with sheer ferocity and stubbornness.

Two blows were enough to tell me that I was about to die.

My first strike, a short jab at the slender, long-limbed Fohoriman with five eyes in a leering face like a skull with an enlarged forehead, was batted aside easily, and I almost lost my grip on the sword. Only a quick withdrawal kept it in my hand, and an equally quick sidestep and parry barely kept the next thrust of that slender black blade from punching straight through my shield and into me. I swung for an exposed knee, careful to keep my elbow tucked and keep the swing tight and short, but the Fohoriman danced out of the way, moving almost leisurely, and took another careless swing at my head.

He was toying with me.

I hadn't quite realized it yet, but he'd also drawn me out through the doorway. I was in the open, and two more of them were suddenly closing in on my flanks, axes held ready. I was about to get cut to pieces, even as another plunged into the doorway.

Then Mathghaman dropped out of the sky.

I don't know if he had climbed the wall and jumped off, or if he'd used some preternatural gift of the *Tuacha da Riamog* to leap completely over it. But he came down on that Fohoriman like the wrath of God, all his weight atop his sword point, driving the blade to the hilts where the Fohoriman's shoulder met his neck.

The monster died with a hoarse wail of despair, already collapsing under the impact. Mathghaman wrenched the blade free with a shower of dark gore, half decapitating the corpse in the process.

The other two that had been closing in on me leapt to the attack. Bearrac had been quick, but Mathghaman was like a lightning bolt, his blade flashing back and forth, flicking drops of blood to stain the snow around us, fending off both attacks. Even possessing such skill, it was quickly apparent that he could be overwhelmed if this went on much longer.

With a lunge, I stabbed at the hulking, long-armed brute with the tusks on his left. I got a piece of him, the point sinking into his side by a handsbreadth before he screamed and danced aside. But I'd given Mathghaman his opening. In the brief moment he didn't need to worry about the one I'd stabbed, he feinted, reversed, riposted, and swept the second Fohoriman's vaguely canine head from its shoulders.

Instead of pressing the advantage, though, Mathghaman stepped back beside me and started to back toward the door, pulling me with him. I struggled at first. My blood was up, despite my exhaustion. But common sense reasserted itself fast. If we got sucked into a fight in the open, it was over.

More of the Fohorimans were pressing in on us, stabbing with swords and spears. Gunny was bellowing for a shield wall. It wasn't anything we'd trained to do, but it turned out to be pretty intuitive. Still, we weren't really ready for this kind of combat, even after our experience on the tor. Not against the Fohorimans.

Another shield was split by an axe that hooked the rim and pulled Synar out of formation when the fox-eared, narrow-featured Fohoriman yanked her weapon back. Only Fennean's quick counterstroke, slashing over Synar's back even as he grabbed his chest rig from the back and hauled him back, saved his life.

Then a spear slithered over top of a shield rim and transfixed Smith through the mouth.

He died with an awful choking, gurgling sound, though the spearpoint had punched out the back of his neck, already severing his spine. I saw his eyes roll up in his head as blood gushed from his mouth, down his chest rig.

He sagged, but he didn't fall. The Fohoriman on the other end of the spear lifted him out of the formation, holding the spear straight up while Smith's corpse dangled from the point. A blue-skinned Fohoriman with fleshy tendrils for a beard leered at me as Smith's blood dripped onto him.

I saw red and lunged forward, halted only by Mathghaman's arm held out across my chest. He stopped me cold, hardly looking back at me as he hewed at another Fohoriman who dared come within reach of his sword. That one fell back, clutching a hand to a thick, doughy throat that had just been slashed open, spilling muddy-colored blood down across its slime-encrusted breastplate.

Then Taramas apparently got tired of waiting for her servants to get carved up trying to overwhelm us.

She let out a high, ear-splitting, hateful shriek. And as she did, the wall in the center of the building cracked, split, and collapsed in on us.

By some miracle, none of us were crushed.

"Back!" Mathghaman's voice roared out over the crash of falling masonry. "Back to the harbor! Stay together! Step!"

Recon Marines are not known for our prowess at close order drill. In fact, we have been accused of being, as an MOS, "Drill Rocks." We can kill people and break their stuff like no other but looking good in formation is not one of our skill sets.

Right at that moment, though, we all seemed to go back to boot camp. Back when drill was important, if only because the Senior Drill Instructor was going to thrash the whole platoon himself if we messed it up too badly. Almost as one, the platoon backstepped, keeping on line, weapons and shields presented to the enemy.

"Step!" Mathghaman wasn't going to pause long enough for the Fohorimans to take advantage. We backstepped. "Step!"

A pace at a time, we fell back across the floor as the Fohorimans flowed in after us. The *Tuacha da Riamog* stabbed and slashed and cut, fast as an eyeblink, still only barely managing to keep the foe at bay while we, fighting gamely but worn down, exhausted, and not nearly as well-trained in this form of warfare, did what we could to support them. Our combined effort slowed the Fohorimans, but not enough. They pressed us back until we were out of the ancient house and backing toward the Tower of Warning.

Without being asked, Gunny and Doc were on either side of Nuala, ready to defend her if we got flanked.

More of the Fohorimans came around the corners of the building, these ones mounted and carrying long spears. They wouldn't need to close in on us to start killing us. We backed up to the base of the tower.

There were no last words. No one had the breath for it. We were all panting, our breath smoking in the cold air that we could barely feel anymore. Every muscle ached, gloved fingers beginning to cramp around weapons.

No, there would be no last words or defiant speeches. There was only a grim determination to take as many of them with us as we could.

We braced ourselves, hunkered behind splintered shields, and waited for the charge.

Gloating, the Fohorimans spurred their mounts toward us.

Then a new horn, high and clear, sounded over the water, and a rain of arrows hammered down into the Fohorimans on our left flank. They hardly scratched the armored or ensorcelled Fohorimans themselves, but they tore into their mounts, killing some and wounding others so that they screamed and reared, forcing their riders to fight to stay in the saddle.

A tall, graceful ship with a white sail emblazoned with a golden sunburst had pulled into the harbor, driven by many oars. More of the *Tuacha da Riamog* stood along the rail, drawing powerful bows with long arrows.

"To the quays! Run!" Another volley of arrows peppered the Fohorimans as Mathghaman urged us on.

Doc was already halfway there with Nuala. Gunny had hung back. He wouldn't leave without the rest of us. He urged the platoon on, chivvying his Marines toward the ship.

Mathghaman, Bearrac, Diarmodh, and Fennean formed a line, swords held ready, retreating toward the quays slowly but steadily as the Fohorimans, hesitant now as the arrows continued to rain on them, tried to close in. I stayed by Mathghaman's side, and Gunny stepped up beside Fennean. Together, we would hold the line to give the others time to get aboard.

"Mathghaman! Now!" The voice that bellowed from the ship was deep and powerful, echoing off the stone buildings. An even thicker rain of arrows fell among the Fohorimans, slowing them further. We turned and ran.

It was a short sprint to the gangway. Eager hands reached out to pull us aboard. Then the gangway was pulled in, the oars surged to back water, and we pulled away as the archers continued to sow their deadly hail among the enemy that roared its hatred from the water's edge.

EPILOGUE

IT was a long voyage. Before we'd even gotten five hundred yards from shore, we heard Taramas and Uergal chanting incantations. Before we'd gotten a nautical mile out, the weather was already turning bad. Black clouds rolled down out of the north, spitting lightning that cracked the sky and hammering us with hail. The wind howled its hate as the Tuacha sailors brought down the sails, massive breakers threatening to swamp even that impressive ship.

The sea trolls made an abortive attack on the ship as we passed the islands to the south during that gale. We had little to do with that fight. The crew handled the trolls with little trouble. A day later, we escaped the edge of the storm.

We didn't have much to do on the way. Mostly we slept. The bone-deep exhaustion of the last few weeks had finally set in. Nuala's visits I'm sure had something to do with it, too. She had put a soft, warm hand on each man's forehead, and when she came to me and whispered words of comfort and peace, I felt all the horror, the fear, the dread, and even the grief of lost teammates fade away, if only for a little while.

I slept as the ship rocked, finally getting through the gale and into open waters.

The weather got warmer as the days went by. Mathghaman and Nuala spent the most time with us, telling us about the world we'd found ourselves in.

Of themselves they said little. The *Tuacha da Riamog* are not human in the technical sense of the word. They are longer lived and have abilities no normal human shares. There are normal humans here, that much we knew. The Dovos were those enslaved in one way or another by the Fohorimans and their Warlock Lords. Even the Fohorimans, they told us, had been human once. Only great evil and dark sorcery had turned them into the twisted monsters that we'd witnessed.

We could understand them, even when they spoke a language unlike anything I'd ever heard. The *Tuacha da Riamog* are born with the "mind speech," a sort of telepathy, I guess. The Dovos don't have it, nor do the Fohorimans, though they have developed a form of sorcery to mimic it. Like all sorcery, though, they told us, it comes at great cost to the one casting the spell and all those around them.

They weren't eager to talk about what Dragon Mask had done. That it was something unforgivable was easy enough to see. I managed to pick up enough information through subtext over the next three weeks of the voyage to figure some of it out.

Dragon Mask had been trying to awaken one of the oldest evils in the world, a creature that was far beyond what the Fohorimans had turned themselves into. Something not of this world, a thing dark, sinister, and unnatural, buried deep beneath the ice sheet the Tuacha called "The Teeth of Winter." Sleeping, and yet in some way still aware, bearing an infinite malice toward every living thing that walked the world above it.

Worse, from what I could gather, it wasn't the only such thing in the world.

I didn't know whether those horrors that had come bursting out of the chamber where Taramas had kept the athame were extensions of that thing or lesser monsters from whatever hellish place it called home before it came to blight this world.

I didn't dare ask. Not at that point.

Gunny brooded most of the way. I knew why. We didn't have to talk about it. We'd left brothers behind. We'd left Marines behind, regardless of what we'd thought of some of them. There was an obligation there. And there was no Big Marine Corps to tell us not to go back for them. If only to be sure of their fate.

If he went back, I'd go with him. There was no need to say that, either.

* * *

Finally, on the morning of the first day of the fourth week since we'd sailed away from the Land of Ice and Monsters—turned out that was what the *Tuacha da Riamog* called it—we saw land again.

We sailed into a deep blue bay, surrounded by green hills blanketed with tall trees. A towering spire of a mountain loomed above it all, with a glittering city of white stone, built around a slender white tower, at its feet. A pale road ran down through rolling green fields studded with stands of trees, to a port of white limestone, built similarly to the ruined Teac Mor Farragah. Sails dotted the waves around the port, and we sailed steadily in. The captain, Nachdainn, stood in the prow and sounded a tall, brass trumpet. A few moments later, after the call had rung out over the waves, it was answered by more horns and bells.

The ship drifted into the harbor slowly, with stately grace, though Mathghaman's face was grim. That was when I remembered what he'd said about their mission to the Land of Ice and Monsters, on that snow-bound mountainside above Taramas's fortress. They had gone seeking one of their own. And they had failed.

We weren't the only ones with unfinished business, it seemed.

He caught me looking at him and reached out to grip my shoulder. Neither of us needed to speak.

We understood each other.

We would sail north again.

Together, *Tuacha da Riamog* and Recon Marines stood to meet the stately figure of King Caedmon where he stood by the quay. He was as tall and brawny as any of the others, his hair and beard white but his face ageless, his eyes keen and penetrating. He lifted his arms to greet us.

I saw Nuala watching us. There was a sadness in her eyes. She knew what Mathghaman would do. And she knew that we were on the same road. When I met her eyes, she smiled and raised her eyebrow, and there was as much command as comfort in the expression. I nodded. What else could I do?

For now, we would rest. But the fight wasn't over.

Peter Nealen is a former United States Marine who now writes full time for a living.

https://www.americanpraetorians.com/

Book 2, *Shadows and Crows* is available now.

Other WarGate Titles Available now:

Forgotten Ruin
Tier 1000

For Updates, New Releases, and Other Titles, visit www.WarGateBooks.com

Made in the USA
Columbia, SC
07 June 2022

61418612R10231